Finn the half-GREAT

Finn the half-GREAT

Theo Caldwell

TUNDRA BOOKS

Published in Canada by Tundra Books,
75 Sherbourne Street, Toronto, Ontario M5A 2P9

Published in the United States by Tundra Books of Northern New York,
P.O. Box 1030, Plattsburgh, New York 12901

Library of Congress Control Number: 2008910108

Library and Archives Canada Cataloguing in Publication

Caldwell, Theo
Finn the half-great / Theo Caldwell.

ISBN 978-0-88776-931-3

I. Title.

s8605.A457F56 2009   jc813'.6   C2008-907122-0

We acknowledge the financial support of the Government of Canada through
the Book Publishing Industry Development Program (BPIDP) and that
of the Government of Ontario through the Ontario Media Development
Corporation's Ontario Book Initiative. We further acknowledge the
support of the Canada Council for the Arts and the Ontario Arts Council
for our publishing program.   ONTARIO ARTS COUNCIL
CONSEIL DES ARTS DE L'ONTARIO

Design: Kelly Hill
Cover illustration: Victor Molev
Cover design: Robert Babos

Printed and bound in Canada

1 2 3 4 5 6   14 13 12 11 10 09

For Harvey

ontents

I   Prologue: Of the Great and half-Great   1

II   A Meeting on Knockmany   47

III   To the Black Loch   85

IV   The Battle of Knockmany   125

V   The Banshee's Song   161

VI   The Necromancer   201

VII   The Maudlin Vale   240

VIII   The Canyon of Heroes   275

IX   Thunder on the Plain   316

Glossary   379

Albion

Black Loch

FYFE

Ben Cruachan

Causeway

Knocknany

Moyle

Giants Ring

Mannin

ALBA

EIRE

Tara

CYMRU

Maudlin Vale

Burren

Canyon of Heroes

Pengersick

Biggen Hill

KERNOW

Treryn

"There were Giants in the earth in those days, and also after that . . ."

I

prologue
of the great and half-great

Finn the half-Great was just that. Greater than some and less than others, he made his way in the world as best he could. But his story, like anyone else's, does not begin with his own first breath. Eons of serious doings passed before Finn came along.

Back when the world was in its morning, greatness was measured out in barrows. Gogmagog was King of the Giants, and his rule was sometimes just and sometimes terrible. (Some might have said he was "just terrible" but, since he was a big fellow with a short temper, Gogmagog's critics were either very brave or very speedy.) The Great Ones, as Giants were fond of calling themselves, held dominion in every region of the Earth except the frozen lands of the north and the untold wilds to the west. They celebrated their valor, dared bold deeds, and exalted brave death – which they generally met before they were very old.

Now, Gogmagog was the largest and strongest Giant anyone had ever heard or thought of. When even he died in combat, it occurred to the other Great Ones that it might be preferable to live, and live well, than to trade life so quickly for a glorious end. They settled into an existence that was less daring but more comfortable, and many years longer.

It was in this way that the Great Ones discovered that they were not subject to the natural ills and waning death of the smaller races that would come along later. They survived. They lingered. In time, they became prideful in their permanence, forgetting their past greatness. "Immortal until proven otherwise" was their boast. It became part of everyday speech. "How are you this morning?" one Giant might ask another. "Immortal until proven otherwise," would come the reply.

The Giants also began to mingle with mortals, and the sons of these unions became men of renown. Among them was Finn mac Cuhail, also known as Finn McCool, son of the Giant Cuhail mac Art and Muirne, granddaughter of Nuada. Lesser in stature than the least of the Giants, yet larger than mortal men, Finn – Finn the half-Great – grew to surpass them both in cunning and foresight.

Cuhail mac Art had been Gogmagog's fiercest warrior when the Great Ones first came to the Isles of Albion. They had freed Albion from the ancient terror that was the Fomorians, also known as the Frost Giants, and they had established the Throne of Gogmagog at Treryn. For his feats against the Fomorians, Cuhail was made Protector of Eire, the smaller of Albion's two great isles. Those who went with him were known as the Fianna, named for their fair hair. The Frost Giants, driven to the frozen lands of the north, remembered him with hatred and fear. He was especially loathed by their chief, Ymir, in size and strength the greatest of his kind, but feared most for his cruelty. For many years, perhaps centuries (the Great Ones were never good at marking time), Cuhail kept the Fomorians at bay, and their hatred of him grew.

One day, Cuhail came across a young woman walking in a golden meadow. She was Muirne, of the Tuatha De Danann. Her beauty was legend, but it had been foretold that Muirne would be the death of her husband, and that her child would be greater than his father. As the Giants and men of those days were becoming accustomed to self-preservation, the prophecy had left Muirne without suitors. Cuhail had never troubled himself with soothsayers and prophecies and other such "hocus-pocus," as he named it. Unless this mortal woman should somehow give birth to Gogmagog himself, he supposed no child of hers could surpass his own greatness. What was more, he loved her, and he would not be dissuaded from marrying her even if he were warned off by the Dagda, King of the Gods.

It was not long before news of this union reached the ears of Ymir, for he had many spies in Albion. He laughed hideously, seated on his icy throne, as he considered how he might turn Cuhail's affection into his ruin. Any time his foes showed mercy or love, Ymir saw instead weakness and opportunity. He would strike at Cuhail through Muirne.

At a time when Cuhail was known to be in the south of Eire, taking counsel with the Captains of the Fianna, Ymir sent his Garuda, a great bird that had broken faith with its noble flock, to snatch Muirne away. Ymir had the bird leave his sword of ice behind, for Cuhail to find. In a panic and a rage, Cuhail sped across the icy shoals to the north. He raced unchallenged through the abode of the Frost Giants and found the Fomorian king seated on his throne, alone, smiling cruelly.

"I see you have brought back my sword," Ymir said, smirking. "Perhaps we can put it to some use."

"So help me, Ymir, if a single hair on her head has been harmed, you'll be as sorry as you are ugly," Cuhail replied. "As it is, I'm going to melt you down for tea!" With that, he hurled the sword of ice at Ymir. But the hilt settled gently in the Frost Giant's hand, and he laughed all the more. Now Cuhail was becoming very cross indeed.

"Return her to me, Ymir, or the sorrows I brought on your vile people in the past will seem like pleasantries."

A memory of their battles flickered in Ymir's mind, and he rose up from his throne in anger. As he did so, Cuhail was reminded of his enemy's monstrous size and form. Just as quickly as he had lost his composure, however, Ymir found it again, and sat back down.

"You know," he taunted, fingering the ice sword, "there are strange things said of this mortal wife of yours."

"Where is she?" Cuhail demanded.

"Oh, she is alive," Ymir replied calmly, "and may she be so until all are sick of the sight of her. No, my old foe, you know what I'm talking about. Where is this son of yours, if he is indeed yours, who will surpass even Cuhail mac Art? Him I must see."

"We have no son," Cuhail growled. "Fight me, if you dare, but stop chattering. You've never been my match. Even now, your evil life is spared only for Muirne's sake."

But Ymir was not through. "It is also said that your name is written in the Lists of the Morrigan, by her own little hand." The Giants believed that the Morrigan, a goddess of ill humor, kept a list of every warrior destined to die in battle. Besides threatening Cuhail with the prophecy, Ymir was taking a swipe at him with the mere mention of the Morrigan. The Frost Giants made no secret of their contempt for the Great Ones' piety, and they rarely missed an opportunity to speak of it in snide tones.

Cuhail was not especially devout himself, but he recognized an insult when he heard one. He drew his sword, famous in song for its swift red blade, and sprang at Ymir, who ducked behind his throne with a craven agility that belied his size. Like most evil things, Ymir cared little for dignity or courage. Cuhail's boast of his superior fighting skill had not been ill-founded, for though Ymir towered over him, the Protector of Eire's strength had always come from his fearlessness.

"Don't you want to know your dear wife's fate before indulging your wrath?" Ymir asked, peering out from behind his chair.

"Why would I believe what you say?" answered Cuhail. "You'd tell me anything to save your vile hide."

"I might," Ymir replied. "But as you have no son, the chief part of my plan is delayed. Take her, if you will, and may rain and fire and ill wind follow you. She is to the east. Not far away. She awaits you, almost alone, at the entrance to the Crystal Caves. She'll wave as you approach, no doubt."

It was in that moment that Cuhail first considered the dangers of the lands he had crossed. The Crystal Caves were home to the Ice Spider, the darkest terror known to walk the Earth. He turned and ran from the Throne of Ymir, the evil king's cackles ringing in his ears.

Back over the shoals Cuhail raced, until at last he spied Muirne from afar. As Ymir had predicted, she waved to Cuhail as he approached, for his mighty frame was stark against the white lands. Drawing nearer, he could see that she was chained by one arm at the mouth of the caves. Sword in hand, he quickened his pace.

But as he came closer to Muirne, Cuhail felt the earth shake, and shadows fell on the cold ground about him. From the surrounding peaks and up from the snowy dunes came a host of Fomorian warriors, hideous to look at and frightful to hear. They had been lying in wait. Now they encircled him, blocking the way to Muirne.

Ymir was not without cunning, and the Fomorians were bravest when the odds favored them overwhelmingly. Cuhail clutched his sword and looked hard at each of the Frost Giants who surrounded him. It was by no means a pleasant look, and it let them know that he planned to destroy them. But in that instant, from the cave behind Muirne, he saw an icy limb emerge. Then came another. It could only be the monstrous Ice Spider, rousing itself to devour the bait chained at the cave's mouth.

Without thought for himself, Cuhail threw Muirne his sword. It landed with a plume of snow at her feet.

"Cut the chain!" he cried.

This was exactly what Ymir had planned. By vile trickery, he had done what no Fomorian could do by strength alone: He had caused Cuhail mac Art to be disarmed. The Frost Giants fell upon him mercilessly with swords and axes.

Picking up the red sword with great effort, Muirne freed herself. She was about to rush to Cuhail's aid, but the Fomorians were too many and she lost sight of him in the fray. She heard his urgent cry on the cold wind, "Run for your life, Muirne!"

Just then, Ymir himself arrived. He had intended all along that Muirne should die. "Get her!" he shouted, as his warriors closed in.

Muirne began to crawl up the mountain that rose above the mouth of the caves. The Ice Spider, roused by the commotion, emerged farther from its lair, and the Frost Giants pursuing Muirne were so frightened by its ghastly appearance that they halted in their tracks. Only thus was she able to escape across the frozen lands of the north.

Cuhail flailed at his enemies with what strength he could

muster, and hurled them this way and that. But at last he was brought down. As life seeped from him, he looked up to see Ymir's face twisted with satisfaction.

"So it ends for Gogmagog's greatest champion," gloated the evil king. "She died quickly, you'll be happy to know." But some flicker in his eyes betrayed him.

"I don't believe you," Cuhail gasped. "So I will be happy – and avenged."

"Take comfort where you will," Ymir growled. "Mine will come from being rid of you." And with that, he smote Cuhail with his sword of ice, shattering him utterly and dispatching him from this Earth.

Blind with weeping and feebly wielding the sword of Cuhail, Muirne made her way back. When she set a weary foot upon Eire once more, she hadn't the heart to return to the home she and her husband had shared. Instead, she set out to find her cousins, skilled in the ancient arts of the Tuatha De Danann, in whose house she would be protected.

She was in no small rush. Though she had not told Cuhail, Muirne was expecting the son who had been fore-told. So she came to the home of her kin in the valley known as Moyle, in the north of Eire. In due time her son was born and, as happened all too often when mortals bore Great children, it was the death of her. In her final moments they placed him in her arms and she named him Demne. That instant, as she looked on him for the first and only time, was the happiest Muirne knew in her too-short life.

Demne was raised by his aunts, Liath and Bodhmall, who taught him poetry and the ways of battle, and by his uncle, Finegas, who taught him to fish. Although his name would change in time, throughout his life all those who knew him well would call him Demne when they wanted to make a point.

He was a happy child. He grew faster than mortal children, though no one told him of his true parentage, and he learned to play his elders against one another in fun. Whenever his aunts, who were stern women, forbade him something, Demne would ask Finegas, who would permit him anything so long as he did not ask too loudly and scare off the salmon.

For as long as anyone could remember, Finegas had set himself on the banks of Moyle's river to fish, every day without fail. He had become skilled in the arts of fishing, and he taught Demne most of all he knew. But from an early age Demne sensed that for Finegas there was more to fishing than the simple task of catching victuals for their table. Whenever Finegas reeled in a salmon, his face would light up and he would whoop with joy, as if it were the first one he had ever caught. He would examine the fish, looking it squarely in the eye, then sigh with disappointment, no matter how immense its size. Demne assumed that Finegas expected too much of himself, and would be disappointed until the day he hauled in the sea monster Leviathan.

One day, as Demne was fishing with Finegas, he asked his uncle why salmon excited him so, and why he was never happy with his catch. Finegas's eyes darted to and fro as if to be sure he would not be overheard.

"There is a magic in this river that I alone remember. Your aunts have never understood why I have sought it here each day since we were children, and they have mocked me ceaselessly for it. They spend their days wielding swords, though no foe has ever found our home, and writing poetry that, to my ear, is truly dreadful. But with each salmon I catch, I draw nearer to a wisdom they cannot comprehend. It is said, and I believe, that Fintan, father of our people, dwells in these waters. He has taken many forms over the ages, and now he has the body of a salmon. It is further said, and I further believe, that the first who tastes this salmon will be given Fintan's gift of foresight. I shall catch this fish, Demne. Then we'll see what my sisters have to say for themselves!" He winked and placed a finger beside his nose.

Having no siblings of his own, Demne thought it odd to spend one's life in a futile pursuit simply to win an argument. All the same, he was pleased to be taken into Finegas's confidence, for he loved him most of all his kin.

Suddenly, the fishing net began to strain. Hurrying to grab it, Finegas struggled to pull it in. He called to Demne, who hastened to his aid, and together they pulled the net up onto the riverbank. They were amazed to see the glorious salmon they had caught. Enormous and tinged with gold, the fish lay motionless yet alive, and somehow aware.

With frantic, joyful fingers, Finegas tore at the nets and lifted the great fish's head so its eyes could meet his own. Demne heard no question asked but, as if in exuberant response, his uncle cried, "Yes!" The old man danced and sang with an abandon he had never shown before. "Demne, fetch firewood, and bring the frying pan from my satchel. For more years than you can know, I have hauled that pan to the river and home again in hopes I'd have this meal!" He laughed. "And now I will be satisfied. Set this great fish over the fire, Demne, but mind you don't eat any of it! Such a gift as this must be prepared just so!" With that, Finegas darted into the woods in search of fresh herbs and seasoning.

Demne set the fire and lifted the enormous salmon into the pan. He could hear the old man's joyful chatter in the woods behind him. "I have had a recipe in mind for this fish, my boy, since before you can imagine. Seasoning is another of our people's gifts. But the amounts must be just right, and picked fresh! It used to be said that I could make a feast from a pile of peat. *That's* how well-liked my spices were! Expert seasoning satisfies a man better than the cleverest of poetry, and you can tell your aunts I said so!"

As Finegas spoke, Demne noticed that the salmon seemed not to cook, though the flame was hot and the pan sizzled. The fish's color did not blacken, and no smell rose from it. The lad touched the scales with his thumb and got a burn, as the fish was very hot indeed. He pulled his hand back and thrust his thumb into his mouth. Thus it was that, quite by accident, Demne was the first to taste the salmon of Fintan.

The great salmon leapt from the pan into the river, and held its head above the waters. Looking into the eyes of the astonished lad, who was still sucking on his thumb, the fish spoke.

"I have waited many years for you, Demne. I am Fintan, of your fathers. I have given you my courage and foresight, there in your thumb, which you may draw upon when you need them. From this day forth, call yourself Finn mac Cuhail, for that is your true name."

By now Finegas had emerged from the woods. Seeing that the bite of wisdom he had sought his whole life had gone to someone else, he was understandably peeved. Fintan turned to him. "Do not be angry, Finegas," he said. "Your part in this tale has been played to perfection, and will not be forgotten. It was your faith that led Demne here, and it was for him that my wisdom was intended. You are as good a son as I might have looked for. But fell deeds lie ahead for Finn the half-Great, and my gifts, together with all the faith of the Tuatha De Danann, may not be enough. Have courage, do justice, and our people shall live forever. Farewell!"

Fintan dove beneath the waters, leaving Finn and Finegas to their astonishment. When at last they could summon words again, Finn asked his uncle about all that Fintan had said. Finegas answered as well as he was able. He told Finn of the trials of Cuhail and Muirne, and of the Fianna, and of the Frost Giants and the terrors of the outside world.

Finn was stunned. He had little practical knowledge of death and war and creatures greater than himself. The instruction of his aunts had been mostly theoretical on these subjects, and there had been scant talk of Giants. He had wondered, of course, why he was larger than everyone else, but his aunts had always answered vaguely. "You are much better fed than we were in our day," Liath might respond, then quickly busy herself with some kitchen task that had suddenly become crucial. Now, Finn was never an imbecile, so he knew this was not exactly the truth. But despite his huge size, he had never imagined that he might own a place in such fantastic tales as he was hearing from his uncle. He felt a rush of pride at the notion that he was at least part-hero. It was Ymir, however, who most intrigued him.

"This is the one who killed my father?"

"The very same, my boy."

They sat awhile in silence. At last Finn spoke again, with a purpose in his voice that Finegas had not heard before.

"I will find this evil giant. And I'll kill him. I will rise above my father, and avenge his cruel death. I see now that this is the reason for my great strength."

Finegas was a peaceful man, and a simple one. Though he could not find the words in his heart, it troubled him that Finn's first thoughts, once he was relieved of the burden of innocence, were of murder and vengeance.

When they returned to the house, Bodhmall and Liath were preparing supper. Bodhmall, the sterner of the two (and this was some considerable distinction), wheeled on them as they entered. "Where have you two been? It is almost . . ."

She had been set to launch fire from her tongue, but something in Finn's bearing made her pause. Though she was accustomed to Demne's size, and was in any case undaunted by even the grandest of Giants, she sensed new power in him. It was as though a hero had strode from her cherished books of old, straight into her parlor.

"Don't be frightened, Auntie. I have just now learned my true history. I had not planned it, but this is the last night I will spend under your roof. There is an unkind debt I must repay."

Now Liath, the younger of his aunts and the one who most hated war, spoke.

"What is it you plan to do, Demne? Do you imagine that the Dagda gave you gifts only to have them thrown away in war? Why is it always revenge first for you fellows? How many hours have we spent at poetry and song? Who has loved the green of our land more than you? Now you would give it all up?"

What exasperated Finn most about his Aunt Liath was that she posed all her statements as questions. Was he supposed to answer? Should the answer be obvious? But he had learned to be grateful. In her way, Liath had taught him the warfare of family discourse.

"I will do what any son would," Finn replied. "What did sons do in those poems you taught me? How else are destinies fulfilled?"

"Do you not know that there are deeper powers," Liath responded, "than you can comprehend? And though you are great in our hidden valley, do you imagine that you are so much in the grand scheme, that you rush to meet the most terrible of foes? Your father, and I must confess that I never wholly approved of him, was more than twice your size, and did he not fall? And now you'd hasten to the north and to death? For what?" Liath was in full flight.

Finegas rose to Finn's defense. "In truth, Liath, the fish was most persuasive. And I've explained to Finn about his father –"

"You old fool!" cried Bodhmall. "You couldn't just teach the boy to fish and cook, could you? No – you had to send him to his death! I suppose you gave him directions to Tara while you were at it?"

"Tara?" asked Finn.

"No one is sending anyone to any death!" snapped Liath.

"What is Tara?"

The others glared at one another and sighed in unison.

"Tara is the hill on which the hall of the Fianna is built," Finegas answered. "It lies to the south. It was your father's seat of power." He looked gravely at Liath and Bodhmall. "Finn is no boy anymore. He has a right to know."

The women sat together as Finegas told Finn the rest of the story. The telling took longer than it needed to, because the old man peppered his directions with insights as to what fish could be found in what stream, and which bait would assure success.

"Oh, a fox on your fishing hook!" Liath exclaimed at one point, but Bodhmall calmed her down.

When Finegas had finished, everyone sat down to supper in awkward silence. As usual, Finn ate considerably more than the other three combined, but he did so without salt, since the salt shaker was at Liath's end of the table and he didn't dare ask for it. So the evening passed.

The next morning, Finn found Finegas and his aunts waiting for him outside. Liath held in her hands an immense scarf that she had knitted during the night. She was skilled with yarns, even by the high standards of the Tuatha De Danann, and could knit quickly when worried or annoyed. The previous night, she had been both.

"Take care that you wear this," she said. "The lands of the north can get nippy." Finn thanked her warmly for the gift and wrapped it around his neck, although he intended to take it off once he was out of her sight. He could hardly go into battle wearing this dainty shade of lavender. But for now, he kissed her forehead and remarked on the scarf's lovely softness as he rubbed it between his thumb and forefinger.

Next came Finegas, bearing a crude map he had drawn. Towns and landmarks had merely been guessed at, while rivers and streams were marked with bold blue strokes, some-times with samples of the bait to be used. Giving Finn a sly look, he whispered, "These are secrets I have shared with no one, least of all your aunts. Keep these spots between us, eh? We'll visit them together when you return." He also handed Finn a satchel of trout "for the road." Finn clasped his uncle's shoulder, then turned to Bodhmall, who was unusually quiet. In her hands was a large gray bundle.

"Demne, this is yours, though I have hoped for many years that you would never claim it." She opened the bundle. Inside, flashing as though awaking from a grudging sleep, was the red blade of Cuhail. "I don't doubt you've strength to wield it. I have taught you what I know of fighting, and many times I have been struck with dread at your great skill. I despise war and death, as will you. But this sword saved your mother's life. Keep it well, and use it justly."

Finn took up his father's sword and the blade shone like a flame. The glow caught all four faces differently: lines of worry on Liath, scars of age on Bodhmall, crags of curiosity on Finegas, and the grin of fearless youth on Finn. He kissed his family, each with love, and set off to the south in search of Tara.

Finn found Finegas's map to be of less use than he had hoped. He kept it close, though, lest he had need of fish, and followed the sun. Crossing to the far side of the river of Moyle, he realized that he was alone. As a child, he had known solitude and hiding places he thought only he could find. But they had all been within the valley of his kin. He was more excited than alarmed at the prospect of independence, and playfully swung the sword of Cuhail as he walked. With no great degree of force (at least for him), he hewed at a large tree beside his path. To his surprise the blade cut effortlessly through the mighty trunk, in a smooth, straight cut, at its thickest spot of knot and black bark. The tree came timbering down at his feet.

Finn stared in wonder at the red blade, which was unscathed, and was saddened. He loved green things; he had no business heedlessly bringing down something that had grown big and beautiful.

Suddenly, from the woods about him, Finn heard voices calling to one another, and footsteps hurrying toward him. A handful of mortal men, raggedy and angry, blocked his path. They only glanced at him, as they were most concerned with the fallen tree. One of them, apparently the leader, turned to Finn in bad temper.

"Oi, did you knock down this tree?"

"I must admit I did. It was an accident, though."

"An accident?" the man shot back. "These trees don't belong to you!"

"And do they belong to you?" asked Finn.

One of the men, not among the swiftest in Eire, noticed Finn's size.

"Hang on," he said, "he's one of those giants! Look at the frame on him! But I thought you were all asleep?"

Before Finn could respond to this curious remark, the leader snapped, "Quiet, you! There is a tree-killer here."

"Now hold on," Finn protested. "I'm as unhappy about this as you are. I am no tree-killer. Accidents happen."

"Yes, they do, especially when clumsy ogres are allowed to wander free." Finn bristled. Though he had never met a full Giant, he knew that the foulest insult to the ears of the Great Ones was to be called an ogre.

"Who are you?" Finn asked.

"My name is Dunbar, and my trees are not free. They bear a price! For starters, you can hand over that red sword of yours!"

As Finn was considering whether to launch this pest over the treetops or merely push past him, another man spoke up.

"Nice scarf!" The man chuckled, and Finn cursed himself – the ridiculous lavender scarf was still wrapped around his neck. He smiled weakly.

"Very fancy!"

"Doesn't quite match your boots, though!"

Dunbar chimed in, "Did your mummy give you that scarf?"

Finn had had enough. In a flash of rage, he grabbed Dunbar by the neck and lifted him to meet his eyes. "Now you listen to me, Dunder," he said firmly.

"Dunbar," the man choked out.

"Either way. If you imagine yourself worthy to wield this sword of mine, think again. Count yourself lucky that you are beneath even feeling its blade. You did not own this tree. It was a thing of beauty and I am pained at what I've done to it. You, however, are a loud bother and a nuisance, and I'd bet all who know you would agree." The others shuffled their feet and tried to look nonchalant. "But if you block my path or insult me even the slightest bit more, I will serve you as I did this mighty trunk" – he drew the man's face closer to his – "without a moment's regret." With that, he dropped Dunbar. "Now, I am looking for Tara and I know it's not far. Who wants to be the one to point me the way?" Finn looked at the others. They all pointed in the same direction, except for the man who had asked why Finn was not asleep, who pointed someplace else entirely. His friend gave him a smack, and he pointed the same way as his companions.

Seeing that the men were quite wretched-looking, Finn reached into his satchel and took out one of the trout that Finegas had given him. He thanked them for the directions and tossed the fish to the man who had first remarked on his scarf. But he underestimated the strength of his throw, and the fish bowled the fellow right over. Finn thought it best to move on.

He passed through the woodlands south of Moyle, being extra careful of the trees, and entered a strange, bumpy meadow. Far in the distance, he could make out the figure of a tall tower perched on a hill. It had to be Tara.

Navigating between the huge lumps in the earth, he made his way up the hill, losing sight of the tower as he did so. It was an awkward ascent, as the hill was steep enough to be a difficult climb, but not quite steep enough for him to use his hands. Giants were fond of making their homes atop such hills because they made it easy to survey the land round about, while ensuring that any adversaries were quite winded by the time they reached the top. As if they were not tall enough already, Giants were most comfortable in high places.

When he neared Tara's peak, Finn heard music – a harp, and expertly played. Oddly, the music seemed more wearying than the upward struggle. It was beautiful to listen to, but unhelpfully relaxing.

When he pulled himself over the top, he could see the tower once again. It was decorated with swirls of white and green, and was topped with a flowing banner emblazoned with a golden harp. The tower stood over a large hall with a thatched roof, surrounded by a gated courtyard. Lying against the pillar of the gate, as if on guard, was a Giant. Fear gripped Finn's heart. It was an honest-to-goodness, big as all outdoors Giant – the first he ever had seen. He remembered his thumb, and the gift of Fintan's courage. He had not yet employed this resource – sucking his thumb seemed undignified – but now he thrust it into his mouth with such force that he almost made himself sick. He was overwhelmed by a nasty taste of black ash. But the thumb soon did its work, and he felt courage once more.

Courage need not displace caution. Finn crept quietly toward the Great One. The nearer he got, the more unsettled he was by the Giant's size. Back in Moyle, where Finn had been the biggest thing that walked, there had been ongoing debate as to his precise height. Bodhmall would crane her neck and say he was close to three arm-spans, while Finegas would argue he was a good deal more, and Liath would yell at them all to just leave it alone and come to supper. Finn could see that this Giant was at least half again as tall, if not twice as tall. The music played on in his ear, and he yawned silently as he tiptoed toward the gate.

When he was near enough to make out details, Finn saw, with no small degree of relief, that the Giant was asleep and breathing softly. It was a misconception much resented by the Great Ones that sleeping Giants snored like thunder. Here this huge fellow lay, soundly at rest, making no more noise than a snoozing kitten. Of course there were Giants who snored, but it was no more common in their kind than among other, smaller creatures. Perhaps it was such a sore point because it seemed to be part and parcel of the image of Giants as clumsy, noisy, and uncouth. A Giant who snored or laughed too loudly or otherwise behaved boorishly was as likely (or unlikely, depending upon the company) to have this pointed out by his peers as any mortal man.

Finn could tell that this Giant had been asleep for some time, for the grass had begun to grow up and over him. He was all but covered up to his knees, and the ivy on the gate had twined into a pleasant pillow for his head. The gate was slightly ajar, and Finn gently pushed it open. It creaked horribly. He winced, but the Giant did not stir.

The courtyard beyond the gates was paved with flagstones of uncommonly beautiful green. As Finn made his way across it to the hall, the music of the harp weighed upon him. Each step felt more difficult than the step before. But on he trudged, until he reached the doors of the hall. They were tall, at least three times his height, and beautifully crafted, coated with gold and carved with scenes from legends of old. One bore the likeness of a large fish.

Finn pushed the door. It was very heavy, like a boulder set in deep mud. He braced his shoulder against it and, humming to block out the wearying sound of the harp, slowly shoved the door open.

The Great Hall of Tara stood as testament to the diligence and skill of the earlier Giants. Its ceiling arched far above Finn's head, inlaid with gold and supported by a dozen white marble columns that ran in two rows from the doorway to a large chair at the far end. The floor was glittering stone of green and white, and the windows on either side of the hall reached almost to the ceiling. Statues of ancient Giants stood between the columns, and a different banner hung over each likeness. These were the colors of the Fianna, who had accompanied his father to Eire so many years before.

Finn dragged his feet from the door to the chair. Although the harp music sounded almost like a voice, no fear that he would be detected or challenged entered his weary mind. The seat of the throne was level with his shoulders – a novelty to him, as he had long ago outgrown the furniture in Moyle. The chair, like the tower above, was swirled white and green. It was square and broad, and seemed to be carved from a single stone.

His strength waning with each passing moment, Finn put his hands on the seat and hoisted himself up. The chair was not especially comfortable, and his arms were too short to settle properly on its armrests. But once he was off his feet, the music of the harp overcame him and he fell asleep.

When he opened his eyes again, he was confronted by a most alarming sight. Standing less than an arm-span away, staring directly at him, was a Giant of magnificent size. The Giant's wrinkled, curious face filled Finn's view, and he wondered if these humongous, quizzical features would be the last sight he ever saw. After a few moments of silence, the Giant spoke.

"Who are you?" he bellowed, in a voice that shook the pillars, and Finn realized that the music of the harp was no longer in his ears. Before he could answer, the Giant drew his face still nearer. "WHO ARE YOU?" Close up, his face was even less appealing. Moreover, whatever strange things he had been eating were huffed into Finn's face with a force that blew back his hair.

"I am Finn . . . ," he began, in what he thought was a conversational tone, only to realize that he could barely hear his own voice. He touched his ears. They had been stopped up, presumably by the Giant, so that the harp's music no longer penetrated. He tried again. "I am Finn mac Cuhail," he shouted, "and I have come here to the seat of my father, seeking aid in my quest."

The Giant's eyes widened – Finn must have chosen his words wisely – and he took three or four paces back. He brought a massive hand to his chin and studied Finn. "Just the same, but half," he said. This puzzled Finn, but before he could ask about it, the Giant continued, "Are you he, I wonder? Or some bewitched and miniature mockery? This is baffling, to be sure."

"Am I who?" Finn shouted.

"Why, he!" the Giant answered.

"He who?"

"You!"

"Who, me?" Finn sputtered, but he realized that this absurd exchange was pointless. This particular Giant could turn even the simplest matter into a brain-stunting conundrum.

He tried once again, more calmly. "Who is it that you say I am?"

Without warning, the Giant's hands shot out and grabbed Finn by the shoulders. The Great One hoisted him from the chair and carried him down the hall. Finn was too stunned to resist, and in any case he was – for the first time ever – utterly outmatched.

The Giant plunked Finn down on his feet in front of the tallest statue. In his wearied state, Finn had not paid much attention to the sculptures. Now, looking up at the details of this chiseled Giant, he was amazed. It was as though Finn himself had posed for the sculptor, though the statue was twice his size. And it held an unsheathed sword in its hand, the blade carved from glittering red stone. The banner above the statue depicted a golden harp on a glowing green field.

"Who is this?" Finn asked.

"It is you. Or is it? That is what I should like to know."

"I believe," Finn responded slowly, "that this is my father. I had never seen his likeness before this moment. But I assure you, I am no less than he!" To add some flourish to his introduction, he drew the red sword of Cuhail from its scabbard.

The Giant misunderstood. He leapt back and drew his own enormous blade, and swung at Finn with thundering force. Finn dodged the blow at the last instant – a good thing, since it would have split him in two.

Finn and the Giant circled one another. Although Finn's skill and speed were unmatched in Moyle, not to mention his size and strength, he felt staggered to be crossing swords with a being so huge. He found himself repeating the rudiments of combat that Bodhmall had taught him: *Knees bent. Back straight. Let your eyes follow the blade. Supple wrists, remember!*

Again the Giant swung and Finn leapt away, but now he had backed into the base of Cuhail's statue. There was no escape. Once more the Giant brought his sword down. As Finn lifted the red blade in a desperate attempt to block him, their weapons clashed. The Giant's sword shattered, leaving the Great One staring in bewilderment at his bladeless hilt.

Finn's sword was unblemished.

"Then it must be you," the Giant said, gaping at the shining blade in Finn's hands. "You fight as you always did. But what happened to you? What sorcery brought you to such pitiful stature?"

Finn saw that the Giant still believed him to be Cuhail, despite his explanation moments before. "I am not Cuhail himself," he explained again, with straining patience. "I am his son. My name is Finn, and my frame may seem puny to your eye but it was adequate for this encounter, wouldn't you say?" He could not resist a little smirk.

"I did not know Cuhail mac Art had a son."

"Nor did I know he was my father until quite recently, but here we are."

"But where is Cuhail? And how did you come to possess Breanain?"

"Breanain?"

"The sword you wield. That is its name," replied the Giant. "Where did you get it?"

Finn told the Giant the whole story, as Finegas had related it, though he left out the details to do with fishing. The Giant was astonished to hear that Cuhail had fallen. "The last thing I knew, Cuhail left for home after his meeting with the Fianna." That had been decades earlier, but as the Great Ones marked the passage of time in centuries, when they bothered to notice it at all, the meeting did not seem to them that long ago. "I am Goll mac Morna, and your father was a dear friend. I alone have kept vigil here. It is best for those who sleep that Cuhail not see them. He would rouse them with ill humor!"

"They are all asleep?" Finn remembered the Great One at the gate, overgrown to the knees, and the fatigue he himself had felt when he listened to the harp.

"Yes," said Goll. "We do not die, you know." Finn detected a hint of smugness. "We may be killed, certainly, but if we are left to our own devices we go on indefinitely. But we have learned to our sorrow that, when our usefulness is spent, we simply fall asleep. The fields of Tara are strewn with my slumbering comrades, under their blankets of earth." Finn recalled the humps in the field below the hill. "Some spy brought news of our drowsy inclination to that filth in the north, and he sent this treachery down on us." Goll waved his huge hand to indicate the harp. "I suppose he likes the idea that he brings us low through the symbol of your father. But for all his trickery, he did not count on the warm spell we've been having!"

"He? Is it Ymir you mean?"

"None other. The icy villain sent enchanted music to our hall to lull us to sleep so he could attack us. As you see, all the others have fallen for it." Goll leaned closer to Finn and flashed a sly smile. "But I have learned how to resist the music. There is some special clover in your ears and mine that blocks its effects. I came upon it at Tara's base, on the bank of a small and hidden brook. That is how I became the sole protector of our hall. I will admit that I left Tara unguarded for a while. I expected the Frost Giants to come slobbering over the plain at any time, so I set out for the north to assess their numbers. When I saw what had happened there, I laughed aloud. Their ice fields are gone! They have melted away! Eire cannot be reached by foot. We are now surrounded by the great, green sea. Oh, how Ymir must have raged at that!"

"So he can never reach us?"

"I wouldn't say that," Goll replied. "There are always other ways. Ymir and his kind are full of nasty ideas. But Fomorian ambition is easily distracted. Their cruelty has no patience. If they cannot get at us right away, I hope and expect they will spend their wrath on one another."

"That won't do," Finn said, half to himself. "I must find a way to get to him."

"To whom?"

"I must find a way to reach Ymir myself, and kill him. I had hoped to find aid here, but . . ."

Goll looked Finn up and down and sighed loudly. "Brave you may be, and Breanain you may have, but your words are folly. You are discouraged? Why? We are safe here, and our enemies are freezing. I understand the appeal of revenge. But from what you say, Cuhail died a brave death – perhaps the last to be had by any of our kind, and no worse than he would have hoped. What's more, I have seen Ymir in his hideous flesh. I know the terrors of the Fomorians all too well. Rush off to them, and I promise you shall feel something far worse than discouragement."

Goll did not seem afraid, but he was oddly willing to leave Cuhail's death unavenged. Perhaps he was worn down by the years of faithful solitude at Tara, or perhaps his valor had rusted away from lack of use. Whatever the reason, Goll the Great had lost his ancient glory.

"You think too little of me," Finn answered. "Each of us has a destiny, and mine was set before my birth. I will do this, whether you help me or not. I'll find a way to the north, and Ymir will shudder at my approach, and he will answer for his crimes!"

"Do you intend to wear that thing around your neck?"

Finn cursed himself. With all the distractions and dueling, he was still wearing Liath's lavender scarf. He untied it angrily. "Will you help me in this task, or has the bravery of the Fianna also gone to sleep under the earth?"

"We are not the Fianna, and you are not Cuhail mac Art. And you and I are very much alone. Even if it were your place to lead them, you could not rouse those who have chosen to sleep, nor rally those who have opted for peace and solitude. Breanain won you our contest, but I see no special craft in you. Out of friendship for Cuhail mac Art I might help you, were it not so plain that this endeavor is beyond our powers."

"How can I convince you that you are wrong? How can I prove that I am worthy to be my father's son?"

"Nothing springs to mind," Goll answered slowly, stroking his chin with his forefinger.

"What if I could accomplish some great feat in the service of Tara?"

"What if pigs could play the harp?" It was clear this was Goll's stock response to what-if questions, and it might have been amusing centuries ago. The choice of words, however, gave Finn an idea.

As Goll watched curiously, Finn strode into the center of the hall and pulled the clover from his ears. The music of the harp flooded his hearing, and weariness struck him like a blow. Bringing his thumb to his lips, he closed his eyes and waited to see what help Fintan might give him.

There was a flash in his mind, and he saw a vision of himself from above. He opened his eyes and looked upward, but all he saw was the golden ceiling. He closed his eyes again and touched his thumb to his mouth and caught another fleeting sight. This time it was a picture of himself from behind. Whirling around, he saw nothing but the doors of the hall far behind him. By now the music of the harp was weighing so heavily upon him that he could barely lift his thumb to his mouth one final time. He saw another glimpse of himself, this time from the front. Without opening his eyes, he shot his hand out and grabbed at the air – and caught something! The music stopped abruptly and there was a loud clang. Finn opened his eyes. Struggling in his grip was a thin fellow, smaller than a man, dressed in the colorful garb of a bard of old.

"Don't hurt me!" the little fellow pleaded. "It was just a job!"

"A job?" said Finn. "Who and what are you?"

"I am Aillen, and I am a musician – a bard, a minstrel. I am not even a very good minstrel, so please do not be angry! I am hardly a minstrel at all! Before I came here, I was doing more in the way of day labor and clerical work than minstreling. It was the harp, not me!"

Goll drew closer and studied the struggling Aillen. "You are one of the Alfar, are you not?"

"Yes. Yes, I am," Aillen replied with embarrassment. The

Alfar, known also as Elves, had populated Eire before even the oldest tales of the Tuatha De Danann. At one time the craft and artistry of the Alfar had surpassed that of all other peoples, but that was long ago. The great civilization they had built became corrupt, and crumbled. Some said a catastrophe had befallen them, while others thought their skills had wasted away through their own laziness. Whatever the case, the Alfar were unwilling to discuss the details of their downfall. These days they were considered a nuisance. They were badly mistreated at times, but they were most often just shooed away or made to feel unwelcome. Scraping out a living was difficult for them. Even their knowledge of the land had diminished.

"And why are you here, wreaking havoc on your betters?" Finn demanded. "Do you know the trouble you've caused?"

"No, I truly don't," Aillen admitted, "but I will go on apologizing as long as need be, if you won't hurt me. It was a job, I tell you! And it was the harp's doing!" Aillen waved at the instrument he had dropped. It was a beauty, gleaming with gold and inlaid with precious jewels of every color. Its strings shone like polished glass.

"What is this job you speak of? And stop blaming your bad behavior on the harp! It is not a living thing with a will of its own."

"I beg your pardon, little Giant," said Aillen, "but you are mistaken. This harp is aware, and it is cunning. What's more, it is altogether evil. It has shattered my will, and ensnared your comrades. Glindarin is its name. Some years ago, as I was foraging on the banks of the river Boann, I saw it glimmering beneath the waters. It had called to me, I know now. When I found it, I was overjoyed. I had been struggling as a keeper of records for a man who sold dirt, but he had fired me, not for any poor service on my part, but because the dirt business had ceased to be lucrative. Dirt was everywhere, he said. The warm spell and melting ice had crippled the dirt market.

"I thought the harp would change my fortunes. I had always wanted to be a minstrel. I will confess that I was the worst – the absolute worst – player of songs, even in my own family, who were all profoundly untalented. But when my fingers touched the strings of Glindarin, such beauty sounded forth that I rejoiced, imagining that it was my own doing. My clumsy hands could do no wrong when they grasped this glorious device.

"I hurried back to my kin. I gathered them about me, took up Glindarin, and played. It was magnificent! Without words, the harp told stories of old, and its music brought happy tears to these sad eyes. I had hoped my family would be pleased and proud that one of us could play such wonderful music. But they were consumed by jealousy. Cursing me for what they called my show of vanity, they drove me away.

"For years I wandered alone through wood and meadow, hoping to find appreciative ears. Whenever I found an audience, Glindarin's song would lull them into a sleep from which there was no waking them. In time I realized that the Alfar alone are immune to Glindarin's charms. Perhaps this is why it sought me out. Since I could never get payment from my slumbering listeners, I took to robbing them. I am not proud of this, but needs must, you know? The Sleeping Minstrel, they used to call me. Perhaps you've heard of me? No? I always thought the name was somewhat misleading, since it was my victims who did the sleeping, not me. I rarely sleep at all. And as I said, I am not much of a minstrel; I simply move my fingers and let the harp do the work. Do you not –"

"Oh, get to the point!" Goll hollered. "Your jabber is as wearying as your music!"

Aillen was miffed, as he thought he had been telling the story rather well.

"How did you come to be here?" Finn asked.

"Ah, yes, that is the difficult bit. Glindarin owned me utterly. I could find no means to support myself beyond lulling travelers to sleep and robbing them. My people are not well liked, as you may know, and few wish to employ us." Goll rolled his huge eyes. "Also, I confess that my vanity would not allow me to lay aside this thing that made it seem I was creating beauty. But I was less and less able to believe that I myself served any purpose."

"I was wandering one day, taking stock of my short-comings, when an enormous bird swooped down and plucked me up. The creature held me in one claw and Glindarin in the other. I thought it was my end, and that I deserved no better. The bird soared higher and higher. The land beneath us was white and icy, and I was terrified and cold. At last we landed and I was dropped before an immense white throne. Seated upon it was a hooded fellow, larger even than any Giants I have seen in this great hall, no offense intended.

"I never saw his face. But he offered me a job! He said that I should come here and play, and keep playing, until such time as he came to pay me. I was thrilled, so of course I agreed. I was just about to offer to walk back to Eire when the giant bird plucked me up once more. He wedged his claw into a certain spot on my shoulder – just here – and I have been sore there ever since. It is not easy to play the harp with a sore shoulder, you know.

"Anyway, here I came. There were not many of you in the hall when I arrived. We Alfar are crafty, you know, and I was able to move about unseen. It is a secret skill we have, so I will not tell you how I accomplished this." He looked from Finn to Goll as if expecting them to be curious. They

were not. "In any case, I began to play. One by one the
Giants made their way to comfortable patches on the hill
and field. They lay down and fell asleep. That was some time
ago, and I have played almost without ceasing ever since. But
still my employer has not come to pay me. I begin to fear that
I will never see any payment!"

"I'll give you payment!" Goll bellowed, raising his massive
fist. But Finn held up his hand, and turned again to Aillen.

"Your squirming villainy has done us great harm," he
said. "But I believe you were drawn into mischief by your
weakness."

"Oh, I was, I was!"

"Silence! Whether you were led astray or not, you have
been a powerful nuisance. But I will give you a chance to
make it up to us." Goll, who had been waiting to squash
the elf, raised his bushy eyebrows at Finn. "This Giant and
I are headed to the north. You will come with us, playing
Glindarin only on my command. Understood?"

"Utterly, completely understood!" Aillen squealed.

"We'll find your employer," Finn continued, "and if you
serve us well, you may yet be paid!" He turned to Goll. "Is
this feat in Tara's service sufficient to earn your company?"
Goll nodded.

Goll fetched a sack in which he placed Glindarin, and
then he visited Tara's armory, returning with an enormous
sword to replace the one Finn had shattered. Aillen was
allowed to walk unbound on condition that he not use any
of his Alfar trickery, or try to escape. Finn tied the sack containing Glindarin to his belt, and the companions set out on
their journey.

When they reached the bottom of the hill, Finn asked
Goll to fetch some of the secret clover that would protect
them against Glindarin's charms. "Stay where you are and

don't watch," ordered Goll, as he snuck off to the far side of the hill. In a few minutes he came trundling back, pleased with himself and clutching a handful of clover. "You weren't watching, were you?" he asked. They shook their heads.

Stuffing the clover into his pouch, Goll led them across the field of Giants in their slumbering barrows, and toward the northern edge of Eire, walking with speed and purpose. Along the way, he told Finn tales of the Fianna, and of Breanain, the oldest object possessed by any Giant. He also told of the stone chair in which Finn had slept at Tara. It was the seat of the Fianna chieftain, and had been Cuhail's alone. No one else had dared sit there. It was said that the stone it was carved from had the power of speech. When Goll paused from his tales, Aillen took it upon himself to sing for their enjoyment, without Glindarin's aid – until they asked him to please stop.

The journey was a happy one for Finn. He was fascinated by Goll's tales, and had seen little of Eire before. He knew Moyle like the back of his hand, but here every brook and field was new to him. From time to time he consulted Finegas's map. Not one river or stream was out of place, but the landscape was poorly represented. Finn loved the green valleys and hills. He lamented that there were not more trees, and felt a pang of remorse for the one he had felled so carelessly. The sun began to fade as the three companions at last reached Eire's northern shore.

"You see?" Goll asked, waving his hand toward the sea, glittering brightly with the day's last light. "We are surrounded by water."

Finn was confounded. He had expected to find trees, so that he could build some kind of boat, but there were none. In any case, he did not know anything about boat-building. He paced the shore, deep in thought, long after darkness fell. The terrain was jagged and unwelcoming, and the wind from the sea was cold. Aillen and Goll had found soft, mossy patches to lie on, but it took them a while to fall asleep.

When Finn tired of pacing he looked for a pleasant place to sit, but there was only sand and rock. Idling about on the chilly coast would not solve his problem. He needed a spot of ancient inspiration. Sure that his companions were asleep, or at least sufficiently snoozy not to see him, he brought his thumb to his lips. With a will of its own, the thumb tucked under his front teeth and pushed his gaze upward to the high cliffs towering over the shore, and he was inspired to achieve his most famous deed. Quickly he pulled his thumb out, unsheathed Breanain, and set to work.

With the first light of morning, Goll and Aillen awoke to the distant sound of crashing metal and shattering rock. Goll grabbed his sword and raced to the shore, with a groggy Aillen speeding after him. When they reached the source of the racket, they saw scores of neatly hewn stones, huge and six-sided, stacked beside the sea. At the base of the rocky overhang a cave of sorts had been created, from which Finn emerged, Breanain in one hand and a stack of carved stones in the other.

"Morning!" he called cheerfully as he added his armful of stones to the others. "I think I've found a solution. There are some trout left in my satchel, just there, if you're hungry."

"What do you think you have found a solution for?" Goll asked.

"How to reach the north, obviously."

"I do not travel by boat!" When Goll had crossed with the Fianna from Alba (Albion's greater isle) to Eire many years before, he had sat at the very back of the boat, keeping his head down, barking at his companions to stop rocking the craft. Of course, they had taken his complaints as an invitation to rock it as much as possible, to see if they could make him sick. Although he had survived the journey without incident, he had vowed never again to travel by boat.

"A little credit, please," Finn replied. "I am not building a boat of stone, Goll the Great. What you must think of me!"

"A bridge!" Aillen exclaimed. "Is that it?"

"More of a causeway, I should think, but yes." Aillen permitted himself a smug glance in Goll's direction. "I suspect Breanain is pleased to be put to good use. We shall make a causeway to the north, and reach our foes by foot."

"Build out into the sea?" Goll asked. "But how far do you expect we must go?"

"Until we reach land. This red blade of mine can carve without dulling, and the Dagda has provided us no mean stock of stone to work with. If we labor together, Goll, it will be a great but achievable task."

Goll looked at the stack of cut stones, and then out to the never-ending sea, and sighed loudly. Finn waited silently for him to recall that he had promised to help. "Very well," Goll muttered, scooping up a pile of stones and trudging toward the water.

"But what am I to do?" Aillen asked.

"Stay out of the way, if you please," said Finn. "Your part will come in time."

Aillen was perturbed. Despite his low standing in the opinion of the rest of Eire, he had a keen sense of pride. He found a solitary rock far down the shoreline where he sat and stewed.

For many days, stretching into weeks, Finn and Goll labored on the Causeway. Whatever resentment Goll had felt for Finn and the project, it was not reflected in his work. Indeed, his strength and diligence were stunning to behold.

As they laid the foundation, Goll waded far into the sea, where it was much too deep for Finn, and meticulously stacked the largest stones, packing them solidly so they would remain unmoved for ages.

As the Causeway reached farther from Eire, it became difficult to judge a straight line. Aillen was only too happy to inform the others that their path was swerving noticeably to the right. After some discussion, Finn and Goll determined that this was not such a bad thing, as they might eventually strike the northern part of Alba, from which the frozen lands would surely be accessible.

The system Finn had devised for cutting the stones and bringing them to the Causeway was largely a matter of scheduling. He would rise first each morning, to carve as many stones as possible before Goll roused himself. Once the Giant was awake, he would take up nearly the entire stack Finn had prepared, and head out across the Causeway. Finn would continue cutting until he had as many stones as he could carry, then take them out to Goll. In the evenings, Goll would advise Finn as to what size and shape of stones would be most helpful the next day.

Aillen was growing increasingly annoyed at being idle. A number of times he tried to serenade the others as they worked, but they asked him to stop almost as soon as he opened his mouth. Once, when Goll was struggling under the weight of a particularly heavy stone, Aillen started singing. The Giant hotly cursed him, threatening to crush him with the rock if he bleated one more note. Aillen complained that if Finn would only lend him Glindarin, he could make music that would please them and lighten their labor, but Finn refused. Seeing that Aillen was upset, though, Finn left his work and gave the Alfar a brief lesson in the arts of fishing.

"This will be your task now," he explained. "We get very hungry at this work, and we're counting on you."

Aillen's small frame puffed up and he solemnly answered, "I won't let you down." Though Finn could haul in far more fish than Aillen with less effort and in a fraction of the time, the little bard's honor was satisfied. And so all three of them worked until at long last, standing on the farthest tip of the Causeway, Finn spotted land.

The final section of the Causeway was laid with astounding speed. Goll and Finn had worked so hard for so long that they had to remind themselves not to be hasty simply because the end was in sight. When the last stones were in place, the three companions set foot on the distant shore. They looked back with pride on their work stretching across the sea.

Finn did not allow himself time to savor his first footsteps outside of Eire. He drew Breanain and looked about, considering which way would lead him soonest to Ymir. The terrain was less green that Eire's, but he could see a ridge to the north and east on which stood many trees. Goll, who had not left Eire in years, nonetheless looked at his surroundings as if he had seen them only the day before. "Ah, yes," he said, "this way." He headed for a path to the north, and the others followed.

As they made their way, Goll explained that they were at the northern edge of Alba, and they could expect the temperature to plummet at any time. Indeed, it was not long before any trace of trees and greenery gave way to frozen plains and sharp ice. The cold became almost unbearable. Many times Finn was tempted to don the lavender scarf hidden in his pouch, but the grief this would earn him from his companions was not worth it. He left the scarf where it was.

"Can we safely say that we are now in the lands of the Fomorians?" he asked Goll at last.

"Yes," said Goll. "These faceless lands are hard to recall, but we are in their domain, to be certain. It would be wrong not to tell you: we are in great danger."

"Very well," Finn answered. "Take out some of that clover so we can plug our ears." When they had done so, Finn removed Glindarin from his pouch and presented it to Aillen. "Play, my little friend, play to your heart's content. Play until I tell you to stop." Overjoyed, Aillen plucked the strings of the harp as they walked, and music of overwhelming beauty flooded the white plain.

The companions trudged on across the frozen lands. Whether the Frost Giants were laid low by Glindarin's charms or were simply not around, no enemy crossed their path. As the light began to wane, however, a dreadful shrieking could be heard over the music of the harp.

"What is it?" Finn demanded.

"We have been spotted," Goll said anxiously. He waited, assessing the approaching threat. "Yes, it is as I feared. He has seen us."

"Who?" Finn asked. "Is it Ymir?"

"No. It is the Garuda. I have fought this creature before, and my life was spared only by blind luck." Finn brandished Breanain, preparing for battle. "Your sword is of no use here," Goll warned him.

"What kind of creature is this?" asked Finn, as the shrieking drew nearer and more terrifying.

"It is a war-bird that was once among the greatest of a noble flock. His strength is hideous. I grappled with his claws, but his true weapon is the air. He will carry you to the skies, dropping you to die on the rocks below. He thrives in this land where there is no shelter or escape."

Finn spied a huge standing stone wedged deep into the frozen ground. He pulled the lavender scarf from his pouch, threw one end of it to Goll, and told the Giant to tie it around himself. Goll curled his lip briefly at the scarf's color, then obliged. Stretching the scarf beyond recognition, and trusting in the skill of the Tuatha De Danann, Finn tied the other end around the stone.

"I see your plan," Goll yelled to Finn over the screeching, which had become deafening. "But you must run from this place. You can't help in this fight."

"I can and I will!"

"No! Listen to me – I will do my best to resist him, but this creature will kill you in an instant, and your quest will be lost. I do not doubt your courage, Finn mac Cuhail, but you must run!"

Finn paused for a moment to wrestle with his pride, then grabbed Aillen and fled north. Goll drew his enormous sword and steadied his nerve for the fight to come. As they ran, Finn and Aillen looked back to see the sky darkened by the shadow of two vast wings descending upon the spot where they had left the Giant.

Remembering the way as best he could, Aillen directed Finn toward the throne of Ymir. This was not easy because the frozen lands were always shifting, and Aillen had only seen them from the air. The sun had faded but this place was never fully dark. Instead, the sky was a dull, unwelcoming blue. It troubled Finn that he had left Goll to fight alone, but he soon turned his remorse to even greater anger and hatred for Ymir. "Keep your harp going!" he ordered, and Aillen played on.

Before long, they could see a sculpted hall of ice rising over the cold, flat land. Taller than Tara, but ugly and lop-sided with sharp, cruel angles, this could only be the home of the Fomorian king. As they drew nearer, they saw that it was more a cave than a hall. There were no windows, and the threshold was a gaping mouth with no door. Icicles hung from the top of the entrance like devouring fangs.

"Stop playing and wait here," Finn said. "I'll go inside and see about your payment." Aillen was only too happy to let Finn go on without him. Finn stepped into the cave, Breanain shining in his hand, while Aillen, clutching Glindarin, used his Alfar craft to hide well.

The inside of the cave was dark, but Finn was pleased to discover that Breanain gave off a red light. He could see that he was going through a tunnel of sorts, with narrow sides and a high ceiling. After a while he realized that he had entered a large, circular hall. He could see nothing but the white floor beneath his feet, and a vague outline of the walls around him. He paused a moment to think, and heard a noise. It was the sound of breathing.

Finn squinted against the darkness to see what creature might be near. As his eyes adjusted, he could make out the dreadful sight of teeth, sharp and terrible, bared in a hideous grin. Gradually the rest of his enemy's form came into view. Seated on his throne of ice, illuminated by a sickening green glow, was Ymir.

Finn could see that the Frost Giant's face was shaped like a wolf's, with jaws that stretched unnaturally almost from one ear to the other. The huge head was white and matted with hair. But the cruel green eyes that beheld Finn were nothing like an animal's. They were filled with amuse-ment and contempt.

"Who is this puny fool who disturbs my hall?" Ymir demanded.

"I am Finn mac Cuhail," the half-Great replied, trying to mask his paralyzing fear, "and I have not yet begun to disturb you!"

Ymir's eyes widened, with more curiosity than alarm. The Fomorian king was accustomed to seeing in dark places, but he had perceived only Finn's relatively small size, not his features. He rose from his throne and slowly approached. His form was grotesque – he was far larger than Goll, at least half as tall again, and he hunched over as he walked, so he might be even taller. His hands and feet were enormous and clawed. His lurching gait made him even more terrifying as he emerged from the gloom. He stopped no more than two sword-lengths from Finn.

"It was said that the son of Cuhail would be greater than his father," he sneered. "It seems that the foresight of the Great Ones is not all it could be." But when the Frost Giant noticed Breanain, he recoiled slightly.

"I see you have not forgotten the red blade my father wielded," Finn said, emboldened.

"I have not, indeed," the Fomorian replied, "but it looks ridiculous in your puny hands. You are too feeble for such a mighty weapon. What is it you plan to do? I wager you can barely lift it. For someone your size, a sling and a handful of pebbles would be more fitting."

Finn scowled, and Ymir smiled nastily and carried on. "I killed your father, as I expect you know. No doubt that's why you're here. But I understand that you were the death of your mother. What a pair, you and I! Working together, we made an orphan of you." Ymir took another step toward Finn, who swished Breanain through the air and braced himself to fight.

Ymir laughed and drew his sword of ice. "There are a number of ways we might do this. I could dispatch you quickly – a courtesy I extended to your father – or you could resist, and annoy me. In that case, things will be much more unpleasant for you. The choice is yours."

As Finn was wishing he were of sufficient size to laugh off this challenge, Ymir suddenly swung his sword. Finn neatly dodged the blow, and Ymir's blade crashed to the floor. The Fomorian could not disguise his dismay at Finn's agility. "I see you have decided to be difficult," he hissed. "Your father was similarly pesky."

Finn seethed at this insulting choice of words. "I will be difficult, and I will make you –" Before Finn could finish his boast, Ymir swung again. Finn sprang away.

Ymir lifted his sword once more. "I have lived too many ages to suffer speeches from a pixie like you. I'll tell you one last time to hold still!" He swung again, but as Finn leapt to avoid the crushing blow, he slipped on the cold floor. Breanain landed a short distance from his hand.

Finn lay helpless at the feet of the Frost Giant. "How oddly familiar this seems," Ymir mused. He raised his sword in a leisurely manner. But he savored his victory too long. Finn had precious moments to regain his senses and to grasp Breanain once more. As the Fomorian's stroke fell, Finn rolled to one side and slashed at his foe with all his might.

Ymir let out a shriek that shook the walls of his cave. Finn, stunned to discover that he was still alive, looked up to see the Frost Giant writhing and cursing in agony. He saw Ymir's huge arm on the floor, severed from its owner, still clutching the sword of ice in its hand. The half-Great regained his feet and, kicking the limb aside, closed in on Ymir.

"What you are feeling at this moment is the sensation of

justice. Now I'll return the favor – hold still and I will dispatch you quickly." Ymir fell to his knees, at which height he was still taller than Finn.

"You have beaten me," he admitted. "You have defeated me in battle. You have surpassed the great Cuhail by doing what he could not do. But I throw myself on your mercy, trusting that you'll also surpass his kindness. Can you outdo your father in strength of heart?" He looked at Finn with the most pitiable expression his cruel face could manage.

Finn stood before his enemy in thought. "I will be honest," he said at last. "I hardly know how to answer you. You are an ancient king and an evil creature. But as you beg for mercy, who am I to refuse? I have taken your honor – what little you had. If you still yearn for life without it, I'll oblige. But hear me – you are dead and gone from this world, as far as I am concerned. You will trouble my land and its people no longer. Are we agreed?" Ymir nodded meekly.

Finn turned and strode toward the tunnel. He did not get far before he felt a scorching sensation in his thumb, as though it were once more pressed against the salmon of Fintan. It was a warning.

He whirled around, Breanain flashing. Ymir had crept up behind him, and brandished the sword of ice in his remaining hand. The hatred in the Frost Giant's awful face gave way first to shock, then to disbelief, as Finn split him in two with one powerful stroke of the red blade. The villain fell in pieces to the floor in a pool of venomous black blood. Ymir, King of the Fomorians, was defeated.

In this moment of triumph, Finn found himself consumed by rage. He grasped Breanain with both hands, raced back to Ymir's throne, and with much cursing and slashing reduced the chair to rubble. He regained his senses when he became aware of a pleading voice behind him. It was Aillen.

"It is done, I think!" the Alfar cried. When Finn turned, his bloodied face, twisted with anger, terrified the little bard. "If I may venture an opinion, that is," he added shakily. "You seem to have won . . . congratulations!"

Finn sighed loudly and dropped his arms to his sides. He closed his eyes. "Thank you for helping me," he said softly.

"Oh, you're welcome," Aillen answered, still shaking. "Any time! Glad to pitch in!" He paused as something shiny caught his eye from the pile beneath Ymir's throne. "Hallo – what's this?" Forgetting his fear of Finn, Aillen leapt toward the prospect of finally being paid out of Ymir's pocket.

He pawed through the rubble beneath the great chair, and gasped at the treasure he found there. The Frost Giant had made a habit of stashing his wealth in odd places, and the lair beneath his throne had been his favorite. There were sapphires, rubies, emeralds, pearls set in gold, crowns, rings, and necklaces. Aillen tried to hide his glee as he inspected each piece. "I'll only take what's fair payment," he said nonchalantly as he pocketed several choice items. Finn took no notice of the booty except for one jewel: a large blue diamond that Aillen held up to the dim light. It was as big as the Alfar's hand, and it shone like a full moon on a clear night. Aillen stuffed it away, muttering that he had gone many years without reasonable payment for his work.

Finn composed himself and slowly made his way back up the tunnel. Struggling under the weight of the treasure he had claimed, and breathlessly insisting that he had taken no more than his fair share, Aillen followed.

When they emerged from the cave, Finn stood under the cold blue sky, closed his eyes, and savored the wind on his face. Long silences usually made Aillen so uncomfortable that he rushed to fill them with chatter, but this time something told him to leave Finn be. Then Finn opened his eyes

as a single thought flooded his mind: Goll! He raced toward
the spot where they had left the Giant. Aillen stumbled after
him, clutching his treasure.

Over the frozen terrain they flew, retracing their steps.
Finn did not ask Aillen to play the harp, as he was no longer
concerned that they might encounter foes. In any case, the
Alfar did not have a free hand or even a free finger to set to
Glindarin. An oversized crown was perched on his head, but
it kept slipping down about his neck unless he hooked it
behind his pointed ear and leaned his head to one side as he
ran. Though he looked ridiculous, he imagined that the
crown gave him the bearing of royalty.

When they reached the spot where Goll had made his
stand, they could see that the land had been torn up by a
mighty duel. The Giant lay motionless, face down before the
standing stone, the remnants of the lavender scarf in shreds
around him. Finn raced to Goll's side and, with effort, heaved
him over onto his back. For perhaps the first time in their
acquaintance, he could see that Goll was smiling. It was a
smile of pure joy and satisfaction.

"Are you all right?" asked Aillen, always the first to pose
the obvious question.

"You can look through the Lists of the Morrigan till your
eyes fall out," Goll replied, "but you will not find the name
of Goll mac Morna there!"

"What happened?" asked Finn.

Goll explained that the Garuda had grown even larger
since their last battle. Each of its claws, he guessed, was the
size of his sword. Many times the bird had grabbed him,
hoping to lift him to the skies and drop him to his death, but
the strength of Finn's scarf had moored him to the ground.
"I will admit there was a moment when I thought I would
rather take my chances alone than end my long years

wearing a lavender scarf. But I have never seen such knit-
ting! And never again shall I make fun of it!"

They had grappled, Goll and the Garuda, and despite his
massive strength, the Giant could tell that he was no match
for his foe. "I was flattened, my sword was shattered, and the
beast's foot was set on me. Just as I was forming a dire curse to
lay upon the brute before he slashed me in two, he stopped.
Just stopped, as though he had heard something. He cocked his
huge head like – well, like a bird – and off he went! I'd say he
forgot I was even there. Who or whatever called him off, I
would like to thank him for his timing! But what of your
mission?" Goll looked at Finn closely. "I see in your face that
your task is done." He sighed. "So it was your destiny, it seems."

Finn helped Goll to his feet, and the three companions
began their journey back to Eire. As the air became warmer,
their hearts were glad for the first time in their fellowship.
Finn's chief concern was that they all have their story straight
in explaining to Liath what had happened to his scarf.

"Couldn't we say it was destroyed in mortal combat with
the cruelest of foes?" Goll asked, but Finn explained that he
had lost or destroyed so many of Liath's knitted things over
the years (some genuinely by accident), that she no longer
considered battle an acceptable excuse.

"Perhaps she won't ask at all," Aillen offered. Finn gave
the Alfar a long look of disdain.

"Here's what we'll say," Finn proposed. "A flock of
Fomorians swooped down on us by night and snatched the
scarf. I grabbed it by one end, hoping to save my beloved
garment. As they pulled, I could see that the scarf was being
badly stretched. Rather than allow it to be destroyed, I let
the Fomorians take the scarf – for the time being – and I'll
snatch it back at some later date."

"But won't she expect to see the scarf again?" Aillen asked.

"My aunt still believes that a pink vest she gave me when I was a boy is being worn by a Fafnir who stole it from me," Finn answered. "From time to time, she thinks she spots him."

They crossed the Causeway slowly, taking time to admire their work. Even Aillen took some pride in the feat, smug in the knowledge that he had been responsible for feeding the workers. When at last they stepped upon Eire once more, their fair land seemed to spring forth with new life and possibility. No more debts or fell deeds before them, the three happily made their way toward Moyle.

Bodhmall was unusually joyful at Finn's return. Seeing him approach from afar, she ran to greet him and threw her arms about his waist, which was as high as she could hope to reach. Finegas was ecstatic also, hugging Finn and clasping hands with Aillen and Goll. Looking up at the Giant, he asked Bodhmall how tall she reckoned him to be. She asked him to please not start with that, and ushered the companions to the house.

Liath was waiting in her chair, just as she had sat the night before Finn's departure. When he entered, along with Aillen and the stooped-over Goll, she could not contain her glad tears. Embarrassed by her display of emotion, she turned the discussion toward matters practical and mundane, such as whether Finn had been eating properly and dressing warmly. It was not long, of course, before she asked after the scarf. The three companions stuck to their story perfectly (Finn had made them rehearse it many times on their journey). When Aillen began to embellish the story as to the number and size of the Fomorian scarf-snatchers, Finn waved his hand sharply for him to stop. Liath looked at the three of them with mild suspicion but she let the matter drop, for the moment.

When they had eaten a meal of fish (Finegas had been saving the spices for it for some time), the companions said their farewells. Goll stretched his arms wide, yawning loudly, and announced that he would head back to Tara for some well-earned rest.

"You'll always have a rightful place atop Tara, by birth and by the strength of your deeds, Finn," the Giant proclaimed. The half-Great was unsure whether Goll was inviting him to return to Tara with him. It did not matter, though, as Finn had seen enough of arms and battle and great deeds for the foreseeable future.

Goll praised Liath's needlecraft unsparingly, and asked whether she might make a garment for him. Liath basked in the compliments, and promised to make him something large and warm. With that, Goll waved to them all and trundled over the hills and out of sight.

Aillen was eager to seek out other Alfar, especially his family. He thanked Finn for including him on his quest, and assured him that in future he would use Glindarin only for good. Then, slinging his hoard over his shoulder and cocking his enormous crown to the sky, he skipped off to the south.

As for Finn, he felt that he had become every inch a Giant, and that it was time to find some high place for himself. He bid farewell to his family once more but swore that this time he would not go far. So it was that he came to the hill called Knockmany, near Moyle. Atop this hill he made his home. In time he would marry, and his wife would be a woman of such strength and cunning that she rivaled Muirne herself. For years beyond counting, Finn lived in peace on Knockmany, knowing nothing of such ominous names as Gawain, Jack in the Green, and the Little King across the Sea. Finn the half-Great considered his destiny fulfilled.

a meeting on knockmany

Towering waves and ungracious winds lashed the Causeway as the Giant strode across the sea. Huge clouts of rain pelted down, and his long black hair and beard blew behind him. But his eyes looked ever forward, burning with resolve. This was Cuhullin, second in size only to Gogmagog among the Great Ones of Albion, stomping toward Eire to settle accounts.

Cuhullin was known to friends as Benandonner, but he was seldom called this, as he had no friends. He was a cantankerous Giant who did not know when to let a matter rest. Indeed, it was the searing memory of an old defeat at the hands of one Finn McCool, a half-Great of far lesser size, that had brought about his trek across the water on this stormy day.

Truth be told, it was not even Finn McCool – it was his wife who had brought Cuhullin low. Oonagh McCool was a woman of infinite cunning. She was one of the Branwyn,

second among mortals only to the Tuatha De Danann, who
had seen the eternal land of Tir na Nog. In those days the
mortal races lived long indeed, though their days were finite,
and she had lived atop Knockmany with Finn, son of Cuhail,
for years.

This was not the first time Cuhullin had roused himself to
find the little Giant whose name had passed into legend with
the building of the Causeway and the overthrow of Ymir.
Years before, he had tried to unite the still-waking Great
Ones of Albion under his rule (he was the largest and
strongest remaining, so this seemed only fitting to him) by
seeking out and defeating other Giants in combat.

He had ventured from his home in the land of Fyfe, in
the north of Alba, and combed the tall hills of Cymru and
Kernow to the south, where the Great Ones of old most com-
monly dwelt. He'd bellow from the valleys below, calling any
Giant within hearing to come down from his hill and fight.
Gogmagog had been dead for some years, so most Giants by
this point had taken to a quiet existence. When they heard
Cuhullin's call, some of them descended sleepily from their
homes out of mere curiosity, or to ask this noisy person to
please keep it down – only to be smacked resoundingly before
they could get their bearings. In this way, Cuhullin overcame
many a baffled foe, batting the bleary-eyed to the ground and
demanding their allegiance.

Other Giants, like the massive Blunderboar, fought
Cuhullin bravely. When Blunderboar descended to the valley
he seemed tall enough to block out the sun, and Cuhullin
wondered if perhaps he should move on to the next hill. But
it was too late, and the Giants engaged in a fearsome test of

strength. They battered each other this way and that, the sound of their blows echoing over the hilltops, until it seemed that Blunderboar might overcome Cuhullin. But Blunderboar was a particularly stupid Giant. When Cuhullin felt his strength fail, he pretended to see Blunderboar's brother, Blunderbuss, approaching.

"Oh – hallo, Blunderbuss!" he called out, smiling. When Blunderboar turned to greet his kin, Cuhullin dealt him a mighty blow on the head, sending him face first to the ground. When he awoke some time later to see Cuhullin standing over him, Blunderboar brought his hand to his thumping skull and admitted Cuhullin's victory with good humor. He looked around, wondering where Blunderbuss had got to, and for many years blamed his brother for distracting him and costing him the battle.

Still others refused to engage Cuhullin at all. For instance, Pengersick was a pale Giant who always seemed to be suffering some sort of illness. He would weakly call down to Cuhullin that he was simply not up to a battle, but might be ready after a few more days of rest and hot broth. Then there was Byrleigh, the forest Giant, who claimed that he was much too busy tending his woods to fight, and that if Cuhullin truly wanted to make himself useful he should seek out the lumberjack Giant Mayhew and chop *him* down, as Mayhew had done to so many trees. But then Cuhullin came to the hill of Castimer.

"What's all this, then?" Castimer called down. "Looking to set yourself up as king of us all, are you? And what sort of claim would you have to that, then?"

"Come down and I will show you," Cuhullin replied ominously.

"Nah, you won't catch me doin' that," said Castimer. "Besides, you could thump me into the dirt – it wouldn't make you any more king than you are now. It's a simple matter of genealogy."

"How do you figure?"

"Well," Castimer went on, "Gogmagog was the fellow in charge, wasn't he? Now he's gone and gotten himself tossed off a cliff. So where does that leave us? Well, who did Gogmagog put in charge, mostly? That would be Cuhail. But then we hear Cuhail's had a bad time of it with those nasty chaps in the north. So who's next?"

"I am!" Cuhullin bellowed.

"Hang on. Here comes Cuhail's boy Finn. He sees what those Frost Giants did to his old dad, so what does he do? He decides to go up and pay them a visit of his own. He's got Dad's red sword and everything. But wait – the way's blocked by water, on account of this unseasonable warmth we've had the last couple centuries. Does our man give up? Not on your life. He takes up Dad's red sword, hacks out a mess of stones like you've never seen, and builds himself a Causeway! So there he goes, stomping north to sort out that lot, and what do they do? They send that bird after him. But he just slips on past, slick as you please. And then he finds himself that big, frosty ogre and you know what he does? Cuts him up into pieces is all, thank you very much. Then he strolls on home, finds himself a hill and a pretty girl, and sets himself up as happy as can be. Then here you come, waking decent folks, calling yourself the king. Oh, very nice. You want to think about that a little more."

"Where do I find this Finn mac Cuhail?"

"Finn McCool? Unless the world's gone even stranger, you're sure to find him on Knockmany. Seems to me that's the sort of thing a king ought to know." Cuhullin smashed his fist on the side of the hill, shaking its very foundation. "And what's that going to get you? Your man is that way!"

Castimer pointed northwest, in the general direction of Eire's farthest point. Cuhullin let out a savage growl, turned, and stomped his way toward Knockmany.

Muttering angrily most of the way, Cuhullin finally reached the spot where the Causeway touched the shore of Fyfe. The journey had taken longer than it might have, for he was not inclined to ask for directions – and he was famous for his nasty nature, so few would have been eager to guide him. When at last he laid eyes on the Causeway, its carved stones stretching out into the sea until they disappeared in the mist, he could not help but be impressed. He quickly recovered, though, assuring himself that he could have done at least as fine a job, if he had felt like it.

Cuhullin's first steps onto the Causeway were gingerly (indeed, he looked about quickly to be certain no one had seen them). He was deathly afraid of water – which discouraged any attention to personal cleanliness, resulting in an odor that other Great Ones generously termed "robust." Although the Causeway was easily wide enough for two large Giants to walk side by side, Cuhullin opted to tiptoe warily along its very center, arms stretched out on either side for balance. Once he had gone some distance into the sea, however, he managed a less ridiculous gait that was more befitting his size and reputation.

What Cuhullin could not know was that the Finn McCool of whom Castimer spoke – heroic and bold beyond his size and strength – had long ago grown soft and happy. Anger and zeal come easily in youth, but peaceful years teach a fellow to smile. This is the way of Giants and men, and Finn was no exception.

And so, atop Knockmany, a contented Finn McCool and his beloved Oonagh were just sitting down to a spot of lunch. As much as Oonagh loved to cook (and in this she excelled beyond even the high standards of her people), Finn loved to eat. He so enjoyed his meals that Oonagh had a job coaxing him to behave suitably at the table. He would cheerfully talk to the items on his plate, addressing the potatoes, meats, and greens in turn. If he was especially enjoying his repast, he might sing. Oonagh would try in vain to explain that such behavior would not be appropriate in front of guests, but Finn could not help himself. In any case, they both knew that, on the rare occasions when they had guests, they were most often the sort who wouldn't mind.

Finn did not like to interrupt himself once he began to eat. If the salt or some essential utensil was out of reach, he would conspicuously stop talking (or singing). Oonagh would patiently retrieve the desired item for him.

"I love you, you know," Finn would tell her, beaming.

"I know it," Oonagh would reply.

On this particular day, as Oonagh went to fetch a favored spoon for Finn, she spotted a Tengu seated on the windowsill. The Tengu were mischievous birds, as well known for their wit as for their pranks. They were short, squat creatures with black feathers and orange bills, and dark eyes that gleamed when they were up to something. How long this one had been sitting in the window watching them, Oonagh could not tell, but she would have none of it.

"Away with you! Shoo!" She waved the bird away. But the Tengu had chosen his spot wisely. From a taunting distance beyond her reach, the bird smirked at her as she purpled with frustration. "Go on – scram! Don't you pretend you can't hear me! Get!"

"Good day to you, Finn McCool," said the Tengu, calmly turning his gaze from Oonagh. "I hope I've not caught you at a bad time." Only then did Finn notice the bird. Oonagh had prepared his potatoes in her unique and spectacular fashion, and he had been singing so happily to them that he had missed the ballyhoo at the window.

"Oh, hallo, Mr. Tengu!" he replied merrily. "Not at all! Please make yourself at home." Oonagh rolled her eyes and set about other business. She had no patience with rascally creatures, but Finn found amusement in the antics of almost every one of the Dagda's children – the Tengu not least.

"Why, thank you," the Tengu said, glancing smugly in Oonagh's direction as he hopped through the window. "I have come about a matter that I suspect you will find most pressing."

"Is that so? Do go on." Finn chomped down the last of his potatoes.

"It would seem that you will be receiving a guest. Not a welcome one, I'll wager, but he's on the way. We've spotted him from the air, you see."

"We're always happy to have guests!" Finn laughed. "There's plenty to eat and drink here, and my stories grow more interesting each time I tell them." Oonagh rolled her eyes once more. "So who is it? Shall I guess?"

"If you wish," replied the Tengu. "Shall I give you a hint?"

"Please do."

"It's Cuhullin."

"Cuhullin, eh? And who is he?"

"Are you sure it was him?" Oonagh asked urgently.

"If there is another malodorous Giant with unruly black hair and beard tiptoeing across your man's Causeway this afternoon, I'll eat my nest." As he spoke, the Tengu kept his eyes low and merely tilted his head in Oonagh's direction. She considered the delivery impertinent, especially in her own kitchen, but her concern outweighed her indignation.

"What could that fearsome brute want with us?" she asked, though she suspected she knew the answer. Oonagh listened closely to the stories told by the birds and animals about Knockmany, and knew the goings-on of Albion far better than Finn did. She'd heard about Cuhullin's mission, but she had hoped he would not bother to come to Eire.

"Sorry," Finn persisted, "but who is he, again?"

"Oh, he's a dreadful creature –"

"Quiet, you!" Oonagh snapped. Turning to Finn, she explained, "He is a Giant, my love. And you're to have nothing to do with him. Do you hear? By all accounts he is extremely unpleasant, and you're not to indulge him, no matter what taunts he may hurl at you. That's all you need worry yourself about."

"But what does he want?" asked Finn.

"Oh," began the Tengu, "no doubt he's spoiling for a fight –"

"What did I *just* say to you?" demanded Oonagh. "And while I'm at it, let me tell you something – I make a very fine Tengu pie. I've won awards for it."

The bird turned away from her huffily, his beak perceptibly out of joint.

"Now, who would be coming here looking for trouble?" Finn wondered. It was a fair question. He had not made an enemy for eons. "Well, whatever his bother, I'm sure we can settle it like a couple of good chaps, and have a laugh about it afterwards."

"I truly think not," Oonagh answered. "This Cuhullin is a nasty piece of work, through and through. Besides, he's far too big for you, my love."

Finn's temper was not so quick now as it had been in his youth, nor his pride so easily stung. But he bristled at this. "And what's that meant to mean?" he inquired, in a sharper tone than he had used in many years.

"It's meant to mean nothing," Oonagh replied calmly,

"except that you needn't be drawn into a quarrel. Leave him be, is all."

"Perhaps you don't know it," Finn retorted, "but I've dealt with some rather large villains in the past."

Oonagh sighed. "Oh, please do tell me again how you chopped that Giant in half," she said. "And this time, I'll make up a dance to it." Neither of them noticed the mischievous twinkle in the Tengu's eyes as they exchanged their first heated words in at least one lifetime of mortal men.

"Ah, well that's it!" Finn huffed, rising from the table. "Finn McCool is never too small for a quarrel!" Oonagh threw up her hands, knowing there was no reasoning with him once he began to refer to himself in the third person. Grabbing his green cap and the walking stick laid by the threshold, he stomped outside.

The sun was full on the hilltop, and Finn brought his cap down low over his eyes as he surveyed the green plains about Knockmany. The view was commanding, and his vision was sharp. When the air was still, a keen listener could hear the sounds of the sea, and this feature had figured prominently in Finn's choice of this particular hill.

Satisfied that his surroundings were safe, Finn headed toward the crest of the hill at a bit of a run, as was his custom. Once at the edge, he leapt into the air, landing on one heel and skidding down the side of Knockmany. It was an impressive maneuver, one he had perfected over centuries. When he reached the bottom, he dusted himself off, adjusted his cap, and turned toward the Causeway. The Tengu fluttered down to accompany him.

The Causeway was no more than a half-hour's stroll from the base of Knockmany. Finn twirled his walking stick cheerfully on the way, regaling the Tengu with the tale of his battle with Ymir. Different versions of the story were well-known throughout Albion. Perhaps Finn repeated it now for his own benefit, to remind himself of his ancient bravery before he faced this new Giant. And if he exaggerated a little – well, like all Giants and mortal men, he came to believe his own tall tales as he repeated them over the years.

The fog grew thicker as they followed the muddy path down to the sea. Though he could not see more than a few feet in front of him, Finn's steps were sure as he strode out across the pebbled shore. Only the salt in the air and the sound of the waves lapping Eire's rocky edge informed him where the land ended and the water began. Dragging his walking stick along the pebbles and occasionally waving it in the air to clear a line of sight, he squinted to find the Causeway. Then came a gust of wind blowing up from the water, parting the mists and revealing the sea; he had found it.

Finn crouched low and peered through the clear air beneath the haze, far along the pathway. At first he could see nothing but an expanse of hexagonal stones stretching into the clouds. But then something caught his eye – a darkness, moving slowly but deliberately toward him. At first he thought it might be a shadow. But as it drew nearer, there could be no doubt that this was a solid form, and impossibly large. Rounded from the top of the head through the massive shoulders, with a black beard and mane that tumbled down beyond the barrel chest, the specter of Cuhullin was a terror to behold. It had been years since Finn had seen a true Giant, and few could rival Cuhullin's size and fearsomeness. With the flicker of an old instinct, he quickly brought his thumb to his mouth. But his courage was not strengthened. Instead, he was seized by a powerful impulse: *Fly home!*

"Is there something you've forgotten?" the Tengu mocked,

as Finn spun on his heel and hurried back toward Knockmany. He scrambled up the muddy path and across the
emerald plain to the base of his hill, and scaled Knockmany
with unaccustomed speed.

Back at his home, Finn paused only a moment and
then, thinking he had harnessed his nerves, pushed open
the large green door and entered. Oonagh sat in the far
corner of the room, absorbed in her needlework. Without
looking up, she spoke.

"I see you're back, my love," she observed. "Did you
settle him?"

"Settle who?"

"Did you not set out to deal with some Giant just now?
I'm asking how that went."

Finn was frantically trying to recall where he had left
Breanain. When the silence after her question became
awkward, however, he grasped for an answer. "There were
other factors involved, my love," he stammered.

"I see," she mused. "As long as all is well."

Finn wondered if he was fooling her. Should he confess
that he was overmatched? Did she know already? Would that
monster come lurching to their door? And *what* had he done
with his sword?

"I should tell you this," he allowed, "if only for your own
protection. There is a chance that this huge fellow may find
his way here. I do not wish to alarm you, my love, but I feel
you ought to know."

"Dear me," she said. He noted that not once had she
looked up from her needlework.

"I have dealt with Giants before, you know," he continued, peering from each window. "Frost Giants, in fact.
Terrifying creatures. You will be safe with me."

"I do not doubt it," she muttered.

"My love? I wonder if I could ask for your help," he asked gently.

"Why, certainly," Oonagh replied, setting her needles aside and rising from her chair. "Now, what is it you'll be needing?"

Finn sighed. "The monster is indeed on his way, but my strength to turn him back may not be all I've made it out to be," he confessed. "Could you help me? What can be done?"

"There's nothing to fret about," she assured him. "Stay right where you are." She made her way to the back room, and came breezing back moments later. In her hand were nine threads of red, gold, and green. She seated herself at the kitchen table, humming softly as she wove the threads into three braids. Then she tied two of the braids around her left arm, and one over her heart.

"Right, then," she said cheerfully. "Go on, my love, and fetch the cradle and baby clothes from our closet, and bring them out here to me." Oonagh had often made her desire for children known. Did she suppose that this was a good time to rekindle the debate?

Finn made his way to a large closet in the back room and, pushing aside some fishing equipment, pulled out the cradle and baby clothes. But what was she thinking of?

He found Oonagh working in the kitchen. The oven was hot, and she deftly moved between kneading bread dough on the tabletop and making cheese from a great jug of milk. "Ah, good, you're back," she said, rubbing her hands on her apron. "Just set those things there, my love, and I'll need you to help outside. Do you see this?" She held up a large lump of white cheese. Finn nodded. "Good. I need you to go out about the hill and pick up as many stones of this shape, size, and color as you can find." He puzzled for a moment before she shooed him out the door with a wave of her hand.

The sun was lower now, and the long shadow of the house creeping across the green hill reminded Finn of his approaching doom. But he trusted Oonagh, so he set to work on hands and knees, digging in the dirt, examining what stones he found, tossing some away and making a pouch of his shirt-front to hold the others. He had gathered several stones when, as he pried another from a patch of loose dirt, something made his blood run cold – a great thump that shook the earth. And then another. Pebbles danced on the ground before his eyes with each pounding blow. He scooched low to the edge of Knockmany and peered down. At the bottom of the hill, slamming his massive fist into its side, was Cuhullin.

Finn scooched hastily back out of sight, then jumped up and ran into the house, trying not to drop the white stones he had gathered.

"He's here!"

"Good," Oonagh replied, without concern. "I'm just about done." She had baked dozens of large loaves of bread and stacked them in two piles on the table. Now she was seamlessly inserting a frying pan (she had many, all of very high quality) into each loaf. "Let's have those rocks of yours over there." She gestured to a huge mound of white cheeses she had assembled on the counter. Finn dumped the contents of his shirt-front next to the cheeses. "Good," she went on. "Now, I've laid out some of the baby clothes. Squeeze yourself into them as best you can. Quick like a bunny!" She set to arranging the loaves (those with frying pans within, and those that were panless), as well as the cheeses and rocks, so that no one but her could tell which was which.

Finn wondered if Oonagh could be serious. If she thought he would face Cuhullin in baby clothes, she had another thing coming. A further pounding blow hit Knockmany's base, however, and Finn did as he had been told; he stuffed

himself into the baby wear, stretching the material unmerci-
fully, and fastened a frilly bonnet on his head.

Oonagh allowed herself a quiet chuckle. "Adorable," she said. "Now see how well you can get yourself into that cradle."

Feeling as ridiculous as he looked, Finn steadied the cradle with his huge hands and stepped in. His knees were up at his chest and he was wretched in body and spirit, but he was in. Oonagh covered him with a soft blanket up to his chin, then went to the window and flung it open wide. She put two fingers to her mouth and let out a long, clear whistle. In this way, she invited the monster Cuhullin to the top of Knockmany.

Cuhullin heard her whistle and paused between punches. He was unaccustomed to invitations. Indeed, it was many cen-turies since he had been welcomed by anyone, and not only because he was most often calling to dispense a beating. He was an ungracious guest in other ways. He talked loudly, often while chewing, and always about himself. He overstayed and refused to leave graciously. In short, he reinforced many of the most notorious and unpleasant stereotypes of Giants.

But Oonagh whistled once more, and there was no mis-taking it – he was being invited. His fist still cocked for the next blow, he began the wearying climb up the side of Knockmany. He had never had especially good balance, so he teetered a number of times, veering off to one side or the other. When he got to the summit, he took the briefest of looks around before bending over, his mighty hands on his mighty knees, to catch his breath.

"Oh, hallo!" Oonagh called as she emerged from the house. "I do hope the jaunt up our hill wasn't too much of a bother."

Cuhullin composed himself. "Oh, not at all," he boomed.

"I only spotted an astonishing pebble – just there – and I was taking a closer look at it." For Cuhullin, this was an uncommonly clever lie.

"There's always time for an interesting pebble," Oonagh replied thoughtfully. "Well, come on. In you come." He followed her to the house. "Mind your head," she added. She had barely uttered the words when Cuhullin, stroking his beard and wondering why she was being so welcoming, walked into the crossbeam of the door. It was a tall transom but he was taller still, and it caught him straight between the eyes, making the house tremble. Stumbling back, his hand upon his forehead, the Giant gave himself a shake and looked angrily about to see who had assaulted him. "You'll want to watch that," said Oonagh, "it's far too low. My Finn can barely make his way through it on his hands and knees." Cuhullin wondered at this remark. "Come on in," she continued. "Carefully now."

Ducking low and turning awkwardly sideways, Cuhullin inched through the door and into the home of Finn McCool. When Finn saw the monster from his place in the cradle, he could barely muffle a shriek. Cuhullin turned.

"Oh, it looks as though the baby's awake," Oonagh explained, as she picked up a piece of cheese and handed it to Finn. She gave him a wink and turned back to the Giant. "Do sit down," she said, gesturing to one of the heftier chairs.

Cuhullin could not look away from the uncommonly ugly infant in the cradle. It was not its bearded and hairy appearance that held his eye – he would not have known the difference between a comely child and a hideous one. No, it was the sheer bulk of the babe that gave him pause. If this was the size of Finn's infant son, how big was the father?

"Come along, then," Oonagh urged him once again. "Have a seat and let me get you something."

"Where's Finn McCool?" he demanded, a tad more sheepish than usual, settling into the chair.

"Oh, my Finn's out and about, doing as he does," she replied as she busied herself in the kitchen. "He takes his time at fishing, then he enjoys a swim around the island to cool himself off." Cuhullin was as much impressed that Finn had no fear of water as he was by the notion that he swam around all of Eire to relax. "Yes, he's just left me here with the baby," she went on. "His supper is almost ready, but let me offer you some while you're waiting." She brought him an enormous plate stacked impossibly high with loaves and cheeses. "It's not much, I know – no more than a mouthful for my Finn – but I wasn't expecting company." She went to the kitchen to fetch a few more loaves, and gave them to Finn in his cradle.

Cuhullin's appetite was legendary, but he was cowed by the mountain of food she had given him. But if Finn could swallow this much and more, Cuhullin would die roaring before admitting that it was too much for him. He lifted a loaf to his lips and took a mighty bite. There was a hideous crunch as his teeth met the hidden frying pan. He let out a howl and dropped the bread with a clang.

"Is it too hot?"

"No!" he managed to mumble, his huge hand rubbing his jaw.

"Thank goodness," Oonagh said. "This bread is a favorite of my Finn – and the baby!" She gestured to Finn, who sank his teeth into one of the solid bread loaves and smiled at Cuhullin as he chewed.

The Giant was becoming concerned indeed as he watched this infant chomp on the same bread that had all but broken his teeth. He reached for one of the cheeses. As he bit down, his teeth made a painful crunch. He threw back his head with a holler.

"What now?"

"Nuffin'!" Cuhullin's hand was gripped tightly over his mouth.

"This is my Finn's favorite cheese," she said cheerfully. "He and the baby can't get enough of it." On cue, Finn munched happily on a piece of real cheese. Cuhullin was alarmed. How could he hope to best Finn in battle if he could not so much as nibble his favorite repast? Even Finn's infant, it seemed, was made of stronger stuff than the Giant!

He contemplated his situation, stretching his wits to their limit. Perhaps he could save face – and teeth – by swallowing the food whole. He picked up another piece of cheese, noting that it was curiously hard as a rock, popped it into his mouth, and gulped it down. The stone landed uncomfortably in his stomach.

"Are you enjoying it?" Oonagh asked.

"Oh, very much." He rubbed his gurgling belly, reached for another rock-hard cheese, and swallowed it whole. As Oonagh kept gazing at him, a pleasant look upon her face, he was obliged to gulp down stone after stone while struggling to return her smiles.

It was not long before Cuhullin's innards began to get the best of him. He felt heavy on his feet, and his teeth ached.

"More bread?"

"Oh, I couldn't possibly." He no longer cared to compete with Finn's appetite. He placed his immense hand on the back of his hefty chair for balance. "You know, I just remembered there is another Giant, even bigger than Finn McCool, that I was meant to fight today. I forgot all about it. Oops."

"Do you mean to say you can't stay?" asked Oonagh. "My Finn will be so disappointed. He was looking forward to meeting you, I know." Finn smiled from the crib.

"I'm afraid so." Finn's hulking infant and the ferocity of his appetite might have cowed Cuhullin into retreat even if he had been feeling his best. But with his belly rumbling and causing him more hurt than he had ever known in his immortal life, he was already defeated. He took his leave of Oonagh with what courtesy he could muster, and plodded out with slow, deliberate steps. With his insides howling, he had difficulty even getting out the door.

When he was sure it was safe, Finn, still in baby clothes, joined Oonagh at the edge of Knockmany to watch the unhappy Giant stumble back toward the Causeway. Many times, when he thought he was out of sight, Cuhullin would pause to sit or fall on all fours. Still, the Giant felt lucky. What if the monstrous Finn McCool had returned to find him in his parlor? He counted this as a little blessing. But never before had the Giant Cuhullin been so miserably bilious.

And so Cuhullin found himself, many years later, crossing the Causeway to Eire on this blustery day. His steps were braver this time, but he was nonetheless nonplussed to be surrounded by water. The rains seemed to be taunting him, for no sooner had he completed his crossing and set foot upon dry land than the sky cleared and the sun shone down on his angry face.

At Knockmany's base, Cuhullin took a few sharp breaths and then, slowly and inelegantly, with sideways steps and much huffing, made his way to the top. There he found Oonagh hanging her wash on the clothesline, in the warm breeze of a lovely day.

"Where's Finn McCool?" he demanded, puffing.

"Why, good afternoon," she replied pleasantly. She did not look away from her clothesline. "I hope you've been keeping well." After she hung the last of Finn's billowing shirts, she clapped her hands twice at a job well done. "If it's the boys you're looking for," she said, "they've taken the hounds down to the Nome for a spot of fishing."

"The Nome?" Cuhullin was puzzled.

"The river, my boy." Though the Giant was eons older than Oonagh, she found the nickname appropriate.

He thanked her for her help, made a gawky bow, and sighed. He stomped back down the hill. For a moment he lost his footing and slipped sideways. In trying to right himself, he turned himself completely around, so that he fell flat on his back and slid, head first and with much cursing, right to the bottom. Oonagh rushed to the edge.

"Are you all right?" she called down.

"Oh, never better, thanks." Cuhullin had come to rest at the foot of the hill and was staring up at the sky. "There are some lovely clouds left from the rain," he said, pointing with his muddy arm. "I just wanted to admire them." Something in Oonagh always inspired him to unusual guile.

"All right, then." Oonagh chuckled and turned back to the house. Once he was certain she was out of sight, he lifted himself to his feet, grumbling, and plodded to the river.

"You won't catch anything but your death of cold that way," laughed Iskander the Cyclops from the shore.

"Well, we'll just see about that, won't we?" replied Finn, chest-deep in the Nome. He strained to keep his fishing gear above the rushing waters. "I'll ask you to remember those words after I've had my success." He cast his line with his arms awkwardly up about his shoulders, and dug his heels into the river's bed against the current.

"You may win the wager," Iskander yelled, "but you look ridiculous. You have to ask yourself – is it worth it?"

"Don't be daft," Finn shouted back. "I look as fetching as ever. But you're right there – I will win the wager. And anyway, how would you know what I look like? You're more than half blind." Iskander was a true Giant, though a small one, and one of the Arimaspians. These were one-eyed Giants from far to the east who searched the Earth for gold (usually stolen from Griffins) with which to adorn their hair. In his more candid moments, Iskander would concede that this was an odd obsession for such a mighty race. Many years ago, he himself had grown tired of the search, deciding that his hair looked lovely enough, and had settled in Eire. The rest of the Arimaspians were scattered across the world, and he lamented that he would never see another of his kind again. But Iskander and Finn were fast friends, and had been so for centuries. Oonagh tolerated most of their shenanigans, and Iskander's ready charm and quick wit were always welcome atop Knockmany.

Something heavy pulled on Finn's line. "Aha!" he whooped. "I told you the finest catch would be found in the middle of the stream!"

"Easy now," answered the Cyclops. "Let's see what you've got before you get to gloating."

Whatever Finn had snared was strong indeed. Even the biggest of catches did not normally pose much of a challenge for him. Though the current and his odd position may have had something to do with it, this time he had to struggle. He was nearly hauled forward several times until, with one last effort, he pulled hard on his line, yanking his catch from the river and sending it flying through the air. With an unholy splat, the fruit of his labor struck Iskander squarely in the face and wrapped itself around his head.

"I'm blinded!" Iskander cried, tugging at whatever it was.

"Don't let it get away!" Finn yelled, wading to the river's edge.

"Get it off, get it off!" Iskander was running to and fro along the bank. He caught his foot on a root, fell onto all fours, and pawed his way toward the sound of Finn's voice. "I'm blinded! Oh, villainy!"

"Ah, stop being so dramatic. You'd think you were the first to catch a fish in the eye. Now hold still."

Knee-deep in the river, Finn reached for Iskander's head as he rolled upon the shore. He had to smack the Cyclops's flailing hands away in order to peel the creature from his face. It was no fish. It was greenish brown, and it had wrapped itself several times around Iskander's head and neck. It was immensely strong, Finn discovered, as he unraveled its coils. When at last Iskander was freed and fell on the bank gasping and cursing, Finn held up his catch for inspection. He had hauled in a mighty snake – a Piast, to be precise – the full length of his arm-span. Its head, adorned with threatening yellow flashes above the eyes, snapped in Finn's direction and let out a horrible hiss.

"AHH!" yelled Finn, tossing the vile creature high into the air, above the trees.

"What was that?" gasped Iskander, his eye wide and his hand on his throat.

"How should I know?"

"You threw it dead at me!"

"I never did."

"Yes! I may be the last of my race, and that could have been the end. Directly at me, you threw it!"

"I did no such thing, you pitiful simperer." Finn stepped onto the riverbank, wringing water from his shirt. "You just didn't get out of the way, is all."

"It is the job of the angler to ensure that those round about him are out of harm's way. In that you failed, Finn McCool."

"Well, I can't do all the looking for both of us," said Finn, dumping water from his boot. "At least I won my wager."

"Oh, I hardly think so."

"Oh, yes," Finn insisted. "Did you see the size of it? Sure as the Dagda made little green apples, that was the biggest catch of the day, and I hauled it from the middle of the stream."

"But that was never a *fish!*"

"Nothing was said of fish. *Biggest*, we wagered. Now come on, don't be a poor sport."

"It's always details with you, Finn McCool." Iskander chuckled as Finn helped him to his feet. Then the half-Great turned toward the woods and whistled for his hounds. Moments later, the pitter-pat of paws could be heard coming through the trees.

Apart from Oonagh, Finn loved nothing so much as his hounds, Bran and his little sister Skolawn ("Skolie" for short). Bran was faithful and obedient, while Skolie was endearing and affectionate, if not so well-behaved. The hounds loved to play with one another, and Bran was exceedingly protective of Skolie. Indeed, his usual good nature would give way at once to fearsomeness if anyone was foolish enough to approach her in a manner that was in any way unpleasant.

They came bounding out of the woods. Skolie was first, her tongue flapping and her mouth stretched wide with glee. She ran to Finn, sniffing him all about and licking his hands. Then she went to Iskander and repeated the process. The dignified Bran emerged from the woods behind her. In his jaws was the limp body of the Piast.

"Good boy, Bran!"

"Has he brought the vile thing back?" asked Iskander.

"It's important to encourage him," Finn said, bending down to pet Bran and take the Piast from his mouth. At first Bran did not want to let go of his prize, but at Finn's gentle urging he relented and joined Skolie in giving the rest of the day's catch a good sniff.

Finn laid the snake out straight on the grass and gave a low whistle at its size. Nothing about it was pleasant. Its color was sickly, its face was alarming, and its strength was unsettling.

"Now, where do you suppose such a thing would come from?" he wondered aloud. "Have you ever seen one before?"

"I barely saw it this time," said Iskander, from a safe distance.

"Such an odd creature." Finn poked at the dead snake with a stick. "It seems more than a bit out of place in the Nome. In Eire, even. I suppose there's always more to know than you think, eh?"

Just then, Bran began to bark in the direction of the far riverbank. Finn and Iskander looked up. Standing on the other side of the water was the mighty Cuhullin. He was noticeably filthy, even for him, and his fists were clenched at his sides. His face was twisted with anger.

"Finn McCool!" he bellowed.

"Oh – hallo, Ben!" Finn called cheerfully. "And how've you been keeping?"

"Immortal until proven otherwise," obliged Cuhullin. "Which is far better than you are about to be!"

"Come on, now," Finn replied. "It can't be as bad as all that, can it?" Iskander, who disliked confrontation, backed slowly toward the woods.

"Oh, yes it can!" Cuhullin shot back. "You cheated me, Finn McCool!"

"Oh?" Finn asked. "And when was that, then?"

"You know very well when," grumbled the Giant. "That was never your supper I was eating. Did you suppose I would never figure it out?" Finn made a show of stroking his chin as though pondering the question, which infuriated Cuhullin all the more. He was touchy not only about being fooled, but also about how long it had taken him to piece things together. In fact, he had never actually figured it out. Over the years, the tale had become something of a running joke, told at his expense throughout Albion. Only recently had it reached his enormous ears. "You've laughed at me for the last time, half-Great! I am stronger than you, by far. In a proper contest I will crush you. The only way you could win is by trickery."

"What's in your head, then, to imagine that I would fight you any other way?"

Cuhullin considered the question for a moment. Then he hollered, "Enough! The time has come to settle things once and for all. Fight me, Finn McCool!"

"Very well," sighed Finn. "Shall I come to you, or would you care to cross over here?"

"It does not matter!" Cuhullin snapped without thinking.

"Fine," said Finn. "Meet me in the middle of the river, and we will have our contest there."

Cuhullin realized that he should not have been so hasty. Watching Finn stride confidently into the river, he tried to swallow his fear of water. It was no easy task. Over the ages, his boasting had gotten him into countless awkward scenarios, but he never learned. As he edged closer to the rushing waters, he hoped his terror would be taken for fearsomeness. He dabbed a toe into the river and quickly drew it out again.

"Any time, then!" encouraged Finn, who was standing

chest-deep in the middle of the river. Cuhullin scowled. He took a few steps back, drew a deep breath, and closed his eyes. Then, with a war yell that could be heard for miles, and with his eyes still shut, he ran for the riverbank at full speed. His first few strides into the water kicked up splashes and sprays high above Finn's head. The war yell continued and his eyes remained closed as he flailed his boulder-like fists, hoping to catch Finn with a blind blow. Standing just out of range, Finn watched the bizarre spectacle. On the bank behind him, Iskander and the hounds stared in puzzlement. Several times, Cuhullin ran out of breath and had to take a great gulp of air to keep hollering. His fists crashed into the water again and again until, with one particularly powerful swipe, he lost his balance and fell forward. Despite his size, the current took him, and in an instant he was swept down the river, around the bend, and out of sight.

"Oh, that's a nuisance." Finn dove into the rushing water and swam off after the Giant. Bran, howling, ran after him along the bank, followed by Skolie and Iskander.

With his powerful arms, Finn outpaced the current downstream and around the bend. He had traveled less than a mile when he found a miserable and drenched Cuhullin, eyes still firmly shut, clinging to a large pointed rock in the middle of the river. Grasping the rock as he passed, Finn swung himself around and took hold of the Giant's huge hand. Cuhullin started hollering once more.

"Enough of that now!" Finn shouted him down. "So you've had your second quarrel with me, eh? Do you think it was worth the bother?"

"Save me, Finn McCool! We'll have no more quarrel after that."

"So you yield then, do you?" asked Finn. Cuhullin paused from hollering.

"Aye," he agreed at last. "If you save me from this wicked river, then I yield."

"Good enough." Finn smiled. "Put your feet down."

"I will do no such thing!"

"Certainly you will. Put your feet down and let's get out of this. Go on!" Cuhullin reached his feet down and, to his great surprise, they met the bed of the river. Standing slowly and releasing his grip on the rock, he rose to find that the water came only slightly above his knees. Finn and Iskander burst into laughter, and the hounds howled along. Cuhullin, drenched and defeated, cursed his bad fortune.

"Ah, the devil swallow me sideways!" he growled.

"Oh, don't be fretting, Ben," said Finn, his face red with laughter. "You could probably have done with a bath, in any case." He clasped the Giant's hand once more and gave it a friendly shake.

Finn helped Cuhullin to the shore, where Bran and Skolie ran to meet them. After much licking and greeting of Finn, the hounds had a sniff of Cuhullin to get acquainted. Iskander greeted the Giant cheerfully, though he got no more than a grumble in reply. They made their way back up the riverbank and gathered the catch and fishing gear before heading home.

Bran led the way, prancing with his head high and proudly carrying the Piast in his mouth. He was plainly eager to present his trophy to Oonagh. Skolie lingered behind, stopping to sniff a stone here or investigate a patch of reeds there. Finn walked between the two Giants, laughing back and forth with Iskander, and doing what he could to lift Cuhullin's sopping spirits.

When the companions reached the bottom of Knockmany, Finn paused. He had been in the midst of telling one of his favorite tales – of a time when he scared Iskander out of his wits by coming through the darkness in the garb of an Obour – when he noticed that the terrain seemed oddly out of place. Bran and Skolie seemed concerned too. Instead of scampering up to their supper, they sniffed about the base of the hill. Presently there were loud, booming voices from the top of Knockmany. Finn and his hounds sped up the side of the hill.

Four Giants sat in a circle atop Knockmany, just outside Finn's door. A fifth Giant, who was heavyset and had a huge beard of red and gray, stood before them, speaking loudly to the other four, though he was not looking at them. Instead, his meaty hands rested on his ample belly and his face was turned toward the sky, as though the heavens were telling him what to say.

"What can I do for you fellows?" Finn panted. The Giants all looked at him. The one who was speaking seemed irritated at being interrupted, but the other four wore faces of relief and weariness.

"Welcome, Finn McCool," answered the rotund, red-bearded Giant, as though it were his responsibility to receive Finn at his own home. "We have been waiting for you." He waved his hand in the direction of the other four, who stood and bowed. As they did so, Cuhullin and Iskander reached the top of the hill, both breathing heavily. At the sight of Cuhullin, the other Giants all recoiled slightly, except one. He stood with his arms folded, a defiant look on his face. He was an extremely small Giant, barely bigger than Finn.

"Please allow me to present my associates," the heavyset Giant continued. "This is Peadair" – he indicated the posturing little Giant – "and may I also present Grimshaw, Girvin, and Parthalan." The Giants nodded in turn as they heard their names pronounced. "And I am Thunderbore." When he introduced himself, Thunderbore's voice deepened and he brought his hand to his chest as though taking some solemn vow.

"I am very pleased to meet the lot of you," Finn replied with a smile. "These are my hounds, Bran and Skolie. Also my dear friend Iskander. And this is –"

"Cuhullin," Peadair interrupted, looking at Cuhullin very strongly. For his part, Cuhullin saw the little Giant as a curiosity, not imagining that one so small could possibly mean to challenge him. In any case, cold and dripping as he was, he for once had no interest in a quarrel.

"We have come," Thunderbore intoned, "to request that you join us in an effort – nay, a calling – a quest, if you will – that concerns us all. The very fate of Eire, Alba, and the world beyond lies in our hands." He looked down at his palms and paused for effect.

"Well, that's grand," answered Finn before Thunderbore could continue. "I think we can make room enough for us all. Let's go on inside and kick it around a bit." He spread his arms wide by way of welcome, ushering the Giants toward the house. Bran picked up the Piast and scampered in ahead of them.

Oonagh was always a wonderful hostess. She never begrudged guests, no matter how large or how many, as long as they brought good natures with them. It was not until Cuhullin and Finn came squishing in that she protested.

"Oh no," she announced. "Not on my floors, you boys." Finn, smiling, held up his catch of fish. "Lovely" – she nodded as she took the fish – "but now find yourself something dry. Ben, I'm not sure what Finn has that will fit. Let's see what we can find you."

As the Giants settled into the big room (and there was just enough room to accommodate them), Oonagh hung Finn's and Cuhullin's wet clothes in front of the fire. Finn emerged from the bedroom wearing crisp dry clothes, and clapped his hands and rubbed them together in anticipation of a merry time. Cuhullin squeezed back in from outside, where he had labored to cram himself into the very largest of Finn's clothes. Oonagh had done a quick job letting out the shirt and trousers as far as they would go. The trousers still stopped well short of reaching his feet, and his belly was not altogether concealed by the length of the shirt. Nevertheless, he was grateful to be dry.

Thunderbore rose in dramatic fashion from his seat beside the fire, once his audience was assembled. "We come to the business at hand," he pronounced. "There is danger upon us. Danger for ourselves, for our homes, and for all we hold sacred. Our land is being overrun. Our waters as well." He gestured to the Piast, which had been laid out upon the floor. Bran lay nearby, keeping careful watch over his prize. "The Little King across the Sea, leader of men and enemy of our people, has turned his dreadful gaze on Eire. All of us here have been affected in some way, or can expect to be soon. Parthalan could tell you how his lands have been taken by little ones with ill intent, and how his rivers are choked with these vile snakes." Parthalan, a medium-sized Giant with brown hair cropped about his ears and deep, dark eyes, nodded in agreement. A farmer, he was an oddity among his fellows in that, rather than high lonely hills, he sought open plains where crops could grow. He was a Great One of few words.

"And Grimshaw," Thunderbore went on, "tells a harrowing tale of near escape." Grimshaw was tall and very lean, and his bearing gave the impression that he had been harrowed for many centuries. His face was especially thin, with long, gray whiskers in lieu of a full beard, and there were bags of weariness under his eyes. He leaned forward slightly in his chair and cleared his throat to speak.

"I was chased from my hill –"

"Chased from his hill!" Thunderbore echoed, smacking his fist into his upturned palm. "Set upon by a mob of mortal fiends – without warning or provocation – and pursued from his home by a forest of torches. We are grateful that he survived to join us here." Grimshaw nodded in appreciation as he closed his mouth and settled back into his chair. "But it grows yet more dire!" Thunderbore continued. "Girvin has seen, and will bear witness, that the Giants Ring has been stolen!"

"It has," Girvin confirmed. He was about the size of Parthalan, with a more pointed face, and his long, black hair swept across his forehead. His eyes were inscrutable, set in deep sockets on his lean visage.

"Stolen!" Thunderbore pronounced once more.

"Hang on," Finn spoke up. "How could the Giants Ring be stolen? You mean all of it is gone?" Iskander, Oonagh, and Cuhullin were also stunned.

"Stolen and gone, as though it had never been there."

"But who could do such a thing?" Oonagh asked. "Who would even be able?"

"Can you not think who?" said Thunderbore. "Could mortal imps move the Ring? Certainly not. Only by the power of the Great Ones could this be accomplished." He was right. The Giants Ring consisted of ancient stones brought to Eire eons before. The origin of the stones was shrouded in mystery, and the Ring itself was a marvel of construction upon a seaside mountain. Legend held that the Nephilim had brought the huge stones from far to the south shortly after the dawning of the world, and arranged them in a circle on a site of mystical power. It had been a sacred place of the Great Ones since time beyond counting. "And that is the worst of it," Thunderbore went on. "For who of us would do such a thing of our own will? None – not even the most treacherous. We must conclude that Great brothers of ours have been taken by the enemy and put to evil purposes. We have heard such reports. And we all know of the sad fate of the Bolster."

"There's no proof to the tale of the Bolster!" Cuhullin protested. He had selfish reasons for speaking up. According to legend, the Bolster was an enormous Giant, perhaps even larger than Gogmagog himself, who had been captured by mortal men and held captive at the pleasure of the Little King. It was said that this huge being was subjected to unspeakable cruelties and forced to fight for the King's amusement. The tale had been told for so long that none could remember if it was truth or merely a fable, or whether there had ever been a Bolster at all. As for Cuhullin, he could not face the thought of a Giant who was bigger than him.

"There can be no doubt the Little King is at work upon our island," Thunderbore went on. "He and his henchman – the cruelest, most vicious, most bloodthirsty mortal man that ever there was."

"Jack in the Green," muttered Parthalan, his eyes to the floor and his arms folded.

"I'm sorry," said Finn, leaning forward. "Who?" He did not notice the look of fear on Oonagh's face.

Thunderbore explained, "There is a monster, no more than half your size but more fearsome than you can imagine, in the service of our enemy. His shears have been the death of countless of our kind. His name is Jack in the Green and he is indomitable. His heart is stone and he is without mercy. He is invisible to the eye, when he wishes to be. His movements are made at the speed of thought."

"Well, we may take comfort in knowing *that* isn't always so fast," Finn said, stealing a glance at Cuhullin, but the others were too unnerved to enjoy his joke. An uncomfortable silence fell.

"If he's smaller than us, what harm can he do?" one Giant was heard to mumble.

"Who said that?" snapped Peadair, who was always demanding to know who had said what, and daring others to repeat themselves. "Why don't you say that again and watch what happens?" Being on the smallish side, he resented any suggestion that a littler fellow could not be fearsome.

"Did you say this Jack fights with shears?" Finn asked.

"Yes," Thunderbore replied. "Sharp, golden, and terrible."

"How interesting," said Finn. "I never thought of shears as much of a weapon. Why would a person fight with shears, I wonder?"

"He used to be a tailor," Grimshaw answered.

"Yes, a tailor," Thunderbore cut in. "A tailor's apprentice, in fact. A young urchin in Alba, taken in and taught a trade. He is altogether evil."

"An evil tailor?" wondered Iskander.

"Most evil, yes," Thunderbore answered. "He was born poor, but now he sits at the right hand of the Little King. How often peasants rise by genius or cruelty!"

"But what interest do they have in us?" Oonagh asked.

"There can be no reasoning with people who believe their time has come," Thunderbore replied. "Mortal men have decided that our lands should be theirs and that our time is past. They have taken Treryn, the castle of Gogmagog, and they have captured and killed us wherever they could. Jack's lieutenants are strong in Eire now. They are led by a man named Dunbar." The name brought a flicker of recognition to Finn's mind, but it was gone almost at once.

"Yet vicious men are only part of the doom we face," Thunderbore continued. "This creature you have plucked from your river is one of many such serpents. No one wishes to cast blame, but it is said that one night not long ago, the Great Hag failed to replace the stone." This was unhappy news. For as long as anyone could recall, it had been the task of the Great Hag, also known as the Harridan, to replace the stone in the rushing spring atop the abandoned hill of Clogher, to the south of Knockmany. She did this at sundown, to protect the waters of Eire from evil creatures. So dependable had she been in this solemn task, said to have been assigned her by the Dagda himself, that none feared for the fate of Eire's rivers. "By some trickery or other, the enemy waylaid her. And their chief ally was lurking off our shore, ready to spoil our waters. Even now, somewhere in the black depths about our island, swims the Jorgumandr." The others gasped. The Jorgumandr was an ancient snake, mother of the Piast. She was thought to be the largest creature that moved, and her disposition was despicable.

"This is all so dreadful," Oonagh said. "But why come here? What is it you would have us do?"

"We seek the wisdom of Fintan," Thunderbore answered, "to aid us in this time of trouble." All eyes turned to Finn.

"Why, certainly!" Finn said helpfully. "I'll try the thumb at once, and see what thoughts it conjures." He brought his thumb toward his mouth.

"Hang on!" Cuhullin boomed. "Just hold everything right there!" His patience in allowing others to run the meeting had been exhausted. Finn froze, his thumb still pointed upward.

Cuhullin turned his glare on Thunderbore. "You've talked a lot of kerfuffle here tonight. You've got the Little King's armies taking our hills and the Giants Ring, snakes swimming up the rivers, and Jack in the Green coming to chop all our heads off. And what proof have you got for any of it? Nothing

but this silly thing." He reached for the Piast on the floor, but
Bran growled. "If you'd come to us with one simple problem,
I'd be more inclined to believe you. But you've chosen instead
to claim the world is coming to an end. I think you're having
us all on. There is no danger. You'd like to rally us, indeed –
then send us off somewhere to do your bidding!"

"With respect, Cuhullin," Grimshaw offered meekly,
"this is not even your island."

Slowly, Cuhullin turned, his massive hands balled into
fists. Grimshaw grew even paler. But before Cuhullin could
do any damage to the frail Giant, Peadair sprang up in front
of him.

"Grimshaw's right!" he shouted. Cuhullin's face grew
red and he puffed up his chest. Oonagh leapt to her feet
between them.

"If you lads think you'll be coming to blows in my parlor,
then you've vastly miscalculated. Sit you down now – the
both of you!" She glared them both back into their seats.

"These tidings are true, Benandonner," Thunderbore
insisted. "And it gives me no joy to report them. I have no
motive except our survival. The world did not grow more
perilous in an instant. It happened as we slept. A little at a
time, the world we knew slipped away. We are all who remain
to battle these woes."

Parthalan suddenly spoke up, though he was still looking
at the floor. "One problem at a time."

"Quite right," agreed Thunderbore. "We must keep our
wits. Finn McCool, if you would be so good, please provide
us with that insight of yours."

"Oh, surely!" Turning slightly toward the wall (as he was
embarrassed by the gesture), Finn thrust his thumb into his
mouth and slurped on it thoughtfully. The taste of black ash
made him wince and images passed through his mind. They

were with him but an instant, and then gone again. He popped his thumb out.

"Well?" Iskander spoke up.

"I see fire and black water," Finn replied. "Nothing more. I should have mentioned," he said, flexing his thumb up and down as he displayed it around the room, "that I don't use this thumb very often. It could be out of practice."

"Fire and black water," Thunderbore mused, stroking his beard.

"I wonder if he means –" Girvin began, before stopping himself.

"Yes?" asked Iskander.

"Nothing, really." Girvin was a wandering Giant and had seen many places. "When you said black water just now, there was a place I thought of. In the north of Alba. I'm sure it's not what you're looking for."

"The Black Loch?" asked Thunderbore.

"Well, yes," replied Girvin, "that is what I thought of, but I doubt it's what you're after."

"You may be right," Finn encouraged him. "Sure I saw water, and it was black – and you've suggested a spot just like that. Well done!"

"I know the Black Loch," said Cuhullin with self-importance. "It is, after all, in my land of Fyfe." He glanced sharply at Grimshaw.

"Is it true what they say about the Black Loch?" Oonagh asked. Cuhullin's mouth fell open, as if he had no clue as to what she meant. "Is it really the home of the Leviathan, as people say?"

"Oh *that*," he answered. "Yes, yes, of course. I've seen him often." Aware of the astonished looks he was receiving, he attempted to embroider his lie. "We Fyfians are all familiar with the Leviathan. I did not know what you meant at first, because the sight of him is so very common. I didn't think it worth noting." Small beads of sweat appeared on his forehead. "We're on quite good terms, I'd say. He's not as large as you'd think. Well – he is *large*, of course. But when you've seen him as often as I have, you forget the size of him. I suppose I am just so used to him. The Leviathan, I mean." The others were gobsmacked. Cuhullin managed a weak smile.

"Could it be," thought Thunderbore aloud, "that Fintan means us to seek out the Leviathan?"

"Well, I've got to tell you," Finn chimed in, "that it's starting to make a lot of sense. I see some black water, and old Girvin knows just the spot I'm thinking of. And here's more fortune – Ben is on friendly terms with the fellow we're supposed to go and see. Sounds like good luck and ancient wisdom, both!"

"Of course!" said Thunderbore. "We must go and ask the Leviathan to fight the Jorgumandr for us! That's one big problem solved right there – wouldn't you agree, Parthalan?" The farmer nodded.

"Excuse me," Girvin inquired, "but why would he do this? The Leviathan, that is. What would be in it for him?"

"You surprise me, Girvin," Thunderbore replied. "Noble deeds require no recompense. The Leviathan's honor is ancient! I suspect he will be eager for such a task. And besides, our Benandonner here is on excellent terms with the creature. He can do whatever convincing is necessary." He gestured toward Cuhullin, who had been gazing about the room nonchalantly, hoping to be ignored. Realizing that all eyes were upon him once again, he felt obliged to speak.

"Well, yes and no."

"Which is it?" snapped Peadair.

"What I mean to say" – Cuhullin was searching for words – "is that I'd hate to trouble the Leviathan for no good reason. That's what I mean. Sure, we're on fine terms. But I wonder how long that would last if I dragged him from his lake for nothing. And that is what I suspect he'd find lurking in our sea – nothing."

"Perhaps you are right," Thunderbore allowed. "Let us assume for a moment that the Piast have sprung from nothing to infest our waters. Let us further assume that the Jorgumandr sightings – of which there have been many, I hasten to add – are fabrications and fantasies brought about by drink. What would you have us do? Nothing? I think not. We must do something, and Fintan's wisdom, which we journeyed here to seek, has been imparted to us. Should we ignore that ancient legacy – of which the Leviathan is a part – and dismiss such wisdom, freely given?" The Giants fell silent.

"Well, those are just excellent questions," Finn said with admiration. Silence again.

"Someone should go with him," Parthalan said, after a good while.

"Right you are, Parthalan," Thunderbore agreed.

"Go with who?" Cuhullin asked.

"You should have a companion on your quest," Thunderbore replied. "And there is but one who is right for the task." He puffed out his chest, causing everyone in the room to suspect that he was about to nominate himself. "Finn McCool, the rightful Captain of the Fianna and scourge of the Fomorians, whose wisdom has shown us the true path, must go with you." The Giants were shocked, and no one was more shocked than Finn himself.

"That's high praise, to be sure," he answered. "But I wonder if it's not a bit of overreach. Every one of you is bigger than me, and apart from the thumb-sucking, I'm not sure I've much to offer. That incident with the Frost Giant was a powerful long time ago."

"Finn McCool," Thunderbore declared, "you are the Chief Protector of Eire. It is your title by right and by deed. None of us is what we once were. But your gift of foresight cannot be matched by any of us. You must do this."

"Hang on a bit, though," Finn answered. "Knockmany is a part of Eire, and I'm the Chief Protector of this bit most of all. Who is to watch over my Oonagh and my hounds if Ben and I go wandering off the island?"

"We shall do it," said Thunderbore with confidence, waving his hand to include the other Giants. "We will stay here and watch over your hill until you return. This task needs doing. You, Finn McCool, are the one to do it."

Finn was flummoxed. He did not want to go. He felt he had been more than helpful by pointing them in the right direction. He thought of all the fishing that would go undone. Looking about the room, he saw the expectant faces of the Giants turned to him. That is, except Cuhullin, who was muttering to himself and shaking his head.

Finally Finn's eyes settled on Oonagh, who had been keeping her own thoughts. She too looked about the room, then back at Finn. She smiled sadly. So it was decided that Finn and Cuhullin would set out for the Black Loch.

το τhe black loch

Knockmany was usually quiet at night. But with so many Giants at close quarters, this night was an exception. The house was cramped, as most of the Giants had stretched out in their chairs to sleep. Cuhullin and Thunderbore, in particular, snored powerfully. Bran curled up with the Piast in the middle of the floor. His paws twitched as he dreamed, perhaps, of chasing it down once again. Grimshaw had decided to sleep outside, saying that he was used to wind and cold. He was soon joined by Peadair, who stomped out, muttering, after his many threats of reprisals failed to quiet the snorers.

Morning crept across the hill to reveal a Great and bleary-eyed company stretching, scratching, and coming to terms with the light. Oonagh was an early riser, and was pleased to display her skills by baking stacks of delicious cakes. This was deeply appreciated by her guests – especially Grimshaw, who wolfed down several helpings as though he had not eaten in an age. Cuhullin bit warily into his first cake, but once he was certain there was nothing to fear, he set to eating with his characteristic vigor.

Finn rose unusually late, partly because he was not eager for this day to begin. Breakfast helped.

"Cakes!" he whooped, seeing them stacked high on the kitchen table, and he tucked in at once. "Cakes, cakes, cakes!" he sang, as Bran circled his chair and Skolie sang with him, in her way.

After the Giants had devoured their massive helpings of cakes and headed, one by one, out of doors, Oonagh sat with Finn at the kitchen table.

"My love," she began.

"Yes, my dearest?" he replied. "These are quite lovely cakes, by the by."

"I am glad you are enjoying them," she said. "I must tell you something. I do not want you to set out on this journey."

"Ah, that's a weight off my mind!" He smiled. "I've no desire to go, myself!" He rested his palms on the table and leaned back contentedly in his chair.

"You must let me finish. I do not want you to go, but I fear you must. That is not to say I believe everything Thunderbore has told us. I do not know what to believe. But I feel there is some task that needs doing, and you are the one to do it. There is something that needs saving. Do not ask me to explain it, because I do not understand it fully myself. But I know that once you leave this hill, I will not see you again for a very long time."

"Away with that talk. Ben and I will go straight there and straight back. It's no more than a couple days."

Oonagh took his hand. "Last night, I dreamed there was a great green sea between us. I was in a tower high above the waves, and I could see you on the other shore. I called to you but you could not hear. And so I sang to you, and you knew my voice. But you could not see me."

"You have a lovely voice, my dearest."

"And then you stepped into the waters," she continued, patting his hand, "and I lost sight of you. You were gone, and I did not know where."

"Well, that's not going to happen," replied Finn, shaking his head.

Oonagh managed a smile. "I will lose you, but only for a time. I will look for you coming from afar. Every day I will expect to see your face, though many days they may be. I shall keep a song for you so you are always with me, though you are beyond my sight."

Finn looked at her for some time as he considered all she said. Even after centuries, he was still enchanted by her beauty. Though her face was grave at this moment, there was no sight more pleasing to his eye. Before he could speak, meaning to comfort her once again, she kissed him with all the adoration that was in her. Then they rose and walked outside together.

"Sure, 'tis a glorious day to begin a quest!" Thunderbore bellowed. He placed his hands on his chest, drew a deep breath through his nose, and sighed loudly, ending with a snort of satisfaction. The Giants, Finn, Oonagh, and the hounds waited for him to continue, as they knew he would. "What a splendid journey this shall be. Such heroes! Such stuff of legend! What great good we shall accomplish!"

"Is he going with you, all of a sudden?" Iskander muttered to Finn.

"I gather he just means it was his idea," Finn said with a shrug.

"If you ask me," Thunderbore went on, adopting a less formal tone and smiling around at them, "this day will be counted among the best our kind have had." He gave a wink to no one in particular. "Wouldn't you say?" He winked again. No one doubted the question was rhetorical, so there came no response. "The ancient wisdom of the Tuatha De Danann has shown us the true path, and this noble pair set out today to defend our island. This is bravery indeed. They shall face dangers unknown. It may be that they go to their doom!" Thunderbore caught a sharp glance from Oonagh. "But more probably they will go straight there and straight back, unharmed," he hastily added. "Yes, this is the most likely scenario. But let it not detract from the glory of their quest!"

Finn and Cuhullin shook each Giant's hand. Grimshaw gave Finn a weak pat upon the shoulder. Peadair grinned broadly up at Cuhullin while their hands reddened with the force of their grip. When it became clear that neither wanted to be the first to let go, Oonagh cleared her throat conspicuously and they separated. Thunderbore shook Finn's hand with importance, as though he were about to present him with some sort of award. Finn then turned to Iskander.

"You'll keep your eye on my little ones here?" he asked.

"Every moment." Iskander smiled, opening his one eye wide to make a show of its size. "This eye sees all, my friend." They each placed one hand upon the other's shoulder. "I will protect them with my life," Iskander added. "Though you won't be gone long. In fact, hurry back. Your wife is a demanding listener, and I'd hate to run out of clever remarks before your return." They laughed together, and Finn moved on to Bran and Skolie, who had been watching him closely.

Kneeling beside them, he wrapped his huge arms around his hounds. He kissed them on their heads and whispered into their ears, speaking to them for quite some time.

Whatever he was telling them was spoken too softly for others to hear, and in any case it was no one else's concern. Kissing them each once more and patting them as he rose to his feet, he turned at last to Oonagh.

"I shall be straight back, my love." Oonagh smiled softly and nodded. She lifted her arms to him and kissed him goodbye.

Then Finn took up his green cap, walking stick, and the more than ample pack of supplies Oonagh had prepared. Cuhullin had likewise been given a wealth of provisions, along with his dry clothes. Finn had told Oonagh she was sending them off with too much food, but she had answered that he should just take what she gave him and stop fussing. Finn and Cuhullin looked around one last time to ensure that nothing had been forgotten and then, each with his own reluctance, made their way down the side of Knockmany.

Their descent was slow. Cuhullin did not want to repeat the previous day's ungraceful performance, especially with several sets of eyes watching him expectantly from the summit above. He chose his steps with extreme caution, at times waving Finn to go ahead and stop bothering about him, and reached the foot of Knockmany without incident.

"This will give us a splendid chance to become better acquainted, eh?" said Finn as they set out across the emerald field. Cuhullin grunted. "Yes indeed," Finn continued merrily, "just two lads and the big wide world, full of adventure. What fun!"

Cuhullin was not overly sociable at the best of times, but he was particularly uninterested in geniality just now. His mind was elsewhere. First, he hoped to make a good impression at the Causeway. He had gotten across it without panicking the previous day, but then his fear had been tempered by anger. He would have to work himself up

into a bit of a rage to face the crossing today. Once beyond
the Causeway, he would have a far graver problem. He did
not know, nor had he ever seen, the Leviathan. He knew no
more of this creature from the deep than anyone else. In
fact, he likely knew less. Despite living in Fyfe for countless
ages, he had never taken the trouble to learn its history.
Moreover, he had only the vaguest of notions as to how to
find the Black Loch.

They reached the muddy path in good time, and
descended toward the water and the foot of the Causeway.

"After you," Finn offered, waving out to sea.

"Well, don't rush now," answered Cuhullin hotly. "No
one likes to be rushed, no matter what's at stake. I am surprised at you, Finn McCool!" He had hoped to work up far
more anger, but this was all he could muster.

"Fair enough, then," Finn replied, without taking the
slightest offense. "Take your time. I hope you don't mind if I
wander around a bit?" He breathed in the fine air and strolled
along the Causeway, stopping now and then to inspect the
placement of the rocks, and tap a few back into place with
his walking stick.

Meanwhile, Cuhullin looked around for something to
make him mad. Blasted rocks! Accursed sky! Smug Finn
McCool! These all irritated him, to be sure, but none made
him furious. He jabbed at the sockets of his eyes with his
finger, hoping to make them bulge – perhaps, if he could
achieve a look of rage, his temper would follow. But it was no
use. Why had he been so foolish? Why, for *once*, had he not
thought before speaking? Now here he was, running errands
for that insufferable Thunderbore, and in the company of
Finn McCool! And who was to blame? No one but himself!
Mindless, stupid Giant, he was! With all his seething, he
found himself well out upon the Causeway before he knew it.

"Ah, there you are," Finn said, inhaling deeply. "Isn't that sea air a joy?" The mist had gathered, so that all Cuhullin could see was the water surrounding the patch of rock on which he was standing, and Finn sniffing and grinning at him. The Giant began to feel unwell. "Well, come on, then!" Finn exclaimed, giving him a friendly knock on the arm and turning once again toward Fyfe. Cuhullin followed slowly, sliding his huge feet rather than picking them up and placing them down in proper steps. Finn took no notice as he pointed at spots here and there, and gave a detailed and unasked-for account of the Causeway's construction.

When at last they reached Fyfe, Finn hopped onto the land. Cuhullin followed, taking short, sharp steps at the last so that he reached the shore at a bit of a run. Placing his hand upon his chest, he leaned forward and breathed deeply. He stamped his feet three times, as if to assure himself that he was again on solid earth.

"Which way then, eh?" Finn asked, looking about hopefully. Fyfe always seemed to him as yellow as Eire was green. The land was drier, somehow, with high, lonely hills that looked like piles of straw. He remembered the range of small mountains to the north, but the peaks seemed lower, as though the land had shrunk since last he'd seen it.

"Now, don't be hasty." Cuhullin thought a moment, trying to recall the general location of the Loch. Nothing but sea lay behind them, to the west – this much he knew – so the Loch was to the east. Something about north occurred to him also. Had he even been there before? He could not remember. He had heard the Black Loch spoken of and seen it gestured toward, but when, and by whom? And were they gesturing with any purpose or just waving generally? If indeed he had been pointed toward the Loch at some point, which way had he been facing? "This way," he announced at last, with false confidence, stomping up from the shore and turning to the north and east.

Finn followed, twirling his walking stick and admiring the views. They traveled all day, along high ridges with sheer drops and through vast golden plains ringed with mountains. Once, Finn felt certain they were passing through a valley they had already crossed earlier in the day. He said nothing of it, however, as his companion was far ahead and trudging with what seemed like purpose. Though he did not know his way, Cuhullin enjoyed being the leader.

"That's quite far enough for today," Cuhullin yawned, as the sun began to set and the shadows stretched. "We'd best find ourselves a hill for the night."

"Where are we?"

"I can't explain every little detail to you, Finn McCool," the Giant replied with irritation. "We are in my lands now. That's all you need know." They were standing in a low meadow, encircled by small clumps of trees that huddled together as though whispering secrets. "How about this one?" He pointed due north, to the highest peak that could be seen. It was sharp and rocky, poking into the sky like a finger accusing the heavens.

"That seems like it would be an awful bother to climb at this hour," mused Finn.

"Our hills are not the gentle slopes you are used to in Eire!" Cuhullin boasted. "Our hills are serious business in a serious land. Now come along!" He turned sharply and led the way. Tired though he was, Finn followed without complaint.

When they reached the base of the hill, they could see that it was tall indeed, and capped with snow. It towered over all others in its small range, and was sheer rock. In fact, it seemed less a hill than a small mountain. The feel of the place was deathly cold, made keener by the lack of greenery.

"You're certain this is the one you want to climb?" Finn asked.

"Yes, of course." Truth be told, Cuhullin had not realized how high the hill was. But now that they were here, he could not weaken. "This is really just a baby hill, by our reckoning," he added, as he swung his foot up to begin the climb.

It was a sharp and steep ascent and Cuhullin had been right on at least one count – Finn had seen nothing like this hill in Eire. Hands and feet had to work in concert, and it was slow going to reach the top. Several times, they needed to stop and hang in one spot for a spell to catch their breath.

When at last they pulled themselves onto the summit – Cuhullin had made a sprint of the final portion to be sure he finished before the half-Great – they rolled onto their backs in the snow, wheezing loudly. Exhausted, cold, and wet, Finn was unconvinced that this hill had been worth the time and effort. He doubted that the Black Loch would be found at the top of such a hill, and they could just as easily have gone around. Certainly they needed some high place for the night, but there were many perfectly serviceable peaks nearby. Why trouble with this monster? Even so, he determined to trust in Cuhullin and make the best of things. The sun was gone now, and so weary were they that they might have been content to close their eyes and drift off to sleep right there – had there not come a blood-freezing roar from behind them.

They leapt to their feet and squinted into the darkness. They could not determine the source of the sound, because it echoed across the range. The moon brightened the summit and they saw that the top was much flatter and broader than they had thought. The roar came again.

"Hello?" Finn offered meekly. Once the word left his lips, he wished he could grab it back again, so pitiful did it sound. Through the gloom he could make out Cuhullin's look of contempt.

"Who goes there?" Cuhullin demanded of the darkness, as if demonstrating the proper form for facing death.

"I go here!" came a booming response. A tall shape approached through the shadows. The blue moonlight traced the slender frame, higher than Cuhullin's but thinner, with long arms. There was a flicker of green eyes. Being approached through cold blackness by an unseen foe was uncomfortably familiar for Finn. "And I go there. I go where I wish. But who are you?" The tall figure stopped no more than a few paces from them, but still they could not make out any features.

"I am Cuhullin! Giant of Fyfe and rightful leader of all Great Ones upon these islands! Who dares to address me?" Cuhullin was much more worried than he sounded.

"Cuhullin, eh? Lovely." This was puzzling. Never, in legend or recorded history, had Cuhullin been described as lovely. Was the figure joking? Had they been expected? Before they could draw conclusions, there was a flash of blue flame, and a Giant's huge face appeared. "I suppose you're here for a fight!" Finn and Cuhullin started. The face was pale, with a white beard that tumbled down to the Giant's belly. The eyes were like two evergreens surrounded by snow. It was unclear whether the Giant was smiling, scowling, or both.

"And who are you?" Cuhullin demanded, once he had recovered himself.

"That," answered the white Giant, "is a fine, fine question. Who am I? Who are you, even?" Cuhullin began to introduce himself again but the Giant held up his hand to stop him. "Yes, you have told me. You are Cuhullin. That is your name. But is that who you are? I have heard this name before, and I suppose you have climbed this hill to seek a quarrel. You seek out many hills, and you fight whomever

you please. Perhaps that is who you are, though you call yourself Cuhullin. Do you see?" They did not see.

"Very well," the white Giant sighed. "You may call me
Baldemar."

"Very pleased to meet you, Baldemar," Finn said. "I am
Finn McCool." Finn could see that Baldemar held an
enormous icicle in his hand, the top of which burned like
a blue torch.

"Are you?" enthused Baldemar. "Finn McCool! How
interesting!"

"Thank you," Finn responded, a little perplexed.

"Come on, then," Baldemar said, turning. Cuhullin had
been expecting a quarrel, but he unclenched his fists and
looked at Finn, who shrugged and followed the white Giant.
He led them across the summit to the gaping entrance of a
domed structure fashioned out of snow. At the door, kicking
at the thin layer of snow upon the ground, he cleared a large
circle of rock and gathered clumps of snow in his hands. He
smoothed and patted the snow into a ball and set it in the
middle of the circle. Then, taking up the icicle once again,
he touched its flame to the snowball, which began to glow
bright blue.

"What is that?" Finn asked.

"This?" said Baldemar. "This is cold fire."

"Does it get you warm?" Cuhullin asked through chattering teeth.

"Not exactly, but it makes it so you don't mind the cold.
Come, have a seat and let's quarrel." He sat down upon the
bare rock, rubbing his palms together and lifting them to the
blue orb.

Cold, wet, and eager to be off their feet, Finn and
Cuhullin set their packs in the circle and sat with Baldemar.
When Finn rubbed his hands together and held them up, he

found that the Giant had described the cold fire aptly. It made him no warmer – indeed, it likely made him colder still – but the discomfort of the cold faded. Remembering his manners, he offered Baldemar some of the edibles Oonagh had packed for them.

"No thank you," Baldemar replied. "I do not eat your kind of food." This remark was delivered with a slightly superior air. In the blue light, Finn could see the Giant's features more clearly. His white beard was huge indeed, much wider than his face, and there was not a strand of hair atop his head, which glowed blue in the light of the fire. His nose was long and sharp, and his deep green eyes darted back and forth from Finn to Cuhullin, as though he was hatching some scheme.

"Nice hill you've got here," said Finn, looking about.

"It's taller than you're used to," Baldemar jumped right in, as though this was precisely what he had expected Finn to say. "And colder. Isn't that right?"

"Yes, actually," Finn replied.

"Have you considered that your hills are too short and not cold enough?" Baldemar asked sharply. "Perhaps they have made you soft."

"Is that what you suppose?" bellowed Cuhullin, bracing himself to stand.

"It is a suggestion, not an accusation," Baldemar said mildly. Cuhullin calmed a bit. "I know what goes on elsewhere," Baldemar continued, "and I know the ways of your kind."

"Are you not one of our kind?" asked Finn.

"No," said Baldemar with palpable pride, "I am a Snow Giant."

"Never heard of a Snow Giant before," Finn mused.

"There are many things of which you have never heard, Finn McCool," Baldemar countered, "but they exist, just the same."

"Fair enough," said Finn. "Are there many of you? Snow Giants, that is."

"There is but one, and he is me."

"Hang on," Cuhullin interjected. "Are you saying you're the only Snow Giant there is?"

"Yes."

"Isn't that interesting," Finn said. "What happened to the others?"

"Which others?"

"The other Snow Giants. Where did they go?"

"There never were any others," said Baldemar firmly. "I am the only Snow Giant there has ever been."

"Curious, that," said Finn. "But if there never were any others, how do you know you are one? That is, how do you know you are not merely a Giant who prefers the cold?"

"I am the Snow Giant because I have said so. I declare that I am different from the others, and so I am. Which is more important – what others say we are, or what we call ourselves?" Baldemar smiled and looked back to the blue fire.

"Can he *do* that?" Cuhullin whispered to Finn after a moment. Finn shrugged.

"That's certainly a way to look at things," Finn admitted. "Here I was, imagining you had to have several of a thing before you could give it a name. For instance, look at Frost Giants. There were plenty of those!"

Baldemar chuckled. "And do you suppose there are none now? Do you? I know what goes on."

"Do you mean to tell me," asked Finn, "that there are Frost Giants hereabouts?"

"I do not mean to tell you anything," Baldemar said. "I mean for you to think on what you already know. This is the way to true knowledge." As Finn tried to find sense in the Giant's musings, Cuhullin, who had meager interest in such talk even when he was not hungry, dug into his pack for some food.

"I wonder, Baldemar," Finn ventured, hoping to change the subject, "if there is anything you can tell us about our current quest. We are on our way to the Black Loch, in search of the Leviathan."

This intrigued Baldemar. "But of course you are," he said. "And you have taken the long way round. Very clever, half-Great. Very clever indeed!"

"Excuse me," Finn asked, "but what do you mean, we're taking the long way round? We're not meaning to be clever – we'd just like to get there and back again." Cuhullin looked up from his pack.

"You came from Eire, did you not? Knockmany, if I am not mistaken? Yes – see how I know things? But you have not taken the most direct route to your destination. If half of what is said of you is true, you did this by design. Whatever your reasons, you have overshot the Loch by some way. Circled around it, in fact, and up my hill." Finn looked at Cuhullin, who nodded vaguely.

"I can't say why we've come this way," Finn answered, "but I wonder what path to the Loch you'd recommend from here."

"You flatter me, Finn McCool." Baldemar laughed. "You presume I am fit to direct you this way or that. Do you surrender your will so meekly?"

"I surrender nothing. I am merely asking for suggestions."

"You surrender everything! You have surrendered to the elements and you have surrendered to my counsel. You were prepared to surrender outright when first you heard me approach!"

"Well, since you mention it," said Finn, "why did you bellow at us so?"

"Is it not my right?" Baldemar asked haughtily. "How might you react if dark strangers came rolling onto your hill in the dead of night?"

"In truth, I'd most likely greet them with a mug of stout and as good a story as I could tell."

"Weakness," muttered the Snow Giant.

"Sorry?"

"There is a notion that all things grow smaller with time. I believe it is true of your kind, most of all. You have been left to your devices for eons, and it has made you soft and addicted to the warmth. You shy away from the rugged battle of fate. This is island-dwarfing. Your famous hill is on an island that you believe is safe. You shrink there, and you forget yourself. You say you'd bring a cup of stout? A cup of surrender, more like." Cuhullin listened as he munched on an enormous cheese.

"Now hang on there," Finn protested. "Incivility is not strength. I expect it may be time to leave." He spoke curtly, rising to his feet.

"Sit down, sit down," Baldemar said soothingly. "Did we not agree to quarrel? Sit down and rest and we'll begin again in a moment. Don't take offense." Finn wondered what he was meant to take, if not offense. But as he did not wish to brave the cold and dark trek to another hill, he settled back down beside the fire. "That's right," Baldemar added. "Be great enough to let it pass."

"Since you want to talk about greatness," Finn said, "perhaps you know something of my history. I am the son of Cuhail mac Art, leader of the Fianna and scourge of the Fomorians."

"Yes, I know all that. But can you speak of others' greatness without mentioning your own?"

"I was just coming to that," Finn continued crossly. "Have you seen my Causeway? And does the name Ymir of the Frost Giants strike you in any way?"

"Of course I know these things. Your great works are the stuff of songs and tales. But once you are dead, they will do no more than make an evening a little brighter for those who are left. You said a moment ago that there must be many of a thing before it can be named. But you seek the Leviathan. There is only one of him, is there not? There is but one Little King, but one Jack in the Green."

"Only one Ice Spider, too," Cuhullin added, still munching away.

"He has a name," Baldemar shot back. "But yes, there is only one of him."

"Fascinating stuff," Finn said with irritation, "but I miss your meaning."

"I mean," Baldemar said, fixing his eyes intently upon Finn, "that there is only one Finn McCool. What greatness can you make of him?"

Finn returned his gaze. The sky was blackness now, with no stars to be seen, and wind hissed across the top of the mountain. He folded his arms across his knees and shrugged toward the cold fire. "I wish to make nothing of him," he said at last. "I wish to find the Black Loch, do what we must, and then return to my hill."

There was silence between them for several moments. The only sound was Cuhullin's chewing. "And while we're about it, Baldemar," Finn continued, "what special place do you hold among the Dagda's children that you badger others in this way?"

The Snow Giant chuckled.

"Do I amuse you?" Finn asked. "Do I seem quaint and silly to you? My hill is too short and warm, isn't that right? What is more, I sing too readily, my wife feeds me too well, and all my tales end happily. When insulted, I bristle, though I'll steer clear of a scuffle if the other fellow lets me. But I have lived long and I have lived well, and I'd rather be a smiling simpleton than a cold-bodied codger any day of the year and twice on Samhain."

"Well!" Baldemar answered after several moments of silence. "There it is, then." He tented his fingers over his long nose. "You'd just like to get there and back again. Isn't that what you said? You'd like to tumble down to the Loch, wake the Leviathan for reasons of your own, then turn on your heel and head home. Well, there are at least two truths I can offer you. One – if and when you wake the mighty creature, he's going to want to know the reason why. I advise that you make your answer short and truthful. Our Leviathan is monstrous and perceptive. He will know if you lie, and you'll wish you hadn't. Two – and this may be more to the point – your purpose is deeply flawed. I confess I do not know why you seek the Leviathan. Frankly, I don't much care. If you have the good fortune to escape the Black Loch in one piece – and this is far from certain – you will see that your life has greatly changed. There are mightier forces at work in the world tonight than Finn the half-Great and his gluttonous friend." Cuhullin, having no idea what "gluttonous" meant, blithely chomped away on two cheeses at once.

"What forces?" Finn inquired.

"You asked before," Baldemar replied, "what special place I hold among the Dagda's children. I tell you that I am no child of the Dagda. If you believe yourself to be one, then that is what you are, and that is what you shall remain: a child. Do you see?"

"That doesn't begin to answer me," Finn sighed. Just as it seemed that Baldemar had begun talking sense, he had gone back to rambling again.

"Does it not? Or does it answer you too well? That is it, I think – I have answered you too well, Finn McCool! You cast your faith high, high into the heavens, and what comes down in return? Silence. I've chosen the highest hill to be found, and dared your Dagda to descend and debate with me. Yet he does not. Is he frightened? Is he merely uninterested? Or can it be that he neither sees nor hears me call him down? This last reason, I think, is enough. One cannot see, one cannot hear, if one does not exist."

"You mean to say that you do not believe in the Dagda?"

"I do not *mean* to say so," Baldemar answered curtly. "I simply say so. And so it is. Do you see?"

"The Dagda," Finn pronounced, "does not appear at the whim of Baldemar. We come and go at the will of the Dagda. In fact, given your attitude, I'd say it's a good thing for you that he didn't show up!"

By this time, Cuhullin had consumed an outrageous quantity of loaves and cheese. He had made an effort to listen to the discussion but, lacking the inclination and vocabulary to call tedium by its name, he had rolled onto his side and fallen asleep.

"You say," Baldemar started again, "that you have lived long, and that you have lived well. I promise that I am far older than you, Demne, and I'll wager my hilltop that I have never lived as well. I have encountered creatures that cannot be described. I have seen many things that would make you weep. Yet I have never seen your Dagda take a hand."

He folded his arms smugly. "You did not seem frightened when I told you the names of the Little King and Jack in the

Green. Either you know nothing of them, or not enough. Do you know of their wizard, Marland? There is no need to make us both awkward by attempting an answer. I see from your face that you do not. But no matter. You say that all you want to do is complete this simple task, so I will help. In the morning, you will see a rough path on the side of my hill opposite where you came up. Descend slowly and mind your feet. At the bottom is what appears to be a yellow field. I am sorry to report that it is a marsh – small creatures leap in to their doom, thinking it a happy meadow – but it should be no more than a nuisance for you. Head due south until you come to a line of trees. You will find that woods and green encircle the Loch. Follow the course of the sun and you will come across the means to summon the Leviathan."

"What means might those be?" asked Finn.

"Never mind the means," Baldemar answered sharply. "Consider, rather, the end. Consider my caution. Consider what you might say if you successfully summon the beast. Choose your words carefully. Be courteous. And, as it might save your life to know it, I should say this – there's no need to mention my name."

"Why not?"

Baldemar let out a long breath. "I like to believe that I am on good terms with most creatures," he said. "I can be a chore, I know it. But it is for the good of all. The Leviathan, it would seem, has a different view. We have not spoken in some centuries, and our last exchange was less than friendly."

"I am sorry to hear that," said Finn.

"In fact, he tried to kill me. I thought the conversation was going rather well, but then he struck. Only my keen reflexes and wealth of experience saved me. More, I cannot tell. The memory is still a terror."

"Well, I shall certainly take heed of all you've said," Finn promised.

Baldemar got to his feet. "I would invite you in," he said, without looking at Finn, "but I think you'd be better off out here. It is colder inside my house. That is how I prefer it. I thank you for a fine quarrel. Good night." With that, the Snow Giant shuffled into his shelter, leaving Finn alone with the dimming blue orb and the sounds of the wind and Cuhullin's snoring.

Finn slung his pack behind him and laid his head upon it. Then he brushed his arms and legs against the ground with vigor to clear the thin layer of snow beneath him. He didn't expect comfort, but he at least hoped not to wake up drenched. His pack was just *that much* too thick to make a proper pillow, and forced his chin down toward his chest. He threw it aside and felt around for something else on which to rest his weary head. His hand fell upon a rock, smooth and flat, no bigger than a dragon's egg. It would have to do – the perfect end to a perfect evening.

He laid his head down once again, folded his arms across his chest, and sighed deeply, gazing at the heavens. A handful of stars had poked through the clouds. As he squinted at them, he thought about how profoundly uncomfortable he was in mind and body. The hard, cold terrain could not be helped. But who did this Baldemar imagine himself to be? What a ruthlessly absurd creature he was.

The Snow Giant was old, or so he claimed, but what did that mean? Finn knew well enough that age itself did not make for greatness. Some gain wisdom from a single word while others linger for centuries, learning nothing and forgetting much. So why did Baldemar irk him so? Was it the cold? Cold could sap both courage and cheer. He missed Oonagh. He missed his hounds. Though he had been gone only a short time, it seemed to him that he had not seen his cozy home in years. He drummed his fingers on his chest and wondered if he could ever fall asleep in such a wretched spot. Just then, Cuhullin began to snore mightily. Lovely, Finn thought.

It occurred to Finn that this might be the highest point he had ever reached – well above Knockmany and the tallest trees he'd ever climbed. Looking up to the night sky, he wondered what one might find above the trees and hills and beyond the stars. Then all at once a smile crossed his face, peace came over him, and he fell into a deep sleep.

There was a rumble. A low sound, unfriendly, it jolted Finn from his slumber. Opening his eyes gingerly to the light, he saw Cuhullin's back. The Giant of Fyfe was kneeling in the snow, not far away, digging in his pack. The rumble came again.

"I'm cursed hungry," Cuhullin muttered to himself.

Finn had been lying on his side. He braced his palm upon the rock beneath him to push himself upright. This was no easy task. A brittle soreness had crept into his bones as he slept, and his muscles had awoken in a defiant mood. Groaning with the effort, he hoisted himself up to sit.

"Goodness, Ben, where do you stick it all?" he asked wearily. Cuhullin continued rummaging. Finn rubbed his eyes with his fists. The morning was cold and clear, and the view from the mountaintop was commanding. It was as though he had been propped upon the tall tower of the world to see what's what. There was a wisp of cloud just below the peak, and below that, yellow fields dotted with hills and trees stretched out to eternity.

With one hand on his back and the other stretching high above his head, Baldemar came yawning out of his cave.

"How's that, chaps?" the Snow Giant asked cheerfully.

"What have you got to eat?" Cuhullin replied.

"A platter of ice can be surprisingly filling. You won't think it's delicious, though." Baldemar traced a circle with his toe, isolating a patch of snow, and flattened it with his foot.

"Bother," Cuhullin grumbled.

"Well, thanks for having us, Baldemar," Finn offered, a little uncomfortably. Truth be told, he was hungry and cold and not quite ready to rise. But after their awkward evening, Finn had a craving to be gone. "We really should be off . . ."

"Pity," Baldemar replied, still not looking up. "I hope it is not our quarrel that quickens your departure. All the same, I trust you will remember all I've said. Fear of criticism is the death of greatness." He flicked his foot, sending a disc of ice hurtling toward Cuhullin. The Giant snatched it up. With another kick, Baldemar served Finn the same way. "Munch on these. They are not food as you understand it, but they'll take the hunger from your minds."

Finn considered the platter of ice for a moment before cautiously bringing it to his lips. When he tasted the odd thing, a surge of cold energy went through him. As Baldemar had promised, it was unsatisfying. Like the cold fire – indeed, like everything Baldemar offered – it held little comfort or sustenance, only distraction. For his part, Cuhullin tossed the disc into his mouth and pounded his fist twice on his belly to help it down.

"Thank you for this, Baldemar," Finn said, as he busied himself with his pack and walking stick. The half-Great avoided eye contact with the Snow Giant in case it set off another unpleasant exchange.

"Not at all," Baldemar replied sadly. He knew that Finn had tired of his company.

When Finn had hoisted his pack onto his shoulders (now much lighter thanks to Cuhullin's private feast), taken up his walking stick, and set his green cap upon his head, he looked once more about the top of the hill.

"Well," he sighed, bringing his eyes to Baldemar's at last, "thanks again. We should be off."

With Cuhullin following slowly, scanning the ground for any stray loaves or cheeses, Finn strode across the hilltop to the descent Baldemar had described. Looking over the edge, he could make out a steep and narrow path, dusted with snow, curling down through the mist and out of sight. He swiveled from side to side, contemplating how he would approach it – head on, sideways, or backward? At last he opted to brace one arm against the side of the hill and hold his walking stick out with the other for balance. And so he started down.

It was slow going at first, but as he got the hang of the ancient steps, he congratulated himself on his deftness. It was only when he heard Cuhullin above, beginning his own descent, that Finn realized that he had planned poorly. The Giant of Fyfe was not possessed of a keen sense of balance. He was also exceedingly heavy. Should he lose his footing and come tumbling down, Finn would be smushed utterly.

Fortunately for Finn, Cuhullin's hunger and irritation at being left behind consumed his thoughts. Muttering to himself, Cuhullin scarcely noticed the uncommon grace and balance with which he negotiated the steep and slippery path.

When Finn reached the bottom, he pushed off from the side of the hill with his palm and foot, and jumped down to soft earth. Large boulders were scattered in the tall grass. He stepped back from the hill, put his hands to his back, and craned up to gauge the height from which he had come and to see past Cuhullin's massive feet.

For a moment, the low mist cleared and Finn could see right back up to the peak. He could not swear to it, but he thought he could see Baldemar looking down at him. What was more, it seemed that the Snow Giant's lips were moving and he was waving his arms, as though he was trying to impart some urgent message. Finn put his hand to his ear. But just when he thought he could make out a word, the mist gathered once again and Cuhullin thumped down from his climb, landing uncomfortably close to him.

"Oi, what's the big idea, half-Great, taking off ahead of me?" the Giant demanded. "Don't you forget who's leading this mission." He jabbed his chubby finger three times at the tip of Finn's nose.

Finn was annoyed at being nearly landed upon and then scolded on the heels of it. He pursed his lips and turned to take stock of his surroundings. There was the hint of a pathway leading away from the foot of the hill, sloping through the tall grass before bending out of sight. "Do you suppose we ought to go that way?" he asked, with a touch of scorn.

"Let's see here." Cuhullin stroked his long beard and tugged his ear. When the logic of taking the path became inescapable, even for him, he spoke again. "I have decided that we shall go this way." He pointed down the path with his whole hand, the huge thumb cocked to the heavens.

"Very well." Finn stepped aside to let him stomp on ahead. Cuhullin puffed his chest out and led the way.

For some time the terrain did not change: tall yellow grass, rugged earth and rocks. It occurred to Finn that this was a land forgotten – perhaps never used. The narrow path disappeared after no more than a few miles. Finn noticed this, but he was quite sure Cuhullin did not. It did not matter, though, because the ground sloped downward from all sides, suggesting strongly where the travelers should bend their steps.

Before long, Finn could see the broad yellow "meadow" Baldemar had described. The unsuspecting eye might easily have assumed that the tall grass sprouted from dry earth. Finn called out to the Giant to wait.

"What's that?" Cuhullin demanded, as he whipped his face about and glared at Finn. "I'll not wait until I'm good and ready." Finn caught up to him. "And what's happened to your memory, half-Great?" Cuhullin went on. "Do you not recollect the conversation we've just had? This is my land and my mission. Now that we've come to the easy bit, don't you try to take control."

"You're right, of course," Finn agreed, restraining a smile.

Cuhullin huffed and turned again toward the tall yellow grass. He thrust his leg out a ceremonial distance to take his first stride. Finn was rather impressed by the number and variety of curses the Giant was able to utter as he fell face forward, before his bellowing was muffled by mud.

Though he was hobbled by laughter, Finn hurried knee-deep into the marsh to scoop out the apoplectic Giant. "Ah, pay that no never mind," he chuckled. "It's no fault of yours that your foot could find no purchase of solid earth. Some fool's put a bog here! Come on and straighten up. Consider it the price of leadership!"

Once he had regained his feet, Cuhullin drew his fingers across his eyes and flicked the mud off. "Why didn't you warn me there was a cursed bog here?"

"I would have," Finn replied, "but I did not want to overstep. I assumed you knew it was there."

"Well, of course I did! That is – I knew there was a bog. But some fool has gone and moved it! It was never *here* before. Curse his hide!"

"Well, never mind him. Let's press on," Finn urged.

With that, the pair continued through the marsh, Cuhullin in the lead. He was less unsettled by this wetland than he might have been; all the same, he trod strangely, lifting his knees high while keeping his toes pointed downward. He kept his arms extended at his sides and bent oddly, his palms turned backward and his elbows higher than his shoulders. Finn might have been forgiven for imagining that he was being guided through the bog by an enormous and ill-tempered goose. Sounds of sucking and squooshing accompanied their steps.

After a mile or two of awkward high-stepping, the yellow marsh gave way to new terrain. Towering trees popped into view out of the low fog and the ground sloped steeply, the mud giving way to solid green earth. Finn and Cuhullin climbed up the embankment and stomped their feet many more times than was necessary, so glad were they to be back upon hard ground.

The trees were clustered together like a wall, their low branches and needles poking down like accusing fingers at a belly. Finn and Cuhullin looked for a gap in the greenery. There was none. Finn remembered that Baldemar had said the Loch was surrounded by trees, so he knew there was no choice but to press through. He turned sideways and, with much effort, squeezed in amongst the trees.

Cuhullin opted for a more direct approach. He lurched toward the forest as though into a wrestling match, prying the trees apart with his massive hands. As for the trees, though they had to yield to his strength, they managed to bend extraordinarily far without breaking. In this way they wreaked their revenge upon the Giant, flicking him fiercely as he passed, while he offered fresh curses from his bottom-less supply.

After much pressing and pushing and flicking and cursing, the trees gave way to open sky and the smell of water. Finn and Cuhullin did not know how far they had come, or even if they had gone in a straight line, but all at once they found themselves on the rocky shore of the Black Loch.

The Loch was so narrow that those with keen eyes could see right across on a rare clear day. But it was very long – at least a full day's walk. None of the Giants had ever sounded its precise depth, though they did like to talk about it.

"Let me put it this way," an unkind Giant might say of a shallow fellow, "he possesses no depth that would rival the Black Loch."

The water was black as blood in the moonlight, befitting a place of mystery and dread.

Standing at one end of the Loch, Finn and Cuhullin could see bits of the shore on either side, while its length stretched out of sight in front of them. Tall trees perched like sentinels on a ridge just back from the water. The shore itself was pebbled and flat. There were sprays of green, and patches of sand that were too tantalizingly small to be a proper beach.

Finn recalled that Baldemar had said to follow the course of the sun. This presented the half-Great with two quandaries. How was he to determine the sun's course in a country without sunlight? And if he did determine the route, how could he convince Cuhullin that the choice had been *his*?

He was not too concerned about tricking Cuhullin; he had made something of a study of doing so over the centuries. To find the direction, he decided to make use of his thumb. Just as he brought it to his lips, however, Cuhullin whirled around to face him.

"Give me a minute," Cuhullin said curtly, as though Finn had been rushing him. Finn swiftly stuck his thumb up in the air as though he were merely testing the winds.

Cuhullin looked out over the Loch, hands on hips, and Finn stealthily brought his hand to his mouth once more. As soon as his thumb reached his lips, he saw a glorious sunset over the water to his right. He took his thumb away and the vision faded to the cold gray of any morning in Fyfe.

"I am supposing," he said, with deliberate bravado, "that we *most definitely* should go this way." He pointed to his left in a forceful gesture.

"Is that what you're supposing?" Cuhullin asked, his voice rising.

"As a matter of fact, yes, I am," Finn replied firmly.

"Do you know what would happen if we went that way?" Cuhullin demanded.

"I have a fair idea."

"You've no idea!" Cuhullin boomed. "Simply none! You'd be the death of us if I let you be our guide. You're a slow creature, Finn the half-Great, and that's the truth. Now I've told you before – this is my country and I am in charge. This is the way we'll be going!"

With that, he turned to Finn's right and stomped away in that direction. Finn grinned and followed, twirling his walking stick.

The rough shore was hard to walk on, and the Giant stumbled several times. "How on earth are we meant to find this cursed creature?" he complained.

"Well," said Finn, "when you saw him before, where were you?"

Cuhullin had forgotten his fib. "Ah, yes, well," he stammered. "That was many eons ago – before you were thought of, Finn McCool! If you knew this land as I do, you'd know that the Leviathan never appears in the same spot of the Loch twice. That's a small secret of Fyfe not many know. Mystical place. All kinds of little things like that . . ."

"So what do you propose?"

"Show yourself, you great, bumbling beast!" Cuhullin bellowed over the water.

"Ah, the mystical call of Fyfe."

Cuhullin began tossing stones of increasing size into the Loch, all the while berating the black water for its apparent cowardice in not responding. Before long, he had run through all stones of feasible size, and set himself to uprooting a nearby tree stump.

"I wonder," Finn said, "if we're going about this quite right."

Cuhullin looked up, perplexed and still grasping the stump. Could there be a better way to summon the Leviathan than cursing and tossing debris into the Loch?

A glint of gold from the midst of the trees that ringed the Loch caught Finn's eye. He hurried over to investigate. Cuhullin followed, carrying the stump he had intended to hurl.

Once again, Finn was compelled to turn sideways and squeeze himself through the thick forest. Cuhullin tossed the stump aside and, muttering defiantly, pushed trees this way and that as he followed.

Some distance into the woods, the trees suddenly parted to reveal a tiny clearing. In the middle of this small, bald bit of land stood a tall, rounded rock upon which Finn could see the thing that had flickered to him on the shore. It was a golden horn. It was not ornate but it had a look of ancient importance. Its color was unblemished, and it glowed brightly in the land so gray.

Cuhullin soon came mashing out of the woods. "What's all this, then?"

"Looks to be a horn," answered Finn.

"Well, that's an odd thing, isn't it?" Cuhullin sounded judgmental, as if the horn's being in the wood were somehow improper. He clambered up the rock and, closing one eye, peered into the mouthpiece. "You blow in here then, do you?"

"I expect so," said Finn.

"Let's see how she sounds!" The Giant made a series of sickening sucking sounds with his lips to loosen up, then put his mouth to the horn. He breathed in deeply and, with all his might, blew into the instrument. Only a barely audible rush of wind came out of the horn's business end. Cuhullin looked the horn up and down. In case he had missed something, he closed one eye and peered into the mouthpiece. Then he took a number of deep, vigorous breaths and blew with a ferocity that bulged his eyes and purpled his face. The sound was no greater than a mouse divulging an intensely personal problem.

"Perhaps you need to purse your lips," offered Finn.

"I'll purse your lips!" cursed a winded Cuhullin, shaking a fist at Finn.

"Here, let me have a crack at it," said Finn as he bounded up onto the rock. He pressed his lips hard together, so that they made a buzzing sound, and blew into the horn. The sound was remarkable, but not at all like a horn. Rather, it was as though instruments of all types – strings, horns, and even drums – sounded together in one glorious harmony, echoing over the land.

Finn stepped back from the horn and turned to Cuhullin, who snarled, pretending he was not impressed. The horn's call hung in the air and seemed to drift on the wind toward the Loch. Just when it was all but gone, it came back as an echo, unlooked-for and powerful. Somewhere over the Loch it had gained strength. Finn was knocked flat on his back. Cuhullin put a hand upon the horn to hold himself upright as the blast of music blew back his beard.

When the sound had passed over them, Finn sat up and shook his head. Then, just as the two were regaining their bearings, another sound came out of the horn. This one was direct and clear and, Finn could almost swear, accompanied by a beam of blue light that came out of the horn in the direction of the Loch.

This new sound shot straight into the trees, and to Finn's amazement, the woods parted. The trees were not burned or broken; they simply moved, root, bark, and branch, to either side, clearing a flat patch of land from the Loch all the way to where the companions stood.

"Well, that was some neat trick!" he marveled.

"What do you suppose is going on out there?" asked Cuhullin.

A white swirl formed in the middle of the Loch. Slowly the circle of water grew and, to their consternation, began moving steadily toward them.

"This cannot be good," Finn said.

"The trouble was you blowing that horn so loud!"

"Ah, yes. I suppose we'd have done better with you wheezing through it a bit longer."

"I was only warming up before you butted in," retorted Cuhullin, "and besides – I won't be slagged by a half-sized pipsqueak!"

"Well, you know, Ben –" Before Finn could get any further, he was interrupted by an unmerciful crash coming from the shore.

Slowly they turned. The Loch itself was no longer visible, at least from where they stood. Instead, all they could see was the body of the most colossal creature they had ever encountered.

The Leviathan stretched from the shore clear to the rock. His blue body was rounded and wide, with a mighty hump upon his back. Massive flippers that curled into claws protruded from either side, and a huge tail went endlessly out behind. The creature's neck, as tall as Cuhullin times two and a half, towered into the sky. At its top was perched an immense head. The mouth stretched wide to reveal rows of spear-sized teeth. Whether the creature was smiling or seething was unclear. His platter-sized dark eyes fixed on Finn and Cuhullin.

"Say something," Cuhullin muttered.

"What ought I to say?"

The rumbling reply came from above: "I often begin with 'How do you do?'"

"How do you do?" blurted Finn.

"Very well, I thank you," came the response, in a tone that was pleasant enough, though it caused twigs and pebbles to dance upon the ground. "How do you do?"

Only now did Finn realize that he was making polite chitchat with the Leviathan himself. "Oh, well," he stammered, "good enough."

He turned to Cuhullin, hoping to pass along responsibility for the conversation. Cuhullin stared up at the massive face of the Leviathan and said nothing.

"Was there something in particular you wanted?" said the Leviathan, in a voice that was tolerant yet firm.

"Well, no," managed Finn. "Nothing. Nothing at all, actually!"

"I see," answered the Leviathan, with waning patience. "I ask because you took the time and initiative to blow that horn. It is an instrument far older than you, and it is not used to being sounded for no reason. So, if I may ask again, what is yours?"

Finn swallowed hard. He looked once again at Cuhullin, who had frozen in place with his mouth open. "Well, since you ask, I did have a purpose."

"That is always a good beginning," answered the Leviathan.

"Thank you," said Finn, finding his rhythm. "That is to say, sir, we came with a purpose in mind. But we did not mean to disturb you."

"Perhaps you didn't, but here we are. State your purpose, please."

"Yes, of course. I am Finn McCool, and this is my associate, Cuhullin – or Benandonner, if you please." The Leviathan nodded, as if this was not news to him. "We have come about a matter of importance. A matter of grave importance, truth be told. We think it's important, at any rate. Important enough to come all the way here and disturb you. Incidentally, your point about the horn, about having a purpose for blowing it, well –"

"You are babbling," the monster said, "and I do wish you would not."

"Sorry. It is simply that I'm awfully nervous."

"As well you might be," the Leviathan replied. "No matter how long my many years have been, I resent every moment wasted upon fools."

"We are no fools!" blurted Cuhullin, without meaning to.

"You are fools," the Leviathan corrected him, "or you have some purpose. If you have no purpose, you are unfortunate. It has been my experience that even fools can be delicious." The Leviathan flashed his teeth ever so slightly.

"Understood," Finn gulped, waggling his eyebrows at Cuhullin lest the Giant blurt out something else. "We have come, sir, to ask for your help. I can put it no more plainly than that. My island is in peril. We were chosen to come and seek you out, understanding, as we did, that you are the only creature capable of saving us from this danger."

"I see. What sort of danger, I wonder."

"We are given to understand," Finn explained, "that the Jorgumandr, that ancient and fearsome serpent, swims even now in the waters around Eire. Smaller snakes choke our rivers. Goodness knows what villainy may spring from that!"

Finn pulled nervously at the hem of his cloak. He felt he had presented the problem briefly but succinctly. Even so, the monster made him uncomfortable.

Slowly, a smile spread across the Leviathan's huge face. Then came a chuckle, and another, until the chuckles blossomed into full-blown guffaws. The monster threw his head back and laughed uproariously into the sky, loudly, deeply, for several minutes. Finn and Cuhullin shrugged to one another.

"Now see here," Cuhullin at last protested. "We've come an awfully long way to see you, with nothing to eat but snow!"

The Leviathan wheezed and chortled until he regained his composure. "Ah, that was rich," he said at last, lowering his head to his flipper and wiping away a tear. "Well worth the interruption. Thank you!"

"If I may," Finn ventured, "whatever do you mean by that?"

"I had seriously considered eating you, I must be honest," replied the Leviathan, still smiling and shaking his head. "But after such a jolly tale as that, I couldn't possibly. It wouldn't be fair payment for a laugh."

Cuhullin was getting really flustered. He furrowed his brow and shook his fist and pursed his lips as he struggled to think of something else to say. Finn, meanwhile, was just confused.

"Sorry," he started in again, "but how are we amusing

to you? What we have described is very real, and very troublesome."

"What you have described," responded the Leviathan, "is very silly. Oh, to be wakened for foolhardiness that one would expect only from mortal men!"

"We would not have prevailed upon you to bestir yourself," said Finn with fragile calm, "if we had known you would mock us. With all due respect, sir, may I ask what's so blessed amusing?"

"You are asking me to save you from the hideous Jorgumandr, is that correct?"

"Essentially, yes."

"And have you ever seen this Jorgumandr that you dread?"

"I thank the Dagda I have not."

"Perhaps you'll hold onto your gratitude until you hear what I have to say. For certain, you have never seen the Jorgumandr. Nor have you, young Benandonner, no matter how long you claim to have lived. Nothing that now walks upon the Earth has seen it. The creature is known to me, of course. For many eons I have endured preposterous stories about its nature and size. Before I say more, how did you come to know this spot and to summon me?"

"The Snow Giant," said Finn. The Leviathan rolled his eyes. "You may know him as Baldemar."

"I know him as a nuisance," grumbled the Leviathan.

"Yes," said Finn, "he cautioned us. He claimed you tried to kill him."

"I did not try to kill Baldemar," the Leviathan said with irritation, "and the way you know this is that Baldemar is still alive. But his talk is balderdash. It was my misfortune that he found me to be a pleasing conversation partner. The horn you sounded would be blown at every hour of the day and night, the water would swirl, the trees would part – again

and again – any time he had some new and preposterous
opinion to impose upon me. At long last, I was obliged to
discourage him from dropping by. He was holding forth on
some tiresome topic, proving once again that any fool may
voice an opinion and most do, when I interrupted with a
little lunge – no more than this." The Leviathan dropped his
face to the companions and snapped his jaws. Finn and
Cuhullin jumped. "You see? It was nothing, but it sent him
scrambling back up to his frozen hill."

"I can see how you'd be tempted," Finn admitted. "He is
tiresome." As soon as he said this, however, he felt sad to be
speaking unkindly of an unfortunate creature.

"I am not as unapproachable as he may have led you to
believe," said the Leviathan. "But I am not used to being
called forth for foolishness. Now, as to the matter of your
Jorgumandr – your tale cannot be correct."

"Are you saying we are liars?" demanded Cuhullin.

"I am saying that you are confused. That's different.
Consider our Baldemar. He is a confused and confusing creature, but not a liar. There is such a being – this much is true.
We know each other well enough, but for reasons I do not care
to divulge, we are not on speaking terms. The Jorgumandr, as
you call him, lives in the deepest spot of the sea – a place
known only to the two of us, I am certain. The snake is large,
at least by your standards. But these fables I have heard – how
the serpent circles whole seas and swallows his very tail – are
fantastic and silly." The Leviathan swung his own tail.

"When last I saw him, he was in grotesquely poor condition. He lay lazily upon the seabed and couldn't open his
eyes, much less conquer your island. And he does not have
offspring. If you knew what I know, the idea that such a corpulent, bloated, infertile creature swims laps around Eire
would tickle you as it did me."

"But where could the Piast have come from?" Finn asked.

"Well, how many have you seen?" said the Leviathan.

"Just the one, myself. But we have tales of many others."

"Interesting."

"In fact," Finn went on, "we understand that the danger in our waters is only a small portion of the problems spreading across these islands. Monsters and mortals and even Fomorians are rumored to be massing together. They have taken our Ring and captured our fortress. This may concern you, sir. If the Frost Giants are awake again, wreaking havoc, who is to say they cannot find and harm you, even here?"

"I think not," scoffed the Leviathan. "It is true that Ymir's brood and the ice and snow attending them were a vexation to me. But since I have been here, those chilly scoundrels haven't disturbed me. They can take a run at a rolling snowball for all I care. My lair has many tunnels and turns known only to me. No army of intruders could match me here. I almost wish they would come and try."

"You dismiss all fears because you think you know better," Finn protested. "I would like to take comfort in what you say, but the things we have heard are too awful. I must believe our islands are in danger. To presume otherwise would be, well, dangerous."

"You may have your own opinion, half-Great, but you cannot have your own facts. What I have told you is true. The Jorgumandr is a sluggish layabout. One Piast in your stream does nothing to disprove this. Mortal men have nowhere near the might to move your Ring, and they could scarcely climb the steps of Treryn. Finally, the Frost Giants who petrify you are slovenly and no more than nuisance-making, if indeed they still exist. Finn McCool, someone has been having you on."

Sensing that Finn was disheartened, the Leviathan added, "But I'll make you a bargain. I know when and how you dispatched Ymir all those eons ago. I am grateful and envious. Much as I would have liked to kill him myself, I am happy that it was done at all. And there was some kindness done for me by Cuhail in ages before you were thought of. So I will repay you. When next I stretch these fins of mine, I will have a swim about your island to see what's doing. If there is trouble, I will take care of it. There will be none, though – of this I am certain. Who or what has sent you on this fool's errand, I do not know. But if it will ease your young mind, I will do this. A favor is paid for with freedom."

"Thank you," Finn replied.

Then there was silence. All three looked back and forth at one another, up to the sky, down to the ground – Cuhullin cleared his throat loudly – but the silence continued.

"Was there anything else?" the Leviathan asked after a while.

"Well, no," said Finn. "I suppose that's all we came for. We are grateful." He found it strange that he felt more unnerved now than he had before the meeting had begun. Something was gnawing at him. He had more or less gotten what he wanted, and with minimal fuss. Was he out of sorts at being made to feel foolish? Surely the words of such an aged and experienced creature as the Leviathan should have reassured him. Odd indeed that they did not.

"Very well," the Leviathan sighed. "Then I will sink back to where I am happiest. My thanks for stopping by. I'll be on guard against your monstrous foes." Finn thought he detected a smirk at the corner of the Leviathan's huge mouth before he slid, with alarming speed, back into the Loch. The Earth rumbled, and no sooner had his head ducked beneath the black water than the trees gathered once more.

"Oh, not these blasted things again!" Cuhullin wailed.

Finn gathered his bearings. "We'll just have to make the best of it," he sighed, "as we did before."

Cuhullin started to tussle with the trees, and Finn followed in his wake. This was not a good idea. Whenever Cuhullin pushed a tree aside, it would snap back at Finn. After a time, he let Cuhullin forge on a good distance ahead. As Finn stood amongst the trees, he felt them pressing in hard on him, as though they wanted to send him shooting straight up into the air. When he could no longer hear or see Cuhullin, he forced his way forward.

At last they emerged from the wood onto a rocky gray plain.

"Which way did we come in?" Cuhullin asked as he inspected a bloody scratch on his arm.

"I don't know," said Finn. He searched for some marker to point the way back to the sea, but he was still distracted by the Leviathan's attitude. Finn had laid it all out for him: the Jorgumandr, the Piast, the reported robbery of the Giants Ring, and the taking of Treryn – not to mention bands of mortal men terrorizing his people across Albion. But if the Leviathan was to be believed, all this was false and idle chatter. Finn would have been more than happy to take a little humiliation if it meant that his hill, his hounds, and his Oonagh were safe. But whom to believe? Thunderbore was full of bluster, true, but did the Giants who had come to Knockmany lie too? He did not think so. He remembered Grimshaw's tired, pitiful face. But had they themselves been misled?

"I think it's this way," mumbled Cuhullin. Fatigue or frustration had made him forgo his need to command. Finn could make out the base of a hill he thought was Baldemar's.

"I think you're right," he said, with mild surprise.

Together they trundled across the plain, finding their way up and back toward the Causeway. They did not speak until they came to a narrow valley that ended at a tall yellow hill.

"See there," said Cuhullin, pointing to the hill. "That is Ben Cruachan. That is my home."

Finn could not be sure, but he sensed that the Giant spoke with a hint of sadness. Before he could admire the hill, or compliment his companion on its fine color or choice location, Cuhullin walked on.

The sun was fading as the companions approached the sea. The smell of salt was in the air, and the ground felt familiar. Here and there in the gathering twilight Finn could see flashes of fireflies, sparks in the dusk. It was a welcoming sight, like bits of warmth and home in a dark and foreign place. He twirled his walking stick and thought of Oonagh and his hounds, and how soon he would see them all.

He jousted with the fireflies, poking at them with his walking stick. Cuhullin was out of sight. Seeing that he was alone, Finn scampered after the Giant.

When at last he came loping down the ridge to the shore, he found Cuhullin there already, looking out to sea. There was something strange about the Giant's demeanor. He did not move or speak, and his eyes were fixed upon the waters.

"Hey-ho, Ben!" Finn chuckled. "Sorry to have fallen back a bit there. Looks like we made it, though, eh?"

The Giant said nothing. Perplexed, Finn glanced around the bit of beach on which they stood. This was the very spot where they had first set foot on Fyfe. He looked up at Cuhullin and followed the Giant's gaze and he saw through the dim of early evening, not far from shore, what had struck his companion dumb.

The Causeway had been destroyed.

IV

the battle of knockmany

It was a solemn scene at Knockmany after Finn and Cuhullin made their long goodbye. The Giants stood together, staring down the hill after the brave companions. Oonagh folded her arms tightly across her chest and gazed instead toward the sea. Bran and Skolie perched upon the brink of the hill, their ears flopped forward and their heads turning this way and that, trying for one last glimpse of Finn.

Iskander took it upon himself to move things along.

"Come on, old girl," he comforted Oonagh, gently placing his hands on her shoulders and leading her back toward the house. One by one, the other Giants turned away from the precipice and followed. Skolie scampered inside after them, hoping to find a discarded bit of breakfast. Only Bran remained, looking down Knockmany after his departed master.

Oonagh cleared away the morning's meal. Iskander and Peadair pitched in but they only succeeded in breaking several dishes, for which they loudly blamed each other. "Please stop trying to be helpful and vacate my kitchen," Oonagh ordered as she flapped her apron at them.

Thunderbore was uncharacteristically quiet. He sat in the large chair in which he had slept, thoughtfully fingering his beard as he stared into the empty fireplace. Parthalan and Girvin slumped in chairs nearby. Grimshaw rummaged through his meager belongings for a pipe and satchel of pipe-weed, then quietly made his way out of doors.

"So!" Iskander said, clapping his hands together and peering about. The only response was Girvin's gentle wheezing as he slouched in his chair. Iskander's huge eye finally fell on Peadair, who shrugged. "Who has a story to tell?" Iskander prodded.

"What kind of a story?" Parthalan asked flatly.

"Why, a merry story, of course," Iskander replied. "Or a song would do just as well. Surely, with all the centuries among us, we've learned a few diversions to lighten the mood. Thunderbore! You must have some fine speech for the lifting of spirits. Let's have it, you old so-and-so!"

Thunderbore continued stroking his beard and staring into space as though he had not heard a word.

"Later, then," said Iskander.

Oonagh finished her meticulous cleaning. She spoke to the Giants softly, her eyes lowered.

"You boys need not stay on my account. You are welcome, of course, but whatever happens will happen, wherever you find yourselves." She turned to the window and rested her hand on the sill.

Seeing that she was as melancholy as the others, Iskander wondered if he had missed something. Why the gloom?

Surely Finn would be straight back. The trek was a bit of a nuisance, but nothing dire. Two days, tops. And nothing Finn encountered could be too terrible for him to handle. He was exceedingly clever when he wanted to be. Besides – Cuhullin was with him. Surely they'd meet no foe who was a match for the mighty Giant of Fyfe. With this squared away in his mind, Iskander resolved that he would get some singing underway:

> Away and gone,
> Far from home,
> O'er mountains and valleys and streams,
> To you, my love,
> I'll ne'er return,
> But I'll gaze on you e'er in my dreams.

> Fare thee well, fare thee well,
> Remember me, dear, ever fondly,
> Fare thee well, fare thee well,
> For ne'er shall we meet again.

> Fare thee well . . .

Iskander preferred to close his eye when he sang. As he opened it at this point in the song, hoping to rouse the others into a reprise of the chorus, he saw that every face in the house, except Thunderbore's, was turned toward him with impatience. He realized this had been an exceedingly poor choice of song. "Yes, right," he muttered. The others sank back to their own thoughts and silence reigned for some time.

Then there came a ruckus. Outside the house, Bran began to bark and growl with a ferocity that frightened even Oonagh. Grimshaw started wailing, not exactly in words, for the others to come and help. The Giants leapt up and rushed out the door – except for Thunderbore, who did not move from his spot.

Clouds raced across the sky, as the wind whirled and bit. Bran was running from one side of the hilltop to the other, barking in each direction. Grimshaw shook, even paler than usual, one arm clutched across his chest; his other hand trembled, holding his pipe in front of his face.

Oonagh knelt and whistled softly for Bran. The hound scurried to her, and she stroked his head as he crouched beside her. The others stood staring, wondering what to make of the scene. Then they heard a noise – a thump. Then a horn, then another thump. As moments passed, the horns and thumps came together in a threatening sort of music.

"What is that?" Iskander asked.

"Sounds like enemies," answered Peadair.

Oonagh looked out across the plains with grave concern. Then all eyes were drawn to the sky. Dark wings appeared to the south of Knockmany.

"Look!" shouted Iskander, as the sinister shape loped across the clouds.

"What is it?" worried Girvin.

Before anyone could answer, the drums and horns started again, unnervingly closer than before. A mass of creatures of various sizes appeared, moving toward the hill.

"I wish you boys would go," Oonagh said. The Giants forgot their fear for a moment, and turned to her in amazement. "There is nothing you can do here but die."

"Stuff and nonsense!" Iskander answered for them all. "Whatever is coming for the hill of my man Finn, we will be here to make its acquaintance. Why would you think any different, silly girl?"

"I do not know any better than you what this is," she answered, "but it is some ugly thing. Go away and leave me to it."

Gradually, the figures on the plain came into focus. They were small, mostly, but here and there were hulking beings. And there were machines with them.

"We're going nowhere," insisted Iskander. "What you must think of us, even to suggest it!"

As he spoke, a shadow fell across his face and a blast of wind swept across the hilltop. The mighty wings of the dark creature blew back the thatch from the roof of the house and shook even the Giants in their boots. As fast as it came, it was gone again, high into the clouds.

"She makes an excellent point," Girvin said meekly.

"Pull yourself together!" Peadair shouted, whirling on him. "Is that what you think of yourself?"

"I'm sorry!" Girvin pleaded. "I wasn't thinking of myself. It's just – nothing that is happening now is pleasing me!" Peadair shook his head and looked back to the sky.

The drums and horns sounded very close now, but a sudden fog gathered near the base of Knockmany. The approaching army was hidden, though its rumble and growl of unseen foes curled up the hilltop.

Oonagh patted her hounds, and worried for Finn. Had he been caught up by this encroaching force or had he made it safely to the sea? As much as she longed to see his face, she hoped he had made it far, far from Knockmany.

"Gather yourselves!" Iskander ordered. "They'll be up and at us soon enough, so let's have our wits about us!" Peadair grinned and clenched his fists. He was the only one. Grimshaw had not stopped shaking, his pipe still in his hand. Parthalan, the farmer – who had no history of fighting that he could remember – stood with his feet planted wide and his fists held oddly out in front of him. Girvin turned this way and that, hoping to see some rescue.

As the first heavy footfalls landed on the slope of Knockmany, the Giants swallowed their fear as best they could. Oonagh laid her head gently on Bran's furry neck and he curled his tail around Skolie, who cowered beside him. Then a noise from the house startled them. Standing in the open doorway was Thunderbore.

What a pity, thought Finn, as he squinted through the twilight at his ruined Causeway. Who or what could have done this? And why? The building of the thing had been a goodly amount of work, and the finished product had been such a boon to all Albion. Thoughtless and selfish, that's what it was, to deprive so many others of a handy footpath! He was cross, but he had not yet realized that this might be a dire problem, and a sign of much more dire problems to come.

"What an onion!" he exclaimed at last. Cuhullin snapped out of his daze and looked eagerly around for the promised vegetable. "If you had any idea how much effort went into that project! Yes, yes, it wasn't all me – I freely admit that. It was more of a group effort than people think. So much work, such a convenience, destroyed – just like that! Unacceptable and unkind!"

Cuhullin realized that no onion was forthcoming, and scowled. His feelings on the matter were, in truth, mixed. He had always resented the praise Finn received for building the thing. His journeys across the Causeway had been harrowing, and when he made it to Eire to see Finn and his folk, things never went his way. But they had been sent on a quest, albeit a short one, and he was the leader. Part of their task was to return and report their findings. How would it look if he, the mighty Cuhullin, went trundling off to the Black Loch to save the world and never returned? It would be an unspeakable blemish upon his reputation. On top of this, the light was fading, and he was anxious for supper. He knew of no nearer place to find victuals than Knockmany.

Finn tucked his thumb under his chin and stared in turn out to the Causeway and down at his feet. Cuhullin planted his fists on his hips and snorted every so often, as if he had just drawn some conclusion, then quickly rejected it.

As darkness gathered about them, the fireflies seemed to multiply. Despite his consternation, Finn found the little flashes a happy sight. Cuhullin did not.

"Away with you, ya bother!" the Giant shouted, flailing his hands at the specks of light flitting around him. The more he swung and swore, the more fireflies seemed to gather.

One firefly was less sure of its course than the others, as if it had a broken wing. The others darted easily in and out of range of Cuhullin's angry swipes, but this damaged fly seemed to rely on good luck. For quite some time Cuhullin cursed and the fireflies buzzed and the wonky-winged one was successful in its weaving. But then the Giant made a lucky strike.

"Aha!" he shouted as he smacked the firefly with the broken wing. The unfortunate thing whirled across the evening sky and splatted into a flat rock beside the shore. Its light flickered and went out. Finn rushed over.

"Easy there, Ben!" he said, scooping up the firefly just as Cuhullin was about to smash it with his fist.

"Hand it over, half-Great!"

"Ah, now you know that's not going to happen." Finn turned away, cupping the wounded firefly in his hands.

"Those blasted things have pestered me for more years than you know!"

"I don't care, Ben. You're bigger and you should learn to keep your temper." Slowly he opened his hands to inspect the firefly. What lay in his palm was less a bug than a very small person. He was white-gold, or at least that was the color of his costume. He had two arms, two legs, and a shock of white hair upon his head. Finn could see two tiny wings, one of which was bent out of shape.

"Careful with us, now!" the creature cautioned sternly, as though it was self-evident that he was some precious thing. His voice was high but firm and, despite his small stature, perfectly audible.

"Sorry!" said Finn.

"There was no need for such a cursed smack," the little person went on, shaking his head and testing his tiny limbs for injury.

"Count yourself lucky there wasn't more than one smack coming to you!" Cuhullin shouted into the palm of Finn's hand. The little creature waved dismissively at the Giant and continued checking each arm and leg.

"Are you all right?" Finn asked.

"Well as can be expected," the manikin replied, standing on Finn's open palm. "I am never quite all right these days. And this big brute was no help." He pointed his thumb toward Cuhullin with two short, sharp jabs.

"May I ask," Finn went on, "what sort of creature you are?" The tiny fellow looked up at him with surprise and blinked, as though the answer should be obvious. When Finn shrugged in surrender, the little one rolled his eyes.

"Why, I am a Spriggan, of course!" he exclaimed. "What else would I be?"

"Ah, yes," said Finn. He knew of Spriggans and their

antics and merry mischief, from children's tales. Decent folk throughout Albion disagreed as to whether the Spriggans actually existed.

"Dandee is my name."

"I am pleased to meet you, Dandee. I am Finn McCool and this is my associate, Cuhullin." Before Finn finished speaking, the Spriggan closed his eyes and tapped his minuscule toe.

"I know you by reputation, Finn McCool. And as for Cuhullin – let me assure you he is well-known to Spriggan-folk."

"And what's that meant to mean?" Cuhullin demanded.

"Simply that we know you," Dandee stiffled a giggle. "I think it should please you that tales of your greatness have reached even our kind."

Cuhullin was angry and baffled. "I would be pleased if you and your pesky kind would flit about somewhere besides all over me!"

"I wonder if you could help us, Dandee," Finn interrupted. "Do you know how my Causeway came to be ruined?"

Dandee looked out at the Causeway. "It's a proper mess," he agreed. "I'm afraid I can't tell you anything about how it got that way. My folk and I only got down to the shore a bit before you did. We were following your man here, and he had all our attention."

"What business do you have following me around, eh?" the Giant bellowed.

"When one's business is mischief, you're a good lad to know," Dandee said firmly, looking Cuhullin straight in the eye.

"Oh? And just why is that?"

"I should not betray the secrets of my folk, but I suppose there's no great harm," answered Dandee with a smile.

"You've been a blessing to us, Benandonner. I admit that you have brought us more joy than any creature on Earth." Cuhullin gave an angry snort. "Your reactions have been priceless. A simple stone slipped into your shoe has sent you into such sensational seething – our laughter lit our lamps for many nights! And hiding your hat brings forth such huffing fury! No one but you has made us so glad, so easily!"

"That was you?" the Giant roared, groping his hatless head.

"Don't spoil it now by being a poor sport. Needs must, you know! We light our fires with laughter. Without creatures like you to warm our bellies, we would not glow and these islands would be in utter darkness."

"I'll give you utter darkness!" Cuhullin lunged for Finn's hand to snatch Dandee away. Finn was taken off guard. He resisted briefly but he was no match for the Giant. Besides, he did not want to see the Spriggan splattered in the struggle. "Ha!" Cuhullin shouted, gripping Dandee in his hairy fist.

"Hang on!" squealed the Spriggan. "Let's not do anything hasty!"

"Make a joke out of me, hey?" Cuhullin roared into the little fellow's face. "Don't you know who I am? I am the greatest of the Great Ones who still walk! What other mischief have you pixies planned for me?"

"I'll tell you," Dandee answered, "but I must ask you to loosen your grip, at least a bit! Even Spriggans need to breathe!" Ever so slightly, the Giant relaxed his hold. "Well, thanks for that, such as it was. We never meant you any harm. Indeed, we never did you any, unless you and your pride are part and parcel. We have discussed tying your beard to your bootlace as you sleep. That is the only prank we have planned, so far. I swear this is true!"

"All right, enough," said Finn, chipping Cuhullin on the

shoulder. "Come on, Ben, let the little fellow be." The Giant grunted. "Honestly," Finn added, "we've got more important things to worry about than your beard and your boots. Go on, now!"

"Do you promise not to go flitting off the second I let you go?" Cuhullin demanded.

"Certainly I do!"

"Well . . . good enough, then." With a suspicious look, Cuhullin reluctantly released the Spriggan.

"Thank you," Dandee wheezed, as he leapt from the Giant's hand onto the flat rock.

"Now, don't you scoot away on us!" Cuhullin wagged his massive finger.

"You obviously know nothing of Spriggan-folk," said Dandee indignantly, "if you think I would break my word." He did a few stretches and deep knee-bends. "If we weren't fond of you at least a little, we would leave you alone. We taunt those whom we enjoy." Cuhullin gave a low growl.

"Listen, Dandee," said Finn, "since none of us is sure what happened to the Causeway, maybe you can help us with something else. My friend and I are most anxious to get back to Eire. Do you know of any other way across the sea?"

"Well, see, there you've asked a good question." The Spriggan brought his wee hand to his wee chin. "I know of ways, certainly. But our ways are not your ways, if you take my meaning."

"I do not. What are you saying?"

"Well, not to put too fine a point on it, we Spriggans are spry. We can go wherever we wish. You two, on the other hand, are heavy-footed Giant types. I wonder if you'd be able to follow me."

"I can follow anywhere you choose to go – just you be sure of that!" Cuhullin boasted.

"Very well. Come along!" The Spriggan leapt up and set himself aglow. "This way!"

Dandee flew off through the night in a jagged line, heading north along the shoreline of Fyfe. His wonky wing made his course a series of dips and turns and weaves. Finn and Cuhullin found themselves ducking and dodging too. The Spriggan was marvelously alight, which was a good thing, since the sun was all but gone.

"Where are we headed?" Finn called with shortening breath, after they had traveled a number of miles.

"The Shifting Stones," responded the speck of light leading them. "We are not long-range fliers, we Spriggans. We find it helps to have rest spots here and there."

Several times Cuhullin caught his foot on a root or stubbed his toe on a rock, and let loose a cacophony of cursing. "How are you back there, Ben?" Finn would call through the darkness, and some profantity would come in reply. Finn took no offense, understanding that if Cuhullin could answer so rudely, he was uninjured.

Up the coast they ran in this imperfect fashion, until at last Dandee stopped and hovered an arm-span in front of them.

"Now here comes the tricky part," he said.

There was little to see save shadows and shapes reflected by the light of the little fellow. The sound of the sea was heavy in Finn's ears. A cool breeze blew up from the water and he shuddered as it caught him unawares. Cuhullin came barreling up behind him.

"What a treacherous pace you've kept up this whole way!" the Giant gasped, struggling for breath. "A body could get hurt running blind up the beach at this hour!"

"Frightfully sorry, Benandonner." Dandee grinned. "I thought you were steady of foot. You'll need to be now, in any case!"

"I can be plenty steady when need be."

"Where are we, Dandee?" Finn peered into the dark.

"These are called the Shifting Stones, but that is something of a misnomer. Not many years ago, this patch of water was frozen solid as rock. Now it has mostly melted, but the gap can still be crossed by those with artful feet." Dandee winked and kicked his heels together. "I don't expect you to find the journey as easy as we do. Blocks of ice come and go, and the traveler must be agile and alert. One leaps from spot to spot, sussing out good luck and hoping for the best. In the morning, I'll try to guide you across."

"There is no time to wait for the morning," Finn said.

"You mean to cross in the dark?"

"Yes, and I would appreciate your help."

"Now hang on. My offer depended on us having enough light to make our way. I can think of none, apart from my kind, who could make this crossing blinded."

Finn turned to Cuhullin and said softly, so that the Great One would not lose face, "You don't have to come, Ben. I'll chance it alone."

"You'll chance nothing without me!" Cuhullin blustered. "Lead on, half-Great, and we'll show him what's what!"

"Fair enough," said Finn. "Now, my good Spriggan, if you'll be kind enough to show me where to start."

"This is such a woeful idea," Dandee muttered as he beckoned Finn to follow him. "See there?" A barely visible clump of ice jutted out into the sea. "That is your first step. It is the only one you can rely upon, as it has not moved in many years. The rest come and go."

"So what does one do?" asked Finn.

"One waits for the morning."

"I have made my decision," Finn said firmly. "So – will you tell me how to begin?"

The Spriggan sighed. "You begin there, as I said. From there, you should find some clump or other about the same distance ahead, to the south – that is, to your left. But no honest Spriggan could claim to know quite what you'll find."

"So take one leap, look to the left for another, then hope for the best after that?" asked Finn.

"Essentially, yes."

"Good enough!" Finn wiped his thumb twice – once on each side, across the front of his jacket – and without a stitch of self-consciousness, thrust it into his mouth. The ice glowed gold and welcoming. "Off we go!"

He leapt from the shore to the clump of ice, his thumb still in his mouth, and nearly overshot his mark. His free arm whirled in circles and he teetered on his tiptoes, struggling to keep his balance. Once he had steadied himself, he craned his neck and smiled back to the others. Dandee nodded, his arms folded in silent judgment.

Finn turned back toward the blackness. Without Dandee it was dark indeed, and his eyes widened in hopes of catching some stray light. He slurped hard on his thumb and another glowing patch appeared, out to the left. He was catching on! He pumped his free arm and built up steam for a jump. This time he landed gracefully. The ice shifted and rolled – not dreadfully, but enough that he had to be alert to stay on his feet.

"Hang on there," Cuhullin called from the shore. "Don't go getting too far ahead!"

"Well, come on then, if you're coming!" Finn struggled to stay upright on the shifting piece of ice. He had taken his thumb from his mouth to answer and found that the spot on which he was standing lost its glow. All at once he was in total darkness, wobbling on a lonely patch in the sea. He thrust his thumb back into his mouth and the glow returned.

He looked about for his next step. Straight ahead, another luminous block beckoned.

The Spriggan said nothing. He had been quite clear that a nighttime crossing was sheer folly. The Giant was trying to think of a reason, apart from cowardice, for allowing his companion to make the crossing alone. If there was anything more alarming to him than the sea, it was the sea in darkness, its sinister waves lapping and daring him to take one step across the invisible line of the shore.

"Ah, hang it all upside down and sideways!" Cuhullin cursed. At the water's edge he squinted at the closest chunk of ice, and took several deep breaths to steel his nerves. "There it is now," he murmured, closing his eyes. "It's naught but a black pool of nothing. Not even Finn is frightened by it. A little pool of nothing, I tell you. Let's have it now, Ben, let's have it!" With that, he leapt bravely into the darkness.

To his surprise, he landed squarely upon his target. He opened one eye, then the other. Seeing nothing but pitch black, he slammed them both shut again. As the sound of water bombarded him, he began to sway on the small bit of ice.

Despite his disapproval, Dandee had been watching hopefully from the shore. Now he whipped a tiny wooden flute out from beneath his glowing wings. He gave it one short blast, and a piercing volley of notes flew over the land and water.

Startled, Cuhullin lost his footing altogether. His heart leapt into his throat as he fell backward. Instead of splashing into terrible water as he expected, however, he was astounded to find himself supported. A swarm of Spriggans gripped him by every available appendage: his arms, his legs, his hair – even his beard.

"Not the beard!" he shouted, in place of thanks.

The Spriggans – many of whom had been cursed and swung at by the Giant earlier in the evening – carefully placed Cuhullin back on his feet. Then, without a word amongst them, they worked in magnificent concert to lift him up and carry him across the water to the second step. They lowered him just enough that both his feet made contact with the scrap of ice, before carrying him off toward the next clump.

"I can do this myself, hang you all!" Cuhullin hollered, flailing his arms. It was no use. The Spriggans were not about to leave him be. As they got their speed up, they needed to rest less and less often. And so they made their way through the night, carrying the bitterly protesting Giant from step to step along the path of the Shifting Stones, touching his feet down here and there to spare his pride.

Finn had made steady progress on his own when he heard the ruckus approaching. He looked back, perplexed by the odd cluster of light with a dark and angry patch in the center. "Ben?" he called out, jamming his thumb back into his mouth the moment the word had left his lips.

"They've got me!" Cuhullin howled. "They've got me, Finn, and they're hoisting me against my will!"

Finn smiled. As always, if Cuhullin was complaining, he was likely all right. Finn continued his own crossing, aided by the wisdom of Fintan, and confident that his companion was in safe hands.

And so Finn and Cuhullin made their way over the sea, each availing himself of a particular magic. It was not an easy crossing for either – not by any means. The Shifting Stones were aptly named; even with the guidance of the Tuatha De Danann and helpful handling by the Spriggans, the clumps were entirely unreliable, all too likely to sink or roll.

Finn found himself on a surprisingly solid foothold.

Sucking hard on his thumb, he looked about for the next glowing spot, but he could not see another step. He sucked yet more powerfully, but the sole result was a mighty slurp that made him grateful to be alone. He removed his hand from his mouth and gingerly tapped from side to side with his foot. He was standing on dry land. He had made it to Eire.

Looking back across the water, Finn could see the shining cloud containing Cuhullin bobbing toward him. As the luminous party came closer, he could hear Cuhullin letting loose some new and imaginative curses. "May the Morrigan read to you by your own wretched light!" the Giant bellowed, as Dandee's company set him down on the shore as gently as they could manage.

"You are most welcome, Benandonner," Dandee said with an inscrutable smile. His pleasant tone sent the Giant sputtering into fresh rage. The Spriggan bowed slightly, just out of reach of Cuhullin's flailing fists.

"Thank you, Dandee, for bringing him along," said Finn cheerfully. "I don't know what I'd do without him."

"Neither do we!" chuckled Dandee, and the other Spriggans all laughed. Cuhullin knew the joke was on him, though he could not put his finger on precisely how. "I do not envy you the rest of your journey," Dandee added. "But dawn is close now. You will have to travel a fair distance in darkness. We could come along a bit of the way."

Finn was about to accept when Cuhullin growled, "Ah, no, you've done more than enough already! Away with you, and leave decent people to their tasks!"

Dandee sighed. "I suppose we must always be at odds. I confess that we protected you as much for our sake as for yours. We don't want to lose such a fine object of mirth."

The Spriggan turned back to Finn. "I am sorry we won't be going with you. May I give you a bit of advice? You may

think you know the creatures of your native island, but
don't be too trusting. There is a mood in the winds. You are
friendly and brave, half-Great, and that is rare. But be wise
also. Not all is what it seems. I will not presume to give you
directions in your own land but, were I earthbound like you,
I would bend my steps that way, straight on till morning."
He pointed to the south and east. "That is all I can offer.
Farewell." Finn raised his hand to wave goodbye, but with
his final words Dandee had extinguished his light and vanished. Like a school of fish, the other Spriggans swerved
into darkness.

"Well," mused Finn, "that was more sudden than I'd
hoped."

"Good riddance to him," grumbled Cuhullin.

There was a thread of moonlight on this northerly point
of Eire, and Finn strained to see a clear and level path. Any
other time, he would have boasted that he was but a few
miles from Knockmany and could find his way home blindfolded. Now he found that the dizzying excitement of the
evening had made him lose his bearings.

"Which way are you headed?" Cuhullin called.

"Home."

The wisps of cloud made the moon an uncertain guide.
Just as Finn caught a glimpse of a hill or plain he thought he
knew, it would become shrouded in blackness. Then he would
see another patch of land that looked awfully like the first.
Despite this, he pressed on south and east, with Cuhullin strag-
gling behind.

In a merciful few hours, the first light of dawn crept
across the island, and Finn grew surer of his direction. "Come
on, Ben!" he called out as he lengthened his strides to leaps.
He bounded through a familiar meadow. He had taken Bran
here as a puppy and, with middling success, tried to teach

the little fellow to fetch; rather than bringing the stick back, Bran would forget his mission, and would trot aimlessly about the field, admiring the sky and the grass. Sometimes he would stretch out and scratch his back, and perhaps make friends with a dandelion, and Finn's commands would quiver into laughter.

These warm memories drove the cold and weariness from Finn's bones. His dark thoughts gave way to the dawn and, happy to be near his home, his hounds, and his Oonagh, he found the world less terrible than it had seemed.

The meadow was long and broad, and at its southern end it dipped into a wooded gully. Finn slid down into the gully on his heels. At the bottom, he stopped for a moment to breathe the sweet air. He looked up at the dripping leaves overhead.

"Where've you bloody gotten to?" Cuhullin was angrily scanning the meadow above.

"I'm down here, Ben!"

Cuhullin plodded to the edge of the gully. "For the love of mercy, can you not stay in sight?"

"Sorry. Come on down – we're nearly there!"

"All right, then, all right – don't rush a person!" The Giant looked for the safest spot to descend, chose a clear patch, and slid his toe over the edge and gingerly down the slope. But what a seemed like a solid patch of ground gave way and his feet shot out in front of him, and he slid down on his back. The ground was soft with dew, so he came to rest quite comfortably laid out on the gully floor, his head and feet elevated as though he were reclining in some earthen hammock.

"Which way is it from here, do you suppose?" he asked, clasping his hands behind his head and pretending that his tumble had been intentional.

"Oh, I needn't suppose, Ben – I know exactly where we are," Finn said.

"Good enough, then!" answered Cuhullin, rising and sweeping the mud off his trousers. "We've lain about here long enough. Time we were moving on, wouldn't you say?"

Finn led the way along the floor of the gully. The sun was well up now, dodging the treetops on the way down to the half-Great's eyes. The day seemed full of promise, and for a time he felt relieved of his panic and urgency. He headed through the gully at a brisk and cheerful pace, less a run than a skip. Cuhullin's legs were longer than Finn's, so it was easy for him to keep up.

The gully ended at a small wooded grove, and Finn scrambled up the stony pathway to the plain around Knockmany. Home was close now. He would have whistled for his hounds, but the corners of his mouth were caught up in an irrepressible grin.

"Blast it all and help me up!"

He turned to see Cuhullin floundering, still down in the gully. The ground was soft and wet and his mighty feet could find no purchase.

"Ah, Ben," Finn chuckled, scrambling back and holding out his hand. "Have you no capacity to move from one height to another?"

"Hoist me and don't be daft!" Cuhullin ordered. "We Giants don't prance around like you smaller creatures. We are too grand for leaps and skips."

"Good enough, then," Finn said, pulling with both hands on the Giant's outstretched arm. After much huffing and wheezing, Cuhullin came flopping up out of the gully. Finn was sent sprawling backward, but he landed on the soft earth and laughed to the morning sky.

"That's enough of that," Cuhullin barked. "Let's be moving on, now!"

"Yes, let's." Finn led the way into the wooded grove. Small as it was, the grove was one of his favorite spots. The trees were ancient and curled. The place was a little wooded jewel, and the sight of it always reminded him that home was near at hand.

Finn could hear crunches and cracks behind him as Cuhullin collided with the boughs of the trees. Even his curses made Finn smile, though he hoped no great damage was being done to the grove.

"I surely hope your Oonagh has something for us to eat," Cuhullin mumbled as they neared the parting of the trees and the plain of Knockmany.

"My Oonagh," said Finn with pride and joy, "will have cheeses and bread and cakes stacked *this high*." He gestured with his two forefingers, indicating a mighty portion. But the Giant was looking past him. His hands still measuring the promised cakes, Finn turned to see what had grabbed his companion's attention.

The sun was nearly full and the grove gave way to the familiar patch of green meadow. The grass sparkled with dew and promise. Finn hoped to spy his hounds galloping toward him, their tongues flying behind them. But no welcoming party came.

When he lifted his eyes beyond the meadow, Finn's heart was struck with fear. Rising above the plain was a deathful mound – black, burned, and empty. Nothing else remained of Knockmany.

"Thunderbore! Thunderbore!" Finn and Cuhullin had raced over the ruined hill and around its base, and found nothing alive. Then the Giant spied the Cyclops' crumpled body face down in a cruel bramble to the east of Knockmany. They turned him over in the thorny mess. At first they thought him dead. He was a pitiful sight, mangled in blood and dirt. Most horribly, his great eye had been put out. As they leaned over him, suffocating with shock and grief, they were stunned to hear a cough and a wheeze from Iskander's blue lips. "Thunderbore . . ."

"He lives!" exclaimed Cuhullin.

"How can he?" marveled Finn.

"Thunderbore . . ."

"Easy now, lad," Cuhullin said softly, slipping his hand under Iskander's head. As a warrior, Cuhullin had been amongst and around wounds all the many ages of his life. He had a little-known gift for tending to the injured, having been so often among their number.

Gently Finn wiped the blood from Iskander's face. Then he and Cuhullin carefully extricated him from the thorns that gouged his arms and legs. Realizing that he was alive, Iskander began to struggle in blind terror against the hands trying to help him.

"It's me, my friend – it's Finn." He held tight to Iskander's right hand. Iskander felt about with his left hand until the palm of it came to rest on the side of Finn's face. The Giant managed a faint smile at finding his friend through the darkness.

"They came," he muttered. "They came for . . . Thunderbore . . ." Before he could manage any more, he slipped back into unconsciousness.

Cuhullin tucked his mighty arms under Iskander and scooped him up. With Finn leading the way, he carried him to a soft and shady spot at the edge of the wooded grove. There they laid him on a patch of moss, and gathered a cluster of leaves as a pillow for his wounded head. They tore strips from their cloaks, and wrapped his injuries with the crude bandages.

"There now," Cuhullin muttered, once he was satisfied that they had done the best they could. Finn knelt next to Iskander. He took up his friend's hand once again and squeezed, so that even as he slept, he would know he was safe.

Finn's mind was a horror of images and fears as he looked over the devastated land. Sometimes, if he had a nightmare, he would force himself to wake when things grew too terrible. He wondered if perhaps this was such a time. But he could not wake. This was real – his ruined hill, his blinded friend, the loss of his Oonagh and his hounds.

Where could they have gone? Who could have taken them? And why? Should he run after them? He would, if only he knew which way to run. The thoughts came too fast now, and he was growing dizzy with worry and grief.

"Who's there? Who is it?" Iskander moaned as he awoke again.

"I'm still here with you," said Finn, placing his hand on Iskander's forehead. "What happened? Where are my people?"

Iskander replied with painful effort. "I knew you'd come back and find me, Finn. I knew you'd be here again."

"Who did this?" Cuhullin demanded. He was standing on a rock not far from the wooded grove, scanning the horizon for signs of life.

"They came from all sides," Iskander said weakly. "There was no escape."

"Tell us, please," Finn urged. "What happened to you all? Where are my people and the others?"

"We stood together as best we could," Iskander answered, "hoping to make a fight of it. But it had been countless ages since any of us were in a battle. I cannot remember when last I fought. I remember I quarreled once over a slice of melon, but that was centuries ago, and it hardly compares. Little people with vicious weapons were first up the hill. Sharp stones struck us from all sides. I saw Parthalan dashed to the ground in a hail, and the instant he was off his feet, they swarmed upon him. Cruel little creatures. Girvin went to help him but they cut him down at the knees. I could not reach them, and they were gone."

"Brave deaths," Cuhullin said solemnly.

"The bravery is not what stays in my mind," Iskander answered, shuddering. "I took my stand close by Oonagh and the hounds."

"Where are they?" Finn pleaded.

"I defended them with all my might. Mortal men, their faces twisted with hatred and their weapons horribly slashing, charged us in wave after wave. I swept them aside again and again, ruining some with my fists and sending others down the side of the hill. But then there came a different sort of creature. I cannot tell you what he was. Just about your size, Finn, but hideously strong. When I saw him approach, I thought you had returned – or that it was brave little Peadair, until I saw him to my left, fighting valiantly. But this small Giant, or half-Great, made right for me. Bran charged him. I tried to keep your hound at bay – I did! But he was too swift for me."

"Tell me he was not harmed!"

"He leapt on this half-Great, who caught him in midair. Bran is no small pup, but this little Giant hoisted him above his head and, I am so sorry to report, my friend, dashed him down the side of Knockmany. I did not see where he came to rest. But as soon as she saw her brother tossed over the crest of the hill, Skolie broke from us and hurtled fearlessly after him. I can tell you no more of them."

Finn asked the question he feared most. "What about my Oonagh?"

"She tried to follow your hounds, but there was no safe way through the spears. I gathered her behind me and readied myself to face this half-sized devilry. I could see that he was different from the others. There was no anger or hatred in his face. I tried to seize him – he was notably smaller, so it seemed to me that the tangle would unwind in my favor. But I was completely overpowered."

"My Oonagh!"

"I am sorry, my friend. I defended her, I promise, the best I could. I was flung headlong over the edge of the hill, into a sea of angry little men. I raged against them, trying to get back to your Oonagh, but they were too many and too cruel and they had the higher ground. They chanted a strange word as they fought. It was 'Arvel,' or at least that was how it sounded. They forced me farther and farther down to the plain. I lost sight of the top of Knockmany and Oonagh and all of our companions. Forgive me!" Finn covered his face with his hands. With a shudder, Iskander continued.

"Once they had me pinned down in the valley, impossible machines approached. They were pushed along by hulking, cloaked creatures – I could not see what they were. But the machines were vicious, great towers of wood and metal with huge hammers and wicked blades that slashed at all angles. I could see men inside, stationed on platforms between the pillars of the machines, guiding them in their brutal work."

For a long while, Finn kept his hands over his face. Forgetting his own pain, Iskander reached out to place his hands upon Finn's arm and comfort him.

"Fighting with machines!" Cuhullin grumbled, glaring across the plain.

"They were made with us in mind," said Iskander. "Just the right height to slash at our knees and arms and throats. Hideous!"

"How is it you survived?" Cuhullin asked.

"I do not rightly know. The men cut low with their machines, trying to topple me even as they slashed and slashed again for my eye. Finally I was cut behind the knee. As I fell backward, I saw the last and most terrible sight I shall ever see – Knockmany was engulfed by flames from the sky. No living thing could have been left upon the hill. Certainly not our attackers or any captives they took. It was a brutal blast of fire! No sooner was I flat on my back than they were all over me. Scores of them, it seemed like. Straight for my eye, they went – straight for it. Then all was darkness. And darkness is all it will ever be."

Brave Iskander was at last overwhelmed by the horror. He brought his bloodied fingers to the dead socket of his eye, fumbled with the makeshift bandage Cuhullin had put there, but Finn drew his hand away. "Easy now," he said. "We will see you whole again."

"And how can that be?"

"I do not yet know, friend. But we will do it nonetheless." Finn's tone was unconvincing.

"You're a kind liar," Iskander said, attempting a smile.

"What of Thunderbore?" asked Cuhullin.

"Yes," added Finn, "you mentioned him several times."

"I did?"

"When we found you, yes," said Finn. "What has he to do with this?"

"He was with us, that I remember. But I do not know why I would – wait! No, he was not. He was not with us. He came out of your house well after we heard the drums. He had a strange and ghostly look on his face as he gazed at us one by one. Then he strode past us all. I remember Peadair demanded to know where he was going. And he cursed Thunderbore most thoroughly when he offered no reply. Thunderbore did not say a word as he walked deliberately to the edge of Knockmany, and down into the midst of our enemies."

"A traitor!" bellowed Cuhullin.

"Yes, I suppose he must be." As Iskander spoke, however, he tapped his chin lightly, as though there was something else he was trying to remember.

"What had he to gain?" Finn wondered. "And whatever it was, how important must it have been to be bought with so much pain! How could he be so cruel?"

"We will find him," Cuhullin promised, grinding his fist into his palm.

"Find him?" Finn shot back. "Hang Thunderbore! We'll find my Oonagh and my hounds! I couldn't give a rotted fish for blasted Thunderbore!"

"All right, then, all right," Cuhullin soothed him.

"We will find them! We must find them! How? Where should we begin to look?"

"If you want my opinion," Iskander ventured, "we should find a safe spot where we can regroup and think things over. Out in the open is dangerous."

"Regroup?" shouted Finn. "Think? Are both of you mad? There's no time to sit and think!"

"Settle down there," Cuhullin urged, unaccustomed to being the voice of reason. The two stood facing each other, Cuhullin with consternation, Finn with desperate rage. Just then, Finn's eye was caught by something behind the Giant. A dark figure was hobbling around the base of Knockmany. He pushed past Cuhullin and raced toward the foot of his hill. Cuhullin sped after him.

"Fellows?" Iskander called weakly, realizing he was alone.

As he neared the dark figure, Finn could tell it was a mortal man, hooded and cloaked. He let out a growl as he ran and readied his fists. But as he came closer, the figure turned and Finn stopped in his tracks. Blinking up at him from under the hood was Finegas.

"Oi," the old man croaked, eyeing Finn's balled-up fists, "were you about to smash me?"

Finn was overcome by the sight of his beloved uncle. He spread his arms wide and scooped him up in a warm embrace, not fighting to restrain his tears.

Cuhullin caught up, and the sight of Finn lugubriously clutching an old man made him more confused than ever. "Who . . . who is this, Finn?"

"This," Finn replied, gently setting Finegas back down, "is my uncle, my dearest relation, and the finest fisherman in Eire!"

"All those people under that one little cloak?" marveled the Giant.

Finegas wheezed deeply, free of Finn's loving but suffo-cating embrace. He drew back his hood and squinted against the sunlight.

"Finegas," he said warmly, extending his hand.

"Cuhullin," the Giant replied warily. Gently he took Finegas's hand with his thumb and forefinger and gave it a shake.

"Ah, Benandonner! Of course!" Finegas smiled wryly and closed one eye as he leaned in close to the Giant. "How tall would you say you are, give or take, eh?" Cuhullin was puzzled by this unexpected query. Before he could answer, Finn spoke up.

"Uncle, how did you come to be here? And what do you know of my Oonagh and my hounds?"

"I have come here looking for you, my boy. And here I have found you. As for your dear ones, I have only imperfect news. Come along with me back to Moyle and we shall speak more in safety."

"Hello?" Iskander called out, attempting to rise.

"Stay there! I'll be right back!" Finn yelled. He turned to Finegas. "What imperfect news? Here is as good a place as any to tell me!"

"But where are you?" Iskander shouted.

"Stay there, I said!" Finn turned to Finegas once again. "Are they alive and safe or are they not? Tell me!"

"Those I have are safe. But come along and let me show you." The old man was already heading toward Moyle, at a pace that belied his many years.

Finn threw his arms up and took off running after Finegas. Flustered and frustrated, he did not think to seek the wisdom of Fintan. Cuhullin scooped up Iskander, draping the blind Giant's arm across his shoulders and letting him use his own feet to limp along.

Down the sloping meadows to the south Finn and his uncle ran, the sprightly Finegas in the lead. "Not much farther now!" the old man whooped.

Finn ran at a good clip, wheezing hard and looking this way and that for clues as to what had happened. Nothing he saw suggested anything but the north of Eire about to bloom.

Cuhullin and Iskander hobbled along behind. The two barely knew one another, so their close proximity made the journey somewhat awkward.

"You are very good at supporting a person," Iskander said into Cuhullin's ear.

"Thank you," answered Cuhullin uncomfortably.

"Thanks for the lift," Iskander added.

"Don't mention it."

Finegas led them through a patch of brush so familiar to
Finn that he could have sketched it on a seashell, and down
onto the hidden path to Moyle. The sweet breeze of the vale
of his youth swept across Finn's face, and for a moment he
forgot his troubles and was glad. He closed his eyes and
breathed in deeply, even as he ran. No sooner did he realize
he was happy, however, than worry for his loved ones struck
him once again like a stone in his stomach.

Finegas ran over a ridge of tree roots and ducked through
low-hanging branches until at last the greenery parted at
Finn's boyhood home. Finn saw a sight that banished all his
unhappiness. Scampering toward him from the house, teeth
bared in a grin and tongue flapping out the side of her mouth,
was Skolie.

He dropped to his knees and spread his arms wide. When
Skolie got to him, however, she ran around and around him,
kicking up grass and dirt in her excitement. When at last she
was done, she planted her furry feet, and leapt up into his
loving arms.

The half-Great hugged his little hound, and applied
many grateful kisses to her ears and the top of her head. Her
tongue was a pink blur drenching his face and neck. He fell
on his back and laughed out loud as she bounded and pawed
at his stomach. It was a wonderful meeting.

"There's more where that came from!" Finegas laughed,
beckoning the others toward the house. "Come along in."
Finn tucked Skolie up under his arm, and followed his uncle
to the door.

Iskander and Cuhullin had emerged into the clearing just
in time to see Finn's reunion with his joyful hound. Cuhullin,
who lacked a perfect understanding of the love of animals,

had curled his lip at the sight of the half-Great rolling on the ground, kissing and speaking gibberish to this creature.

Finn ducked under the transom and stepped into the house. Skolie wiggled under his arm and he set her down to scramble across the parlor. Bodhmall, who had been laying food on the table, turned as they entered. She seemed to Finn very old now, having for some reason aged far faster than her sister and brother. She sighed deeply, set her stack of plates upon the table, and shuffled toward Finn, arms wide. Gently he put his arms about her. She waved her hand in the direction Skolie had scampered. His eyes followed her gesture to a soft and cozy cushion, lovingly and skillfully made, on which lay Bran. Liath knelt beside him, stroking his head.

Finn knew at once that something was wrong. Bran did not spring up and come to greet him. The hound only lifted his head and peered across the parlor for a moment before dropping his chin once again onto the cushion. Finn looked to Liath. She smiled sadly and nodded.

Finn knelt beside Bran. He wrapped his arms around his hound, scratched delicately behind his ears, and traced his fingers along the top of the dog's head in a way that only he knew. Bran let out a little wheeze of contentment. Then Finn gave him a kiss upon the nose and whispered many kind and secret things into his ear.

"Blast it all!" Cuhullin, attempting to help Iskander into the house, had misjudged the height of the door. The Cyclops spilled forward onto the floor as Cuhullin, one hand upon his forehead, clenched the other into a fist and thought about smashing the door frame.

"Oh, no you don't!"

Still scowling, the Giant peeked through his fingers to see Bodhmall looking at him sternly. He had never met this woman, but in those four words he knew her. Slowly he unballed his fist.

"How is my little person?" Finn asked.

"I'll be all right, I think, thanks," answered Iskander from the floor.

"Not you!"

"Oh, good enough, then," Iskander muttered. "I'll just paw about blind on the floor in a room full of strangers. Outstanding." Cuhullin ducked in and helped the Cyclops to a large chair in the corner of the parlor.

"We found this brave little fellow," Finegas said, kneeling to join Finn by Bran's cushion, "a good half-league from here. It was clear he'd had a nasty fall. But he was struggling to make his way here. Weren't you, boy? And his good little sister was helping him along. She was right by his side, licking the top of his head while he rested."

"My brave little hounds," Finn said softly, giving Bran a pat.

As the half-Great and his uncle attended to the pups, Liath quietly made her way across the room to Iskander. She took his hand in hers and said a few words of introduction. Then she set about cleaning and dressing his wounds with more skill and thoroughness than the others had managed.

"And what of my Oonagh?" Finn asked. "Did you find nothing of her? Please say you have some news!" Finegas shook his head and looked away.

"I believe that she lives." Finn and Finegas lifted their eyes to Bodhmall, who had spoken these words with conviction. She leaned wearily upon the table, but there was strength in her expression.

"How can you know this?" demanded Finn.

"With age comes a sense of things. I cannot explain it,

and you are too young to understand it. We do not control what will occur, but we can see it clear as the day."

"Then tell me," urged Finn, "what do you see?"

"Oonagh lives," she assured him. "But she is far away. You may find her and bring her home again. I can see that she has not died. I see it."

"But where is she?"

"To find her," answered Bodhmall, "you will need help – beyond the skill of any under this roof. There is hope yet, I know it. The ways and means of the matter, I must leave to higher powers." The old woman shuffled to her chair. She had grown even paler as she spoke, as though she were struggling under some oppressive weight.

Finn wondered what higher power she might mean. Like many warriors, Bodhmall was devout. Finn hoped she was not merely urging him to pray to the Dagda that all would be well. "To what power must I turn?" As he spoke, he saw that Bodhmall had fallen into a deep sleep in her chair. Then at last he remembered the wisdom of Fintan. Without a thought for modesty, he put his thumb in his mouth. But it was no use. There was no image, no wisdom, no taste of ash. Just a dirty thumb and a pang of despair. Dejectedly, he pulled his thumb from his lips.

"I know whom she means," Finegas offered slyly, as though he could not wait to be questioned further.

"The Banshee," Liath interjected, still tending to Iskander's hurts. Finegas scowled.

"The Banshee?" said Finn. "Is that what you were going to say, uncle?"

"We'll never know now," Finegas sniffed.

"But the Banshee," Finn protested, "does she not foretell only death?"

"That is a cruel misconception!" Liath answered sharply. "Strange things have passed by our valley in recent days. Stranger, even, than any of us has ever seen – and we have lived a long time. Mortal men, clattering contraptions, loping Giants, and wings in the air. In truth, we do not understand their meaning, despite the many years among us. The Banshee lives in the Burren, and she is skilled beyond all others in divining the way of the world. Go and seek her out, Demne."

"She is known to us?" puzzled Finn. "How so?"

Liath looked up to the ceiling and flapped her hands, searching for the proper way to explain it. "We are distant cousins, suffice it to say," she sighed at last.

"Good enough, then," Finn said. "The Burren? Have I been there before?"

"Not unless you were very lost or very desperate to be far from trees and green," answered his aunt. "It is to the south and west, near the edge of our island. The journey is long and the destination is uncharming. But for all the Banshee's wisdom, that is the place she chooses for her home."

"I can find you the Burren," Finegas chimed in proudly. "It seems like a dry and lifeless place to those who do not know Eire as I do." He shot a glance at Liath. "But the skilled man of our island can yet suss out water and life on its craggy face. Leave it to me."

"Thank you, uncle." Finegas smiled. "Are you going to tell me the way, then?"

"What, now?" Finegas said, his smile draining away. "Not just yet. In the morning I shall draw you one of my special maps." He winked and touched his finger to the side of his nose. Finn nodded and smiled, pretending to be grateful.

By now, Cuhullin had grown quite uncomfortable. A good deal of time had passed with others doing the talking and making the decisions. Besides, he could find no suitable spot in which to sit. The house had been built, of course, with Giants in mind, but the Great One of Fyfe was larger than any who had ever squeezed under its roof.

"Sit and let me feed you," Liath announced to the room, as she helped Iskander to his feet and toward the table. At this commandment, Cuhullin's spirits brightened. Ducking lower than he really needed to, and with his hand held protectively over his forehead, he made his way to the largest chair. Finn was reluctant to leave Bran, but Liath added, "Now, Demne." As he rose and came to the table, little Skolie took his place upon the floor, nestling warmly beside her big brother.

Liath and Bodhmall had prepared an abundance of food in anticipation of the companions' arrival. They had not known just who or how many would be appearing at their door, but they knew that in times of trouble, it was never long before kith and kin came knocking. Cakes, cheeses, and bread were piled high on platters in the center of the table. For once in his long life, Cuhullin paused to savor the scene before beginning to devour it.

"On you go then, Demne," Liath urged, when she noticed that Finn was not eating. He was sitting silently at his customary place, his eyes down-turned and his hands upon his lap. "Tuck in, my boy. You need your strength."

"What good is my strength without my Oonagh?"

"You'll not have one again without the other, so please do eat up." She had set a small special plate by Finn's place. On it was a helping of the most beloved dish from his boyhood: peas and cheese. Besides the fact that it rhymed and was exceedingly delicious, little Demne had always enjoyed the patterns he could create by pushing this delicacy about on the plate. Eyeing this serving, Finn marveled that his aunt imagined that such deep hurts could be soothed by mere food – even the most delectable. Still, to oblige her, he took up his spoon and started in. Liath smiled and piled a plate high for Iskander.

They ate together in silence, save for the sound of Bodhmall gently snoozing in the corner. Finn was surprised to discover that the dinner was buoying his spirits. As he ate and regained his strength, he found that he was fretting less over what had happened to his beloved, and planning and plotting more as to what to do next. The peas and cheese were gone in short order, though he did pause near the end to trace Oonagh's name with what little was remaining.

Finn's blind panic was gone and his paralyzing sadness had retreated. Anger lingered, but he put it to use. He resolved that he would find his Oonagh – and that those who had taken her from him would pay.

V

the banshee's song

Voices were all around her, but Oonagh did not recognize the languages they spoke. Here and there a word would catch her ear, yet there was no context to give it meaning. Some creatures boomed. Others screeched. It was impossible to tell if they were quarreling, agreeing, or celebrating something hideous.

Specks of gray light poked through the shroud that covered her face. Though she had been given no choice in the matter, she did not regret that she was blindfolded. Nothing that engaged her other senses made her want to see too.

The wagon on which she found herself creaked along ominously, as if toward a scaffold or a dolmen. Her hands were tied behind her back, with rough ropes in tight loops and knots, as though she were some lethal thing whose escape could not be risked. The creatures beside and about

the cart were in no way pleasing to the nose, and Oonagh
hoped that, wherever she was being taken, the place would
have a profound supply of soap and water.

The long, trying journey had begun when she was blindfolded atop Knockmany. Iskander held her back from
following her hounds through the vicious throng. Little men
surrounded them, hurling abuse at the Giant and eyeing her
with evil intent. Then Iskander's huge hands let her go and
swung around to fight. The contest could not have lasted
long because, before she knew it, Iskander was gone, and a
little Giant looked down upon her.

What Oonagh saw in this new creature's face could not
properly be called pity, but something suggested that he
understood her fate and the fear she felt. He was about the
size of Finn, though broader across the shoulders, and dressed
in a more military and menacing manner than her own
beloved would have chosen. Shocks of red hair sprouted from
beneath his helmet, which seemed a size too small for his
head. He bore no weapons, she noticed, and his open hands
moved toward her slowly. She did not panic, so deliberate
were his movements. Just as he was about to take hold of her,
however, several mortal men came within range, brandishing
their arms. Never taking his eyes off Oonagh, the creature
sent them flying with a single swipe.

The little Giant took Oonagh up, firmly but without
hurting her, and carried her through the fray. She strained
for some sight of the hounds or Iskander, but all she saw was
chaos. Suddenly she spied Peadair. He was punching and
plowing his way through the mortal men, daring them on
and pronouncing his opinion of them as he went. Oonagh
called to him and, miracle of miracles, the pugnacious Giant
heard her. Seeing that she was being carried off, he called
out angrily and started in her direction.

Oonagh did not know how close he came to rescuing her. A hood was pulled down over her eyes, and the sight of the Giant's determined face through the crowd was the last thing she saw. Then her hands were bound. She felt herself being carried down the hill, and the same strong set of hands, presumably those of the little Giant, placed her on a solid board on some moving contraption. It was not long before she heard and smelled the sea.

She was hoisted again, this time by many weaker but less gentle hands, and loaded into a boat. Instructions and arguments were hurled back and forth until, after some time, Oonagh could feel they were underway. Groans and grunts surrounded her, so she supposed this was some kind of rowing vessel, propelled by strong and ill-tempered creatures. It was only now, as she realized she was leaving Eire, that she began to worry in earnest. She had feared for her Finn and her hounds all along. But as she felt the boat pulling away from the island that was her home, brave Oonagh began to fear for herself.

The journey across the sea was a smooth one, though she cared little whether the waves were friendly or not. Her mind raced from one unhappy place to another. The sight of Bran disappearing over the hill flashed horribly before her. She wished she had kept hold of brave Skolie after that. And most of all, where was her Finn? What had they done to be so cruelly separated?

At long last the prow of the boat struck land. Oonagh was thrown forward by the shock of it. Once again hands were upon her, lifting her out of the craft. Up a short hill they went, with much jostling, until finally, with loud argument among her captors, she was placed on the wagon where she now sat. Whether minutes, hours, or the whole of a day had passed, she could not tell. She was dizzy from grief and disoriented from being blindfolded.

Then she heard a sound. A loud, deep voice called out and the wagon came to a sudden halt. This time, Oonagh understood the words.

"What is all this?"

"We've brought . . . you know," some shifty-sounding creature croaked.

"Oh you have, have you? Then come with me, and do not stray from the path I lead you, understood? Nothing to your left or right is any of your business. If you forget that, you will wish you had not. Come along!"

The wagon lurched forward once again. Oonagh could make out indignant muttering. They had gone a fair way when she heard the deep voice again. "That's far enough! I'll take it from here. The rest of you, look to your guides and head straight back the way you came. If I see you here again, it will end poorly. Go!" Oonagh could hear the murmurs fading with footsteps behind her.

When the deep voice spoke again, it was softer. "This way, please." There was a moment of silence before she realized that the voice was addressing her.

"Well, that's a silly thing to say," she answered, in a tone less sharp than the words themselves. "My hands are bound behind me, and I can't see which way you mean."

"Of course," came the accommodating reply, and she heard what sounded like the snapping of enormous fingers. At once, her bonds were cut by swift and skilled hands. "Please," the voice added pleasantly, as she felt a cold touch upon her shoulder. She reached out and her hand was taken gently by some huge and icy creature.

Still blindfolded, Oonagh stepped off the wagon and went where she was led. Whatever type of being was helping her along, it was larger than any she had encountered before.

Indeed, she realized that she barely had hold of the smallest part of a finger. The creature seemed to suffocate all warmth around him. Being next to him made her shiver. Despite his size, he neither rushed nor pulled her along, but guided her at her own pace.

She felt rounded cobblestones beneath her feet; no jagged or uneven edges caught her. The noises she heard suggested industry and efficiency – the clanging of metal and the crisp issuing of commands – in contrast to the grunting rabble who had captured her. Voices came from beside her and above, suggesting that some great building or tall towers were round about.

She was taken in through a door and up a circular staircase, and felt herself enveloped by the cool silence of solid stone. From the top of the winding stair, she was guided down a long hallway where the only sound was the echo of footsteps – her own, and the massive clomping of the creature who accompanied her. A door creaked open and she was gently urged through it. The huge and frosty hand was then removed. When Oonagh the door latch shut behind her, she felt she was alone in a room.

She became aware of a wisp of a sound from the direction of the door, and turned toward it. Just as she did so, the sound came again, this time from the opposite side of the room. She whipped her head back around.

"Who's there? I can't see you!" There was a flick and a snip behind her head and the blindfold fell from her eyes. Blinking against the light, she peered around to see that she was in an opulent hall, presumably part of a grand palace, with high, arching ceilings, and magnificent tapestries upon the walls. The room was lit by soaring, pointed windows on two sides, as well as immense chandeliers bearing innumerable blue-glowing candles. The room

had fallen silent again, and nowhere could she find a hint
as to the noise she had heard, or who had freed her eyes.

A massive stone fireplace stood in the center of the room,
and above it hung the most ornate tapestry Oonagh had ever
seen. A large white stag stood upon a blue field, one hoof
raised. It was circled by many smaller stags, all reared up on
their hind legs. The needlework was astounding – perhaps
beyond even her skills and those of her people. More
remarkable than the perfect stitches and glowing threads
was the soul and pity of the piece. The jeweled eyes of the
central stag looked plaintively out from the field, and
Oonagh felt as though the surrounded beast were gazing
straight into her heart.

"Toothsome Oonagh."

A narrow man, dressed with elegant simplicity, was
leaning in a corner she had inspected just moments before.
The only decoration on his green garb was a single red
feather stuck into his cap, which he spun thoughtfully on his
finger. His face was white but not pale, and his yellow hair
was flowing but neat. He was in no hurry to say more.
Oonagh could think of nothing to say, the two considered
one another across the room in silence. "I see you admire my
work," he said at last. She was alarmed to find that he was
suddenly right next to her, though she had not seen him
move. He was not menacing. He was just close. "I made this
tapestry many years ago, with a dream in mind. It was an
early and clumsy work, I admit, but I am flattered that it
pleases you."

"I don't know if I'd call it pleasure, but it affects me," she
responded.

"Fair enough," he allowed. "You noticed it, and that gives
me some simple joy." He turned to face her. "I am Jack, and
I am your humble servant."

"Oonagh McCool," she answered, extending her hand. It was an awkward gesture; he was standing so close to her that she had to bend her elbow out to the side so her fingers would not collide with his chest. With the same speed he had displayed in crossing the room, he retreated a few steps and bowed, taking her hand and gently kissing it in one smooth movement.

"A long-awaited honor," he said, straightening once again to meet her gaze. He was slightly cross-eyed, and he enjoyed watching others' discomfort as they struggled to decide which eye to meet. Oonagh looked from one eye to the other, while he took his time before speaking. "Jack in the Green, you may know me as, though I never introduce myself as such, and I am not so called by my friends."

"Yes, I know the name," Oonagh said apprehensively, resolving to look into his right eye no matter what.

"You do? And what do you know about it?"

"I know it is the name of a killer," she answered, "and the name of the reason I am far from my home and those I love. Is there more I should know?"

"So lissome, and yet you wound me," said Jack, bringing a hand to his chest.

"That was no wound," she shot back. "But press me and you may learn the difference. Why have you brought me here?"

"Well, first, let me say that I am no killer," said Jack. "I am a tailor. A simple and humble profession, I know, but it gives me pride. Yes, I admit I have been responsible for the end of many unfortunate and deserving creatures. But our reputations shouldn't rest on what we do once or twice upon a time. I have no doubt you feed your husband well. Does that make you nothing more than a cook?"

"Rubbish," said Oonagh. "Do you know what grief you

have caused already? Do you know what pain you have
caused even me, whom you do not know? And you compare
it to baking a pie! I've asked you a proper question, and I'd
be glad to hear no more of your mangled philosophy. Why
have you done this?"

"You are wrong that I do not know you," he responded
with an oily smile. "You do not know me – that much is
clear – but Toothsome Oonagh is a creature I have admired
for some time."

"What can that possibly mean?"

"Surely you are aware that your wisdom and beauty are
known throughout these islands. Do not demean us both
with false modesty. You are a glory of a woman. I set two birds
free from my window. I told them to bring back some
scrap of loveliness, to show me it still could be found in this
world – it had been a melancholy time for me.

"The first bird was a dove, and she returned with a remarkable flower. The petals were red, gold, and green. It smelled
and looked sublime, and I even supposed I heard some lovely
music coming from it. But I already knew about beautiful
flowers. The dove seemed so proud of her discovery that I
could not bear to let her see my disappointment, so I killed
her. Then I had her tastily prepared by my kitchen and made
her my supper, to show there were no hard feelings between us.

"The next morning, the other bird returned. It was a
raven, this one, and the wretched thing perched on my sill
half-dead from exhaustion. In his beak he bore a simple gift:
a single strand of golden hair. Where could this have come
from? What could it mean? I questioned the bird at length,
and he said he'd been to Eire, to a hill of emerald green on
which lived a woman of surpassing beauty. You were hanging
washing on a line and he had snatched one strand of hair
that was caught up by the breeze. A queen of nature, he said

you were, going about your business with royal grace. He did not know your name, but he swore that your very life was proof of the loveliness I sought. The raven said this with his final breath, as the journey had been the death of him. Untouchable and lovely Oonagh of the Emerald Hill."

"Oh, rot," Oonagh humphed. "Where have you brought me? Stop your nonsense and tell me."

"This is my master's house," the tailor replied. "He has many mansions and, in his kindness, he has given me the use of this one. I tried to make it my own in ways here and there, such as this trifle of a tapestry that you admired. But I am merely a humble tenant."

"I have a house all my own," answered Oonagh. "Did you know that? Oh yes, of course you do, because your wretched bird saw me hanging out the washing in front of it. But I am not there now. And do you know why? Because some slobbering band of petty villains came and dragged me away. I know who you are, and I saw what was done to the Great guests at my home. You are a killer. Vicious little cowards – you think you're heroes for cutting down creatures whose only crime is being bigger than you. I have heard of the trouble you are spreading upon these islands. You are not the only one who learns from the birds and trees. Disgraceful, puny man. What did you expect from me but hatred?"

If Jack was dismayed, he did not show it. The tailor's smile never wavered, as if her every word was precisely what he had expected to hear.

"You are quite right," he said, "but for the wrong reasons. All I have done, I have done for love: love of land, love of man, love of a woman, and love of a dream. It is true, there are many creatures greater than I am. But that does not make them innocent, any more than their greatness is a crime. There is a time, Toothsome Oonagh, to all things. The season is turning, but new worlds dawn every day. And we must embrace them, seize them, or we too fade and die. You ask why I have brought you here. We have lived too long in the shadow and fear of hulking goliaths whose only claim to power is the brute strength they were born with. Our islands have been their playthings and battlegrounds, according to their whims, for ages beyond counting. And what of those creatures *without* stupendous size or monstrous strength? Do they cherish their lands and loved ones any less? Of course not. But what place do the wants and fears of little people hold in a land of Giants? Less than none, as we have seen. My dream is to right that wrong."

"What a relief," gasped Oonagh. "Here I thought you were some nasty villain waging war on those I love. But since it was all in the service of some noble end, I feel worlds better. What a rat you are."

He flashed her a new sort of grin – less joy and more teeth – and resumed twirling his cap upon his finger. He could not hide a flicker of malice in his eye. But before she could speak again, he vanished.

"You're getting too far ahead, and you don't even know where you're going!" This was the latest in a series of reprimands Cuhullin had shouted to Finn. The half-Great ignored him. It was true that he had gotten carelessly way ahead. It was also true that he did not know exactly which way he should run. But he sensed that he was headed to the south and west, and he wanted to close as much of the gap as he could between Moyle and the Burren before nightfall.

It had been a long day already. Finn had not slept much. Despite Liath and Bodhmall's repeated requests that he rise and find a proper bed, he refused to leave his spot on the floor beside Bran. He lay with his arms around his hound, Skolie stretched out nearby. Liath had led Iskander to a room in the back of the house, where she had redressed his wounds and sung him to sleep. Cuhullin, meanwhile, had arranged himself in an awkward diagonal fashion from one corner of the parlor to the other. The Giant of Fyfe had snored mightily, but the others were either too old to hear or too exhausted to mind.

At dawn Finn had dashed around the house, haphazardly hurling provisions into his upturned green cap, and made for the door. To his surprise, Liath was standing in his path.

"That's how you think you're going out?" she demanded. "Alone and with no proper food in you?"

"This is serious business, aunt."

"Indeed, but not so serious that you can't have a breakfast. Sit you down, Demne, please, and let's get you something reasonable."

He felt foolish standing just inside the door, his cap filled with an impractical assortment of utensils, cheese, and some impenetrable nuts that Liath used for cooking. Without her noticing, he returned each item to its place.

After a brief breakfast, they discussed who would go with Finn to find the Banshee. Cuhullin was coming along, and that was that. Not only was he determined to lead another outing, but he was profoundly uncomfortable in this place, surrounded by a lovingly bickering family he did not know. Finegas said he would like to join them, but that was quickly squelched by Liath, who admonished him to talk sense. Bran too made hopeful noises, as though he were well enough to make the trip. Finn patted the hound and whispered into his ear that his solemn task would be to protect those left behind. Bran lifted his head proudly from his cushion. Indeed, though he had not patted Finegas, Finn had whispered something similar to his uncle, sparing the old man's pride. Finegas had smiled slyly and, as though it were some fine secret, had slipped a map into Finn's hand.

Most surprising was Iskander, who tottered, unaided, from the back room. He leaned on the door frame and spoke with conviction.

"Who thinks they're going anywhere without me?"

Every face in the room turned to him. No one knew who should answer, or how. At last, Finn spoke up. "My friend, you cannot . . . ," he began.

"Either you're taking me along," Iskander cut him off, "or I'm pawing my way to the Burren by my lonesome. You decide what your conscience can bear." There was little else to say at that point, so Finn smiled at his dear friend's loyalty, then led the way outside. Without a word, Cuhullin put his shoulder under Iskander's arm and helped him along behind.

Once outside, the leave-taking was more solemn, as they all nodded in silence to each other. Suddenly Finegas whooped, "Whoa, hang on!" and darted into the house. Finn and Cuhullin shrugged at one another. Iskander, despite having been told not to by Liath, firmly and repeatedly, during breakfast, scratched at the bandage over his eye. "Here it is, here it is!" Finegas called out excitedly. Under his arm was a large, straight object wrapped in cloth. With both hands, Finegas presented it to Finn. The half-Great's heart quickened when he peeled back the cloth and saw a flash of red. He reached in and raised aloft, for the first time in many years, the mighty sword of Breanain. "Don't you remember?" Finegas asked. "You left it here for safekeeping and for me to give it a lick of polish. Good thing I kept it safe, eh? Especially since you'll be needing it now. Came in handy that I remembered, too. There are lots of ways a person can help!"

"Thank you," Finn said quietly. With one last look to his aunt, sword in hand, he set off running toward the west. Cuhullin took a deep breath, hiked Iskander a bit farther up onto his shoulder, and jogged on after.

This was how Finn found himself, hours later, in a beautiful but unknown patch of Eire, being barked at to slow down. The sun was high, and he stood on a bare outcrop of rock overlooking an expanse of green meadow. Breanain was still unsheathed and flashing in his hand.

"So where to from here, eh?" Cuhullin asked. He and Iskander had adjusted themselves so that the Cyclops no longer had his arm draped across Cuhullin's shoulder. Not only was the Giant of Fyfe much taller than the Cyclops, which made for uncomfortable bending and reaching, but neither one of them was nimble. They did not hold hands – not by any means – but grasped one another by the forearm in a manner befitting two warriors. "You were in such an all-fired hurry to get to this spot," Cuhullin added. "So where are we?"

"Give us a moment to catch our breath and get our bearings," Finn replied firmly, feeling winded for the first time.

"You know I'd offer my advice," Iskander said wryly, "but every spot looks the same to me just now."

"Thanks for the thought." Finn shaded his eyes with his arm and peered upward to track the course of the sun. He looked back at the way they had come and forward to the new horizon. None of this helped. When he had taxed his wits all they could pay, he unfolded the map that Finegas had drawn for him. Seeing him resort to this measure, Cuhullin snorted and found a place for himself and Iskander to sit.

The map was no more useful than Finn had expected. In fact, it was a fair sight less so, because the Burren was not even indicated. It seemed that, in his eagerness to identify

the finest fishing spots in the west of Eire, Finegas had forgotten the map's main purpose. Rivers and streams were
drawn in rich blue and, as was the old man's custom, bits of
bait were attached to the map here and there, atop the best
spots for their use. Along with the bait and riverworks there
were scribbled bits of advice and admonishment, such as
"Sing a ditty before dropping your line here," and "Tell NO
ONE of this spot – F." Finn shook his head as he refolded the
map. He tried not to feel ungrateful, though he allowed
himself the wish that his uncle could think of things other
than fishing and spices.

As Finn squinted across the meadow, something caught
his eye. He could make out a black speck. It was small, to be
sure, but what grabbed his gaze was the speed at which the
speck was moving. Darting this way and that, it covered vast
distances in a blink. Its path was not direct, but as it zigged
and zagged across the meadow it became clear that the speck
was headed for them.

"What is that?" said Cuhullin.

"What is what?" Iskander asked.

"I don't know," Finn answered. "I just caught sight of it.
But it's on its way here!"

"Well, that will be just fine," Cuhullin grumbled, grinding his fist into his palm. "There's been too much running
today, and not nearly enough slugging!"

"Whatever it is, Ben," the half-Great said, "it's too small
for you to be slugging it."

The black speck was drawing closer, but whether its
speed was achieved by wings or by some blur of legs was
impossible to tell. At last it came to rest out of sight, directly
beneath the rock on which Finn and Cuhullin were standing.
They craned their necks and listened. They heard the
sh-sh'ing of whispers.

"Hello?" Finn called down. The whispering stopped.

"Show yourself!" Cuhullin commanded. A faint yelp came in reply. "At once, I say! If I need to climb down there, you'll regret it!"

"Uh . . . hello?" came a reedy voice.

"Yes, we've already said hello," Cuhullin barked. "Who and what are you?"

"Sorry, yes – is Finn McCool up there, by any chance?"

"We already know who is up here," Cuhullin answered angrily. "What I want to know is who is down there!"

"Of course, you're right, I'm sorry. We are – that is, I am – an old friend of Finn McCool. Did you say he is there with you?"

"Yes, I am here," Finn said. "And who are you? I don't recall any friends who move at your speed. Seems like something I'd remember."

"Well, yes, you're right," the little voice answered. "I didn't always – that is to say, I do not travel alone anymore, so I move a mite faster now. Actually, it's not me at all, if you want to know the truth. There's an arrangement. I would invite you to come down and say hello, but I worry that your Giant might smash us."

"As well he might," Cuhullin sniffed.

"There will be no smashing," Finn promised, "unless you give us cause. But you say you are a friend, so you shouldn't worry."

"I will worry, regardless," replied the voice, "but do please come on down."

Finn spied a narrow path to the right of the outcrop, and sheathed Breanain for the first time that day. It occurred to Finn that he had nothing but the word of this speedy character that the meeting would be peaceable. Congratulating himself on his shrewdness, he drew his sword once more and carefully climbed down the path. Cuhullin grumbled and headed back to fetch Iskander.

The way was pebbled and steep. Finn braced himself with his free hand on the side of the rock. The last step down was a bit too far to be negotiated comfortably, and he was unsure whether to leap or clamber a little longer. He pressed himself against the side of the cleft, and using the hand that held Breanain, swung down and dangled for a moment above the ground. In that instant, he saw two sets of eyes peering at him from the shade under the rocky overhang.

Finn released his hold on the rock and clomped down onto the lower level. He heard a gasp of alarm. The eyes were still on him, though he could not make out the faces. "Well, are you coming out or aren't you?" he asked impatiently.

"We'd like to," came the reedy voice, "but are you certain we'll be safe?"

"I have already said so! Now stop messing around and come out!"

"All right, all right – but just remember, you promised!" With that, two timid creatures came blinking into the light. One was on all fours, matted with shaggy gray fur, and stood not much higher than Finn's knee. It was a little goat, with wee rounded horns poking through the fuzz atop its head. The other creature was also small, not much taller than a man, and walked upright. His clothes were dusty and ragged, though a heroic attempt had been made to keep them mended. It took a moment, but Finn found a flicker of something familiar. It was Aillen.

"Hey there!" Finn exclaimed, raising his arms high, sword still in hand, not considering how frightening this greeting might seem. Aillen and the goat ducked back under the rock. "Oh! Sorry!" Finn sheepishly lowered his weapon.

"We apologize!" Aillen squeaked.

"Now, what are you saying sorry for?"

"Anything and everything. When in doubt, we say we are sorry. It is a strategy that has kept us alive. Whatever we have done to make you raise your hand, we heartily and unreservedly apologize."

"Agreed," bleated the goat.

"You've done nothing. Don't be daft."

"Sorry for that! We don't mean to be daft!"

"Enough. Stop apologizing or you really will make me cross. Come on back out here."

"Of course, of course!" Aillen said, leading the goat back into the open.

Finn smiled. "Welcome back, my friend. It has been too long since we saw each other. But what happened to make you so timid?"

"You flatter me," Aillen said. "You surely recall that I could never be confused for a hero. My timidity is nothing new. May I present, please, my associate – Alistair."

The little goat bowed to Finn. "How do you do?" he said, his eyes averted.

"Immortal until proven otherwise, thank you," Finn replied. "I am pleased to make your acquaintance."

"Out of the bloody way down there!" Cuhullin came tumbling down from the rock, dragging a bewildered Iskander behind him. The two skidded straight through the conversation before coming to a halt in a cloud of dust. "Well, I've managed to get the blind fellow down safely." Cuhullin dusted his clothes and helped Iskander to his feet. The Cyclops, dazed, rose and shook his head.

"Are you all right, my friend?" Finn asked.

"Never better, never better," Cuhullin answered, not imagining that the question could be meant for anyone but him. "And who are these little rock badgers?" He frowned down at Aillen and Alistair, who started to tremble.

"We're very sorry . . . ," Aillen began.

"None of that, now!" Finn cut him off. "This is Aillen, the famous bard of the Alfar," he said with a wave. "And his companion, Alistair the . . . goat."

"Escape Goat," Alistair offered meekly.

"I beg your pardon?"

"I am sorry, but I am an Escape Goat." As tales of this slight fellow were only sparsely known in Albion. The Escape Goat was a swift beast who was always getting blamed when things went awry, but miraculously managed to be absent when repercussions came down.

"Fair enough," said Finn. "These are my friends Benandonner and Iskander."

"An honor to meet you both," Aillen said humbly, as he and Alistair bowed low.

"Thank you," mumbled Cuhullin. His eyes darted suspiciously between the two strangers.

"You must tell me, little bard," Finn said, "what happened to you? When last we saw one another, you were burdened with treasure too great for me to count or you to carry. Yet now you appear in such a wretched state."

"Not to worry about me," Aillen replied. "I still have ample treasure to last the rest of my life – provided I am killed sometime later today."

"But what happened to your crown, and your diamonds – and your harp?"

"Where to begin?" Aillen ran his fingers through his whitened hair. "Things began well enough. Such adventures we had, eh Finn? And so lucrative! But I have learned since then that not everyone can shoulder good fortune. After I left you, I returned to my people – to my family, no less – and it was marvelous. I was well received. Dare I say it? – I was popular! One could suppose this was partly because I handed gold out to everyone, but I did not do this to be well liked! It had been so many years since I had seen my own kind – and years beyond memory since they had treated me with kindness – that I doled out treasure to keep them from harming me. People are pleasanter when you give them gold. They enjoyed my jokes. Even my music made them glad, for once! It was a happy time.

"But smiles turn to frowns once the coins are spent. When there was no more gold, I sold the larger pieces of treasure, one at a time. The riches I had were vast, but my kin had speedy hands. Then there was no more to sell. Suddenly they found my music less pleasing. I was no longer so amusing. I was driven away again – this time with more vigor – and had I not befriended good Alistair here, who knows where I would be!"

"I am terribly sorry for your troubles," Finn said.

"Thank you," answered Aillen ruefully. No one spoke for a little time.

"As for us," Finn ventured, tired of waiting for Aillen to find the courtesy to ask after him, "we have seen hard times of our own. We heard tales of a merciless sea serpent. Then, when we went to investigate, our Causeway was destroyed, my hill was put under siege, and my beloved was stolen from me. Now we are doing the best we can to find her. We are headed for the Burren to seek the counsel of the Banshee." The little bard bristled. "What is it?"

"Nothing," Aillen answered hastily. "Nothing at all. The Burren, you say?"

"Aye."

"I don't recall seeing you in those parts before," Aillen mused. "And a person of your height – I would have noticed."

"How do you mean?"

"I mean you'd be the tallest thing there, beyond even the grandest dolmen. The Burren is the home of my people, the Alfar. It is a flat and lonely land, and that is how we like it. It is a bleak expanse of crag and stone. We retreated there long ago, because there are no trees from which we can be hanged, no water in which we can be drowned, and no earth in which we can be buried."

"So you know the way there?" asked Finn.

"We know it better than we wish to recall," said Aillen, putting a consoling arm around Alistair.

"Then you must show us the way!"

"Now hang on, half-Great!" Aillen protested. "We know where it is, but the Burren's the last place our feet and hearts would wish to take us! What would make us head there?"

"How much do you like the state of your bones? Would it be worth your while to keep them as they are?" Cuhullin asked ominously.

"Easy now." Aillen cautiously swung his leg up over the back of the Escape Goat. "Don't be hasty, Giant!"

"My name is Cuhullin" – the Giant closed the gap between them with surprising quickness – "and I'll be as hasty as I like!"

"Settle down, Ben." Finn held onto Cuhullin's tunic. "I have worked with this little fellow before. All he needs is to be talked with." Cuhullin snorted, keeping his eyes upon the Alfar. "Tell me, Aillen – what good works have you done since last we met?"

"Good works?" wondered the Alfar. "Does dodging disaster qualify? If it does, Alistair and I are above even you huge lads!"

"What I am saying," Finn continued, "is that we are engaged in a quest for the good of us all – to save our islands. You did a turn for the world when you helped us build our Causeway. What say you to helping out once more?"

"If you mean to appeal to my nobility," Aillen answered, "you are misguided. Appeal to my friendship, or even my shame, what little I can still feel. I have been chased off so often that nobility has been driven from my heart. I care nothing for saving the world. Indeed, I could make a strong case for seeing it crumble."

"I'll appeal to your bloody skull!" Cuhullin bellowed, lurching forward. Aillen clutched the Escape Goat's mane and, in a flash, goat and rider were out on the meadow, well beyond reach.

"How did he do that?" marveled Cuhullin.

"He meant nothing by it!" Finn called to the pair. "Come back, old friend! Let's talk some more."

"Thank you, no," answered Aillen. "You are an old chum and I'm happy to talk with you again. All the same, we can become reacquainted from a healthy distance. You wish to find the Burren? Well, I suppose I can come to the rescue once more – for old times' sake. Follow me!" With that, Alistair reared up and Aillen gave a heroic wave of his arm. The Escape Goat took off across the meadow, this time at a less blinding speed. Finn was puzzled for a moment, but as they grew smaller he raced after them. Cuhullin grabbed Iskander and followed.

"Lovely," mumbled the Cyclops. "More running in the dark."

The path twisted through the meadow to a deep, forested valley and led down to a tiny stream. It occurred to Finn how little of his islands he had seen, despite his many years. For days, he had been led and directed and bossed about in lands that were supposed to be his own. He wished he had some wisdom of the world around him, now that trouble had come calling!

After a good while of traveling, Aillen allowed the space between them to narrow. Little by little, he slowed Alistair to a more reasonable pace. As Finn got closer, he and the tiny bard spoke happily of trees and years and all that had happened. Never did Finn stop fearing for Oonagh, but he was comforted to see his old friend, and it seemed to him that Aillen was truly glad of the reunion too.

"You three up there! Keep a civil pace for the rest of us!" Cuhullin was finding it difficult to keep up. "We're not all built for speed!"

"We're slowing down, Ben, don't worry," answered Finn.

"You'd best be. I will catch you eventually, either way!" Finn ignored him.

"If I may say," said Aillen, "your Great friend seems a tad touchy."

"He is that."

"If I let him draw a bit closer," Aillen continued, looking at Cuhullin puffing along, arm in arm with Iskander, "do you suppose a song might cool his mood?"

Finn recalled the horror of Aillen's singing, but he was diplomatic. "You know, he is not awfully fond of music – no matter how sublime! Even your talents might not amuse him."

"All the same," Aillen answered, "I think a song might do him good." With that, he slowed the Escape Goat yet further and drew a battered lyre from his satchel. Finn brought up both hands to dissuade the bard, but Aillen paid him no mind. He plucked the strings, hummed a few notes, and started in:

As eons go by, we get smaller and smaller,
But a long time ago, the world was much taller.

> *There were monsters and trolls and mermaids and*
> > *fauns,*
> *And Centaurs and Spriggans and Elves and so on.*
> *And there were Giants as well, in the Earth in those*
> > *days,*
> *Cold, lanky creatures, very set in their ways.*

These first few lines weren't dreadful. Finn was pleasantly surprised to hear that the Alfar's skills had improved over the years. It seemed this song was some sort of satire. In the past, his songs had been so impenetrably earnest that they were nearly unbearable.

> *They rumbled round the Earth, bravely fighting and*
> > *dying,*
> *Now they're all underground, slumberly lying.*

By now, Cuhullin and Iskander had caught up, and the whole company moved on together at a moderate pace. Alistair's head swayed to the music. Aillen swung his leg over the Escape Goat's back with a flourish, riding sidesaddle as he went into the refrain:

> *Time flies on! Time flies on!*
> *Never more shall we see thee again!*
> *Time flies on! Time flies on!*
> *Under mounds you sleep to the end!*

> *The Great Ones are gone, never to return,*
> *The world is peaceful once more!*
> *Yes, the Great Ones are gone, never to return,*
> *Let the spirits of all creatures soar!*

The little bard did not notice that bushy eyebrows were rising all around him. Even Cuhullin understood the song's meaning. "What's all this?" he demanded.

Aillen froze, his arm poised to strum again upon the lyre. "It's very popular," he said indignantly.

"It is?" wondered Finn. "With whom is this nasty song popular?"

"Well!" gasped Aillen. "With everyone! Do you mean to say you have not heard it?"

"I'll not be hearing it again, I can tell you that!" Cuhullin roared. Finn held up a hand to calm him.

"No, little bard," he said, "I promise that none of us has heard that tune before. Did you write it?"

"Oh, I wish I had!" Aillen sighed. "I'd be far better liked if I had come up with that all on my own! No, it has made its way around the island in recent years. Catchy little thing, isn't it?"

"It did have a nice melody," Iskander offered. "But it's wildly offensive, of course!" he added hastily.

"Little bard, tell me," Finn persisted, "where did you hear this song, and who is spreading it around?"

"You surprise me!" Aillen answered. "Creatures of all sorts hum this song! Although I like to think I have given it a little – something – to make it my own." Cuhullin made angry noises but Finn cut him off.

"It was not that we didn't like your version," he explained, "but the words did not speak very well of us, in case you didn't notice. I think it would be best for all of us if no more popular songs were sung for now."

"Suit yourself," sniffed the Alfar. He flicked Alistair's mane and the Escape Goat trotted on ahead, not at a blinding pace, but swiftly enough to let the others know that feelings had been hurt. Finn threw up his hands and followed. Still grumbling, Cuhullin took Iskander's arm once again.

So it was that the five made their way together across the green lands of Eire, veering south and west on their way toward the Burren. At long last, as the sun began to fade, they reached an odd rift where the rich and lively terrain ended abruptly, replaced by a plain of pale and jagged stones. As far as the eye could see, there was no green, no water, no trees, no sign of life.

"What's all this, then?" Cuhullin asked.

"This," sighed the Alfar, "is my home. It isn't much, I know, but it is no worse than we deserve, I suppose. We less live here than survive. This, my friends – if I can still call you such – is the Burren."

"Of course we are friends," Finn answered absent-mindedly, surveying the bleak terrain. "How on earth do you manage to live in such a place?"

Aillen was proud to hear the amazement in Finn's voice. "Oh, we have our ways," he said. "You were seeking the counsel of the Banshee? Well, it's a lucky thing you've got me with you! Not too many could find a straight path to her abode. Come on, then, but mind your step – this land is treacherous to the toes."

"Blast it all!"

Before the Alfar finished his warning, Cuhullin slid his foot across the border of the Burren, caught it on a crag, and fell over. Not wanting to infuriate him further, Finn and Iskander did not comment. Even the Alfar saw the need for a diversion.

"Thank you, Alistair, as always," he said, leaping nimbly off the Escape Goat's back and landing on the dry rock of the Burren. "I'll go this last bit on my own." Cuhullin dusted himself off while the others pretended not to notice.

"I've left you behind for too long, old friend," Finn said
to Iskander, taking the Cyclops by the arm. "Would you
forgive me and come with me now?"

"Certainly!" said Iskander cheerfully. With that, the two
set off after the Alfar. Only Alistair lingered, and cautiously
approached Cuhullin. The Giant of Fyfe, angrily brushing
the Burren's dirt and pebbles from his beard, looked down to
see the Escape Goat blinking up at him.

"The secret," Alistair said quietly but firmly, "is to take
small steps. I hope you will try that, as you will have more
success, sir."

"Thank you," answered Cuhullin, a bit surprised.
Alistair bowed his head and, without another word, trotted
off after the others. Taking small steps – unnaturally small,
at first – the Giant followed. Just as the little fellow had
promised, his feet found purchase.

There was not much to mark one spot from another on
the vast Burren. The expanse was like the face of the moon.
The featureless horizon put Finn in mind of his travels, so
many years ago, through the frozen lands of the north.

"How could trees ever grow in such a place?" he wondered.

"They do not grow here," Aillen said mournfully. "Trees
were once carried in full-grown, and it was our lot to watch
them die."

After a long while, Finn could see a thin plume of smoke
rising from a point on the horizon. They drew nearer through
the gathering twilight, and saw that the smoke rose from the
chimney of a lonely cottage. It was a tall structure, made of
stone and earth, with a roof of rock shingles.

"What is this place?" Finn asked.

"It is the home of Herself," Aillen replied. "I told you I
would take you there! You see how difficult it would have
been to find, nestled in amidst the stone as it is? Yes, it's a

jolly good thing you found me!" Alistair and Cuhullin caught
up. Their aspect suggested that they had been having a pleasant chat.

"Well then," sighed Finn, "thanks for your help." He
began leading Iskander toward the cottage.

"Hang on now!" Aillen cautioned. "Where do you
imagine you are going, unintroduced? You want something
from her, hey? Well, you'll be getting nothing but trouble if
she does not know you. Fortunately for you, once again,
you've got me to make the introductions!"

"Fair enough," Finn said. "Lead on, Alfar, and make us
known to her, please." Aillen nodded sharply, then strode
with importance toward the cottage. They could see the
crooked figure of a man busying himself outside the door. He
was old and slow, and despite the heavy footfalls of the
Giants he did not seem to notice their approach. He was
muttering angrily to himself as he paced back and forth,
sweeping at the ground with his feet.

"Hi-ho, Wrisley!" Aillen called out. The old man looked
up, surprised. He narrowed his eyes to see who had spoken.
He seemed to recognize the little bard, and a narrow smile
creased his face. But when he noticed the Giants and the
half-Great, he stepped back. "Not to worry!" Aillen assured
him. "These friends are large but good. We've come to see
the missus about a matter up to the north. Is she in?"

"Yes, she's in," the old man snapped. "She's *always* in,
isn't she?" The others had drawn up close behind the Alfar,
and the old man stared at them, scrutinizing their faces.
"What are all your names, then?" he demanded, as though
investigating some crime.

"Well," Finn spoke up, a little taken aback by the man's
tone, "I am Finn McCool. And this is my dear friend
Iskander of the Arimaspians – he was blinded in the matter

my little friend spoke of. This is Cuhullin, the Great One of Fyfe. And not to be forgotten, this is Alistair." The old man looked suspiciously at the Escape Goat, who met his gaze fearlessly. Finn could see that they knew one another. After an odd silence, Finn added, "This is a lovely spot you have here, sir. Have you lived here all your life?"

"Not yet," the old man answered abruptly.

"Fair enough." The half-Great was growing impatient with the old man, but more so with Aillen. If the Alfar knew this man already, why was it left to Finn to make the introductions, endure the glares, and move the conversation along? Time was not their friend. "Do you know the Banshee, then?" he asked awkwardly.

"Know her? I should hope so!" The old man looked up at Cuhullin. "Great you are, but I doubt you'd have the courage to be married to a wife who knows all. A spot of ignorance in this house would be as comfortable as a warm blanket and a mug of stout drunk in peace for once!"

"Wrisley!" A woman's shrill voice called from inside the cottage. "Leave them be and let them by! Off with you now to your pipeweed and your moping! Go on!" With one more suspicious glance at Alistair, the old man turned and shuffled away, shaking his head. "Do come in, lads, do come in," the woman added. "Smartly, now! Don't dawdle in doorways." Finn looked round at the others and, with a shrug of his shoulders, ducked into the cottage, Iskander in tow. One by one, the rest followed.

The cottage was crowded but not messy. Rows of books lined the walls, and odd carvings and statues were all about. Most of the decorations looked as though they came from far away, so peculiar were their designs. A glittering orange suit of armor, holding some strange star-shaped weapon, stood watch in the far corner. The cottage itself had been built a courteous height, to accommodate Great guests, and Cuhullin appreciated this more than anyone. In the center of the main room, nestled in a comfy chair behind a table, was an older lady. That is to say, she should have been old. Her hair was gray, and disobedient strands strayed in all directions despite an apparent attempt to tie them in a bun. Her skin was wrinkled, and she sat hunched over, withered hands tucked under her chin. But her eyes told a different story. They twinkled with life, inviting the companions to conversation.

"How do you do," Finn said. "I am –"

"Yes, Finn," she interrupted, "we both know who you are, so let's not take time with introductions. What do you want me to do for you? Iskander, Benandonner – do sit down, lads. Ben, help him to a chair." The Giants were agog. They had never met her before, yet she addressed them as though she had spent all their lives with them. Alistair stood beside Cuhullin while Aillen, suddenly sullen, fidgeted just inside the door. "Yes, Finn?"

"Well," Finn said, a little discomfited at her abruptness, "I have come to ask for your help. You see, my love was taken from me."

"How dreadful for you. How can I – boys, DO sit down, please! It's distracting with you all milling about. How can I help you?" As the startled Giants hopped around finding places to sit, Finn sat across from the old woman and tried to find his words.

"I need to know what to do. Where to go to find her. How can I bring her back to me?"

"Well," she said, "first you must be sure what it is you are looking for. Your love, you say?"

"Yes, that's right," Finn answered plaintively. "She is gone from my hill and I do not know where she is. So much has happened that I do not understand. Why would she be taken? What wrong have I committed?"

"Mm-hm." The woman tapped her bony finger on her lips. "So all this happened because of you, personally? You lost your love by some fault of your own?"

"No!" he protested. "That is not what I meant at all . . . I only . . . what do I call you?"

"I am the Banshee. And I go by many names, not all of them nice."

"I am told that we are related, you and I."

"Yes," the Banshee said, "but let's not dilly-dally as to how. Our family is . . . complicated."

"Fair enough," said Finn. "Please – can you help me?"

"Now that, of all things, I do not know. I can explain the situation, but I cannot understand it for you. You want to know how to get what you want. You call it your love, and I shall not quibble with that for the moment. Suffice it to say, these things that have happened are not about you. The world is a very big place, and you are only a little fellow, after all." Finn bristled and straightened up in his chair. The Banshee did not seem to notice or care that he was many times higher than she.

"What you want is to make things as they used to be in your corner of this Earth. Is that not so? That is what you want me to help you do, but it is a small plan, Demne. Make no small plans for they stir no hearts! You are not the eye in the world's storm, but you have some part to play. You can never be too small for the Dagda to use – but you can easily be too large." She shot a quick glance at Cuhullin. "Tell me if what I have said is untrue."

Finn hesitated. Was this a question or a dare? "It is true!" he sputtered at last. "But what of it? I don't wish to play a part in some great plan! I only wish to save my Oonagh from whoever has taken her, then repay them for what they've done. That's all I seek!"

"But do you not see," she laughed, "that this is the way of the Dagda's plan? All creatures chase their petty ends, and in so doing they push along the fortunes of the world. Of the many things going on about you, all you have considered is that which strikes *you*. And you know only enough to be angered by it. That is the thinking of a child, Demne, and the time for childishness is past. Everything we have known is crumbling around us. Creatures with gifts must take a part. You were given an ancient wisdom, and you have gifts within you that you still do not know."

"And I do not care!" Finn shot back. "At least tell me that she lives! Can you do that much?" The Banshee smiled and shook her head. "What does that mean?" he asked with panic.

"She lives." The Banshee's tone conveyed that Finn was missing the point. "That news should cozy your corner of the world for a moment." Her thin lips closed and she looked casually about the room, as if she were considering rearranging the furniture.

"So? Now what?" Finn stammered.

"Now?" she asked with mock astonishment. "She has not stopped living since I last spoke, if that is what you are asking."

"How do I find her? And how do I bring her back?"

"There was a circle of stones that stood on this island since before Cuhail was thought of," she said. "Now they are gone. You have not asked what power did this, though you should have done so with quivering fear. Your half-brethren are killed and worse, yet you have not stirred. Even the one towering work for which you are known has been undone, yet you do not question how. Each year you live, you see a little less. You have had merry times, but you may amuse yourself into extinction. Deny your gifts and you shirk your obligations. You are half-Great in more than stature. Baldemar is a bore, I know, but he told you much the same. Let me ask you: If you knew your love would be happy and safe in the place where she is now, would you still beg me to bring her back?"

"She is my love," Finn answered softly. "How could she be happy without me?"

"There is so much you don't understand, Demne. I don't mean to hurt you. I only want you to consider more than your own wants. More often than not, I find the truth through song. Would you like to hear?" The old woman leapt from her chair and across the room with unexpected agility. Arms outstretched and long, jagged sleeves flowing behind her, she seemed to fly. A massive, ornate trunk sat beside the fantastic suit of armor. The Banshee, not a tall woman, was barely the height of it. With no apparent effort, she lifted the lid of the trunk and peered inside. "Let's see here," she mused. "Where did I leave it?"

"Leave what?" Finn asked.

"A very special music-maker," she replied, rummaging in the trunk. Aillen lifted his head. "Ah! Here it is!" The Banshee produced an instrument so glorious that, although it was centuries since he had seen it, Finn recognized it at once. Glindarin, the harp, shone through the room as though waking from some lovely sleep. Aillen whirled to face the door.

"Hang on there, little bard," Finn said, remembering. "Wasn't that thing yours?"

"What thing?" the Alfar asked indignantly, his arms folded.

"That harp – didn't you used to –"

"NO!" The Alfar's suddenness and volume changed the mood of the room. "That is to say, it is not mine any longer.

Times have been hard, you know. Some things that were mine no longer are. I have sold off many things."

The Banshee ignored Aillen. "What we will do is sing a song of what is to come. Iskander, dear, you will write down my words, please."

"Me?" the Cyclops blurted. "How can I write anything?" He waved his arms in a show of his blindness.

"Oh, dear me, you are still blind!" she exclaimed. "How foolish of me! Hang on – let's see what else we have in here." She set the harp on the floor, taking no notice of Aillen's eyes upon it, and rummaged in the trunk again. "There it is!" She held high a flashing blue diamond. At the sight of it, Aillen smacked his forehead and smeared his fingers down his face.

"Hey, now – wasn't that diamond also –" Finn began.

"Yes!" the Alfar snapped, stomping outside. It was indeed the prize jewel he had found beneath Ymir's throne. Plainly, he was not interested in discussing his change of fortune.

"Now just relax, dear," the Banshee said to the Cyclops. "Sit there and put your head back – that's it." Finn, Cuhullin, and Alistair craned to see what she was doing. She hunched over Iskander's head and tore away his bandages, but the flurry of hair, elbows, and jagged cloak kept them from seeing her precise workings. At last she straightened up and stepped away. "There now! Look around and tell me how it is."

Iskander lifted his face. For the first time since the horror on Knockmany, there was light. But the world shone differently now. Objects appeared from many angles at once and, though he could not put it into words, the Cyclops saw stories from the past and the future. Some said his kind possessed the gift of second sight, meaning that they could see what others could not, but this was something else. When he looked at a thing or a person, he saw a piece of where it

had been and where it was headed. He blinked at the ornate
suit of armor in the corner. At once a field of tiny men, with
flags and banners all about, appeared to him clear as day.
When he rubbed his hands over his face, the vision was
gone. When he turned to the others, they gasped to see that,
where his great blind eye had been, the beautiful blue jewel
was now firmly fixed.

"Well, that's champion!" Finn exclaimed. "Can you see
with that in?"

"I can more than see," Iskander replied, holding up his
hands to marvel at them. Only when his gaze fell on
Cuhullin did a hint of sadness cross his face. He turned to
the Banshee. "Thank you. Thank you so much! How ever
can I repay you?"

"It is not me you'll be repaying," she said enigmatically.
"But payment will be made." She took up the harp once
again. "What we need is a rainbow at night. Have you
never seen one? They are pure white, and they always tell
you something. You are lucky fellows, for I feel one coming
on!" With that, she glided out the door of the cottage.
"Take a scroll and a quill from the table there, Iskander.
Come along please, boys."

The night was cold and clear, and the air was of that
encouraging sort that makes the world seem possible after a
long, dreary day. Finn breathed in deeply. "Over there!" the
Banshee cried. Every head turned up to the dark sky, though
only Iskander spotted it at first – a glowing white arch
stretched across the charcoal heavens.

"But that harp of yours," Finn said, "doesn't it just put
people to sleep?"

"You say that," the Banshee replied, "because that is all
you have seen it do. Iskander, dear, are you ready?"

"Yes, I think so." The Cyclops struggled to flatten a scroll

of parchment against the evening breeze. The quill he held
was a delicate feather, too fine a thing for his bulky hand,
and he had not written anything down for ages. "Please don't
go too quickly."

As the Banshee drew her slender fingers across the strings
of the harp, the most splendid music spilled forth, filled with
harmonies and hope. She closed her eyes and, lifting her face
to the glow of the white rainbow, she began to sing:

> You *cannot go back the way that you came,*
> Need *is must, but your road is not the same.*
> To *reach the other side,*
> Find *the Wyvern to ride,*
> The *dragon will half yield to your name.*
>
> Stone *of old will be shattered by steel,*
> Giant *of gifts just in time will reveal*
> To *his friend who's unseen,*
> Save *the half-Great from the Green,*
> Her *fate lies behind the Golden Seal.*
>
> Do *what you will, do what you cannot,*
> Not *without blood will freedom be bought.*
> Take *care for your friend,*
> The *wee ones will send*
> Sword *and spear to undo all you wrought.*
>
> There *are times that try your very soul.*
> Is *survival to be your only goal?*
> Another *day will yet see*
> Half *of all that you may be*
> Great Finn McCool, *when you are made whole.*

When the song was over, the Banshee strummed a little longer and hummed to herself. She swayed gently, eyes closed, as Glindarin's glorious tones filled the night sky. After a time, the music faded and the old woman slumped forward as though asleep.

"Well, that was . . . lovely," Finn said at last. And it was true. The Banshee's singing voice was wonderful – especially compared to the hectoring tone of her conversation. "But what's this song meant to mean? A sword was mentioned. And was there something in there about a dragon?"

"Yes, there was," Iskander answered, scanning his scribbled notes. "Right near the beginning. There it is."

"What could a dragon have to do with us?" Finn wondered.

"It depends on which dragon," Alistair mumbled.

"What was that?" Finn asked.

"A dragon can mean many things," the Escape Goat explained. "Well, more to the point, different dragons mean different things. But I think she said, did she not?" He looked to Iskander and his scroll of parchment. "The Wyvern got a mention in there, unless I am mistaken."

"Well, yes, I think so." Iskander was running his huge finger along the lines of his notes.

"What is a Wyvern?" asked Finn.

"Why, he is one of the five dragons, of course!" Alistair answered, as though shocked by the foolishness of the question. "Or – I'm sorry – or were you joking?"

"No, I wasn't joking," Finn said. "I know nothing of dragons, except from my aunts' songs and stories. What can you tell me about them?"

"Oh, where to begin?" Alistair sighed. "Well, there are five, as I said, and not all of them are approachable. I only know them by reputation, mind. The sight of a dragon inspires me to uncommon haste."

"It says here," Iskander read, "that we are meant to ride this dragon. Can that be so?"

"Do what you cannot!" the Banshee exclaimed, emerging from her trance. "Do you boys never listen? Dragons and swords – I knew that was what you would notice. But these are details, details! Look for the deeper meaning, always."

"Well, since it was your song," Finn ventured, "why don't you explain it to us?"

"I'll be explaining nothing out here. It's deathly cold!" She shuddered. "Come along inside, boys, all of you." She took up her harp and glided toward the cottage door. By the white light of the rainbow and the moon, Finn, Iskander, Cuhullin, and Alistair exchanged glances.

The half-Great let the others go in ahead. Just as he was about to duck inside, he felt a tug on his sleeve. He turned to see Aillen's pale face looking up to him.

"I am sorry," the little bard said softly, "for the way I acted earlier. Times have been hard, you cannot know. It pains me to see any of the treasures I once possessed. All the same, it does not excuse my being such a bother. Can you forgive me?"

Finn smiled. "You are a good fellow," he said, setting his hand on Aillen's shoulder, "and I am fond of you. Times are hard for all creatures, and even the best of us sometimes act in ways we don't mean. You have been a big help to us already, and I am thankful." Aillen clasped his small hand on top of Finn's, and the half-Great thought he saw a tear welling in the Alfar's eye.

"Thank you," said the little bard, before slipping his hand away and stepping into the cottage. Finn followed.

Inside, the Banshee already had tea steeping in a pot. There was a welcome smell of home and sleep throughout the house. The Giants arranged themselves in large and comfy chairs beside the fire. Alistair sat with his hooves tucked neatly under him, by Cuhullin's feet. Aillen took a cup from the Banshee and sat on the floor next to his goat.

"Come along in, Demne," the Banshee called to Finn. "Here's your mug, and have a seat, dear." The half-Great obliged, taking the cup and settling in next to Iskander by the fire. As he did so, he noticed the old man they had met earlier, brooding over a book beside the hearth. "Let me tell you, lads," she said, "what you may have missed."

"Oh, she's lovely at that," the old man muttered.

"Pay him no mind," the Banshee said, with a wave of her hand. "He imagines my gifts are solely for the purpose of annoying him." The old man sank his chin indignantly into the palms of his hands. "Now, Great and small, to business!" Finn took a sip from his mug. The flower-scented beverage unjangled his nerves and put him in a mind to listen. "Your love is in Alba, Demne. Maybe my ditty didn't make this plain, but it is so. You will have to tax your strength and cunning to bring her back."

"Alba? How could she have gotten there? And what for?"

"Please don't interrupt," she said, raising a gnarled finger. "You must find the Wyvern and engage him to take you there. I will not trouble to fill your head with details of this ancient creature, as the remembering of them would trip you up when you meet him. Most of what you need, I have already given you, except this: other Great Ones, whom you don't know, must come and aid you in your quest. There must be no more than eighteen of you, and you will find greatest advantage, in this and all things, by the number three. Heed my words and always look for the deeper meaning. In finding it, you will find all else that you seek. Now – questions?" The Giants sat in silence until Iskander meekly brought up his hand. "Yes?"

"What does the name 'Arvel' mean to you?"

"It means sadness," the Banshee said. "Arvel was a boy, and he is wept over. To others, mind you, his name means other things. It means anger, guilt, and vengeance. I know this name rang in your ears in your darkest moment. That is not all I can tell you, but it is all you need know. What else?"

"How do we find this Wyvern?" Finn asked.

"If I may," Aillen spoke up, rising to his feet. The Banshee gave him a sideways look of amusement. "I know exactly where the Wyvern currently makes his home. I cannot tell you how I came to this knowledge, but I would consider it an honor to guide you Great Ones there." He gave a little bow and sat back down beside Alistair, who gave him a nod of encouragement for a speech well delivered.

"Thank you, Aillen," the Banshee said. "A brave and welcome offer. Well – there it is, gentlemen. You came for my counsel, and I have given it freely. You will stay what is left of the night here. In the morning, Demne, go to seek your love and much more. Do so with my blessing, little Giant."

Moonlight gleamed on hard metal. An eerie silence, unbecoming such massive industry, filled the night air as towering beams and mighty blades shunted into place. From the window of the castle tower, Oonagh squinted to see what great levers and pulleys were conducting this colossal work.

She could not sleep in her prison palace. Though she could find no way to escape, she was able to wander through the rooms and hallways undetected – or at least unhindered. And so she found herself in the tower, spying on this sinister scene.

Oonagh knew she had not lost her wits. All the same, she could not comprehend why she saw no men or machines in the courtyard, moving these huge pieces of metal and wood. Some contraption was being constructed – a cruel thing, and immense. But she could neither hear nor see the workers.

Then she saw a shape standing on a rampart below. It was a man, a very tall one, and slender, too. His back was to her, and she could see long white hair tumbling from beneath his pointed hat. He wore a dark cloak, and in his hand was a crooked staff. As she watched, Oonagh realized that he and he alone made the parts of the massive machine move through the air. He waved the staff this way and that, as though conducting a monstrous symphony. The contraption, all teeth and clubs, gradually took shape before her disbelieving eyes.

Then a beam that surely had been the trunk of the heartiest tree in Albion froze in midair, high above the courtyard. Oonagh looked down at the man, who stood motionless, holding the staff before him. His head began slowly to turn. Horrified, she saw that he had spun his face right round upon his neck and was looking up to her. Through the cold darkness, their eyes met.

The wizard smiled.

VI

the necromancer

Y ou will grow in the valley – the soil is good down there."

Finn tried to look as if he understood these words, but the effort made his face hurt. "Thank you," he answered. The Banshee laughed.

"Now, don't pretend you know what that means." She wagged her finger up at him. "You will see, my boy, you will see."

Iskander and Cuhullin were munching the last of the sumptuous breakfast they'd found on the table when they woke. None of them could remember when or how they had bedded down for the night. All they knew was that they had been gathered by the fire, listening to their hostess, and then awoke refreshed, blinking into the morning light and smiling at the fine smell of food.

"Ah, good, you're all awake!" Aillen hollered, trotting up to the cottage on Alistair's back. "We have been up for hours. But I suppose you larger folks need your sleep."

"Where did you go off to?" asked Finn.

"Ah, we know many places in these parts," said the Alfar slyly. "You needn't worry where we were, little Giant. It was a place too small for you, and one you'd never see, even if you passed it a thousand times."

"Fair enough." Finn shrugged. He had wanted to be alone before the Giants awoke, hoping for a moment's peace and clarity. Now everyone was up and the morning was beginning all at once.

"Did you lads have enough to eat?" the Banshee asked. They all nodded. "Good lads. Now, I bid you fly with wisdom." She glided back into the cottage. The companions had begun to notice that she made a habit of ending conversations abruptly.

"*Pssst!*"

Finn looked around. "*Over here,*" a croaky voice beckoned. Lurking by the side of the cottage was the old man. His face was brighter now, and he waved at Finn to come closer.

"Yes?"

"Keep it down, keep it down!" the old man admonished. "She could hear a sparrow belch in a typhoon!"

"Sorry."

"Don't be sorry, just listen closely – I know what happened to your Causeway."

"You do? How was it destroyed?"

"That I can't tell you. I simply mean that I know it is in disrepair. I am Wrisley, by the by. Sorry we were not properly introduced last evening but, well, when Herself is on her high horse, there's not much room for polite conversation. Marriage, eh?" Wrisley gave a short chuckle and a wink. From beneath his cloak he pulled a small woven patch, tattered and faded, decorated with a hammer and saw. "I suppose you know what *that* means?" He held the patch up proudly.

"It's very nice," Finn said. "But I'll need a tad of help as to its meaning."

"This is the solemn seal of the Jobbers Guild. And you, young fellow, are chatting with a lifetime member!" Wrisley waggled his eyebrows.

"Congratulations," said Finn, trying for enthusiasm. The Jobbers were a diligent yet unproductive collection of tinkers, uncelebrated throughout Albion for the caliber of their work. When they explained why a promised task was not yet complete (as they often did), they would famously preface their remarks with "Here's your trouble," and point out some problem of their own creation.

"My brothers and I will get that Causeway fixed up lickety-split!" Wrisley said, winking. "It's a fairly simple job." He hitched his thumbs into his belt and threw back his shoulders. "While we're at it, I'll have a look at your foundations, too. Diamonds to dandelions, that's where we'll find your trouble."

"Thank you," Finn answered, backing away.

"When you're talking price," Wrisley went on, "let's just say you're lucky that you're talking to me. Other craftsmen – and I don't want to be saying anything I shouldn't here – but other craftsmen will go ahead and give you a price, and that's fine. But how do you know what you're getting for that amount? And how can you be sure of the quality of their work? You can't – exactly! I'll talk it over with my brothers and we'll see what we can come up with. I'm not making any promises, you understand. But between you and me, I can tell you we'll find a price that will make you very happy." He delivered these last few words in a raspy whisper.

"Wonderful stuff, Wrisley, thank you," Finn said, shaking the old man's hand in farewell. Before Wrisley could start again, Finn spun on his heel and headed back toward the others.

"And say hello to your uncle for me!" Wrisley called after him.

"What was that all about?" Iskander asked Finn as he returned.

"I suppose he is helping me with some repair work," Finn explained. "But back to business, lads. Aillen, will you show us the way to this Wyvern?"

"Certainly!" The little bard hopped onto the Escape Goat's back. "Alistair and I have been itching to move along since this morning. This way!"

The Alfar took off toward the east. Finn and Cuhullin jogged along side by side but Iskander dallied behind, still fascinated by all the sights he could capture with his new eye.

"Come along, blast it!" Cuhullin would shout back from time to time, and the Cyclops would abruptly straighten up and abandon whatever pebble or patch of dirt he was perusing.

They moved briskly through the morning. Alistair alone was tireless, but whenever they stopped to rest at a stream or a shady spot, the Escape Goat had the courtesy to pretend that he was winded too.

"Is it much farther?" Finn asked, gasping beside a bending brook in the noon sun.

Aillen answered with irritating thoughtfulness. "It depends upon whom you ask."

"I am asking you," Finn growled. "Is it much farther?"

"Not really, no," the Alfar mumbled.

The land grew gradually greener, the farther from the Burren they traveled. The company moved in single file through a small glen, with clover and grass cropping up around them. Suddenly there came a strange noise from a cluster of trees beside the rough trail. Alistair froze in the lead. The noise came again – this time a little louder and more chilling. It was a voice, and not a happy one.

"Hello?" Finn called out. A pitiful moan came in reply. "Can we help you?"

"Help?" bellowed Cuhullin. "Who are we helping, not knowing if they are friend or foe? These are dangerous times. Use your wits!" The Giant tapped his temple with his finger. But Finn crept past Aillen and the Escape Goat to suss out the source of the sound.

"It's a friend coming to see you," he called ahead.

"I have no friends!" came the mournful reply.

"Well, I'm coming to see you, regardless," Finn answered, "so don't do anything rash once I get in there." When he took hold of the low-hanging tree boughs that shrouded the sorrowful creature's hiding place and lifted them away, he found a shocking sight. Lying on the ground, in a crumpled and bloody mess, was all that remained of Thunderbore. "Merciful Morrigan!" Finn cried. "What has been done to you?"

"Can't you just kill me without making me answer? My shame is worse than my wounds." His many hurts were pitifully bandaged, by himself or by some other unskilled hand.

"Who's in there? What is it?" Cuhullin peered over Finn's shoulder. "You! Treacherous villain!"

"Easy now, Ben!"

Iskander arrived, and Finn and Cuhullin stepped aside, allowing him to have a look with his bejeweled eye. For a long time, the Cyclops stared at the hapless Thunderbore in silence. "You were foolish," he said at last.

"I know it, I know it!" Thunderbore wailed. "But it was not my intention to go wrong! You must believe that!"

"What does he mean, Iskander?" asked Finn. But the Cyclops turned away. "Now look here, you," the half-Great said to Thunderbore. "What have you done? Why did you send us on that errand for no reason? And why are you here, in this horrible state?"

"I thought . . . I thought I was being wise," Thunderbore gasped. "Could I please have some water?" Aillen reached for his tiny canteen and passed it to the ailing Giant. "Ah, thank you, little one. If only all your size were so kind!"

"All right, you've had your sip of water," Finn said. "Now let's have the rest of it!" Cuhullin regarded Finn with a certain displeasure. Battle wounds always appealed to Cuhullin's sense of honor. He had spoken hotly when first he saw the treacherous Giant, but he would never badger a bleeding soul. Whatever Thunderbore had done – and it was doubtless heinous – it seemed to the Giant of Fyfe that Finn could let the interrogation wait until his injuries had been tended.

"My love was taken while we were away. Did you know that? Spit it out!"

"I am sorry for you, Finn McCool," Thunderbore managed to say. "Sorry for your love, and for what I have done to you. I intended to be clever, but tragedy struck. I admit that I knew more than I told you all. But I did not lie! I promise you! The little folk have been raging."

"Yes, we know that," Finn snapped. "My friend here saw them before they blinded him. And he also saw you wading in among them!"

"I was going to negotiate! I had spoken with them before – that is something I had not told you. My plan was noble! They had taken our brothers' hills. The Ring is gone, too. You can see for yourself."

"I don't give a flying fig about the Ring! Where is my love, and why was she taken?" Finn was ready to tear apart what was left of Thunderbore.

"I think I know," Thunderbore offered meekly. "I know you wish to harm me, but I can't move to defend my poor self."

Thunderbore's voice was a ragged whisper. "I had heard that vicious little ones were stirring in these islands, and so I took it upon myself to seek them out and come to terms. I may not have many gifts, but talk is one of them – or so I thought. I traveled far to the south – none of you knew of this – and I met with the man who leads them. Dunbar is his name. We sat in counsel, two together. Another man stood behind him, though I could not see his face. He was hooded and cloaked, this second man, and he never spoke. But it appeared, somehow, that he gave Dunbar his words. He meant to be reasonable. Dunbar, I mean. Though I sensed he was angry beyond words, the hooded man controlled him. Dunbar said their demands were fair and overdue. But then your name was mentioned, half-Great. Dunbar knew you, and he named you as one of his terms."

"And you agreed?" said Finn, aghast.

"No, no," insisted Thunderbore. "We do not know each other well, Finn McCool, but I have known of you since before you were born. Cuhail was my chief and my friend. This man Dunbar and his hooded master made it clear that you were to be delivered into their hands. They did not say why and I did not dare to ask. I could not allow the son of Cuhail to be bargained away like an extra block of peat for a faithful customer. But I knew how to fool them. That is, I thought I knew. I would lie and pretend that I agreed – I did not tell them anything they did not know. They knew your hill, your love – even your hounds. I suppose you could say that my negotiations bought you time!"

Thunderbore looked hopeful. Seeing that no one was buying the idea, he continued. "I hatched a plan. I knew you were noble and would never leave your home in the face of danger. So I decided to send you away – to the north, if possible, for your foes approached from the south – so your pride and your person would be spared."

"My pride and my person?" Finn demanded. "Who are you to measure their value? I would gladly trade them both to have her back!"

"I know it, I know it," Thunderbore groaned. "But I did not imagine they would appear in such numbers and force! They seemed so reasonable that I thought they would pop by in a small group and ask you to come along quietly. I never imagined that any harm would come to those you love. Having had a hand in bringing it all about, I decided I should go and parlay. That's where I was going when you saw me, Cyclops. But this time I was set upon and hauled down, battered and bound. Then I was dragged toward the water. I knew they had some wicked plan for me. It was only by the grace of one that I was saved!"

"Yes, how about that?" Cuhullin asked angrily. His sympathy for Thunderbore's wounds had faded. "How is it you are here, free and alive, if you are not a traitor?"

Thunderbore cowered and raised his hand as Cuhullin's shadow fell over him. "It was . . . it was . . ."

"Oi, what are you doing to him?" A ball of wrath came hurtling from the woods and struck Cuhullin full in the chest. He tumbled backward and, before he could regain his feet, the foe was on the attack. Pounding and pummeling Cuhullin was Peadair. Cuhullin waved his arms as he struggled up to one knee. The smaller Giant was speedy. No sooner did he land a fist on Cuhullin's jaw but he was around behind, smashing his ribs and shoulders. At last, Cuhullin got up and began to throw punches of his own, in wild and powerful swings that blew back the beards of those all about.

Peadair darted and dodged, which was a good thing for him, as a single one of Cuhullin's blows would have made him a memory. Fearless and grinning, he moved in beneath Cuhullin's fists, landing knuckles under his chin, then dancing away unscathed. Indeed, things might have gone badly for the Giant of Fyfe had a forbidding flame not sprung up between the fighters.

"Enough, lads!" Finn held the blazing Breanain aloft. "I don't want to put an end to either of you, but if you make another move to quarrel, I'll take at least one!"

"What were you doing to him, eh?" Peadair demanded, staring up at Cuhullin.

"I wasn't doing a blasted thing besides looking for some answers," Cuhullin shot back. "And why do you care, anyway? Were you part of this too?"

"Part of what? Our brother is hurt! What else is there to be part of?"

"Settle down, lads, please," said Thunderbore weakly. "It was good and loyal Peadair who saved me. He battled through the throng to my rescue! He knocked them good and proper, I promise you! And then he brought me here, and he has tended to me with kindness, though I have asked him many times to be on his way – I can feel my fate in my bones."

"Is this true?" Finn asked Peadair.

"I suppose it is," the little Giant answered. "He is one of our own and he is hurt, no matter what he may have done. We look to our own here on this island."

Finn knelt and spoke to Thunderbore. "You said you might know where my love has gone."

"I might, yes. Dunbar is a vassal of the Little King. The evil company was moving to the water, and there were boats waiting. If Oonagh is alive, and I expect taken to Alba, then you'll need look no farther than Caerleon, which in happier times we called Treryn."

"Gogmagog's Treryn?"

"The same. They took it, and now they have given it a new name. It is hardly a palace anymore. The Little King struts, and Jack kicks up his green toes as he plots and schemes. They will have taken her there as a trophy. Oh, the indignity of it all!"

"I don't care about dignity," Finn said coolly. "I have heard plenty of this Jack already, and he can kick up his heels wherever he likes. But if one hair upon her golden head is out of place, there will be no more tales of him, I promise!"

"He is vicious, you know," Thunderbore warned.

"So everyone keeps telling me," answered Finn. "Now listen – we are headed to Alba! Thunderbore, I believe you when you say you meant for the best, and I hope you have told us the truth. Peadair, you are a brave and faithful brother. You could help. Will you join us?"

Peadair shook his head. "This island is my home, not Alba. I am sorry for your loss, but Dunbar is stirring up sorrow here. It is up to me to suss him out and thump him good and proper. Eire forever – and Fyfe just a little longer." He nodded and smiled to Cuhullin. To everyone's surprise, Cuhullin smiled and nodded back.

"That is a pity," Finn said. "Is there nothing we can say that will convince you? You said we are all brothers." Peadair shook his head again. "Very well," said Finn. "If you change your mind, we will be glad. We are headed for the home of the Wyvern, guided by these little fellows here –" He turned to indicate Alistair and Aillen, but they were nowhere to be found.

"Did you imagine we would stay nearby for all that?" Aillen emerged from beneath a patch of leaves, brushing specks of dirt from his arms and shoulders. "Giants punching each other and shouting back and forth!" The Escape Goat appeared, and gave himself one long shake from the tip of his nose to the end of his tail, then back up again.

"Oi, hang on," Peadair exclaimed. "I know you!" Aillen took several steps backward. "You're the little blighter what put all those Giants to sleep way back when. There was a reward on you, did you know it? Not that there's anyone left to collect it from now! Whatever became of you?"

"Oh, well, I moved on from that line of work," Aillen said nervously. "That was only a temporary thing. I am glad all of you are awake now, though!"

"If you won't come along," Finn said to Peadair, "then we'd best keep moving. Is there anything we can do for this one before we go?" He pointed with his thumb to Thunderbore.

"Rest and understanding is all he needs," answered Peadair. "I've taken him this far and I'll see no harm comes to him. Good luck and be safe, lads, and we'll see you all back here after it's over." He gave Cuhullin a friendly slap on the back. No one said a word when Cuhullin returned the gesture, but they all marveled at the change between the two Giants.

Then they were off, Alistair and Aillen once more in the lead. Cuhullin came along behind them, and Iskander walked beside Finn in back.

After a while, they came to a narrow path at the side of a tall green mountain. The path ran under a canopy of tree-tops to a hidden valley so steep that they had to descend in single file. The air was cooler and rang with birdsong. At the far end of the valley, beneath the foot of the mountain, was the gaping mouth of a cave.

"Easy now, please," Aillen whispered. "We don't want to pester him, and none of you can get away so quickly as we can."

"Who's getting away?" grumbled Cuhullin. Aillen signaled him to shush.

From the darkness of the cave they heard a low rumble. They froze, and Alistair adjusted his hooves for a quick departure. A billow of smoke curled out of the cave and caught Cuhullin square in the nostrils. He reeled and released an unmerciful sneeze.

"Bless you." The voice came from inside the cave.

"Thank you," said Cuhullin, rubbing his sleeve along his upper lip. The ground trembled. A broad and scaly snout came sliding out of the cave, followed by a wide face topped with dark horns. The rest of the creature revealed itself slowly, until the tip of a humongous pointed tail at last slipped into the sunlight. It sat on its haunches and looked down upon the company. This was a true dragon, to be sure. Blue in color, he was larger than the lot of them put together – higher than the Giants stacked on top of one another, and impossibly squat around the middle. He was shaped like some gigantic teapot. Huge wings unfurled high and wide from his shoulders, and he tapped the tip of his tail upon the earth. He smiled faintly, as if he were awaiting a proper conversation.

"Are you the Wyvern?" Finn asked cautiously. The dragon snorted a puff of smoke.

"Let me give you a guess: I am either he, or a Stonefish who has done tremendous overeating. What do you think?"

"I see your point," answered the half-Great, "but I did not want to assume. My name is Finn McCool and these are my companions – Cuhullin, Iskander, Alistair, and Aillen."

"Pleased to meet you," said the Wyvern, linking his surprisingly tiny hands across his chest.

"You know," ventured Finn, figuring to break the ice with small talk, "I always understood that your kind – dragons, I mean – had no arms. But there you have them, neatly folded." Behind him, Cuhullin and Iskander studied this new creature up and down, while Aillen and Alistair backed away at a pace so subtle that it was barely visible.

"Yes, it's true," the Wyvern agreed, "that is a common misconception. We do have arms, but they are very short. These stubby things of mine, though, are long enough to hold a good book, and for me that is ample." As the dragon spoke, small clouds of smoke from his nostrils punctuated his words.

"Ah, so you're a reader, then?" said Finn. "I love a good story too. You know, apart from the arm thing, I don't know much about dragons."

"I cannot speak for the other four dragons," the Wyvern told him, "but yes, I enjoy a good story. I love to read and wander by a singing brook, but it is difficult for me to do so unnoticed. No sooner have I found a spot I like than some heroic busybody from the nearest village rouses his fellows and they come hurtling after me. Over the centuries one ceases to take it personally, but it's still a nuisance."

"I am sorry," Finn said. "Why would anyone be alarmed by someone as calm and approachable as you? Even your color is a soothing shade of blue, if I may say so."

"Ah, thank you," the Wyvern sighed. "But I was never happy being called blue. Red, gold, black, blue, and green – we've passed into the language – but I have always thought of myself as more of a teal – a civilized shade. But blue is what they call me, and who am I to blow against it?" He gave a small snort of flame, which caused Aillen and the Escape Goat to retreat more hastily.

Cuhullin protested, "We've just had a hard time with fire, and we don't need more from your snoot!"

"Sorry," the Wyvern replied. "I was merely punctuating my point. What hard time have you had?"

Finn jumped in before Cuhullin could say anything more. "My hill was burned. Knockmany, it was called, and I loved it. But now everything green and good has been burned away."

"I know Knockmany," said the Wyvern. "I am sorry. I wish I could tell you that all is soon to be green and good again, but that is no more than a hope. Where did the fire come from?"

"From above, it would seem," Finn replied.

This seemed to disquiet the dragon. "That's not good news."

"How so?" said Finn. "What's the matter?"

"Well, I know your hill, as I said. It was burned black. From above? Not many could accomplish this. Even we five dragons have only limited fire. We can heave out flame in short bursts, which is impressive and a fine way to end arguments. But to produce enough fire to consume your hill – and to do it while in flight, no less – that is a feat beyond any of us except one."

"So one of you dragons is to blame?" Cuhullin growled.

"If a Giant does something wrong," the Wyvern answered, "are all of you held responsible? Some in these isles think so. Would you blame me, for the acts of my fellows?"

"Perhaps not," admitted the Giant of Fyfe. "But count yourself lucky that I don't!" The dragon smiled ever so slightly. "You think that's funny? Maybe you'd like to squabble in earnest!" Cuhullin raised his fists.

"Settle down, please," the Wyvern said, holding up one of his little arms. "You may be Giants, but the lot of you would be no match for even the least of my kind. I am not boasting or trying to be difficult. In fact, I am deadly bored by confrontation." Cuhullin was not satisfied but, wisely, he put his fists away.

"Which dragon has the most fire?" asked Finn.

"He excels in fire, in ferocity, in form, and in misery," said the Wyvern unhappily. "Domovor. Red, for those of you who care about our colors. It wouldn't surprise me if he could devour the rest of us together. If not for him, there would still be six of us." The Wyvern's face grew dark as he spoke of the red dragon. "One feels an affection for one's own kind – no matter how far wrong they may have gone."

"It is troubling," said Finn, "that the mightiest dragon is our enemy. We need your help in getting to Alba."

"To Alba?" said the Wyvern, rearing up. "Ah, no. I may be the only creature in these islands who doesn't claim to have some sort of second sight, but there is one prophecy I was given, and I believe it. Alba is to be the death of me, and the little one who does me in is to spend forever as a hero. Nowadays I suppose you all know a bit of how I feel, eh? But this is more particular. My death and the celebration of it are to mean more than my life has ever done."

"But we were told that you were the one creature who could help us. Our way back is destroyed, and time is our enemy. Please, can't you help us?"

"Little people are ravaging our islands. One of them holds my doom in his wee paws, and you want me to fly into the thick of them? And, I would bet that my brother the Domovor is among them. We are not close, he and I. Did I tell you that? And it is unhealthy to be unclose with him."

Finn began to bring his thumb to his lips, unconcerned that he was doing so in plain sight – maybe Fintan would help him negotiate with this monstrous coward. But then the Wyvern spoke again.

"I see that you are disappointed. I am not a superstitious creature – at least, I do not think I am. Isn't it funny how we imagine ourselves all one thing or none of another, and how very wrong we may be? But a song was sung for me once, and it scared me well and truly. It told a tale, unremarkable enough, but I did not see its deeper meaning at first. When it was deciphered for me, the song froze my bones. I am no coward, half-Great, though you may think so."

"This song," said Finn, "who sang it to you?"

"A sage woman." The Wyvern closed his eyes. "One who is wise and all-seeing. One whose kindness to those with less vision is legend."

"I see. So – an authority, then?"

"Very much so."

"And you wouldn't argue with her, even a little?"

"No – why do you ask?"

"Well, tell me this," Finn challenged him. "Did this wise woman have a husband? Was he henpecked but good-hearted? Did he offer you a reasonable rate on any repairs you might be needing? Was her home a spot of life on a gray and rocky plain? Did she sing her song to the moon and did you sleep and dream when she was done? In short, good dragon, did the prophecy that frightens you come from the selfsame Banshee who sent us to find you now?"

"She sent you?" the dragon marveled. "How can that be, since she told me to fly far from Alba in fear for my life?"

"Perhaps she told you the truth so that your courage would be tested when we came. She is wise and all-seeing – you said so yourself – and she is good. If she says you will carry us to Alba, who are we to argue?"

The Wyvern placed one elbow in the palm of the other hand, and tapped his chin with his slender claw.

"If I may," Iskander offered from the back of the group.

"That is not precisely what she said." Finn shot the Cyclops a look.

"How do you mean?" asked the Wyvern. The Cyclops threw up his hands in apology to Finn before answering.

"Well, what she actually said, as I recall, is that we were to find the Wyvern to ride. There was nothing specific about our destination." Seeing that Finn was fuming, he added, "But, all things considered, Alba seems like the most logical place. Since that's where we need to get to, I mean." He smiled weakly.

"I'll tell you what," said the dragon. "Your father, Cuhail, was a help to me in times that most creatures have forgotten. You're right about the wise woman. I don't doubt she meant our calamities to collide – that is, my death and your lost love. But I am not so brave as all that. So I can take you, yes, but not as far as you would like. We can fly from here to the Isle of Mannin. It is not what you asked, but it is closer than where you are now. And as your friend has pointed out, it's no less than the Banshee said I should do. Can you accept this, half-Great?"

"You ask as though it were up to me," Finn snorted. "If that is all you will do, I have to accept it. I am grateful, mind you."

"Don't despair, " chuckled the dragon. "Things work together for good. Now – who is coming along?"

Finn turned back to the Giants. "My friends, you have been loyal and true. I can't expect you to do more. If you don't come along, I will understand." Cuhullin and Iskander blinked back at him.

"Have you got rocks in your skull?" boomed the Giant of Fyfe. "Where did you get the notion that you'd be moving on without us?" Finn clasped his companions each by the shoulder.

"I suppose," came a meek little voice from below, "that you'll be wanting us to come along as well?" Aillen and Alistair crept forward, looking apprehensive.

"I could not possibly ask you brave souls to do more than you have already done," Finn reassured them. The bard and the Escape Goat did their best to hide their relief. "Besides, it will be an awkward ride already, we three clumsy oafs clambering all over this poor dragon. No, you good lads stay here and guard our island. We will all see one another again in happier times." He turned back to the Wyvern. "Now then – how are we to go about this?"

The dragon surveyed Finn and the two Giants thoughtfully. "I think, for balance," he said, "the littlest of you should ride upon my neck, and I can clutch the other two, one in each claw."

"You mean to say," Cuhullin bellowed, "that I am to be hauled up into the air by a claw and flown over the drink?"

"Now, Ben," Finn soothed him, "this should be your easiest trip yet. Remember those blasted pixies last time? That looked pretty tough. And though you're brave about it, I always knew my Causeway was too narrow and low to the waves for your comfort. Here we have a mighty beast, sure of foot and wing, willing to fly us along. I'd say that's a gift!"

"What I plan to do," the dragon explained, "is get some air beneath me, then take hold of each of you fellows from the ground. Don't worry, there's little chance of you being harmed."

"Little chance is less comforting than no chance," Iskander observed.

"Lucky thing you're so brave!" Finn said, clapping his friend on the shoulder. They noticed that Cuhullin was on his knees next to Alistair, saying a private goodbye.

"All right then." The Wyvern bowed his head low in

front of Finn. "You hop on first." Finn stepped around the
dragon's neck, threw his leg up and over, and sat on top. A
thin mane stretched down from the top of the Wyvern's
head, and he grasped the long blue hairs. "Gently, please,"
urged the dragon. "Now then – up we go!" With that, he
spread his mighty wings and began to flap them up and down
in earnest. The force of the wind sent Aillen and Alistair
bowling backward. Slowly and smoothly the dragon lifted
off, stirring the leaves in the grove. "Stand close together and
let me get a grip," he called down to the Giants. Reluctantly,
Cuhullin and Iskander shuffled next to one another. "Lovely,
perfect – now hold still." The dragon's legs were massive and
long, in contrast to his stubby arms. He stretched them,
curling and flexing his huge, clawed toes. Iskander watched
in alarm and fascination while Cuhullin crammed his eyes
shut. Then the Wyvern took hold of them and lifted them off
into the sky.

The door creaked open, apparently of its own accord. The
torch on the corridor wall burst into flame and flickered in a
rush of air that might have been the wind or a whisper.

"Yes?" Oonagh called out, less in fear than in impatience.
The air stirred again. "Very well," she sighed, rising and stepping out into the corridor. She descended the stone staircase,
and the torches all flamed as she passed. Oonagh did not
need the light anymore. She had made a study of the castle
during the days and nights of her captivity.

At the bottom of the circular stairs was a solid wooden
door. As she approached, it too creaked open on its own.
Daylight flooded into the gray palace and warmed her skin.
She went out into the courtyard where she had seen the

assembly of horrible machines. The place looked different now. The machines and their parts were gone, and the court-yard sparkled and shone like a frosted meadow. It was warm, though, and as Oonagh squinted against the light she saw that the courtyard was filled to knee height with white and black marbles. "What's all this about?"

"Thank you for coming, Toothsome Oonagh."

The voice was sickening. Jack in the Green appeared in front of her, his cap courteously in his hand, and bowed slightly. What was meant to pass for an endearing smile was pasted across his face. Oonagh felt her upper lip curl.

"What do you want?"

"It occurred to me," Jack answered pleasantly, "that there's been too much talk of my admiration – for you, that is. Attention must be paid to how you feel and what you want."

"What are you on about?"

Jack furrowed his brow. "I mean to say, I gave you no choice in all this. I realize that now, and I would like to make amends. I want you to choose – or at least have a hand in the choice. There are two of us in this, after all."

"There's one imbecile I've counted, but what two can you mean?"

"Always ready to be cross," Jack chided, as one might speak to an adorable child. "I will make you a wager – but will you agree to my terms?"

"How is that a useful question," Oonagh answered, hands on her hips, "when you haven't named your terms, and when I don't trust you anyway?"

"My terms are these. If you win the wager, you may walk free from this place and I will renounce all claim to you, however strongly I feel the fates wish us to be together. Sound fair?"

"Sounds suspicious. And what if you win?"

Jack smiled. "In that happy case, it is you who will do the renouncing – of the life you're well off out of – and agree to marry me."

Oonagh knew he was swift and vicious – but was he clever? She stroked her hair in a show of feminine caprice. "I suppose so," she half-giggled, shrugging her delicate shoulders.

"Please don't suppose," said Jack. "Do we have a deal?"

"We do, Jack."

"Very well," he said, muffling his glee. "A simple bet it shall be. I will pluck two marbles from the many you see here – one white, one black – and place them in this little pouch. Then you will slip your fair hand into the pouch and pull out one marble. Pull out the black, and you are free to return to the dark night of the life you have known. But pull out the white, and we will be wed before sunset touches that tallest tower. Agreed?"

"It seems a ridiculously simple bet on which to risk one's whole life and love!"

"It's not so simple," said Jack. "It was no small effort to fill this whole courtyard with marbles. And when you consider all that trouble for the sake of grabbing just two, you'll admit that it's taken a lot of trying. What do you say?"

"I say that I will do it, and I will abide by what comes."

"Excellent," Jack hissed, and he flapped open his little pouch. Then he leapt, slowly enough that she could watch him, into the midst of the marbles. Eyes closed, he glided his palm over the little orbs, turning his face to the sky as though appealing for higher wisdom. Oonagh did not tell him how ridiculous he looked. Finally he snatched up two marbles, one white and one black. But in the flicker before he dropped them into the pouch, he tossed away the black one and took up another white. His hands were so speedy that not even Oonagh could see what he had done. But in his eyes she saw that some trickery was afoot.

"There you are, Toothsome Oonagh." He held up the little pouch with the two marbles inside.

"Give me a moment," she replied, and she looked up to the tower Jack had mentioned. It was high and majestic. Its top was pointed, with red shingles and a mighty banner sporting a golden hen upon a blue field. "All right then," she sighed. "Let's have it."

Jack held out the little pouch, his eyes blinking hard. Oonagh turned her face away, thrust her hand into the bag, twisted it this way and that, and brought out her fist with slow drama. Jack snapped the pouch shut and eyed her hand eagerly. Her arm trembled, and she brought her free hand over her eyes, shielding her sight. But as she was about to open her fingers and reveal what lay in her palm, a fainting dizziness came upon her. She swooned and fell forward, and whatever she held went flying anonymously into the sea of marbles.

"Frightfully sorry," she said, regaining her composure with suspicious suddenness. "But it doesn't matter – whatever color you've got left in the bag, that must be the opposite of what I chose. Open it up and let's have a look!"

Jack was displeased. He clutched the bag tight to his chest and snarled. "Was your life so lovely before?" he asked.

"Lovely or not, it was mine," she answered, rising and straightening her skirts.

The two eyed each other for a time, Oonagh unblinking and Jack clinging to his pouch. Words were not needed for both to understand what had happened between them. They had gambled and they had cheated, and she had bested him. As the sunset touched the top of the tallest tower, Jack shook his head sharply, then vanished.

"I would not want you thinking that I am not sympathetic to what you are trying to do. It's just that dragons are susceptible to prophecies, especially when they're about our own death and the end of our kind. Did you know that our own language has no future tense? The closest we manage is the past that has yet to happen. I find that a little conversation makes a journey more pleasant, don't you?"

They were flying fast and high and the wind was strong, so it was hard for Finn to make out what the dragon was saying. There was an awkward pause while he wondered whether he had heard the words correctly. "Yes!" he blurted back.

There was no sight of land through the mist and cloud below them. Finn had no fear of heights; indeed, he rather liked them. But this was far higher than he had ever found himself, and he might as well have been underwater for all he could see. Iskander and Cuhullin dangled from the dragon's claws.

"We are starting our descent in a moment," the Wyvern advised his passengers. "Keep your knees good and bent so that your landing may be as soft as possible. Knees up, now!" They plunged through the clouds, and all of a sudden the mists parted to reveal the brown and green of Mannin's Isle. As he got close to the earth the dragon leveled off, and he deposited Iskander and Cuhullin on the ground at a bit of a run. Iskander managed the landing just fine; indeed, he had the foresight to start his legs pumping before touching down. But Cuhullin was bowled forward into several ignominious somersaults.

The Wyvern's feet came down gently, and he lowered his head so Finn could swing his leg over easily and step onto the ground. "Welcome to Mannin," the dragon said, waving a stumpy arm. The company looked around at the uneven patch of ground plopped in the middle of the sea. There were no hills, exactly; mounds, more like, as though the soil in this spot could not be bothered to rouse itself into proper points. "There is nothing to see but more of the same. No living thing except one person, to be found in his cottage. He knows we're here already, I'll wager."

"Who is this lonely person?" Finn asked.

"He has many names, and does not care to be called by any of them. That is why he lives alone. But this fellow sees things that others do not. Hears them, I suppose I should say. He can help you to understand the wise woman's words."

"How's that?" inquired Iskander.

"Enough talk," the Wyvern replied. "Let us find him and he can show you!" He lifted off once again, flying low to the ground, his wings beating slowly. The others followed him across the unremarkable terrain.

Finn wondered whether this was time well spent. It was irksome enough that the Wyvern had not taken them to Alba, but now they were being dragged out of their way to meet some crafty curmudgeon. Just then, he noticed a long line of aged rocks. They were rectangular, with features worn by weather and years, though they had been carved by something other than nature. There were about two dozen, each twice the half-Great's height and as wide as he was tall. "What are those?"

"The man can explain it all," said the Wyvern.

They came to a cottage of black, unwelcoming wood set in a patch of mud. The Wyvern landed at its edge, and when Finn and the Giants caught up to him he was already in conversation with an old and grouchy-looking person. He was tall for a man, and wrapped in a dark cloak. He wore a short black hat with four corners, and his long gray beard raced down his chest as if in retreat from the scowl on his face.

"Well, why can't she do her own work?" he demanded.

"What do they want from me?" The Wyvern made a sooth-ing gesture with one of his tiny arms and the man's voice came down to a more polite level, but now his words were lost to the others.

"May I present," the Wyvern said, turning to them and forcing a smile, "Finn the half-Great, Iskander the Cyclops, and Cuhullin the Giant of Fyfe." They each bowed to the old man, who snarled a little more with each introduction. "Sirs," the dragon went on, "before you stands one of the true treasures of our islands – a man who has forgotten more of the ways of the world than anyone else has ever known. And I hasten to add, he has not forgotten much! Yes, this man who stands before you, rich in wisdom and in years –"

"Ah, save it to wash the hogs with!" the old man inter-rupted. "I suppose you'd best all follow me. Come on, then!" He stomped toward the cottage, muttering angry words to himself. The Wyvern nodded reassuringly and gave the companions a wink.

"This is where I leave you," he said. "I have done as I promised, and I think this man may help you mightily, despite appearances."

"Are you certain you cannot go farther?" pleaded Finn. "Our task is a daunting one, and we need your strength and years. Is there anything I can say to convince you?"

The Wyvern shook his head. "I know where my death awaits me. I must avoid that place, at least for a time, until weariness or crushing curiosity leads me there. Farewell, Finn the half-Great. May we meet in better times!" With that, the dragon spread his wings and lifted up into the clouds and out of sight.

"Well, let's go and see what this miserable fellow has to tell us," Iskander said, after the dragon had disappeared. He headed for the cottage, and Cuhullin followed.

Finn was feeling very low. For all his pleading, he had convinced no one, large or small, to come along and help him. Iskander and Cuhullin, of course, were with him, and for that he was grateful, but one was his dearest friend and the other was pursuing some personal point of honor. It was also not lost on the half-Great that neither of them had any other place to be. He hung his head and followed them to the little dwelling.

The mood in the house struck him at once. The Giants stood wary-eyed against the wall just inside the threshold. The main room was filled with dark green light from a glowing copper bowl of water which stood upon a three-legged pedestal. Cobwebbed shelves ran along the walls, holding jars filled with murky liquid and the remains of bizarre creatures. A long table stood at the far end, with tall chairs lined up on each side. Seated at the head of the table, in the chair of honor, its mouth stretched in a ghastly gape, was the decaying corpse of a full Giant. The companions squinted through the dim green light at the hideous thing, and were alarmed to see, in the center of the dead thing's skull, the socket for a single eye.

"What's all this?" Iskander demanded furiously.

"This," the old man answered, turning from his rows of jars to the table, "is my home. And you can learn or leave." The swiftness of the reply, and the firmness with which it was delivered in the face of the Cyclops's spitting anger, surprised all three. "Now sit you down at the table, and let us speak of things you do not understand." It was an insulting invitation, to be sure, but that was not the only reason they hesitated. They did not want to be next to the terrible dead thing. They arranged themselves on the farthest chairs, with Iskander facing his departed kin.

"Who . . . who is this?" he asked.

"It's rather like a mirror on the future, is it not?" chuckled the old man. "Or a glimpse of the deep past?" He sat next to the corpse, at the other end of the table, and fixed Iskander with a hard look. "Cyclops, you had second sight before my sister set that stone in your socket."

"Your sister?" wondered Finn.

"Yes," the man answered. "Do you suppose I don't know that jewel and where you've been? She is my sister, but let's not bother about details. Our family is . . . complicated." Finn had heard these words before. He squinted at the man to find some family resemblance to the Banshee. "My sister divines her futures and fables in her own ways. For me, I give the dead the respect to let them tell their own tales."

"But how can this poor fellow speak?" Finn asked.

"You think in a straight line, your kind," sniffed the old man. "We are born, we live awhile, and then we sleep or die – is that not the way of it? How much you miss, seeing the world in this way! Learn to see time from above, and you will fare far better."

"Thanks for the tip."

"Now, I am told by our winged friend that you have been brought to my home as a stop on some mighty quest. You have questions for me. Or do you even know what to ask?"

"Arvel," Iskander muttered.

"Speak up, lad! What is it you're saying?"

"I have a question," the Cyclops said. "Who is Arvel? What is this name, and why was I cursed with it?"

"There now, that is a question. And let us see if we can find an answer!" Leaning backward in his tall chair, the old man ran his fingers over the rows of shelves and plucked out several rolls of dusty parchment. He unrolled them flat upon the table. The sheets were blank. He produced a long black feather from his sleeve and traced circles in the air over the parchment. "We will seek out this Arvel, eh? See what he has to tell us." As he spoke, he turned his face to the ex-Cyclops. "Will you be good enough to read aloud?" He touched the feather to the parchment and began to scribble. His strokes were sharp and straight, then round and furious until black, adamant lines soon filled the page. His eyes rolled back into his head, and his breathing became shallow and strange. When at last he spoke, his voice was deep and quite unlike the tone he had used before. "We are seeking Arvel. Will he come and speak with us?" The green light in the room darkened. Cuhullin, especially, became uneasy.

"What's happening, Finn?" he whispered.

"I don't know."

"Arvel!" the man went on in his unsettling voice. "Are you there? Will you come and speak to us? Arvel, how did you die?" Iskander gasped. The man's quill began to move with greater purpose. "How did you die, Arvel?" A word was scrawled.

"*Giant.*"

The voice that spoke the scribbled word had not come from the old man, or from some disembodied spirit floating amongst them. It had come from the mouth of the dead Cyclops. His decayed lips had not moved, but the voice had come through him, all the same.

"You were killed by a Giant?" the old man went on, while Cuhullin struggled to find his breath. "Are you a man?" Another word was scratched down.

"*Boy.*"

Iskander brought his hand over his mouth, and a tear began to well beneath his diamond eye.

"You are a boy, Arvel?" the man continued. "And you were killed by a Giant? Who killed you, Arvel?" Two more words.

"My *friend.*"

"What friend killed you? How did you die, Arvel?" Now

the scribbling grew furious. Sheets of parchment flew from the table. Without moving its head or even its mouth, the corpse read aloud a word here and there.

"Friend . . . killed . . . Giant . . . killed . . . friend . . . killed . . . me . . ."

This was too much for Cuhullin. Clutching his chest, he leapt up from the table and raced for the door. He slammed the fist of his free hand into it and tumbled outside. The old man dropped his quill and smacked both palms on the table. He looked around like a man awaking in the middle of the night to the thought that he has forgotten something crucial.

"Who went where?" he demanded. Any life there had been in the dead Cyclops was gone, and it sat dusty and dispirited as ever. The light in the room returned to its green glow – which, after the events of the preceding moments, was surprisingly comforting. "Do you fools want your answer or do you not?"

"Sorry for the interruption," Finn replied. "But this was too much for our friend. We do want answers, and we are grateful that you are willing to help us, sir. By the by, what should I call you?"

"I'd prefer you call me nothing at all and be on your way," the man grumbled, snapping his quill back into his sleeve and gathering up the parchment. "But if you must stay and speak, you may call me Durriken. Ah, the living!"

"Well, Durriken," Finn went on, "the dragon thought that it would be a good idea to drop us here. He seems to think you have some special wisdom. Our mission is difficult, and we would be grateful for any help you can give."

"Mission?" The old man sniffed. "Do you know what your mission is? My wisdom may seem special to you, since you know next to nothing and I know something more than that. You have stumbled around your island, and lost time at the Loch. Is that not the extent of your mission so far?"

"Uncharitably put, perhaps," replied Finn indignantly. "How do you know of our trip to the Loch? And why is it lost time? The Leviathan himself has agreed to reconnoiter around our island."

The old man laughed. It was a wheezing chortle, filled with mocking and empty of joy. "Do you suppose that the Leviathan did you a favor? You are more a fool than I had heard!"

"Why do you say that?"

"The Leviathan is a prisoner," said Durriken. "When you told him about the snake in the waters, what was his reply?"

"That the Jorgumandr was fat and slothful, not a threat of any account."

"Oh, that's a laugh!" The old man wheezed and chuckled again. "I suppose he wishes that snake were fat and slow! It is a lie, Finn McCool, and the dweller in the Loch knows it well."

"Why would he lie to me? And why is he a prisoner?"

"The Dagda is a daring bargainer," Durriken answered. "At times, he wagers well; other times, he deals poorly. There was a contest held, before you were thought of, and my, was he shrewd then. The gods needed a king, but there are precious few ways for mighty creatures to compete without ruining the world. So it was decreed that a race would be held. Have you never heard this before? Lir, god of the sea, chose the Leviathan as his champion. The Dagda took the Jorgumandr. They would race once round the world and the winner would decide the king of the gods. Lir chose wisely, or so it seemed, for he supposed the Leviathan would know the quickest route. The mighty creature had learned every crevice of the deep during the early ages of the world, while the snake knew to eat and devour but little more. So the race began, and the Leviathan was well ahead. But with victory in sight, something caught his attention. He veered from his course and disappeared in pursuit of some distraction. That's when the snake overtook him and won the race. The Dagda was king, and Lir was furious. He seized the Leviathan by the neck – this may seem implausible, but the gods are greater than you think – and plunged him into the Black Loch. Only when his horn is sounded, and when he is called upon with pure intent by a creature in need, is he allowed to leave his watery prison. He did you no favor and he told you no truth."

"So I am a fool?" Finn sighed. "Is that it?" He pushed himself away from the table and sat looking down at his lap. "Tell me, Durriken, do you have anything useful to tell us?"

"Do not treat yourself so harshly," the old man said, although his tone was less comforting than his words. "You are not a failure, you just do not know. I can help you. If you went to see my sister, you heard one of her screeching songs, yes? What did it say?"

"We have it written down, do we not?" Finn turned to Iskander. "My friend?"

"Ah, yes," the Cyclops answered, shaking his head as if he were waking up. "Sorry. You wanted the words? I have them here somewhere." He rummaged in his pockets and produced the scroll he had scribbled at the Banshee's home. "There you are, then!"

Finn unfurled the scroll on the table and smoothed it with his hand. The scrawled words were barely legible.

"Give it here," Durriken snapped. He looked the scroll up and down. "This was it?"

"Well," Iskander said meekly, "it was all I got."

"I could have sworn she sang more than that," Finn mused, peering over the old man's shoulder.

"I didn't ask to be secretary," Iskander protested. "The wind was high, her words were coming fast, and that rainbow was captivating for a fellow looking through a new eye for the first time."

"Excuses," sniffed the old man. "Well, let's see what we do have." He spread both hands wide on the paper and squinted at it. He looked it up, down, and side to side, then pronounced, "Silly."

"What is?" asked Finn.

"You, for one, but this ditty, most of all. Simplest, silliest song she's ever sent. There's nothing to it!"

"Explain, please."

The old man sighed. "Here, have a look." Producing his quill once again from his sleeve, he traced a line over what words could be made out. "See? Who could miss that?" Finn perused the paper:

> **You** cannot go back the way that you came,
> **Need** is must, but your road is not the same.
> **To** reach the other side,
> **Find** the Wyvern to ride,
> **The** Dragon will half yield to your name.
>
> **Stone** of old will be shattered by steel,
> **Giant** of gifts just in time will reveal
> **To** his friend who's unseen,
> **Save** the half-Great from the Green,
> **Her** fate lies behind the Golden Seal.

"Have you ever seen anything so childish?" complained Durriken.

"What does it say?" asked Iskander, straining to see.

Finn read aloud, tracing his finger down the page, "You . . . need . . . to . . . find . . . the . . . Stone . . . Giant . . . to . . . save . . . her. Who's this Stone Giant?"

"I swear," Durriken sighed, "if she would simply *tell* people what they ought to know, life would be a fair sight easier! The Stone Giant, my unlearned guests, is older than the oldest thing you have ever heard tell of from the oldest person you have ever met. He can be summoned from this island – at least, that is how the story goes. Now I see why she wanted you dropped here. She thinks she is oh so clever!"

"Please, sir," Finn implored, "what are you saying?"

"To complete your high purpose, you need to summon this ancient thing, though I can't imagine what he'd want with you. He can be summoned from here, as I said, but only if you –"

"Oh, brilliant!" Finn exclaimed, before the old man could finish.

"What's that?" Durriken said, taken aback.

"Since this whole mess began, that's how it's been – summon this, go see that, beg for help from the other. And it's gotten us nowhere! I need to get from here to Alba, find my love, and thump the life out of the tailor who took her. Why is this so difficult? I don't care how old this rotted thing is, and I don't care if he can be summoned, or whether he wants to have tea with me or not!"

"Tsk tsk," muttered Durriken. "Do you suppose the world is happening only to you? We have all had loves. What makes yours so special?"

"Wonderful," groaned Finn. "Another lecture on my smallness, too!"

"I will not lecture," Durriken said, "but it is your soul, not your blood, that makes you. If you wish to fret about your love while your half-brethren lie slain, then your smallness is your own curse and creation. I do not lecture, mind, for I do not care."

"What am I supposed to do?" Finn demanded. "There's a quarrel in the world, and I did not start it."

"Do you not know how little wisdom rules the world? I cannot tell you why things are so difficult, but I am telling you what *is*. As you catalogue your misfortunes, consider that they have at least made you aware of your time. From all the centuries whiled away in leisure atop your hill, is there one day you can call to mind, remembered in its entirety? To see time flatly is foolish enough, but not to notice it at all – that is a true waste. As you suffer, half-Great, be grateful that you now have a better notion of where you are and what you are about."

Finn replied coolly, "I shall be as grateful for that as I am for you not lecturing."

"Well," Durriken retorted, "I shall tell your friend here the truths of the Stone Giant. If and when you are inclined to hear them, he may pass them on." He fixed Iskander in his gaze once again. "There is a pebble that must be freed from within a stone, not far from this dwelling – I shall take you to it, but listen to me now. How you are to free the pebble, I cannot say, but it will be an act of sacrifice. The pebble will summon the old fellow from the sea. These years he dwells in low places. His kind were summoned to watch over the dawn of the world, and he is the last of them. A noble race, quite like you were before you became so precious with your lives."

"So we were better creatures," Iskander burst in, "when we sought out brave death?"

"No, you were stupid. But please don't interrupt. He may ask you your business, or he may already know, or he may not care. He is a weary thing, and heavy. Your plight may be unknown to him, but there is nothing new to his eyes. Find him, if you will, once your friend is through his huffing."

"Who's huffing?" Iskander began, but just then Cuhullin arrived short of breath and doing his best to disguise it.

"Sorry about that, lads," he wheezed. "Just needed some air. What did I miss?"

"Are you all right, Ben?" said Finn.

"Never better! What a question!"

"Welcome back, Benandonner," Durriken said, rising from the table. "So sorry we lost you earlier, but perhaps this will amuse you." He pulled a stool up to the green-glowing bowl of water and arranged his cloak to sit. "I have heard many tales of the death of Gogmagog, and I say vanity was the killer." The Giants snorted, for Gogmagog had been nothing near to handsome. "I do not mean that your king was comely, but pride played a part in his downfall. Many who lose for lack of wit call the victors knaves and tricksters. What was it you said before, Finn, about finding and thumping that tailor? You said it should be simple. Let us see just how simple it has been. Tell us, Benandonner, if you recognize anyone." He closed his eyes and twiddled his fingers over the bowl, as if it were an organ he was about to play.

Finn and the Giants stood by at a cautious distance as the green water began to swirl and cloud. Shapes appeared, and letters, though too briefly to be built into words. Then faces, rolling and turning, filled with urgency, unable to impart their desperate messages before sinking back into the darkness.

Durriken twisted his fingers, drawing them upward again and again over the bowl.

One face lingered. It came up and up through the sickly green water, eyes closed and mouth agape. Suddenly the eyes popped open, startling the companions.

"Who are you? What do you want?" it said. The face was less menacing than confused. Cuhullin clapped his hand over his mouth and his eyes bulged. He was too stunned to bolt from the room again, much as he would have liked to. "Where am I? Please?"

"Blunderboar." Cuhullin mumbled the word into his palm. Finn and Iskander turned to him, perplexed and alarmed.

"Ben?" the face pleaded. "Is that you?" His hand still over his mouth, the Giant of Fyfe shook his head. Words failed him when he saw his one-time friend so pitiful and disembodied.

"Benandonner is with us," Durriken said. "But who are you, and how did you come to be here?"

"Here? Where am I?"

"You are dead," the old man replied helpfully. The face looked even more panicked, its wide eyes darting this way and that, in search of some escape. "Please tell us why."

"I was – I was with my brother!"

"Yes," Durriken prodded, "go on."

"Blunderbuss and me – we were together and hunting. He was ahead of me. He was running."

"Yes, go on, please."

"Then he fell. He fell out of sight. I caught up to him, and the ground gave way beneath my feet. A great gaping hole, it was, that someone had dug deep and covered as a trap for us. We argued between us – that is our way, my brother and me – over whose fault it was that we found ourselves in a pit. Then we heard a voice call down. 'Blunderboar and Blunderbuss, what are you doing down there?' 'Quarreling,' my brother said. 'Help us out of here or be on your way.'

"Then we saw who had called down. It was a man all in green. He stood at the edge of the pit, smiling. 'Stop that now. Your quarrel is with me.' He held up his weapon – a pair of golden shears. We laughed. He was so small and his weapon so ridiculous. 'Come down and quarrel, then,' Blunderbuss called up. And he did, he leapt in between us. But we could not get hold of him! We could not see him, except when he'd stop a moment and taunt us with that vicious smile! Cut after cut, Ben! One instant he'd be before us, grinning, and we'd hurl our fists. Then, quick as lightning, he was on the other side, bleeding us away. I saw Blunderbuss go down on his knees, weak and pale. And the cutting did not stop! I could not see him and he would not stop! He killed us, then! He killed us!" Blunderboar looked as desperate as the faces that had first appeared in the bowl.

"Thank you," said Durriken, as Blunderboar sank back out of sight. "Did that seem simple enough?" he asked, turning to Finn.

"Where did he go?" worried Cuhullin.

"To the same night that awaits us all," the old man replied. "'Immortal until proven otherwise.' Is that not what you say? It seems our Jack has found the proof."

"You devil," whispered Finn.

"Now, now, half-Great," Durriken said calmly. "There is but one path through the thorns to the stars. A night of shame or glory is within your hands."

"If glory comes after death, I am in no hurry," Iskander muttered.

"That's the end of it," the old man announced abruptly, rising from his stool. "Let us go and see about your pebble."

He ruffled his sleeves and strode out the door. Finn and
Cuhullin looked at each other, and Iskander took one last long
look at his decaying kinsman at the table. Then they followed.

Durriken was crouched at the edge of the dark circle of
earth, digging through the long grass that grew around it.
Finally, finding a blade of grass that pleased him, he straightened up. He took the blade of grass between his thumbs,
brought it to his lips, and blew a loud, warbling birdcall that
seemed familiar to Finn.

"What was that?"

"One last lesson," the old man replied, "and you ought to
thank me for it. I told you earlier to see time from above, and
here I have called a bird from a past you barely remember.
Come on, now!" This time, Durriken headed toward the
sound of the sea, the Giants on his heels. Finn followed too,
but he lagged behind. For all the old man's wisdom, Finn was
coming to hate him.

"Close enough!" Durriken instructed as they reached a
sheer drop at the land's end. He stood beside one of the
massive rectangular rocks. Finn saw that it resembled a head.
This one had fallen on its side, and its markings were more
ornate. "Great ones, stay put. Finn, you come along here."
Finn slouched over to where the old man was standing.
"Have a look in there and tell me what you see." Durriken
pointed into the ear of the huge head.

Finn peered through the tiny opening into blackness.
"I see nothing," he said impatiently.

"Look harder, please."

Finn turned his head from side to side, giving the light
a chance from every angle. Then, at last, he saw a small,
white dot deep within. He plunged his arm into the hole to
feel for it.

"No use doing that," the old man chuckled. "It's too far down. I'd bid you ask Benandonner to try, but he'd be stuck at once, wearing this head on his arm the rest of his days."

"What am I to do?"

"Whatever you are prepared to," Durriken replied. "I said there would be some sacrifice involved."

Finn had had quite enough of this codger. Without another word, he drew Breanain from his belt and held it high. Then, with all his might, he brought the sword crashing down upon the stone. There was a flash of blue light. A cloud of smoke and dust engulfed them all. When they could see clearly again, the stone head lay cleft before them, and a single white pebble sat amidst the rubble. But in Finn's hand was a bladeless hilt. Proud red Breanain was shattered.

"How can this be?" Finn gasped.

"Would you like to hear the explanation, or would you prefer to complete your task?" asked the old man. "I thought so," he went on, when Finn did not answer. "Take it up, then, lad, and fling it into the sea."

Finn tore his eyes from the broken blade, stepped in among the rocks, and picked up the pebble. He looked at it a moment. Then he turned his face toward the sea, reared back, and hurled the little stone into the water. It disappeared into the darkness, and there was nothing. Then there was something. A swirl – a blossom of foam – and the waters began to part.

VII

The Maudlin Vale

t had been an awkward lunch. Splendid dishes of every description were spread across the table. The finest flavors from the far-flung places of the world sat all but untouched.

"What truly troubles me," Oonagh said, "is that I do not know what it is you want. You have me here. You have taken all that was mine. Why, then, this fuss and circumstance?" She drummed her fingers on the embroidered white cloth and eyed her dining companion across the length of the table. The room was resplendent, with sunlight pouring in through the window, flowers of all colors, and unobtrusive servers sidling close to the carved columns and tall drapes.

"Do you not like it?" Jack asked, grateful for her first words.

"Oh, don't be a dunder." Oonagh sighed. "That is nowhere near what I said, and you know it." Another silence.

"Of course I like it. What fool wouldn't? My dislike for you, however, remains profound."

"I can accept that."

"It was not an offer."

"Very well," he said, pushing his chair back from the table and standing just swiftly enough that she could see his anger. "You wish to know what I want?"

"I wish to leave," she answered, staring firmly back at him. "But if I must stay and listen to you, then yes, that is what I want to hear."

"I want you to look at me kindly. That may seem too high a mountaintop now, but from there you'd see other horizons. You'd see yourself, and this world of ours, as I do. And it is ours, Toothsome Oonagh. For years you have been with a slothful, selfish lot. Would I please you more if I sang at the table? Or let you serve me for centuries while I leave you childless?"

Oonagh's eyes narrowed. "Fling yourself from your wretched mountaintop, and that would please me plenty."

Jack grasped her arm, firmly but not cruelly, and led her up the winding stone staircase to a landing with two wide glass doors. He pushed through them and they found themselves on a large terrace high above the courtyard.

"That would please you, would it?" he asked.

"Yes."

"Very well," he said. "Wait here." He disappeared inside the palace. The terrace was broad and beautiful, with shining flagstones in rainbow colors. The railing seemed very high to Oonagh, but on her tiptoes she was able to peer over it. There was a commanding view of the yard below, and the green plain beyond the palace. Something was being done on the field, with ropes and rocks and pulleys and men, but even her keen eyes could not make it all out from this distance. The wind blew back her hair and she thought of happy times, looking from atop Knockmany to the sea, waiting for Finn to trundle home.

She heard a whistle from above. "Is this high enough for a flinging?" Jack stood on the tallest tower, more than twice as high as the terrace. Oonagh gasped. His feet appeared to have precarious purchase upon the red tiles of the roof. He clung to the flagpole that bore the blue and gold standard.

"You'll break your fool neck," she called up. "And the rest of you, too!"

"You said it would please you to see me flung from some high place. Let it never be said that I denied Toothsome Oonagh. Bring up your little hand, then drop it thus." He let go of the flagpole and gestured, nearly losing his balance. "And when you do, I swear, I will fling myself down. I mean what I say."

Oonagh was vexed. Much as she wanted the end of Jack, it was quite another thing to bring it about herself. Then she thought of her brave hounds, and the Giants who had pro-tected her. And she thought of Finn. Her hand shot up in the air, and Jack's face hardened. But her arm shook. Images of those she loved flashed in her mind, yet she could not bring her hand down. At last, she shook her head and placed her hand on her chest. Their eyes met – hers full of defiance and anger, his full of tenderness and sorrow. And he leapt.

It was a hideous thing to watch a body fall from such a height. Agonizing seconds of wondering what to do, where to run, and knowing there was nothing and nowhere. Oonagh peered, horrified, through her fingers. Jack disappeared from sight as he fell past the tall railing of the terrace. She raced to the edge and craned to see the courtyard far below. There was no sign of him.

"I am glad you couldn't do it."

She whirled around. Jack was leaning against the post of the glass doorway. Whether he had flown or had been saved by some higher hand, she did not know. Still, there he stood. The smugness was gone and he looked at her with pure reverence. They held each other's gaze in silence for some time. Oonagh smiled.

"The Dagda gave an eye for wisdom," the old man said. "Where do you think it went?" This was an odd remark, so nobody answered. Durriken looked down at the broken red blade. The others were watching the parting sea.

The seabed was laid bare between two walls of water. Then a jagged crack began to form along the exposed earth, and the plates of the world moved apart. The water should have rushed into the gaping crevice, but it waited, motionless, for the one who was coming.

Before long, he arrived. First, a groping hand of stone reached out of the darkness. It was almost the size of Finn. Then another hand. When both hands had found solid spots to clutch, they heaved the mighty being into the light. His head was huge and flat on top, and very like the statues dotting the island. Finn fretted that, once this towering thing saw the cleaving he had performed upon his decapitated kin, he would be outraged.

At a weary pace, the Stone Giant brought one immense knee, then the other, up out of his ancient pit. He sat back on his heels and brushed his palms off on his thighs. Blue sparks flew. He heaved a sigh and raised his face.

"Hello there." His morose voice shook the earth.

"Hello back," Finn shouted. He felt the eyes of his companions upon him, as if they had elected him spokesman.

"Thank you for coming." Cuhullin and Iskander winced. Finn whispered, "If you don't like my choice of words, one of you heroes can do the talking."

"Not that I had much choice." The Stone Giant shrugged. "And not that it will matter. There is trouble up here again. There always is."

Finn looked to Durriken, but the old man was no help. He spun on his heel and headed back to his dark cottage. Finn addressed the Stone Giant. "You speak as a creature with experience, but perhaps I can tell you exactly what trouble we've been having."

"It is always the same trouble," the Stone Giant said. "Yours is nothing new." He looked up at the walls of water on either side. "Do you want to get going to wherever you're headed then?" he asked. "This here won't stand forever."

"How did you know we were going somewhere?"

"I told you. Your wants are nothing new. You will find out for yourself – they always do. I know that you want to go from where you are to where you would like to be. No one is ever happy where they are. Whenever you're ready."

"Very well." Finn was taken aback. Just then, Durriken came hurrying up with a long, dusty bundle in his hands.

"Wait a minute!" he cried. "Don't be off just yet! I have something for you!" He brushed past the Giants. "I know, Finn, that you do not care for me, despite our short acquaintance. It's quite all right – I am not for all tastes. For what it's worth, I offer you this." He held up the bundle. "May it serve you well, as it has done others over many years." Finn took the bundle from the old man's upstretched arms, surprised at its tremendous weight. Not only was it far heavier than it appeared, but he marveled that such a frail old fellow could hold it at arm's length without a sign of strain.

"Thank you," Finn said, perplexed. He peeled back the

wrapping to see a gleaming blade, black as midnight. At that moment, he could have sworn he heard a low groan from the Stone Giant. But the big fellow didn't seem to be watching. The sword was magnificent and powerful, and the blackness of its blade consumed all light within its reach. The hilt was golden, decorated with rubies of uncommon size. It was heavier than Breanain, and longer, too. Finn swung it a few times through the air, and found that it stirred passion in him. He tested the new weapon, slashing and parrying invisible foes.

"Hang on there! Ho, now!" shouted Cuhullin, cocking his fists and jumping back as Finn ventured too close.

"Oh, sorry, Ben. Just getting the hang of it, is all. Didn't mean to ruffle you!"

"You ruffled nothing," growled the Giant. "Just keep an eye, is all I'm saying."

"Will do," agreed Finn, sheathing the sword. "Thanks for this," he said to Durriken with genuine appreciation. "It is a kind gesture. What can I pay you?"

"Use it well. That will be payment enough." Durriken's face was sour as ever, but he sounded sincere. "Let me offer you one thing more." From beneath his cloak he produced a golden horn, beautifully bejeweled, with a ring of white pearls around its sounding end. "This horn has saved greater creatures than you are or know. I give it to you as a trust. You may blow it once, and only at direst need, and help will come to you. It has other powers, and a spirit within, of which you need not know. Once and once only, mind."

"Thank you again." Finn bowed and took the horn. He wanted to say something more to the old man, but did not. He turned to the Stone Giant once again. "Now then, sir, whether our troubles are new or not, you are correct – we must be going. If you are willing to help us, let us be off to Alba!"

"Good enough," groaned the Stone Giant, creakily rising to his feet. "Clamber on, then." He reached out his hands to touch the edge of the land, making a bridge of his arms for the companions to crawl up onto his shoulders. This was an awkward moment for Finn and the Giants. They hardly knew this big fellow, so none of them wanted to be first to step on him. The Stone Giant waited. At last Finn decided to get things moving. He stepped onto the back of the Giant's huge hands and slowly edged his way up toward the shoulders. "Is it the three of you coming?" the Stone Giant asked him.

"Well, yes, I believe so."

"Then one of you'll need to make your way up to the top of my head, one of you, and I'll have the others on my shoulders." The two Giants looked uncomfortable with this plan. Muttering, Finn took hold of the Stone Giant's ear and swung his leg up and sat, surprisingly comfortably, on top of his head. "Don't worry about me," the Stone Giant said. "I've been old and tromped-on since before you can know." He tapped his hands on the land to hurry them along.

Before he climbed on, Iskander took one last look back at the dark cottage. Then he stepped onto the Stone Giant's hand and worked his way up to perch on his shoulder.

The walls of water had not escaped Cuhullin's notice. He heaved a sigh and began to climb up. When all three companions were settled in place, the Stone Giant turned from the shore of Mannin and faced the open sea. The walls of water on either side gave way, and the waves crashed in high around his chest. Cuhullin tucked his knees up close. Finn turned back to see Durriken watching them, his expression inscrutable.

The Stone Giant moved smoothly and slowly through the water. The rough rock of his hide offered little grasp.

"So," Finn ventured. "You came up from beneath the earth, did you?"

"At first, yes."

"That's nice. It must be peaceful down there."

"Peace is not to be found upon the earth or beneath it. Peace is within, or not at all."

"Fair enough," Finn conceded. "We were told that you and your kind were summoned to watch over the dawn of the world. Fascinating stuff! Are you one of the Nephilim?"

"No," the Stone Giant answered firmly. "We are different. But you are correct, we were here before the beginning, and now I am the last who remains. We were resented. Yet, for your tomorrow, we gave our today."

"But you are still needed!"

"Deep graves are filled with indispensable creatures."

Cuhullin was not enjoying the trip. Still clutching his knees to his chest, he balanced precariously on the Stone Giant's shoulder. His instinct was to complain, but where to start? The water, the hoisting, and the huge and strange Stone Giant all irked him. But even he could see that there was nothing to be gained by going on about it now. "Marvelous," he muttered to himself.

Iskander, meanwhile, was lost in thought. His time in Durriken's cottage had done much to thin the veil between life and death, and this is an unsettling sensation. He looked down at the waves passing beneath him. This precious new eye had the power to pierce through water. He could see fish and rocks deep beneath the surface, even to the seabed, and as he watched, the burden of night became a little lighter.

"Where in Alba do you plan to take us?" Finn asked after a while.

"There is a place," the Stone Giant answered, "that I care for very much. It is a green valley reached through an inlet, and you will find a few of your kind there. It is not a happy place, I warn you, but it is safe."

"We are not looking to be safe!" Cuhullin's indignation rose above his fear.

"Your brothers there," the Stone Giant said, "have hard-won wisdom of the world. Though they are safe from foes where they dwell, they fight with shadows."

"Bah," snorted Cuhullin. "Who has ever been slain by a shadow?"

"Greater ones than you know."

"Speaking of fights and quarrels," Finn chimed in, "you might prove valuable to us in our quest."

"Are you speaking to me?" the Stone Giant asked.

"Certainly," said Finn. "You are powerful and know the ways of the world."

"There is little to know," the Stone Giant said, "except that you act like wolves to each other. I wish you would learn the craft of gentleness. But you will only learn from experience."

"All the same," Finn persisted, "even if you don't fight, your very presence would help us bring others to our cause."

"You are right, little one. I won't fight. We defend, we do not harm."

"There it is, then!" exclaimed Finn. "This is your ideal task! If you side with us, you will be defending the great history of our islands. You will protect and preserve all that is green and good for generations to come! Those who have died, or have yet to live, surely deserve better."

"Yes," the Stone Giant mused, "the living do get their way." Then he waded on in silence.

Finn was annoyed. He thought he had presented the case

for action rather well. But the Stone Giant was unmoved, even uninterested. This was a fine predicament. If he could be stirred, the Stone Giant could break the mortals' lines and retake Treryn on his own.

"What sorts of things are you willing to protect? What I have described seems, at least to a little fellow like me, precisely the sort of stuff that deserves defending."

"I protect no particular interest," the Stone Giant replied, "not even one so high-minded as you think yours is."

"Then who decides what and whom you defend?"

"I defend life, and the freedom to be tragically wrong. You are what you are, and if I knew as little as you, I might well behave the same way. I know you have a scheme. It is the way of your generation, no need to be sorry for it. We are different from you. You may despise me for not protecting the precise things you deem worth defending."

"It is not a matter of opinion," Finn protested. "There is good and there is evil. I am not the one who makes them so! Do you stand for good or not?"

"You seem clever for your age, so I know you were not listening. Good and evil do not enter into it. Freedom to live is all."

What grand-sounding nonsense, Finn fumed. Ancient, soggy statues from underground might be able to afford such sentimental philosophy, but real lives and loves were at stake!

A green shoreline came into view through the mist. Cliffs rose up on either side and the Stone Giant waded between them into an inlet. The water was still deep around his chest, even as the open sea narrowed to a river, but he pressed upstream against the current. Trees towered along the riverbank, and a sprawling canopy of leaves sheltered the companions.

The sound of voices came from amidst the greenery, but not in words. Instead, they spoke in short, sharp exhalations, like the last exasperated sound of someone turning on his heel and abandoning a pointless argument.

"Not far ahead, I will leave you," said the Stone Giant. "The path is straight here. You will not need weapons. Beware and listen. The soil is good here."

"What did you say?" asked Finn.

"You were not listening."

"I was listening," Finn said, "I simply want to know –"

Before he could finish, the Stone Giant stopped abruptly and his three passengers were thrown forward, off his head and shoulders and onto the soft green earth.

"Couldn't you give us a word of warning?" Cuhullin shouted, rubbing the back of his head.

"You young ones are hard of listening," the Stone Giant scolded. "Did I not say I would be leaving you soon? Hear me for once, all of you. Those who dwell in this vale do not welcome company. But this is the purest place on the Earth. He mourns honestly who mourns without witnesses."

Finn tried one last time to bring the big fellow on board. "Will you not consider the welfare of those who don't have the luxury of ducking beneath the ground?"

"I have pondered for eons and ages," the Stone Giant said. "You will not change, and the world will little note if you do. But I am weary and you are young. I wish you the best, though I will not stay. Goodbye." With that, he sank beneath the water and out of sight.

"Very well," said Finn. "Alone."

"Not alone." Iskander was still dusting himself off from the tumble. "We're still here, you know."

"Yes, of course you are," Finn answered. "What a silly thing to say! You are still here, both of you, and I am glad and grateful. Thanks." He reached up and clasped the two Giants upon the shoulder.

"He'd have been super to have along, no question," the Cyclops admitted. "A strong, solid fellow, big as all outdoors, would be handy. But a chap that size won't be going anywhere except by choice. You did your best."

"And look where my best got us."

"Where?" Cuhullin demanded through the willow branches.

"Some sad green place," Iskander answered. "Our friend said the path was straight. What do you say we find and follow it, and see where it leads?"

"He said we would need no weapons," Finn mused, feeling the hilt of the black sword. "What a strange sort of place."

The three companions searched through the greenery for any sign of a trail. Just then, there came a rustling from the bushes. Heavy footsteps – heavier than Cuhullin's would be if he wore boots indoors and threw a tantrum – made a clump of boughs ahead of them begin to shake. Cuhullin readied his fists, Iskander lifted his palms to the heavens, and Finn, despite the Stone Giant's advice, grasped the handle of the black sword.

The branches parted. Before they could react, a Giant of medium size tumbled through the greenery and fell flat on his face in front of them. His gray hair uneven, as if cut by clumsy hands with a dull blade. His clothes were dirty and ragged. Most notable was the size of his feet. They were enormous, defying any boots to contain them. Huge burlap sacks were wrapped around them, tied with rope just above the Giant's ankles. The companions realized right away that he meant no harm. He looked mildly embarrassed.

"How do you do," Finn said.

"Immortal until it's over." The companions puzzled a moment at this unorthodox reply. Before they could ask about it, he went on: "You are new to the Vale, I see." He rose to his enormous feet, dusting off his clothing. "I know most creatures hereabouts – even those who don't wish to be known, or even known of – and I have not seen any of you before. I would say welcome, if we were in a happier spot."

"And we would say thank you," answered Finn. "May I present Iskander from the east, and Cuhullin of Fyfe. I am Finn McCool. What may we call you, sir?"

"I am Clumberfoot," said the Giant. "Not many things please me, but I may be pleased to meet you."

"Thanks for that," said Finn. "We are most pleased to meet you. We have just arrived, and none of us knows or remembers your land very well."

"I know my own island well enough!" Cuhullin argued.

"Of course you do," Finn agreed, "but this particular patch seems a bit too green and soft for a rugged fellow like you. Perhaps our new friend here has explored it more recently." Cuhullin, satisfied, nodded.

"I have explored the Vale, it is true," said Clumberfoot. "And that sets me apart. Most here keep to themselves. Misery loves to be alone."

"Misery?" wondered Finn. "Who's miserable?"

"Those who do too much mulling. You've come to a mulling sort of place. I promise I am the friendliest person you'll meet, and I'm not that friendly."

"You're perfectly pleasant," Finn assured him. "Perhaps you will be good enough to show us around? We are seeking reinforcements, as we have great tasks to do."

"Great tasks don't interest us. Talk of them stirs tempers. I shall show you around, if you wish, but mine is the warmest welcome you can expect."

"You've been plenty warm, and thanks."

Clumberfoot looked Finn up and down, his eyebrow cocked. "There are some who may not give you a hard time. Come with me and I'll introduce you." As he turned to go, he snagged his huge feet on a clump of earth and tumbled down once more. "Sorry about that. It is my way." Finn tried to help him up, but Clumberfood quickly righted himself. "There are things about ourselves that we cannot change," he said sadly. He turned again, more carefully this time, and set out through the greenery.

They followed along, hacking their way through the leafy boughs of the Vale. The Cyclops was behind Finn, and Cuhullin brought up the rear. It was hard to keep sight of Clumberfoot through the thick brush, but the thumping of his footsteps made his location clear. The only other sound was Cuhullin's cursing as branches and vines whipped him.

"Who are we going to see?" Finn called to Clumberfoot.

"Brothers," the Giant answered. "Not of mine. Brothers to each other, I mean. I have no family."

"Sorry to hear that," Finn said.

"Thank you."

From time to time, Clumberfoot's steady, thumping pace would be interrupted by a rustling among the trees. In contrast to Cuhullin, though, he didn't curse. He merely muttered instructions to himself to watch his step.

"We're coming to it now," he called to them. "Slow down. I'll go on ahead and call you when it's safe to follow."

"Good enough, then," Finn shouted.

"What does that mean? Does that mean yes?"

"Well, yes."

"You ought to say that, then," said Clumberfoot, firmly but not unkindly. "Folks get hurt when people aren't clear with one another."

"I suppose you're right. Sorry, Clumberfoot."

"Good enough," Clumberfoot said, and darted ahead through the woods.

"Finn?" Iskander called through the greenery.

"Yes, friend?"

"We are in a very odd spot," the Cyclops observed. "Wouldn't you say?"

"I would. One of the oddest we've seen."

"I've seen odder," bragged Cuhullin, but before he could continue, Clumberfoot shouted

"Come on ahead, lads. Find your way through." With careful steps, Finn and Iskander made their way toward his voice, trailed by Cuhullin, cursing.

They stumbled into a clearing. A tall, square rock stood in the middle. Clumberfoot, his back to them, was gesturing as he spoke with someone unseen. When Clumberfoot heard the companions approach, he moved aside. A Giant's face, fringed with a straggly beard, peered over the rock.

"What do they want?" The words did not come from this strange Giant, nor from Clumberfoot.

"I don't know yet, I haven't asked them!" This was definitely from the strange Giant.

"Then oughtn't you better ask them before the sun goes down?" demanded the hidden voice.

"Always in such a rush," said the straggly Giant. "Someone should explain the value of patience to you!"

"I don't want to get involved," offered a third voice, meekly.

"I am Finn McCool." Finn extended his hand and walked slowly toward the one Giant he could see.

"Are they coming this way?"

"A little one is, yes. Now quiet down and let us make his acquaintance." A huge hand came whipping out from behind the rock and gripped Finn's. Just as he was beginning to panic at the imminent loss of limb, the hand gave his a gentle shake and released it. "I am Lubomir," the Giant said.

"Good to meet you," Finn began, but the unseen voice chirped again.

"How little is he? Let's have a look!" Much cursing and arguing and bringing up of ancient grievances came from behind the rock.

"I don't want to get involved!" the third voice cried once more.

A mass of dirt and heads and arms emerged from behind the rock. But when the dust settled, Finn was astonished to see that they were, in fact, one immense body with one massive arm on each side and two legs, but with three heads all in a row across the shoulders. They wore a tunic of eggshell white on which was emblazoned a blue castle with three towers, built upon a rock.

"Tell your brother to be more careful!" scolded the Giant on the right.

"Tell *your* brother to respect his elders," chided the Giant on the left.

"I don't want to get involved," squeaked the Giant in the middle.

Clumberfoot yelled over them, "May I present Lubomir, Luboslaw, and Lutz."

"We have already met," Lubomir said, casting a snide look over the middle Giant and directly at the fellow on the far side.

"It is easy to meet folks first," that Giant replied, "when one is always pushing and nudging and making oneself obnoxious."

"I am Finn McCool," the half-Great called out in a friendly voice, for the benefit of the two brothers he had not met, "and these are Iskander and Cuhullin."

"Cuhullin?" Luboslaw demanded. "Cause-of-trouble Cuhullin? What's he doing here?"

"Nothing, so far," the Giant of Fyfe grumbled, "but if you mean to insult him, he may do plenty." He shoved his way past Iskander and glared at the three brothers.

"Oh, please don't let's start anything," implored the middle Giant. "I don't wish to be involved in any quarrel!"

"My brother Lutz," Luboslaw said, "is a friendly coward. I suppose cowards must be friendly. I am no coward, but I can be friendly to those who deserve friendship." Cuhullin did not understand his full meaning, but he could tell he was being goaded.

"If you start in with this troublemaker," Lubomir called to his brother, "you are on your own." Luboslaw hung his head.

"That's better," snorted the Giant of Fyfe, seeing that he had won, even if he did not know how.

"We'd like to be friends," Finn offered, "if you'll have us. Not just the three of you – and Clumberfoot, of course – but everyone in this charming green vale. May we sit and tell you why we are here?"

"I'm not sitting down with him," Luboslaw muttered.

"Well then," Lubomir said, "stay standing, if you are able, but the rest of us could use a good sit."

"We don't even know the others," Luboslaw protested, "and the one we know of has been a bully since before we came here." Cuhullin did not fire up this time because he didn't realized that Luboslaw was speaking of him.

"Please let's not squabble with them," pleaded Lutz from the middle. "Or, if you must squabble, leave me out of it."

"A vote, then," Lubomir announced. Luboslaw groaned and rolled his eyes. "All opposed to having a seat with the strangers?" The brothers' left arm shot up. "One opposed. Very well. All in favor of sitting and having a chat?" Their right arm and right foot both came up. "Two in favor! Abstentions?" The toe of their left foot lifted ever so slightly off the ground. "The motion is carried – we sit!" Their right leg flew out from under them, and they landed with a thud on the soft ground.

"Thank you," said Finn. He motioned to Iskander and Cuhullin to make themselves comfortable on the grass. Clumberfoot maneuvered his way to the ground.

"We seldom speak to anyone but each other," Lubomir explained. "And sometimes we don't talk at all. We've gone centuries in silence. But Clumberfoot has been a friend to us when nobody else was, even when we were not friends to each other. And since you come with him, we will speak to you."

"We have come to your valley to seek help," said Finn. "Not merely for ourselves, mind – though the heaviest stakes are mine – but for you, and for the sake of our kind in these lands. Trouble came while we slept. Now fire and hatred are spreading across the world."

"Fire and hatred are nothing new to us. They are older than the hills. Do you propose that we can end them?" asked Lubomir.

"Not forever," Finn replied, "and not everywhere. But in our spot of the world, perhaps."

"That will be lovely for you," Lubomir sighed. "As for us, we were never welcome in your spot of the world. That is why we came to this one. We see a good deal less of fire and hatred here."

"Fair enough," said Finn. "Tell us something of yourselves. What hatred are you hiding from?"

"We are not hiding!" Luboslaw shot back. "We may get tired of angry looks, or even pity, but we did not come here to hide."

"Why did you come here, then?"

"Don't you make choices each day? Did you not do some choosing of your company? We are no different. We could not choose or unchoose the company of our brothers, obviously. But we could choose to absent ourselves from curious and judging eyes. Would you begrudge us that?"

"Of course not," said Finn. "I suppose I hadn't considered your situation."

"No one ever thinks of anyone's situation," Lubomir said. "If they did, we might not choose to be here. Here, we have no friends or enemies except each other."

"That seems cozy."

"We have a way among ourselves," Lubomir went on. "It is far from perfect, but we cope."

"Indeed," Finn said. "I see you have a way, certainly. I must say that I am glad you won the vote and chose to sit."

"He wins every vote," Luboslaw grumbled.

"How's that?" asked Finn.

"What my younger brother means to say," Lubomir interjected, "is that I'm in charge of more limbs than he."

"We both have two limbs!" Luboslaw shouted.

"I stand corrected. We each control two limbs, the arm and leg on our own side. But it is Lutz, in the middle, who holds the balance of power."

"Don't bring me into it," Lutz said, shaking his head. "I abstained from the sitting down."

"Lutz can always be counted on to stay out of things. Our left foot is his domain. Abstention is his kingdom."

"At least I am in charge of something," Lutz sniffed.

"You know I wasn't being harsh," Lubomir soothed him. "The world needs middle voices. Our mother loved us, but no one else has since." The heads nodded. "We have made a fair trade. The world doesn't love us, so we do not love it.

You're on a quest to make the world a better place. We don't care how much better it could be. You have come here seeking help, but this is no place for heroes."

"What will you do, then when fire and hatred find you here?" Finn asked.

"That won't happen," Lubomir assured him. "None come here except those who wish to be alone."

Finn spoke carefully. "There was a time when I believed as you do – that a fellow could keep to himself and be left alone. I lived a happy life for many ages. Calamity crashed on me through no fault of mine. Little people with hatchets and hate found me. Well, that's not true – they found my loved ones, which is worse!" Tears came all at once, and he buried his face in his hands. The brothers and Clumberfoot were unmoved, but Iskander reached over and patted Finn gently on the back. Cuhullin shifted from foot to foot.

"Sorry for that," Finn said, after he had regained his composure.

"He mourns honestly who mourns without witnesses," Lubomir said flatly. The others recognized the words at once.

"Where did you hear that?" Iskander asked.

"It is one of the oldest truths we know," said Lubomir. "And I have heard and repeated it many times."

"Is there nothing you can do to help us?" Finn implored.

"There is always something," said Lubomir, "but what is it you want?"

Luboslaw chimed in. "Why would we help them?"

"I did not say we would, I merely asked what they would like. Are we too busy to hear the answer?" Luboslaw brought their left arm across his portion of their chest. Had he been in charge of their whole body, he would have folded both arms – but he was not.

"We believe my beloved is at Treryn, or whatever those who now hold it are calling the place. They have done more than this, and will do more yet, but her fate is all that concerns me."

"I see," said Lubomir. "What else have they done?"

"They have killed our kind wherever they have found them."

"*Our* kind?" sputtered Luboslaw. "What kind would that be?"

"Giant-kind," said Finn, surprised at the question. He looked to Lubomir, expecting the reasonable brother to take his side.

"Luboslaw asks a fair question," Lubomir pointed out. "He means that we and other Giants are not one kind. Giants have always spurned us for the crime of being hideously different. What I mean is whether you are a Giant at all."

Finn had never thought of this being in question. "I am," he insisted.

"You are what?"

"I am a Giant if I say so," Finn said a little crossly, sitting up taller. "That is all you need to know. If I were not one, that would hardly be your business anyway. I claim the right of any creature to say what I am. You may call yourselves the Treble Giant for all I care, and what would it be to me?" As he finished speaking, he became aware that his face was hot and his voice was raised. He wondered if Baldemar would laugh or applaud, or both.

"If you say so," said Lubomir calmly. "They have killed our kind, then. Anything else?"

"They've also taken the Giants Ring. We don't know how or why."

"Oh, I know about this!" Lutz piped up. His brothers turned to him in surprise. "The rocks they were moving.

I know the Ring from when we were lads. The same rocks, I saw them."

"When was this?" Luboslaw demanded. "What did you see?"

"You two were asleep, as usual," Lutz answered a little smugly. "We were lying under the stars near the inlet of the river. The moon was full and bright over the water. I heard the sound of boats and oars. They were strange craft, wide and flat, with huge sails that caught the moonlight. And I could hear whisperings. I did not wake either of you because you can never be trusted to keep quiet. As they came closer, I could see little men crawling all around the ships, with tremendous cargo that was secured by ropes. The men on the ships signaled to men on the shore who were arranging some contraption of logs. Then the bows of the ships dipped onto the land, in a way I had never seen boats do before. The men on shore set the logs in a row, and they rolled the cargo from the ships. They were blue stones, and I knew them. The stones of the Ring. The stones would roll to the end of the logs, then the little fellows would take hold of the rearmost log and run it to the front. In this way, they moved stone after stone of the Ring onto the land and through the Vale, out of my sight."

"Why is this the first time we have heard this tale?" said Lubomir.

"Well, you two are impossible to speak to," Lutz answered indignantly. "There's no telling you anything without a quarrel."

"Who would quarrel?" Luboslaw asked angrily. "You could just tell us what you saw! Where's the quarrel in that?"

"Sirs, please," Finn interjected. "Forget who saw what and who was asleep when. Don't you realize what Lutz is telling you? These little people are in your valley already – at least, they have been here. We're strong, but they're wickedly smart. You were going on about how your Vale was of no use or interest to them, and in fact they hauled the Giants Ring right through it!"

"So it would seem," said Lubomir thoughtfully. Luboslaw was still glaring at Lutz, who wore a faraway expression, as though the last several minutes had never happened.

Finn had an idea. "We are advised by an ancient wisdom – the Banshee herself, if you want to know – that we should rally our brothers, including you, if you will come, to strike back at these little evil-doers. She told us we should number no more than eighteen. Whether you are one of us or three is not for me to say. You must decide what you will do and be."

"I expect we would be of precious little use," said Lubomir. "But there is one known to us, here in the Vale, who might be. He is a relatively new arrival, and keeps to himself even more than the rest, but he has the size and strength for striking. Would that be of some help, I wonder?"

"It would indeed," answered Finn, "and I thank you for thinking of it. If I may say so, though, you three seem more than formidable yourselves. Who is it that surpasses you in strength?"

"I did not say that we were not strong," Lubomir corrected him. "When we work with one mind, I do not know that any Giant can stand against us. But, it is not in our nature. We have seen more of fighting than we care to recall. However wary we've been of entering a quarrel, once we're in it, our enemies have had good cause to fear us." He and Luboslaw moved their arms in concert, crossing them firmly across their huge chest, just under Lutz's chin.

"I believe you," Finn replied. "So this other fellow is strong, and fierce besides?"

"We don't know," answered Lubomir. "He seems dangerous and sad. Angrier than sad."

"He sounds like the sort of fellow we need," said Finn. "I have shown my sorrowful side here, and perhaps this valley is just the place for it. But I am angry too. Lead on, and we will gratefully follow!"

"Hang on, then," Luboslaw cut in. "I don't recall us taking a vote on it! You two have cooked up a deal, but the rest of us have a say in where we go and whom we introduce to whom!"

"True," Lubomir replied. "Protocol must be observed. If you would like a vote, then you shall have it. All opposed to leading these fellows to meet our angry Vale-mate?" Luboslaw's hand shot up. "One opposed. All in favor?" As before, the hand and foot on Lubomir's side came up. "Two in favor. Abstentions?" Nothing. "Abstentions?" he repeated. "Lutz, do you abstain?" The left foot stayed where it was, upon the ground.

"Deadlock!" Luboslaw whooped. "The motion is not carried. There is no clear majority! They can find their own blessed way!"

"Lutz, didn't you hear me?" Lubomir prodded. "It is your turn to vote."

"You know," Lutz replied, his eyes closed and his tone lofty, "I hear you all the time, even when you think I am not listening. For instance, I heard very clearly what you said earlier about my abstentions. I may not have an arm or even a shoulder to call my own, but I do have opinions."

"I did not mean offense."

"Well, it was very rude."

"It was, I suppose," Lubomir conceded, "especially in front of others. Can you forgive me, please?"

"I can," said Lutz, his eyes still closed.

"Thank you," answered Lubomir. "Now, how would you like to vote?"

Lutz pretended to think. "I firmly abstain," he said at last, and raised their left foot with ceremonial importance. Luboslaw sighed with exasperation.

"He's forever coddling Lutz," he griped, "and this precious fool always falls for it."

"That's enough of that," Lubomir said. "The votes are counted and the decision is final. We will lead them, and let there be no complaints." Luboslaw gave one last huff before enlisting his leg and arm to help the three brothers get to their feet.

"Thank you again," said Finn, also rising. "And thank you, Clumberfoot, for bringing us here." Clumberfoot did not answer, as he was working hard to right himself – extending his hands, leaning forward as far as he could, hoping to bring himself to his feet without tipping face forward. It was clear that he had practiced this for some time, as he wobbled for only a moment and stood up without danger of falling.

"You are most welcome," he said, with a little smile of satisfaction – the first sign of pride or pleasure they had seen since making his acquaintance.

Iskander and Cuhullin lumbered to their feet too. Cuhullin studied Luboslaw with curiosity, as he often did when confronted by a hostile stranger. The Giant of Fyfe always underestimated how many foes his belligerent ways had made for him throughout Albion.

"By the by," Finn wondered, "who are we off to meet?"

Lubomir answered, "We know him as Timberfor."

"This is something I would like to give you, and I ask no payment for it."

What a suspicious way to present a gift, Oonagh thought. Who pays for a gift? Grinning, Jack cast his cap aside and held out an ornate purple sash decorated with diamonds.

"Thank you," she said, taking the precious item gently. The jewels were arranged in letters and runes she did not know. Whatever story they told, she supposed the tale must be grand – or at least important – to merit such majestic telling.

"Make a fool glad and put it on," he urged her. Oonagh obliged. What harm could it do? She draped the sash over her shoulder and smoothed it with her hand. Her first thought was how ridiculous it looked on her humble, sensible dress. But Jack was beaming. "Thank you for that," he said. "This is an old and special thing, and it means a fortune to me that you will have it. I have asked plenty of you, I know. And as you have said, I have also taken without asking. Forgive me all that, if you will, but only let me see you wearing this."

"You want me to wear this all the time?" Oonagh asked incredulously.

"Yes, please."

"It is lovely," she allowed, "but no one wears anything all the time. It is a strange thing to ask."

"I do not pretend to be ordinary."

"Good enough, then." She raised her eyebrows.

They were standing in the paddock of the palace stables. Over time, Oonagh had more freedom to move about the grounds. Jack had appeared to her here – unexpected, as was his custom. Wherever she went, she could hear doings and voices, but the creatures and their business were kept from her eyes. The encounter with the wizard building his contraption had been the exception, and she imagined that discovering him had been no accident. She supposed that escape was possible, but where would she go? She was not given to mad dashes, and so she stayed put and bided her time.

"Does it become me as much as that?" she asked, holding the fringe of the sash up to her long, golden hair.

"As much as that and more. You know, you really are a marvel."

Oonagh did not respond at once. By nature she was defenseless against flattery, but something in the way Jack served it up left her cold. "Thank you," she said stiffly, hoping to discourage him.

"I mean," he went on, not taking the hint, "the way your beauty glows wherever you are. And your wisdom, too – you think I do not see it, but I do."

"Yes, thank you very much," she replied, cooler still.

"Do you know what a woman's greatest power is?Her mystery. You could have had me dead, and you did not. Yet now, as we speak and you wear my gift, I feel you closing off from me – why? I do not know, and it fascinates me."

"I dislike you. That's why. Does that help any?"

"You say that," he laughed, "but you are unsure. Ha! You are a mystery even to yourself!"

"And you are a jackass through and through. But I suppose it is a good thing that I am such a marvel, or you might kill me for a remark like that."

"Kill? Who said anything about killing?"

"Don't play the innocent with me. I've seen you cheat and lie. Your self-regard is proof that you deceive even yourself."

"Self-regard?" Jack seemed staggered. "I am a humble tailor. And I am not so vicious as you imagine. Indeed, a sense of humor does not go amiss in my line of work."

"Your line of work is killing."

"But with a jocular outlook." There was an awkward silence as she looked at his eyes and wondered which one was wandering.

"I know what evil lurks within you," said Oonagh. "It crossed your face when we first met, though you hoped I wouldn't see."

"It's true, I know, I am not perfect. But so what? Do you possess no evil of your own?"

She thought of her Finn, her hounds, and her home. And she looked at this man before her, who had taken them away. She could not answer.

The Maudlin Vale was especially miserable by night. Wisps of sobs and pitiful voices drifted through the darkness, and now and then some beloved name. No one called out to another, or expected to be answered, but the cries were desperate nonetheless.

When it came time to stop for the night, the three brothers said nothing to Clumberfoot and the companions. They simply halted, murmured briefly to one another, then settled down with their back against an ancient willow and closed all six of their eyes.

"Are they done?" Cuhullin demanded. "Why are we not moving? It's just a bit of nighttime!"

"I suppose they're tired," Iskander answered. "Fellows? Is that it?"

Clumberfoot shushed him. "They are done for the night, I'm afraid. Nights are dangerous times hereabouts. Feelings run high."

"What should we do?" Finn asked. "Just wait out the darkness?"

"You must be tired yourselves," Clumberfoot said. "The Vale is broader and deeper than you'd think, and it takes time to get through it. What's more, you don't want to startle the fellow we're headed to see. Sleep does not come easily here, but close your eyes and rest awhile. It will be light before you know it."

Reluctantly and with much grumbling, the companions searched for a rootless patch to stretch out on. Finding one was not easy, for there was almost no light from the moon or the stars; the canopy of weeping trees was too thick. Cuhullin protested about not pressing on through the darkness, but as Clumberfoot had predicted, he was readier for sleep than he thought. Soon the Giant of Fyfe was snoring loudly, not far from Finn's feet. The racket did not much bother the half-Great, though, because it drowned out the mournful sobs of the unseen Giants round about.

Finn's eyes were heavy as he squinted up to the dark tree-tops. He worried, as always, about his Oonagh. The wind parted the boughs for a moment and he saw one lonely star looking down at him. But as soon as it appeared, the wind changed and the heavenly thing was lost from sight.

"The stars, like us, are beyond the clouds," Clumberfoot murmured, as if giving directions in a dream.

"What?" Finn asked, but a long snore was the only reply. In his weariness, the half-Great wondered if he was dreaming himself. He closed his eyes and rolled onto his side, letting out one last sigh as he thought of his beloved.

When his eyes opened again, what seemed no more than an instant later, they were greeted by gray morning. He had not dreamed, that he could remember, and he did not know if he had even slept. The heaviness of the Vale was upon him like a blanket.

Iskander and Cuhullin snoozed nearby, but Clumberfoot

and the brothers were nowhere to be seen. Just as Finn began to imagine that the four had left him and his friends to their own devices, a familiar thumping shook the ground.

"Good, you're all awake," Clumberfoot observed. "We were just over to see –" Before he could finish, he caught his huge toes on a clod of earth and came tumbling down. "Days come and this will happen," he said softly to himself, laid out upon his stomach. "We pick ourselves up, just like anyone else." Slowly and carefully he righted himself, his face hardening as he forced himself not to avoid the others' eyes. "We were just over to see," he began again, pronouncing each word deliberately and distinctly, "the fellow you are going to meet. He is not in good humor, I warn you, but I do not suppose you expected much else."

"What do we care if he's in a bad mood?" grumbled Cuhullin, rubbing the back of his neck. "He should be concerned about our mood, sleeping on dirty great roots all night!"

"I'll take the roots over your snoring, Ben," Iskander groaned, stretching.

"Yes, Clumberfoot, we'd like to come along," Finn said. "Where is he?"

"This way, please." Slowly the Giant made his way through the thick trees, careful not to trip. The weary companions followed him down a gentle slope.

Not long into the journey, Finn realized he was hungry. Before he could say so, Cuhullin's mighty stomach rumbled, speaking for them all. "There's naught to eat where we're headed, I'm afraid," Clumberfoot called back to them. "We don't much fuss about food in these parts."

They came to a clearing where the trees gave way to bare rock. A waterfall splashed in the distance, and the rugged earth dipped sharply into a gaping green gorge. The three brothers stood with their back toward the drop-off. Lutz's face was a blank as he searched the sky. Luboslaw studied their boots, clucking his tongue. Lubomir was talking with a Giant who was seated in front of them.

All the others could see was the broad back of this new Giant, as he sat hunched on a rock. Orange hair tumbled from beneath the worn brown leather cap upon his head. Lubomir's lips were moving, though Finn and the others were too far away to hear his words. He lifted a finger of greeting to them, never taking his eyes off the new Giant or seeming to lose his train of thought. Seeing this, Clumberfoot raised his hand and pursed his lips as though he were about to whistle.

"Don't be shushing us," Cuhullin protested. "We've come a long way through vicious, whipping trees, and we won't be told to keep quiet!"

Finn addressed the Giant's back. "How do you do, friend?" No reply. In the regular world, in regular time, neglecting to respond would be a rude breach of Giant custom. But these were irregular times, and the Vale was a peculiar place. "Lovely day, isn't it?" he added, to kill the silence.

"The wise speak when they have something to say; fools speak when they have to say something." The Giant's meaning was sharp, though his tone was dull. Finn knew he had been insulted.

"So the cleverest sit rudely and say nothing?" he retorted. Again, no reply. "Your name is Timberfor, we are told, and we do not wish to be your enemies. We have too many enemies. Perhaps you do too. Even the strongest of us needs more friends. May I be your friend?"

"Boring," Timberfor sighed.

"I am no bard or jester," Finn admitted, though he wondered if Aillen would fare much better with this crabby chap. "But I would rather shake hands than cross swords."

"We've no need of swords to handle this grouser," Cuhullin

said. "If he won't speak civil, maybe he'd like to swing fists!"
But Timberfor would not be provoked. Finn looked to
Clumberfoot and the brothers, who all shrugged. Lubomir
raised his eyebrows and glanced at Cuhullin as if to say that,
if he'd kept queit, the conversation would be going better now.

"We didn't come to argue," said Finn. "Our time is
wasting."

"Then go away."

Finn could see that this fellow would not be moved to
conversation, and he wondered if he was worth their time
and effort. But he thought of his unbroken string of failures
in bringing others to their cause. If he could not even stir
this recruit to speech, what hope was there for their mission?
Unhappy, as ever, at having to resort to this means, he
brought his thumb to his lips.

In his mind's eye, Finn saw a dark-haired boy with
smiling eyes. A tiny lad, full of life, he ran, laughing, down a
hill. This was a happy sight, and the half-Great was glad of
it. It was a vision of goodness, full of joy in the present and
hope for the future. Then it was gone.

"Who was the boy you knew?"

None of them was prepared for the reaction. Timberfor
leapt to his feet and whirled on them with fire in his eyes. His
huge arms were spread wide, ready to take them all up and
dash them over the cliff.

"WHO ARE YOU TO ASK ME?"

"I am sorry –" Finn began, badly startled.

"I WILL KILL YOU WHERE YOU STAND – ALL OF
YOU!"

"I didn't say anything," Iskander pleaded quietly.

"GO NOW! AND DO NOT RETURN!"

Finn and the Cyclops found themselves shuffling toward
the shelter of Cuhullin's shadow. Even the Giant of Fyfe did

not relish a tangle with someone so fearsome and infuriated. His success in combat had often come from his own anger and eagerness to fight. Confronted by a Giant even angrier than himself, he lost his advantage. Timberfor – a ball of fury, seething with strength – held the companions in his glare. Cuhullin braced himself for battle, resolved that the moment Timberfor's foot came off the ground, the fight would be on. From the corner of his eye, Finn could see that Clumberfoot and the brothers were strangely unmoved.

"There was no harm meant by the question," Lubomir said mildly. The tone and timing of his words had an astounding effect. The fury seeped out of Timberfor just a little, and he looked away. "We were the ones who brought them along," Lubomir added, "so please do not be cross with anyone but us. Words come for any number of reasons, and we do not know theirs, in all fairness. Come along, now." Timberfor lowered his arms. He sat down again upon the stone, this time facing the companions.

"How did you come to ask me this?" he asked, more civilly. "Were you sent to find an answer? Are you enemies?"

"We were not sent, no," Finn replied, "and we knew nothing of you when first we set foot in your valley. We are not your enemies and we don't envy them. At times I catch a glimpse of hidden things, and that is how I came to ask. I am truly sorry to have upset you."

"I see," said Timberfor, looking at the earth between his feet. "Now you have asked, and told me why. So leave me be."

"That's not any kind of answer," Iskander blurted. Finn quickly raised his hand to the Cyclops, who clapped his hand over his mouth and shook his head in apology.

"You're right," said Timberfor. "It's not. I don't like to give answers. I don't like to speak. I don't want to be your enemy, either, so the less you know of me, the better."

"We'd like to hear your story," Finn prodded. "Perhaps you'll start from the very beginning, and we'll see if we are friends at the end?"

"I had a friend," Timberfor muttered.

"You did?" said Finn. "Tell us about him!"

"I . . ." Timberfor lost his words a moment and swallowed hard. "I killed him."

"I see," Finn said carefully. "May a person know the reason why?"

"A person may know any number of things," Timberfor said sadly, "but never does one know why. Since he is gone, nothing has any reason." The Giant's change from fearsome to forlorn had been sudden but sincere. Finn could see a suffering like his own; worse, even, because he had yet one treasure that Timberfor was without – hope.

Finn moved closer, and sat himself, uninvited, on a corner of Timberfor's stone. "I have lost my love," he said, "but I may get her back again. I do not presume to ask whom you have lost and how, or why you have come here. I ask you for nothing, in fact. My friendship is here, if you have use for it. We will help you, if we can. Elsewise, we will be on our way." Timberfor stared at his shoes. Finn began to get up.

"There was a boy," Timberfor said suddenly. Finn sat back down. "And he was my friend. I do not know how to seem friendly, so I never had friends. My hill was high and lonely, but the sun would strike it gently in the afternoons. That was when he came. He was always smiling, and so I would smile too. We would play and talk. He was not happy down with the mortal men. I don't know how he found me, but I thought it was a gift from heaven. And a pie! One time he brought me a pie – not large, you know, but too much for him to carry, and so he dragged it up the hill by rope. How ridiculous he looked! A good boy! I ate the pie in little bites, so he would think it was more than a mouthful. It is a good thing, having friends. Then he turned for home again. The sun was setting and he said he had to beat the darkness home. So he turned to go, and I was sorry he was leaving, though grateful that he had come to play with me again. So I touched him gently upon his head with my hand. And that was enough. Who could know he was so fragile? No, he was not fragile – I am an oaf and an ogre! He was my friend, and now he is gone." Timberfor covered his eyes with his hand. He took a deep breath and went on. "Then the little men who had made him unhappy in his life came with torches and swords to find me. His father led them, and he spat his own name at me – Dunbar. I fought my way through them, though I was blinded by tears. They chased me and I ran on and on. I have been gone a long time now." He rested his forehead in the palms of his hands.

"I am sorry for you, Timberfor," Finn soothed him. "The boy is in happy sunshine now. I know you didn't ask, but I've told you all the same."

"Thank you," said Timberfor, not lifting his head. Every Giant's face was forlorn. This fellow might be angry, but he was also in mortal sadness. Perhaps this was the right place for him, and it would be unkind and selfish to pry him away.

Then Iskander had a thought. "Excuse me," he ventured, "may I ask one thing about this boy?" Silence came as consent. "What was his name?"

Timberfor looked up, perplexed. He stared deep into the jewel of the Cyclops's eye before answering softly, "Arvel."

VIII

the canyon of heroes

It was a dizzy height, but Oonagh's mind was clear. She shuffled delicately across the narrow ledge to the lonely tower she had seen out her window early in her captivity. The waning moon did its best to light her steps, and it glinted upon the polished flagstones of the courtyard far below. Wind whistled through her hair and whipped the banners on the turrets. They flicked and flapped as though waving to distract her. But Oonagh was steady of foot and soul.

Many nights she had noticed lights flashing in the tallest window of the lonely tower, but never once had she observed anyone entering or leaving, and its door stayed bolted shut. The narrow ledge she inched along was the only approach she could see.

It was cold now, and as she reached the middle of the ledge, where there was no shelter at all, she felt the chill all the more. She paused and crossed her arms across her chest.

There was a smell of autumn in the night air, and she closed her eyes and breathed deep. This could have been any crisp evening in Eire, after she had packed Finn and the hounds off to bed, when she would pad about Knockmany, singing to the stars and seeing what they had to say.

The wind kicked up. Ordinarily it would take a typhoon to unsteady the agile Oonagh, but her purple sash caught the gust like a sail. She tried to draw it back in, but the billowing sash pulled her up onto her toes. She circled her arms furiously against the fall, to no avail. Over she went, plummeting toward the unforgiving flagstones.

"Good evening."

Oonagh had clenched her eyes closed, and she pried them slowly open now. The courtyard was filled with shadows, so she only saw shapes, but she recognized the voice. She felt around and discovered that she was being held gently in two enormous hands. The palms were thick and rough, fringed with long hair.

"Good evening," she replied, a little shakily.

"Are you all right?" She placed the voice of her rescuer. It was the same humongous creature who had accompanied her, when she was blindfolded, to her quarters on the first day of her captivity. Now, as then, his tone was neutral and polite.

"I am, thanks to you," she answered. "A jolly good thing you were walking by. Silly of me to be doing what I was, I know."

"If you are all right, I'll set you on your way." With that, he placed her carefully onto her feet in the courtyard and started off.

"Hang on! What do I call you?"

"Oh, I don't think you'd like me," the hairy hulk answered.

"That's not what I asked," she retorted. "And anyway, why wouldn't I?"

"Because I am going to kill your fellow." He spoke these words with an eerie calm and turned to go. His silhouette in the moonlight made him look like a moving mountain. Taller by half than Cuhullin, he was impossibly wide, and matted with white hair.

"When my fellow comes here, I am going to tell him you said so," Oonagh shouted at the monster's back, finding her voice but not her composure, "and then you'll be sorry!" She knew it was a hollow threat. Finn was large by mortal reckoning, but he would be no more than knee-high to this behemoth.

"Tell him whatever you wish," the thing replied, stopping in his tracks but not turning to face her.

"Why would you save me and then say such a thing? Why not just let me drop?"

"That's a lovely sash you're wearing." Slowly, the monster turned. When the moonlight caught his face, Oonagh could not help but bring her palm over her mouth at the sight of him. His face was pointed like a wolf's, with a mouthful of teeth like spears. His right eye socket was empty and shrunken, and his snout veered off to that side, crowding the scarred hole. His left eye was covered by a bulging patch, black and adorned with sharp stones. The monster lifted his nose to the moon and sniffed deeply of the night air.

"The scarf is not mine," she answered, managing her nerves. "But anyway, how would you know it? Can you see me?"

He smiled nastily. "I can," he said.

"And just what has my Finn done to you that you should want to do him harm? He is the kindest fellow in these isles, you vile brute!"

"He well may be. I have not met him. But he owes me a life, so I shall take his." He turned to leave.

"Wait!" she called. "Whose life?" The monster lurched away. "Hang on – what is your name? What are you?" He stopped and faced her again, his hideous face drowned in the dark. Only his teeth flashed.

"My name is Balar, and I am at your service." He gave a little bow. "Good evening." With that, he disappeared into the night.

"If I understand you properly, our problems are bigger than we knew." Finn spoke slowly, one fist under his chin and his other arm folded across his chest.

"Your problems are what you make them," Timberfor said.

"Well . . . that's just silly," Finn snapped. "I didn't make Dunbar my enemy and invite him to stir up mischief in Eire. I am sorry for him, to be sure. But I had nothing to do with making these problems. How is saying so helpful?"

"I'm not trying to help." Good thing, thought Finn, for what this troubled Giant had told them had only upset the companions. Iskander, especially, was out of sorts.

Arvel was a ghost and his father, Dunbar, was their enemy. After he had chased Timberfor from his hill, Dunbar had wandered through Albion, ruined in mind and body. His sorrow had quivered into hatred, and he had fallen into the service of Jack and the Little King as chief Giant-killer in Eire. Many mortal years had passed – no one could say how many – since the tragedy on Timberfor's hill, and Dunbar, as men are wont to do, had fed and watered his hatred until it grew to include all the Great Ones yet living. Hunting Timberfor without success, he settled for slaying every other Giant he saw. Timberfor cared little for his own life but he would not lay it down without a fight. And so the misery of one mishap had become the doom of many.

"Could it be," mused Lubomir, "that you may help each other in these troubles? That is to say, this half-Great and our Giant brothers have come here, where few speak or stir, seeking soldiers. And you, my friend Timberfor, have found no peace in this place because your past pursues you wherever you go. Might you be friends? Only you can know."

"I had a friend," said Timberfor softly.

"You did," offered Finn, "and I am sorry you lost him."

"What does that get me?" Timberfor snapped.

"That's enough of that from you," Cuhullin boomed. "This little fellow is with me, and you're done threatening him." The Giant of Fyfe towered over Timberfor as he sat, and held a clear advantage in the early going of a scuffle. More than this, Timberfor knew that Finn meant to be kind, and so he cooled his temper.

"I am sorry," he muttered, picking at his bootlace. "I told you already, I do not know how to seem friendly."

"But you seem a decent fellow," said Finn, smiling. "Do not worry about the rest."

Cuhullin stepped back, and Clumberfoot, who had been uncomfortable at all this raising of voices, breathed a small sigh of relief.

"Now, what about this clever fellow's idea?" Finn wondered. "We know where we're headed, you're not sure where you ought to be, and we've stumbled across each other's path. Do you think you'd like to come along with us?"

"What use would I be?"

"More use than you are now, sitting here and stewing."

"Very well," the troubled Giant said, "I suppose I'd best keep moving anyhow. Lead on and I will follow." He rose slowly. "Thank you for having me," he said, nodding to

Clumberfoot and the brothers, "but I can see you would like me to go now. I don't blame you. Farewell."

"Hang on there," Clumberfoot protested, "don't say that. You are always welcome here, and anyway it's not up to us who stays or goes. We live in the Vale but it does not belong to us." Luboslaw snorted. "It's true," Clumberfoot insisted. "We do not mean to drive you out. In fact, I envy you going."

"Why not come along?" Finn said at once.

"I . . . I mean," stammered Clumberfoot, "that I envy his being able to go. It is right and good that this fellow should be on his way. I think we all agree on that. What he seeks is not here. As for me, I have found shelter from angry eyes, and that is enough to give me peace."

"For now," Iskander blurted. Clumberfoot looked at the Cyclops with injury in his eyes. Then he looked down at his enormous feet.

"Yes," he said. "For now."

"And you may have peace again," Finn said, "if we accomplish this task. Peace is purchased with interludes of unpleasantness. This is such a time, and we'd welcome your help."

"He means war," Lutz muttered.

"Yes he does," Luboslaw loudly agreed, "and it's not the sort of talk we welcome here! Take that mongering down to the Canyon. We want none of it!"

"I will take my talk," answered Finn softly, "and the rest of me, and whoever of you will come, away from this place in a moment. Just indulge me a little longer. Where is this place you are telling me to go, where they talk of war?"

"The Canyon," Luboslaw snapped. Finn and the others looked at him blankly. "Down there," he added, jabbing his finger in the direction of the steep drop-off. "They're awake all hours, clanging with hammers and plotting by fires. It's a bothersome place and we stay out of earshot, as best we can." He cast cross looks at Timberfor and Lubomir. "Every time we wander near here, it's a mistake."

"We are not wandering," Lubomir noted calmly. "We came here on purpose, having voted on the matter. That said, you have a point. War and rumors of war have been uninteresting to us. But to save our peaceful place, perhaps we should leave it awhile."

"I don't want to get involved," Lutz announced.

"We may be involved already," Lubomir countered. "Perhaps it is time to act."

"Oh, listen to you," Luboslaw scoffed. "You're always right at the wrong time. When it was cowardly for us to come to the Vale, you couldn't drag us here fast enough. Now, when we're content where we are, you want us to go running off with some band of troublemakers."

"I am glad we agree," Lubomir replied. "On everything but timing, that is. Does any of you know the way down to the Canyon?" He looked around at Timberfor and the companions.

"Well, no," said Finn. "I for one don't know anything about the Canyon, much less how to climb down there."

"I know all about it," pronounced Cuhullin. "This is my island, after all. I know every inch of it!" Iskander and Finn looked dubious. "But they may have changed the path since last I was down there," he quickly added. "Blasted men!"

"Luboslaw," said Lubomir, "since you suggested it, what kind of fellows would we be if we did not see them down there?"

"I suggested nothing!"

"Did you not? Who was thrusting his finger toward the place not a moment ago?"

"I'll thrust my fist toward you in a moment, slyboots!" Luboslaw shouted, full of menace.

"That's better!" Lubomir agreed. "If we're headed down to all those warmongers, you'll want to keep that fighting spirit up!"

Luboslaw let out a roar and flung his arm across their chest at his brother's head. Lubomir parried with his arm and kicked out their left leg with the right. The Treble Giant collapsed in a heap, with much cursing to be heard, and Lutz pleading over it all, "I don't want to get involved!"

After more tussling, the brothers found themselves with both arms locked and their mighty legs linked at the knees. Luboslaw bellowed, the veins in his neck bulging. Lubomir smiled back with infuriating reasonableness.

"So if I understand you correctly," he said, as if he were asking for the sugar at teatime, "you would prefer not to go?" Luboslaw let out a roar of exasperation. "Very well," Lubomir added, "let us settle this in a civilized fashion."

"No more voting today!" Luboslaw growled.

"As you wish." Their legs and arms started to untangle, and their neck veins to unbulge. "Let us count fingers. You throw and I'll throw. Whoever we land on will be the one to decide."

"Do you think I am meeting you for the first time?" Luboslaw sneered. "You'll do a quick count of the fingers, then start counting from whichever one of us makes you land on yourself. You pulled this trick not two centuries back. Aha – you thought I wouldn't remember, but I do!" He sniffed. "All right, I'll play your game. But first, let's decide where we'll start counting. How's that, then? Not so clever now, eh?"

"We'll start on Lutz," Lubomir said.

"I don't want to get involved!"

"Well, you'll have to, for once!" Luboslaw shouted into his little brother's ear. "Very well, Lubomir, let's have it."

The two brothers brought their fists up and down several times, looking suspiciously at each other. Once they had built up a good head of steam, Lubomir counted them off.

"And a one . . . and a two . . . and a three . . . and throw!"

Luboslaw held out only his stubby thumb. From Lubomir's hand, not one single finger extended.

"What's that, then?" Luboslaw demanded.

"That is my throw," Lubomir replied. "Zero. Let's see then, what's yours? Ah, one. So let's count off here – starting, as agreed, from Lutz. One!" Lubomir pointed daintily at the center of Lutz's forehead. The middle Giant was stunned, and his eyes crossed a little as they fixed on the tip of the finger. "You choose, brother. Do we stay or do we go?"

"I don't want to get involved!"

Lubomir urged Lutz gently, "Say nothing, and you have chosen. Say something, and at least you have been heard."

"What kind of nonsense is that?" Luboslaw shouted. "You heard him! He doesn't want to get involved."

"Very well," Lutz said. "If I must choose, then I shall. I have made it clear to you for ages that I disapprove of making decisions. Before I decide, let me say to you both that I think you are very unkind to place me in this predicament. There – I've said it, now let's not dwell on it. I wish to go, to move on, to the Canyon or wherever. At the very least, perhaps I can find some place and time to be by myself without your constant quarreling."

"A wise and fair choice," Lubomir said. "I am sorry for putting you in that spot."

"Hang on!" Luboslaw protested. "None of this is fair! You planned it somehow that we would land on Lutz, and you knew what he would choose. And anyway, who ever said you could throw zero fingers? I might have thrown zero too, had I known that. Then where would you start counting, hey?"

Finn, Cuhullin, Iskander, and Timberfor packed up their things and followed the brothers to the edge of the drop-off. Then a polite cough caused all seven heads to look back.

"If I may," Clumberfoot said tentatively, "how long do you think you will be gone?"

"Who can say?" Finn answered honestly.

"War is an uncertain business," Cuhullin added, as he flexed his massive arm.

"All right, then," Clumberfoot replied. "I was just wondering."

"You should know, my friend," Lubomir advised, "that the way down to the Canyon is delicate and precarious."

"Yes, yes, I know," Clumberfoot agreed. "Now I remember. Yes, you're right. Never mind."

"If you'd like to come along," Finn offered, "you know we would be glad to have you."

"No, no, Lubomir is right. The path is much too difficult for me with these . . . disadvantages. I should stay here. You fellows go on ahead. I would only be in the way."

"I will look after you."

They turned to Timberfor. He beckoned to Clumberfoot, and the matter-of-fact look on his face and the tone of his voice made it clear that the tripping Giant would be part of the troupe.

"Thank you," said Clumberfoot softly, and he shuffled to join Timberfor at the edge of the drop-off.

"Well, that's settled then," Lubomir sighed. He pointed to a narrow gap between two jagged rocks that stuck straight out from the side of the cliff. "That is where we begin our descent, threading that needle. There are other paths into the Canyon, to be sure, but my brothers and I can promise you, this is the safest." Luboslaw nodded, and Lutz shook his head as though remembering a nasty accident. "I propose that we lead the way, and you follow one at a time."

"Certainly," said Finn, plotting that this time he would let Cuhullin go ahead of him. The Giant of Fyfe, meanwhile, huffed and steeled himself against yet another bout with unnerving heights.

With astounding dexterity, the three brothers worked their arms and legs in concert to clamber down the drop-off. Iskander was about to follow when Finn clasped his hand across the Cyclops's chest, nodding surreptitiously in the direction of Cuhullin. "After you, Ben."

"Right," snorted Cuhullin. Looking down, he let out a slow, breathy whistle at the sheerness and depth of the drop, which wound down through greenery and out of sight. Realizing that his reaction might be taken for timidity, he pounded his chest with his fists. "Here we go, then!" he growled eagerly. He crouched down, taking hold of the stones. Closing his eyes and whispering a few words of encouragement for his own hearing, he descended cautiously after the brothers.

"Now you, friend," Finn said to Iskander. The Cyclops smiled and followed Cuhullin, though without the drama. For a full-grown Giant, Iskander was uncommonly nimble. "Me now, I suppose," said Finn, seeing that Timberfor and Clumberfoot were engaged in some whispered discussion. He did not look down; rather, he turned and took hold of the rocks as he had seen the others do, and slowly lowered himself, trusting his feet to find purchase. Only when he was too far down to change his mind about preceding the final two Giants did he realize his error. He had learned when they departed from Baldemar's mountain that climbing down before Cuhullin was a bad idea. Now he was immediately beneath Clumberfoot and his enormous extremities. Nothing he had seen of Clumberfoot's dexterity inspired confidence, and just one of those huge feet would squash Finn in an instant. "Bother," he muttered, and it occurred to him what a silly last word that would be.

Long vines hung from the Vale down to the Canyon. Finn held himself in place with both feet and one hand and gave them a testing tug. Most of them pulled right out of the rock, and Cuhullin made his feelings known about the rain of green- ery landing on him. But when Finn found a secure vine, he was able to slide down fast, nearly catching up with Iskander.

The air grew cooler the lower they got. The Vale had seemed deep, but the Canyon was a stranger to the sun. Finn was sure he would see his breath, were it not so dark.

At last, as he slid down in the blackness, his feet landed flat on the Canyon floor. But he had no more than a moment to savor this obstacle overcome before he heard an ominous rustling above him.

"Look out below!"

Finn flung himself forward, straight into the chest of a sur- prised Cuhullin, who caught him in midair. Before the Giant of Fyfe could admonish him to watch where he was going, there was a mighty *clomp* behind him. Cuhullin set Finn down and together they squinted through the darkness. Clumberfoot was grabbing at the air for balance as his upper body swayed like an oak in a high wind, while his enormous feet stayed planted. When he had steadied his top half, he smiled.

"I told you you'd be all right," Timberfor called down. "Just lead with the feet – don't fight them!" The red-haired Giant landed next to Clumberfoot and clapped him on the shoulder.

"Yes, you were right," said Clumberfoot, very pleased. "Thank you."

The floor of the Canyon was littered with leaves. Sturdy trees that had no need of sunshine stood over the company, as in judgment.

"Are we all down?" Finn asked through the darkness. Before anyone could answer, they heard a shout.

"Stay where you are, please! We have you covered."

"Who's giving orders?" Cuhullin demanded.

"We've been expecting you," the voice replied. "In fact, you're late. Please be cooperative. We don't want to hurt you."

"I'd like to see you try!" No sooner had Cuhullin spoken than a large arrow came whistling through the darkness, just past the end of his nose, and lodged in a tree trunk beside him.

"Hold your fire!" ordered the voice.

"Sorry! Sorry!" another voice called back. "Lost my grip!"

"Don't kill them before we've had a chance to speak. Now, fellows, would you come along with us, please? We have much to discuss, and time is wasting."

"But who are you?" Finn asked. The two voices had come from opposite sides of the cluster of dark trees, and none of the companions had seen anything of these interlopers. The three brothers stepped out of the shadows into a rare bit of light. With them was a tall and sturdy Giant with long dark hair and a tangled beard. Leather straps slung over each shoulder crossed his bare chest. A massive broadsword was upon his back, and he spun two small daggers in his hands.

"I am Caddock," this new Giant announced.

"Caddock," Finn repeated. "I am Finn McCool. How do you do?"

"Immortal and that's the end of it," Caddock said, giving his daggers a flourish of a spin.

"Who shot that arrow at me?" Cuhullin demanded.

"If I were shooting at you," the second voice answered from the darkness, "you'd be dead already." Two new Giants presented themselves at the far side of the conversation. One was tall and slender, with tumbling blond hair and fine green clothes. In his hand was an ornate bow and on his face was a look of entitlement. Next to him was a squat Giant whose bearing was full of apology. He was hunched over, shabbily dressed, and his face was smeared with muck. He clutched a jeweled quiver filled with golden arrows, the obvious partner to the slender Giant's bow.

"Would I, now?" sneered Cuhullin, whirling on this new pair. "And who are you?"

"My name is Taliesin," said the tall Giant, giving his golden mane a shake. "And this is my associate, Swynborn. I am an archer, among many other things, and I am pleased to meet you." Cuhullin snarled in reply.

"Introductions accomplished," Caddock interjected, "please come along with us. The brothers can vouch for us. Let's go." He sheathed his daggers at his sides and slipped back among the stout, stern trees that passed for greenery in the Canyon, Taliesin and Swynborn on his heels. The other Giants looked to the brothers. Luboslaw and Lubomir nodded reassuringly, while Lutz pretended to study a leaf that hung close to his face.

Finn shrugged to the others. "If these fellows say so. They are the ones who brought us here, and following the locals beats standing here staring at each other."

With that, the Treble Giant led on, and the companions followed through the cold gloom of the Canyon.

There are places that are unwelcoming but, once entered into, will not let a person leave. Oonagh sensed that this was true of the lonely tower, so she was not unhappy that she had failed to arrive there. It was not like her to allow her mind to wander, to lose poise and balance, as she had done while inching along the ledge.

She turned over the words of the monstrous Giant in her mind. They frightened and sickened her, but his calm pledge to murder her Finn made her furious. How had he known to catch her then and there? And how could he see her plainly with no eyes? Surely he possessed some hidden sight. Did it tell him that he would be killing Finn?

The sun was up as high as it would go, but the day was stubbornly gray. Oonagh was alone in the courtyard and, as was becoming more common, she could hear mighty military maneuvers being conducted on the plain beyond the palace walls. She looked up to the tallest tower, where the blue banner bearing the golden hen flapped joylessly in the cold breeze. There was no sound from the dark, lonely tower, but always she felt she was being watched. The tower's sleeping malice felt like a dare – and Oonagh often accepted dares. She gave her head a shake of determination and strode across the courtyard to the tower's base. Though it might be a prison or a trap, she knew it held answers.

The high, pointed door was sturdy and thick, with a hefty lock. With one furtive glance to each side, Oonagh whipped the slim wooden pin from her hairband. She had never picked a lock in her life, but she was dexterous and determined. The pin fit easily into the top of the keyhole, and she poked it about, hoping for a lucky catch. The mechanism was so rusty that even the proper key might have had a job to pry the lock open. She brought her ear to the keyhole and jostled the pin with more precision. Flipping the end of the pin upward, she felt it grab a cranny. She flicked it quickly sideways and the door creaked open.

To her surprise, she found no stairway leading up to the top of the tower. Instead, a narrow row of steep stairs, nearly a ladder, wound down to some unlit cellar. What a curious construction, she thought. She was undaunted by the quiet darkness of the place – she had little fear of the unseen. Her deepest fears were for the fates of those she loved. She felt around the top step with her toe, and started down.

Something like moonlight trickled through the downward passage. This seemed strange, as it was daytime, albeit rather gloomy. Oonagh could not find the source of the faint light all around her, but she was grateful for it.

The staircase took a sharp turn and the passage opened into a grand underground hall. It was a circular room, abandoned but heavy with ancient importance. The arched ceiling was held high by a ring of ornate stone pillars. In the center of the floor, Oonagh could see the source of the light – a huge, elaborate seal. Though a coat of dust covered it, the majesty of the thing shone through. She knelt at the edge of the seal and brushed the dust off with her palm. At once it glowed a brilliant gold, so bright that she had to shield her eyes for a moment. Then she busied herself with both hands, wiping away the film of centuries.

When she was finished, the room seemed to be filled with sunlight, as if her dusting had moved it from night to day. She put her hands on her hips and scrutinized the magnificent seal. A dragon was in the center, its wings spread wide in majestic flight. Its ruby eyes flashed with fearless wisdom. In its claws was an unfurled scroll on which were written two words – "Numen Lumen." The dragon soared over two rounded diamonds and the seal was ringed with bold letters spelling words Oonagh knew and longed for – "Immortal until Proven Otherwise."

The seal's light flickered on the far wall of the chamber.

Oonagh noticed a small door – too small for any Giant – crafted out of wood that looked far newer than the rest of the room. The door was square across the top, unlike the pointed windows and thresholds throughout the rest of the palace. Thinking she would once again be obliged to pick a lock, she readied her trusty hairpin. But when she approached the door, she found that it was unlocked and slightly ajar. The crossbeam was barely higher than her head and the threshold was no wider than half her arm-span. She slipped her fingers into the narrow space between the door and its post, and pulled the door slowly open. The hinges gave an unmerciful creak that rebounded off the high walls of the chamber, and she stopped for a moment, in disbelief that her action had brought about such a ruckus.

As she turned back toward the door, adjusting her grip, she heard a whisper and felt a rush of wind past her ear. Whether it had come from behind her or from the far side of the door, she did not know. She whirled around, but the chamber was still empty. She wondered if Jack might be near, since unsettling, nasty wisps so often signaled his arrival. But there was something colder to this gust – like a grave but well-meant warning. A small voice, like the coo of a dove, sounded in her ear. She whipped around both ways, but again she saw no one.

One last time, Oonagh hooked her fingers inside the door. She gave it a single, mighty pull, and with a screech it opened wide. She staggered backward. As soon as she had regained her balance, she crept up to the threshold and peered inside.

The first sight that met her eyes was a face. Pale and beautiful, it was the visage of a woman lying on her back with her eyes closed. Oonagh was surprised that she did not jump with shock, but the woman's face was too entrancing and peaceful to be startling. Her arms were folded across her chest, and her delicate white hands held the perished remnants of a bouquet that likely had been quite lovely. Hair like a raven's wing curled down from her head and around her shoulders. She was draped in a white robe, with shining red slippers on her feet. Then something caught Oonagh's eye, and it gave her the shock she had earlier been spared. Peeking out from under the withered flowers and her queenly hair was a lovely, embroidered purple sash.

Oonagh's trembling fingers felt for the sash on her own shoulders. It was identical. As her alarm began to retreat, she noticed that the small tomb was much deeper than she had first thought. She could make out the slippered toes of another woman, very like the first. The two were laid out end to end upon engraved stone slabs. She crept into the tomb to take a closer look, and became aware that there were other women as well. All told, there were six beautiful corpses, three on either side of the room, laid out in identical vestments, including the purple sash. Two women were golden-haired, three had dark locks, and the one farthest away on Oonagh's right had spectacular red curls that shone with life even in this dark place of death. As Oonagh stepped cautiously toward her, one final horror met her eyes. At the end of the tomb, one last ornate slab stood. It was raised slightly and perpendicular to the others, standing between the two rows. It was vacant.

She turned, her hands groping for the light, and ran out into the chamber. Once out of the tomb, she flung herself against the screeching door, slamming it shut. Panting, she rested her head on her wrists.

"Lovely."

At the far end of the chamber, leaning against one of the mighty pillars, was Jack. His eyes were fixed upon the seal on the floor and in his left hand he twirled a pair of golden shears. "Such skill they showed, in their day," he added. "You see, this is the Great Seal of the Giants of old."

"It looks more like a dragon than a seal."

"Well said," Jack laughed, though a moment too late to have gotten the joke. "Your wit is a welcome guest in these old halls."

"Guest, am I? What an odd word, implying choice."

"You have chosen to wear that sash," he replied casually. "It occurs to me that I did not properly describe its significance. I believe you know that I serve at the pleasure of Artek himself."

"The Little King."

"Artek," Jack repeated by way of correction. "And I am proud to be a humble member of his household. This palace, in which we are pleased to have you, has been entrusted to me personally by him. The jeweled language on your sash speaks of my service to the King. You are not the first to wear such a garment, I admit, but by wearing it you are bonded to me."

"I see," she said. "And had you planned to share this information with me, before I found a roomful of dead women?"

"Tragically mortal," he sighed. He pushed off from the pillar and sauntered toward her, still twirling his shears. "You see, I am older than I look. But I was a boy once. I lived in peace with my mother. We had few possessions, though we had love.

"Then a Giant came to our village. At first, livestock was all that disappeared. Then, one by one, he stalked and devoured the people living round about. The strongest men of the village went out with torches to bring him down. None of them returned. Then the Giant came to our poor home, and I was the only one remaining to defend us. I had just become a tailor's apprentice, but my prospects were already in doubt because the tailor himself had been eaten by the Giant. I had my shears, and that was all. Out I went, trembling, to face the hulking thing that stood in our front path. He sneered at me and spoke roughly. 'You'll be no more than a mouthful,' he said, 'before I eat whoever else is inside.'

"I knew I had to win this impossible fight. When he tried to take hold of me with his huge hand, I leapt with all my strength. Before I knew it, I had jumped up and over him, to the other side. Terror helps us find new skills. Then, with my little shears, I struck. This seemed to make him mad, and I almost regretted it. He chased me all around, but he had no hope of catching me – I was too nimble and frightened. I would let him get close, and then I would strike again. He roared and cursed, but he began to slow as he bled. So much blood in him! But in time I got it all, and he lay dead on our path. It was not a fight I had wanted, but I learned from it that I have a duty to protect those smaller creatures who cannot defend themselves."

"Splendid," said Oonagh. "But how does that begin to answer my question?"

"I have fought many Giants, and I have never lost. I do not age or grow ill, either. For better or for worse, I am without death – at least, thus far. Time and the Great have no antidote for me. But I am powerless against love, and the need for it. I loved others before I saw you, I confess openly, now that you have seen the truth. I loved each of them, in their day. Now there is you, and there is nothing so precious in my eyes."

"I understand," Oonagh answered. "You would make me a queen, giving me every treasure but freedom."

"You have freedom. You have had it all along, more than you enjoyed in serfdom on your ogre's hill. I have given you . . ." He snorted with impatience. "My love, I would prefer that you look at me when I am speaking."

"And I would prefer that you not speak at all," she answered calmly, not lifting her gaze.

"There it is. You treat me in a way that would be forbidden to anyone else. Such freedom!"

"You confuse power with authority, and you have always done so, I suspect."

"Power is character. I found mine when I was called upon to defend my home. It seems so long ago now, and I wonder at times what became of that frightened boy. Fear and I have grown estranged." He chuckled at himself. "Oh, such dull talk. I know I am awkward and demanding and short of temper, but my traits have served these islands well."

"So you make virtues of your vices," observed Oonagh. "But you can't feel joy. True joy is a serious thing, and you are no serious fellow."

"Was your Finn serious? Is my fatal flaw that I don't suck my thumb? Yes, I know all about his inherited wisdom and childlike ways. As for me, I am imperfect but I try. Can your Finn say the same? He strove for no more than another fistful of food. I may fail, but not for lack of nobility. And when I succeed, as I intend, the ages to come will be amazed."

"Succeed?" she scoffed. "At what? Destroying everything grander than you are? You are my enemy, and I am yours, so send me to join these departed women. Take my life, along with my love and freedom." She ripped the purple sash from her shoulders and dashed it to the floor. It landed on the ruby eyes of the golden seal's dragon. Instantly, it burst into a spout of flame and was gone.

Jack stopped spinning his shears, and looked at her hard. At last he spoke.

"So be it."

"Here they are!"

Finn and the others stepped out into a large clearing of trees in the middle of the Canyon. Before them, seven Giants in battle gear sat in a circle around a low fire. At opposite sides of the ring, two of the Giants sat on stones a little higher than the others. One was old, with a long gray beard and squinting, skeptical eyes. The other was not young, but he appeared the very picture of youth in comparison to the first. He had flowing, golden hair, and wide, lively blue eyes. He wore a green tunic and red cape, and it was he who announced the arrival of the companions to the circle. "We were beginning to think you would never come."

Caddock strode in among the seated Giants and took what appeared to be his set place in the circle. Taliesin did the same, but filthy Swynborn did not take a seat of his own; he stood respectfully behind the archer Giant, his grimy hands clasped formally across his waist. The other Giants were unfamiliar to Finn. Their lean and leathery faces wore faraway looks. He wondered if he ought to wave or introduce himself, but the gray Giant spoke up.

"You do not have the floor," he said humorlessly to his younger counterpart, "so it is given to me to welcome our new arrivals. Cuhullin, of course, is known to all of us." The Giant of Fyfe was surprised and pleased to hear this. In all the running and fighting and following of directions, his appetite for recognition had gone untended. The Giants in the circle nodded to him with respect. Cuhullin couldn't remember any of them. His memory for grudges was unlimited; for faces, less so. "And Lubomir, Luboslaw, and Lutz we know also. You are well met, sirs." The brothers nodded to the assembly one at a time. "And also, of course, little Finn McCool. I would ask that those of you unknown to us state your names clearly."

"I am Iskander, friend of Finn," the Cyclops said.

"Welcome, friend of Finn," the golden-haired Giant replied.

"Again," sighed the gray Giant, "I must remind you of protocol. You will have ample time for greetings when the floor is yours. Next, please?"

"My name is Clumberfoot," the tripping Giant offered meekly. "I cannot claim any friends, but I am pleased to meet you all." He looked around, hoping to find someplace to rest his shy gaze.

"And you?" the gray Giant prodded Timberfor, who kept his arms folded and his eyes to the ground. "Please?"

"Who needs to know?"

"Now look," the gray Giant said firmly, "the meeting has already been disrupted, and protocol requires an introduction."

"You say first then, hey?" Timberfor answered sharply.

"That . . . that is not the way of it!" the gray Giant sputtered.

"I am Ronan," the golden-haired Giant cut in cheerfully. "We are pleased to meet you. I see you have met Caddock, Taliesin, and Swynborn already. May I also present my brothers in arms, Trebiggen, Killorgin, Korrigan, Onslow, and Quint." They were rough characters with muddied faces and fierce weapons, and to look at them one would have thought they had never heard a delicate voice in their lives. Trebiggen commanded the most immediate attention because he was simply enormous. Although he was seated at the far side of the fire, his deep green eyes were higher than Finn's. His bare shoulders balled out from under his leather vest, and the width of him was almost enough for two of the others.

Killorgin and Korrigan sat next to one another, muttering private musings, Korrigan leaning his hand on a long green spear, and Killorgin fingering the handle of a large cask. Onslow and Quint were a matched pair with cropped

auburn hair and dark, deliberate eyes. "And this," Ronan
added, lifting his palm toward the older Giant opposite him,
"is the venerable Thumos." The gray Giant seemed torn. He
gave a sharp polite nod, though his expression made it clear
that he was unhappy about it. "If you do not wish to tell us
your name," Ronan went on, "that's quite all right. You
come as a friend of friends, and that is good enough. When
you choose to tell us, we'll be pleased to hear it."

"Thank you," said Timberfor, looking Ronan squarely
in the eye. The golden Giant smiled and turned to Finn and
the others.

"Better late than never, you fellows," he chuckled. "We
had half a mind to go along and get you."

"Late?" wondered Finn. "That's the second time you said
you were expecting us. How did you know we were coming?"

Ronan laughed. "At what point do you suppose you were
not being watched?"

"By who? How?"

"Little Finn McCool," Thumos interrupted wearily, "it is
not for you to question. But since my young counterpart has
seized the floor, I will yield to him the remainder of my time."
He waved his hand toward Ronan as though making a half-
hearted effort to bat a fly. Then he folded his arms and looked
away, shaking his head and moving his lips.

There was no way for Finn to know, and Cuhullin
could not remember, but Ronan and Thumos were two of
Gogmagog's most celebrated generals in Alba. As with all
Giants, no one knew quite how old they were, but Thumos
had opted for the role of elder statesman and Ronan was all
too happy to yield it to him. They had played their parts for
centuries, and their bodies told the tale – one graying and
slow, the other youthful and energetic.

Thumos was a lover of rules. For him, it was not enough

that anything should simply be permitted – it had to be either mandatory or forbidden. He was forever huffing about this protocol or that, and while the others attempted to show him suitable deference, his fussing was often a source of mirth. But nobody could argue with the results of his methods. For ages Giants had fought in disorganized bands without ranks or columns, until Thumos introduced order to their battle plans. But as the number of fighting Giants had dwindled, he had not adjusted his style of command. He continued to insist upon the fine points of military decorum, directing invisible armies, talking of flanks and phalanxes, even when his forces numbered no more than four or five fellows.

Ronan was rarely without a smile, but when his face did turn dark, those around him knew he meant business. He inspired and enlivened his fellow Giants, and his companions adored him for his good humor and strength of heart. He welcomed Finn and the others with genuine warmth, and it seemed to the half-Great that he was the distillation of all that was good and noble about their kind. "Sit you down, you new fellows," he invited them, "and let us help bring you up to speed."

Finn and the rest cautiously found places next to the battle-hardened Giants in the circle. Trebiggen was the most welcoming of the bunch, though he did not smile – he nodded steadily as they made themselves comfortable, looking each one in the eye. Clumberfoot was slow to approach the group at first, but after closing his eyes and having a little talk with himself, he shuffled toward the fire. Timberfor was last to come along. He stood at a distance with his arms folded until his eye returned to Ronan, who gave him a friendly look and waved for him to join the group.

"Thanks, friends," Finn offered around, on behalf of the new arrivals.

Ronan cleared his throat. "Please allow me to begin by expressing my admiration for one of your group in particular." He looked at Iskander. "I am sorry, sir, for your misery at Knockmany. You fought with bravery that inspires all of us, and these are folks who know a thing or two about courage! You should never have been left so outnumbered, yet you tried to the last against an impossible foe. Well done, Cyclops, and so say all of us!" The other Giants cheered. Trebiggen slapped Iskander on the back with a force that made him lurch forward and nearly jostled his jeweled eye from its socket.

"Thank you," he said softly.

"You did not know then, nor, I expect, do you know even now, just who and what you were matched against. Will you hear it?"

"I will," answered the Cyclops.

"There were wings in the air," Ronan said. "Did you see them? They were the wings of the red dragon, and I know you have heard something of him by now. He burned your hill, Finn the half-Great, and it is only by the Dagda's grace that you were not there to be destroyed. You saw something of the enemy's machines. They are diabolical and fierce. And men, of course, came to kill you. They never rush at anything so swiftly as they do at murder. But you stood strong before them, and that is an inspiration to us all. I think you know that courage may be needed soon again."

"Excuse me," Clumberfoot interjected, "but may I ask what you're talking about? I did not know about any of this when I met up with these fellows, and none of it sounds very nice. Sorry to interrupt, but this all sounds fairly important."

"We here in this Canyon," Ronan replied, "are the last who remain to defend our islands. Years ago, we fought huge foes to make these lands free. Now our enemy is more sinister, and we are far fewer. You did not know anything of this war, you say, and I believe you. Whether in the Vale, or beneath the sea, or asleep upon their hills, our kind have turned away from what we were. I wager you are a good fellow, Clumberfoot, and I am sorry to tell you that there are those who hate you."

"I see." Clumberfoot wrinkled his brow.

"May I ask one thing?" Iskander cut in. "In the battle, there was a fellow I have thought of many times since. He was not large – about the size of our Finn, no offense to my friend – but he was strong as the hills. What do you know of him?"

"You are speaking of Gawain," answered Ronan. "He is the strongest fellow on two legs, and I don't envy you tangling with him. He owes his life to Jack in the Green and he will do anything the tailor asks. Gawain's strength is born of loyalty. There is no feat he cannot accomplish to fulfill an oath. His tale is not a happy one, and it would have been over long ago but for Jack. Though he doesn't hate us, we must consider him our enemy. It's a pity, as I expect there's some good in him."

"Well," mused the Cyclops, "I'm with you on his strength. But I got no sense of good from him. No doubt you're more sensitive than I so you'd see him more clearly."

Ronan laughed at this. "I don't know how sensitive some would call me, but I do sense there is more to Gawain than meets the eye. But he isn't our chief concern. There is a wizard, too. He built the machines that hewed down your friends, and he has done more that you don't know about. He is as old as we are, and the highest counselor to the Little King. Marland is his name. He and Jack are of one mind, though he does not answer to the tailor. I'd warn you to beware of him, but no one knows how he comes and goes. He could be in the midst of us in an instant, so no warning from me would do any good."

"What of this Jack himself?" Iskander wondered.

"Ah, there's the onion," sighed Ronan. "He is swift and vicious, and there is no dealing with him. Jack in the Green is the best fighter in these isles. His weakness is that he knows it. That's not much of a weakness, I know, but at least it is something. He led a sad young life, but what he has made of it since erases all pity. A bosom friend to the son of the King, he grew to be a perfect murderer. Killing has made him rich and won him favor. The Little King even gave him Treryn to kick up his heels in."

"Such a collection of miseries," Iskander said. "Wizards and machines and tailors with phantom speed. How do we begin to fight such foes?"

"With the keen weapon of courage," Ronan replied. "With courage, we can't fail."

"Fail at what?" Finn blurted. Realizing that all eyes were upon him, the half-Great wished he could reel his words back in. "Sorry, but I must ask. Ronan, what are we to *do* – besides be brave? And why did such great and powerful fellows, with strength and riches and conquests and wisdom, come to destroy my lovely hill in Eire?"

"Our kind can win any quarrel, if we band together as the brothers we are," said Ronan. "We have strength we have forgotten, and I pity our foes when we remember. As to why our enemies came to your sweet corner of the world, you have ancient foes, Finn McCool, and they have not forgotten you. The Frost Giants stir even now in Albion. Balar of the Evil Eye leads them, in the company of his savage brother, Bergelmir. They are in league with Jack in the Green, and the price they have been promised is your head."

"Why don't they just come and get it, then?" Finn asked. "Who needs an army and machines to put an end to little me?"

"Your name is more respected than you know," Ronan said. "You are a hero to some, and the Fomorians wish to make no mistake."

Finn sighed. "Since before I was born, foes have over-estimated me. Things would have been much easier all round if they had known how small I truly am. But please, help us understand what you are planning. Strong as you say we are, we don't make much of an army. Are we waiting for reinforcements?"

"If reinforcements come, they will not be turned away. But don't expect them. It's just us, for now. Don't fret, though – we're prepared."

"Prepared? For what?"

"We are prepared for the worst," Thumos interjected. "Though it may be worse than that."

"Worse, indeed!" Finn lamented. "There are armies and Frost Giants and every vicious thing aligned against the few of us!"

"But . . . ," Clumberfoot began.

"But what?" Thumos snapped. Clumberfoot did not continue. "Go on, then. You've spoken up without having the floor, so you may as well finish. *But what?*"

"But are our enemies not planning too?"

"Well, of course they are!" Thumos answered hotly. "We must always, always keep in mind that no matter how sound our battle plan may be, our enemies have a vote as to whether it succeeds."

"Is our battle plan sound?" Clumberfoot was trying to sound brave. "What is our battle plan, anyway?"

"Do you all just talk whenever you wish?" Thumos sighed, throwing up his hands. "We will tell you the battle plan when you are ready to hear it. Clear enough?"

"Sorry," Clumberfoot mumbled into his chest.

Thumos looked around the circle to make certain he had the company's full attention. "Let us discuss our options. Charging headlong on high words, hoping that all will be well, is no battle plan. We must take whatever time we need, and survey the ground. We all yearn for victory, but it will not do to be brave and dead. The foe have built machines. They have a dragon, we expect. Frost Giants lurk among their ranks. We have to take all these one at a time. I agree that time is not our ally – you see? I am not so unyielding. But we mustn't rush. Hasten slowly, I say."

Thumos's words had struck home. Even Lubomir and Luboslaw turned their faces toward each other – over the head of Lutz, who was gazing down at their shoes, trying not to be involved – with looks of approval.

"As you see," Thumos continued, looking squarely at Ronan, "prudence is palatable to our brothers. Will you be reasonable at last?"

Ronan smiled. "Yes, you are winning, but I am about to speak. There is not a coward in this company, but you fellows have seen enough of war to know what happens to plans once the battle is joined. Analyzing every angle is a recipe for loss and wastes time. Our beloved Thumos says himself that we have already prepared for the worst, and for that we owe him thanks. His talent for order is a gift to us all. But if we prepare up to the moment when the enemy is on our doorstep, the only useful plan then will be for retreat. Is that our way?

"Trebiggen, I remember you leading us through that Fomorian legion at the battle of the Nairn – you are as fearless as you are strong. And Caddock, who can stand against you in close fighting? Taliesin, our archer, and Swynborn, his noble companion. Killorgin, you are a fearsome sight in battle, and Korrigan, you are the master of the spear. Onslow and Quint, you are thinking warriors, creative and deadly. Now we are joined by the mighty Cuhullin! Could we ask for a greater reinforcement? And with him are the brothers, with the power of three in one. Clumberfoot, you are a pure fellow and we are grateful to have you. Your nameless friend has the look of a hero in his eye. Iskander has proven his bravery, defending Knockmany against all odds. And not least is Finn McCool, slayer of the dreaded Ymir with a single stroke! I almost pity our enemies!" He grinned at each face by the fire, and every Giant sat a little taller on hearing himself named – all except Thumos.

"You flatter us, Ronan," the gray Giant said ungraciously. "I am not saying you do not have our interests at heart. But you tickle these fellows with compliments to get your way. We have planned for disaster, yes, but not yet for victory. I mean to introduce a notion of defensive flanking. It may require some days of drilling, but I would rather do things right than in a hurry."

"May we all live so long." While the generals had been talking, Killorgin had taken many surreptitious sips from the cask he was holding. Drink rendered him wordy. "Ronan gives us hope, and you dash it with your dithering. That is always the thing with you!" Korrigan gave the overly refreshed fellow a tap on the shoulder to quiet him down, but Killorgin was not done. "Every plan but your own seems absurd to you. But you hear none of us complaining! I believe in our victory. I believe it because it is absurd." Killorgin's manner went abruptly from angry to lugubrious. "You may not believe," he sobbed, "but I do!"

"Oh, that's enough!" Taliesin rose. "Whenever you lot figure out when we are going to fight and how, come and find me!" He took up his bow and stormed away, shaking his head and muttering. Swynborn grabbed the quiver of arrows Taliesin had left at his place and scurried along behind him.

"They are ready now, Thumos," Ronan said gently. "Can you not see that? You can plan and drill us into the ground, but you can't make more of us. We have all the strategy in the world, if our hearts are strong!"

As Thumos and Ronan continued their quarrel, Finn rose quietly from his spot by the fire and left the circle, and walked alone into the dark woods. Behind him, he could hear the discussion going on and on. All this arguing did not bode well for the battlefield. But his despondent thoughts were interrupted by the whizzing of weaponry somewhere in the thick forest. He followed the noise until the trees parted to reveal a clearing lit all around by torches. To his far right were bales of straw, bundled and stacked to form a wall, here and there dotted with circles of red paint. To his left he saw Taliesin steadying his bow to release an arrow, and Swynborn behind him. The arrow went buzzing through the clearing and lodged in a more or less random spot of the wall.

"Jolly good shot!" Swynborn called, and ran to the bales of straw. He took a good look at the lodged arrow and let out a low whistle of admiration. Then he stooped and took a brush from a small pail of red paint, and drew a bull's eye around the arrow. "Will you have a look at that? Glorious shot!" He plucked the arrow from the wall and trotted it back to Taliesin.

"Thank you," the archer said serenely, accepting the arrow.

"And in such dim light, too! Really something!" Finn began to back away from this peculiar scene, but he stepped on a twig. Taliesin squinted into the gloom but Swynborn's eyes found the half-Great right away. "Have a few shots on your own," he urged the archer, "and I'll be straight back to collect them for you." He trotted toward Finn.

"Sorry to interrupt," Finn said.

"Oh, not at all, not at all. We were fixing for a break soon anyhow. Perfect timing, really."

"All the same, I should be moving on and leave you to your . . . practicing."

"Suit yourself," the Giant agreed, walking a little way with Finn back into the forest. "You may have noticed," he went on, placing his unwashed arm across Finn's shoulders, "that our approach is somewhat unusual."

"I am not an archer," Finn said, "so I don't know what is usual and what is not." This was honest enough, though one did not need to be a deadeye wand-splitter to see that painting the target around the arrow was not normal.

"Good, good," Swynborn answered cheerfully. "That said, the time comes to all of us when we can no longer do the things we once could. Do you know what I mean?"

"Absolutely," said Finn, hoping to end the conversation as quickly as possible, since Swynborn's arm was heavy on his shoulders and the Giant smelled rather fiercely.

"When we see such a time come for a friend, we have choices to make. Now, I take the view that if a Giant – or half a Giant, excuse me – feels good about himself, well then, he can accomplish anything. But if he begins to fuss about his limitations, he will go precisely nowhere. Take as an example our Taliesin there. For ages, he was the greatest archer of our kind. But over the centuries his eyesight has begun to fade. This is not common knowledge, I should add – not even to him. I alone – and now you, I suppose – have become aware of it. So what am I, his friend, to do? Fortify his confidence, I say!"

"So you deceive him, making him believe he can do what he cannot?"

Swynborn nodded happily. "What are friends for?"

"Right," said Finn thoughtfully. "Good enough. I'll be off and leave you to it." He took a few quick steps forward, hoping Swynborn's filthy arm would fall from his shoulders, but the Giant held firm.

"Before you go," Swynborn added, "may I impress one thing upon you? My dear friend's limitations are not known to others. I fear it would hurt him to hear that he has poor eyesight. Could I ask you, please, to keep this between us?"

"I will say nothing."

"Good fellow." Swynborn smiled, at last dropping his arm. "See you after a bit, Finn McCool." With that, the unwashed Great One trotted back toward Taliesin.

As Finn walked on, the ground beneath his feet sloped steadily downward, and he was surprised that the Canyon cut deeper still. The air was dark and cool, with the smell of mist all around. He could hear running water up ahead. He followed the sound, his ears being of more use than his eyes in this shadowy place, until the land dropped away into a chasm. He stopped just in time, hearing pebbles tumble down before his toes. He peered into the pit, imagining that this must be the lowest place on Earth that was still above the sea. The sound of water was louder now, and his eyes adjusted to see the glint of a waterfall catching and reflecting what dim light it could as it cascaded into the abyss.

Lowering himself to the ground, Finn got set to shimmy down into the pit. It was a dirty climb, with little in the way of root or branch to cling to, obliging him to dig his fingers deep into the clammy earth.

Once at the bottom, Finn could see a dark, swirling pool at his feet. He knelt down, cupped his hand to the water, and took a drink. A chill shot through him, as though the water flowed from the deepest and coldest cavern of the world. He gasped as the heat fled from his chest, down through his toes, and right out of him. He rolled over onto his back, took a deep breath, and collected his thoughts.

The waterfall towered, magnificent above him. It started from a single trickle over a rock higher than the point of his descent, and joined other tumbling streams to form a wall of white foam that crashed into the dark pool. The sight and sound of it was entrancing, and it held Finn captivated.

Through the falling water, Finn saw a flicker of light – at least, he thought he did. He got to his knees, rubbed his eyes with his fists, and squinted into the falls. Enough moments passed that he began to feel his senses were playing tricks on him, and then the flicker came again. It was a golden glimmer, far behind the water, and it grew from a series of flashes to a sustained glow. From there the light spread long and wide, until the whole cataract was illuminated. This seemed odd to Finn, though not so odd as to cause alarm – until the huge eyes appeared.

They peered out from high in the waterfall. They blinked but did not focus on the half-Great right away. It occurred briefly to Finn that this might be a good time to make a break for it, but before he could act, the eyes had him. They held him transfixed as they became clearer through the mist of the falls. Slowly a face joined them, then a mighty armored frame and a mane of golden hair – all this no more than an image of golden light shining through the water.

Finn was more perplexed than ever. It was as though he were looking up to a mirror image of himself, though twice his size, and something in the back of his mind told him he had experienced this before. He raised his hand slowly, to see if the reflection would do the same. No movement came

from the glowing image except a slight furrowing of the eyebrows. Finn snatched his hand down again.

The immense fellow studied Finn's every aspect. After a
good long look, he spoke. "Where is the red sword I left for
you?" The specter's eyes were set on the black blade slung
from Finn's hip.

The half-Great was stunned. He opened and closed his
mouth several times before any words emerged. "I broke it,"
he answered at last.

"You broke it? Have you any idea through how many centuries and battles I wore that weapon? And you break it in a
single campaign?"

"I – I didn't mean to."

"What use is it to say that?"

"Sorry," said Finn. "I wasn't thinking of the use, I was just
thinking of something to say. Are you – are you Cuhail?"
Suddenly he remembered the statue in the hall of Tara so
many centuries before.

"I was," the apparition said firmly. "And your mother
named you Demne."

"She did," the half-Great said softly. "Though I never
knew her – or you. Nowadays, everyone calls me Finn."

"I know it," said Cuhail, allowing a little smile to find its
way across his face.

"What are you doing here? How did we both come to be
in this place at once?"

"Now, that I do not know. But I have learned many
things since I breathed my last, and I know all things are one.
I know the place where I am and the place where you think
you are, but no reason why we should be here together. Tell
me, Finn mac Cuhail, why are you not among the heroes?"

"Those fellows up there?" Finn pointed to the ledge from
which he had descended. "Heroes? I was with them earlier.

They're sure proud of themselves. Though I suppose they were your comrades, so I shouldn't speak badly about them."

"Of course they're proud," Cuhail answered. "They're heroes. What about you, my son? Why have you come so far from your home, and why do I find you here alone?"

"I'm alone because I wish it. I am no company for heroes. I never have been."

"You are too hard on yourself," Cuhail said thoughtfully. "You did kill the monster who killed me."

"I killed one villain, yes, but that is all I can claim. You won many wars before you were brought down."

"It is the same war."

"And anyway, I'm not interested in war. My enemies took my love and I'm raging to get her back. That is all I know and all I wish to know!"

"Ah, they did much the same with me," said the Giant. "I knew it was a trap – even a brute like me is not utterly out-foxed by Fomorian slobberers – but what choice did I have? We are forever chasing after our women, and that is always, always the right thing to do." He sighed. "You want your peaceful corner, but who gave it to you? Ages before you – before me, even – there were those who traded their peace-ful corners for yours. You had your green and happy hill, and you may someday have it again. That is more than some ever see. You are raging after your love, and I hope that you find her. But do not disdain to do the good of the world while you chase down your dream."

A movement on the ridge high above caught Finn's attention. He put his hand to the hilt of his sword. There was nothing to see but shadows and the silhouettes of large boughs. Just as he convinced himself it was his imagination, he spotted a pair of eyes glinting greenly down upon him.

"Who is that?" he shouted. The eyes disappeared. Finn turned back to the falls only to find that he was alone. "Father?" he called into the tumbling water, but his voice sounded ridiculous.

It was a hard moment. Had he known he would see Cuhail in this place, he would have made a list of questions to ask. But now he was by himself again, and it had all happened so abruptly that he wondered if his father had been there at all.

Once again, Finn thought something was moving on the ridge. Whoever this was, Finn blamed him for cutting short his conversation with Cuhail, and he scrambled back up to give chase. When he reached the top, however, he found that he could not remember his way. He veered through the tall, dark trees, trying to retrace his steps back to the circle. Just as the panic of being lost began to seize him, he fell into the clearing where Taliesin and his friend had been practicing. They were gone. Finn ran around the circle, trying to remember the way to the heroes' fire.

"A herald! A herald!"

This was a voice Finn had not heard before, and he beetled after it through the dark woods. Not more than a hundred paces away, he found the meeting circle, right where he had left it. The Giants were still assembled, but a new one was with them, hunched over with his hands on his knees, struggling to catch his breath. He was trim and tall and he wore a green cap with one red feather shooting back on either side. On his feet were light leather moccasins tied tightly from his ankles up to his knees. His face was lean, with a pointed chin and nose that looked fashioned to split the wind. Curly brown hair tumbled from beneath his cap. He gave a few short coughs as he summoned his air.

"Who is this?" said Finn.

"He is Sprydon," Ronan answered, "and he is the finest of scouts." The golden Giant leaned toward the gasping fellow. "Who is it you saw, my friend?"

"A herald, I say," Sprydon choked, "and he is heading here now under a flag of truce."

"Here?" Thumos sounded indignant. "How does he know we're in the Canyon?"

"However he knows, he knows," Sprydon replied. "He'll be here any moment. He's fast – I barely beat him!"

Just then a figure stepped out of the shadows and into the midst of the Giants. Though he was alone and unarmed, and far smaller than the smallest of the Great Ones assembled, a cautious silence fell over the whole group. Iskander recognized the newcomer right away. It was Gawain.

"I come with a message," the little fellow said slowly and clearly, not troubling to look any of the Giants in the eye. "Jack in the Green means no harm to any of you, and he wishes there to be no violent quarrel."

"Well, that's a first!" Killorgin blurted. There was a grumble of agreement from the others.

Gawain waited patiently for the commentary to subside before continuing. "He offers you war or dice."

"What devilry is that?" Thumos shouted.

"One toss," Gawain went on, "with the winner to take the spoils."

"And what do we get if we win, hey?" Korrigan demanded.

"Never mind that," Thumos corrected. "What would your Jack want if we lost?"

Gawain replied as though reading regulations from a parchment. "If you win, Jack will leave Treryn, as you call it, taking his army and weapons with him. If you lose, however, he merely asks that you do the same – remove yourselves from these islands, never to return."

"Preposterous!" Thumos shouted. "Insulting and preposterous! Impossible, insulting, preposterous, and dishonorable!"

"Hang on," Ronan interjected. "Is that the same thing, Gawain? If we win, Jack leaves a home that was never his. If he wins, we are to leave the lands that were ours before he and his kind came to be. How is that a fair deal?"

Before the little Giant could answer, Killorgin shouted into his ear, "How does it feel to betray your own kind?"

Gawain closed his eyes a moment before looking straight at Ronan. "Fair or not, it is the deal Jack is offering." He turned and observed the circle. When his eyes fell on Finn, he stopped. The two regarded one another in silence, and it seemed to Finn that Gawain knew something he did not. He could not recall meeting this fellow before, but the somber, knowing look on Gawain's face stirred the half-Great's curiosity.

"Out of the question," Thumos thundered. "Gawain, go back to your master and tell him honor prevents us from doing what he asks. No Giant here shall risk his home and pride on a game of pitch-and-toss!"

"Hang on!" Finn jumped in. "Who's to say it can't be done? Would you rather die than take a chance at having what you want in a moment?" Thumos turned to him in outrage. Finn added, "War or dice seems a fair choice to a fellow who wants to live, does it not?"

"To a fellow who wants to live without pride," Thumos answered through gritted teeth, "certainly."

"Fine!" Finn retorted. "Go get stabbed through the head and keep your honor. Will that make you happy? Good!" Finn and Thumos turned their backs to one another, their arms folded, and the whole company stayed a moment in silence.

"Is that your answer, then?" Gawain asked at last.

Ronan looked back and forth between the quarrelers, then round the grim faces of the group, before answering. "I am afraid so."

"Very well," said Gawain. "It will be war."

Thunder on the Plain

reen mountains in autumn bow down before
    the moon,
Shall we look for the stars to fall any time
    soon?
Not in the springtime nor in the deep winter's chill,
Fade away, fade away, but return when you will,
Forever and our moment are hewn.

Oonagh sang to the graying sky through the narrow window
of the lonely tower. The chill air nipped her fingers on the
poor harp she had found in the corner of her cloister.

He will not come again till the hills are reborn.
Can we see the heavens through a sky that is torn?
Not a voice heard to rage at the death of the light,
Die we all, for now the sun is caught in the night,
Yet hope is summoned up with the horn.

My love, come back to me from the place where
you are,
Heart of mine says where you've got to is quite too
far,
Is the spring that we knew never to be again?
Almost there, our hope was full and lovely and
then,
Broken just within sight of the star.

Her words drifted down from the high window and danced across the plain beyond the palace. There, men and beasts made ready with machines and weapons.

Jack had dragged her up into this small room in the lonely tower. He had not killed her, as she had expected, so she presumed she still had some use in his plans. But she was dizzy with grief as she sang, and the gray walls of her tiny prison appealed to her as the very anteroom of death.

It was a mighty army in ill humor that carried out maneuvers below. The loveliness of Oonagh's voice could not penetrate the clang and clamor that consumed all other sound. Towering machines rumbled into place while captains shouted instructions. Drums were beaten, and beasts dragging armaments moaned in complaint. So many men filled the field that little green could be seen. Huge, hooded Giants moved among the mortals with heavy weapons. All in all, the gathering was a complement of destruction.

Ronan whistled for his riding beast. Finn and the Giants heard a rumble and braced themselves for whatever was about to arrive. The snapping of twigs and boughs came closer and closer as the beast's strides rattled every tooth in the Canyon.

When the last of the dark tree trunks was pushed out of the way, a massive gray creature galloped into the Giants' midst. He was many times the size of the largest pig anyone had ever heard of, though his features were perceptibly porcine. The snout was the shape of a shovel. The ridge of his back was as high as Cuhullin and the top of his head was half that height again. Four legs like tree stumps surrounded an impossibly large belly. A small, curly tail snuck out from his back end, mocking the heft of the rest of him. His eyes were deep and dark, kindly yet vacant. He blinked at the assembly before finding Ronan. He plodded over to the golden Giant, dipped his huge head, and nuzzled against his shoulder.

"What manner of creature is this?" asked Clumberfoot.

"This," Ronan replied, stroking the creature's shovel-snout, "is the River Horse. He and I have been friends for many adventures, and I would not think of going to war without him."

"Our enemies do not decide when we go to war," thundered Thumos. But Ronan paid no mind to the gray Giant as he swung his leg up and, with a flourish, leapt onto the River Horse's back.

"My friends," he proclaimed, "it is time to remind the world who we are!" His regal bearing on the River Horse was a sight to behold: flowing cloak, glowing mane, and a smile that suggested that all things were possible. "Are you ready to find our enemy and show him what we are made of? Will you follow me to victory or brave death, in the footsteps of those who went before us?"

"Let us at them!" shouted Killorgin. "Just let us at them!"

"That is the spirit of my Great friends!" Ronan cried. "Forward to triumph and to glory!" He spurred the River

Horse and the portly beast thumped off through the dark woods. The others took up their weapons and supplies and, with rousing cheers and many slaps on backs, they followed. Thumos was last; he stood at the edge of the clearing, arms folded. When all the Canyon's regulars had gone after Ronan, the gray Giant shook his head and stomped after them.

Finn and the newcomers did not follow right away. Though he was never far from a fighting mood, Cuhullin had been taken by surprise at the speed with which the heroes stormed off to war. The Treble Giant was also at a loss. Timberfor and Clumberfoot stood side by side in silence, and Iskander shrugged and smiled at Finn.

"So that's it," Clumberfoot mumbled at last. He shuffled toward the center of the clearing, and with a few taps of his enormous feet he snuffed out the fire. "Shall we be off as well, then?"

"They'll get half a league before they realize we're not with them," Lubomir guessed. "All the same, I suppose we came here for a fight."

"I did not vote to come here," Luboslaw muttered.

"Well," sighed Finn, "they are the best chance we've got. Coming, lads?" He waved to the others and set off through the dark woods. The eagerness of the heroes had carved a path that was not hard to follow. Iskander and Cuhullin trailed Finn at once, followed by the Treble Giant. Timberfor and Clumberfoot brought up the rear.

Before long, Finn and the companions were again within hearing of the heroes' whoops and battle cries. So a small troop of Giants, armed with courage and slogans, set out to face a mighty army of men, machines, and goodness knew what else.

After a fair walk, Finn saw one of the heroes not far ahead. The straggler was moving slowly, shaking his head as he went. When the half-Great and his companions came nearer, they could see that it was Thumos, marching without enthusiasm.

"Fools, bloody fools," the gray Giant muttered. As Finn approached, Thumos turned to him. "I know we disagreed earlier, but not by much. Honor is too dear a thing to be chanced on a toss of dice. Besides, Jack in the Green is a notorious cheater. Did you know that? But even though we could not accept his dare, that does not mean we ought to march straight into defeat!"

"Who says defeat?" demanded Cuhullin.

Thumos curled his lip. "There is no point in rushing and making mistakes. We must prepare! Too rash, too rash, these young fellows are. Your father understood this."

"My father would likely do a good many things differently. But he is not here now, and we are. That is the thing of it, Thumos. Much as you may wish for greater companions, we are all you have."

"Surely you are not for this mad rush?" said the gray Giant. "I heard you are wiser than that."

"I have a question." Finn and Thumos stopped quarrelling to see who had spoken. To everyone's surprise, it was Lutz – even his two brothers turned their heads to him. "You mentioned the Banshee earlier, and said she warned that there shouldn't be more than eighteen of you. I did a tally back at the fire, before that Sprydon came jogging in, and it seems we're over that limit by one. Unless – did she mean to count me and my brothers as one? What about fractions? Did she mention fractions?"

"Who's a fraction?" Luboslaw protested.

"It was only a question."

"She did say eighteen." Iskander tapped his chin with his finger.

"Yes," agreed Finn. "And you are three separate fellows, that is certain. Sharing a shirt does not make you all one. What should we do about this?"

"You know," Iskander suggested, "she only said it in passing. Maybe it wasn't important. Besides, we've got too few already – isn't that what everyone has been saying? So now we send someone away? That's just silly."

"No one is being sent away," Finn declared. "If our numbers trouble anyone, let him feel free to leave. Otherwise, we'll all stick together and do what needs doing."

They had quickened their pace and were drawing near the heroes. The boasting and backslapping were unabated. Ronan, on his River Horse, led the way through the dark woods, and the ground sloped steadily upward out of the Canyon. Killorgin's voice was loudest, in turns angry and sad, full of antipathy for the enemy and admiration for his friends.

Thumos and Finn marched side by side in silence at the head of the rearguard. Cuhullin and Iskander were right on their heels – the Giant of Fyfe had balled his fists, even though the battle was still a few miles away. Behind them marched the Treble Giant, but Timberfor and Clumberfoot were not in sight. Finn peered past the others to see that Clumberfoot had tripped and fallen. Timberfor was clutching his shoulder and bending his knees to bring him upright again. Finn was about to double back to help, but Timberfor popped poor Clumberfoot out of the mud and onto his feet. Both Giants laughed with good humor. It was a fine moment, and Finn was glad he had seen it.

"Hold, my friends, and take a moment!"

Ronan raised his hand in what Finn supposed was some military gesture, which the heroes all seemed to recognize. "We are near the place, so let us reconnoiter."

The Giants were lined up roughly two abreast on a steep slope. Only Ronan, on his piggy mount, could see what lay over the hill. The half-Great could see precious little except the backs of Quint and Onslow in front of him, and the belly of Cuhullin behind.

The tall, dark trees had gradually given way to low, trunked growths that could not commit to being all tree or all bush. Ronan whistled softly, and the Giants fanned out to join him at the crest. They did so with plenty of jostling and stern orders as to where to look and put their feet, until they were gathered around the golden Giant.

Once they were assembled on the crest of the hill, what they saw was magnificent and horrible. Treryn was a wonder to behold. Finn was the only one of them who had never seen it before. The soaring walls and towers shone gold against the clearing sky. Gogmagog's ancient home was a mile at least from one end to the other, with sparkling turrets standing watch all along. Huge blue standards billowed atop every tower and spire, bearing the image of a golden bird. The palace compound was shaped like a star, with one mighty drawbridge in the middle, ringed by menacing iron teeth warning that only friends had best approach. A vast army of men was spread out upon the plain before the palace, in square formations. Assigned to each team of soldiers was a huge slicing machine built of wooden beams and massive blades, operated by the men with lines and pulleys and pushed into place by hooded Giants.

"This is no fair fight," Ronan said at last. "They will need a few more of them!" The company chuckled, with the exception of Thumos, though Killorgin laughed loudly enough for them both.

The ridge on which they stood descended to a wide river that separated them from the plain of Treryn. Ronan spurred the River Horse to search for a suitable crossing, and the company followed in single file. But just as the descent was underway and Giants were spread down the slope from top to bottom, horns sounded from atop the walls of the palace. The Giants froze in their tracks.

The horn blasts were not calls to battle, or peals of alarm. Rather, they were ceremonial, signaling that some event was about to begin. With tremendous precision the squares of troops, along with their Giants and machines, spread out into a circle around the far edges of the plain. Finn and the Great Ones stood in amazement. In the center of the plain of Treryn, in just the form it had stood in on the good earth of Eire for ages beyond counting, was the Giants Ring.

The outer portion of the Ring consisted of blue stones that formed a perfect circle around the inner structure. Halfway within this circle, white stones were arranged in an order that was understood only by the wisest of the wise. The main portion of the Ring was in the middle. Thirty obelisks, each the height of the hugest of Giants, stood in a circle, and stone crossbeams spanned each pair. Every section of the Ring had some ancient purpose, though the Giants had forgotten just what each bit was for. All the same, the Ring remained a cherished treasure, and the moving of it from Eire to Alba – however impressive a feat that was – angered the Great Ones immensely.

The heavy drawbridge began to creak open, slowly lowered to the ground by enormous chains, spanning the spike-filled ditch that separated the palace from the plain. Four men, dressed in ceremonial blue and walking two abreast, led a procession out of Treryn. Behind these four, three ragged men – forlorn, filthy, and chained at their necks – were brought out under guard. Behind them came a tall, solitary drummer beating ominously upon a timpani slung round his neck. Finally came several strong soldiers, each wrestling with a heavy chain that was fixed to something massive and high above them.

Slowly the soldiers' mighty captive emerged. Bound at the arms, legs, belly, and neck, he was the greatest Giant since Gogmagog. He was as wretched as he was enormous, pale from lack of sun and draped in scraps of ratty clothes that had become tatters over the centuries. The hair of his head had fallen away in clumps and he moved with a limp on his left side. Most unhappily, the fellow had been blinded. He cocked his head to make sense of the sounds of men and drums about him. The Giant's miseries notwithstanding, the sheer size of him made the soldiers who held his chains look ridiculous. No might of theirs could possibly hold this fellow in place, had he the mind and spirit to be elsewhere.

"Bolster."

Trebiggen spoke the name softly, as if remembering it from a dream. It was so many ages since the Bolster had been taken from them, and his bearing had become so pitiful, that few of the Great Ones could hope to remember him well. For his part, the huge captive could recall little of liberty, and not much at all of what he once had been.

"Can it be?"

"Are you certain?"

"Only Gogmagog was ever so large!"

The three ragged men and the Bolster were led into the Giants Ring. The men were brought to the far side of the inner circle and each one was given a long, pointed stick, similar to the spikes that studded the ditch outside the gate of Treryn. The Bolster, meanwhile, was made to stand at the near side of the tall stones. The drummer's beat quickened as the guards and soldiers prepared to release the chains. The timpani built to a roll, and the drummer ended with one great clash. The captors released their chains, and a bloodthirsty cheer went up from the throng that stood around the Ring.

Immediately, the three men ran for shelter among the tall stones of the Ring's inner circle. The Bolster stretched his arms out and rolled his head back and forth on his trunklike neck. He sniffed the air for his prey, then lurched toward the circle of stones, groping with his tremendous paw. The men darted back and forth among the obelisks, unable to decide on the best hiding place. When the Bolster reached the edge of the circle, he placed his left hand upon a stone crossbeam, leaned in toward the center of the structure, and listened. The cheering throng quieted down, and the men in the circle became still and silent. Suddenly, some sound or smell caught the Bolster's senses, and he roared to the sky. He plunged his hand into the circle and felt about. The crowd whooped and hollered once more.

The men jabbed at the Giant's hand with their sticks – an ill-calculated move, as the spikes could not penetrate his skin but their prodding gave the benighted Bolster clues as to their whereabouts. He snatched up one of the unfortunates by the heel, hoisting him out of the circle of stones. The others hurled their makeshift spears, which bounced harmlessly off the Bolster's belly as he brought the squirming man up to his face. Spectators who were ignorant enough to suppose that eating some unseen, wriggling foe would be only natural for a Giant gasped. Instead, the Bolster sniffed the upside-down fellow, even as the man cursed and madly swung his fists. Then, in one sharp motion, he snapped his arm straight up, flinging the flailing man far into the sky. His victim was no more than a speck to the lookers-on when he reached his highest point and started back down again, plummeting like a comet. He struck the earth with a sickening thud.

No sooner had the first fellow met his end than the Bolster fished his hand in among the tall stones again. Almost at once, he caught hold of a second man. This time, he simply dashed him the length of the plain.

The last of the condemned men found it impossible to hold still and meet his fate. Unarmed and alone, he scampered from the shelter of the tall stones. This might have been a prudent plan, had he been able to master his fear sufficiently to flee in silence, but he shrieked in horror as he ran. Within a few strides the Giant scooped him into his palm, which he drew up, flipped, then slammed to the ground.

There was silence on the plain after the echo of the Bolster's blow had faded. It lasted only a moment, though, before the crowd erupted into cheers. Horns and drums started up, and weapons were brandished. The Giant's guards approached cautiously, though the blinded captive stood perfectly still and showed no sign of further danger. They took up his chains once again, and guided him back toward the gate of the palace.

Once the Bolster had disappeared inside, the Giants on the ridge were left to their thoughts about the grotesque work to which he had been put. Shame and anger fought for supremacy in their minds after seeing their brother set to monstrous murder. The poor victims evoked something like pity too, though the Giants did not know the men's offenses.

"Follow me down, lads," Ronan called, and they focused again on the task at hand. In single file they made their way to the river's edge, where the golden Giant was waiting for them, still seated majestically on his mount. "Today we have seen how our enemies would have us," he announced. "Blinded, in chains, and set to their vicious will. I know that you cannot stand the idea. We will ford this river, and we will make our enemies remember!" He punched the air. His courage was contagious, and the Giants, who had moments before been dispirited, once again warmed to the thought of victory.

"Have you given thought as to where you'll make this crossing, General?" said Thumos. "That water is deeper and faster than you know, and any one of us slipping into it would not be seen again."

Ronan grinned. "My old friend, you are the eternal enumerator of our disadvantages. Where would we be without you?" He steered his mount toward the water to survey the course and current of the river. After a moment he raised his arm and rendered his verdict. "We shall cross the river at its shallowest point," he said. "Just there, by the –" Before he could finish, a gray hare scampered up from the water's edge and straight across the path of the River Horse. The terrified beast reared up on his hind legs and gave a shriek of fright. Ronan wrestled with the reins, but the creature was uncontrollable. Again and again he rose up and kicked his front feet, building his fear into a frenzy.

"Be calm! Be calm!" Ronan shouted into the creature's ear, but it was no use. With one final thrust, the River Horse threw him off. As the Giant went down, he pulled hard on the reins to try to keep his balance, and this was his terrible undoing. The River Horse toppled backward, landing with all his weight upon Ronan and rolling over him. The poor beast scrambled to regain his feet and, still in a panic, fled down the riverbank and out of sight.

It had all happened too fast for the Giants, who were accustomed to slow, strong movements. No one, not even the speedy Sprydon or the nimble Caddock, had thought to move in to help Ronan when he first started struggling. Now it was too late. Filled with regret and shame, they beheld the tragedy on the ground before them. Ronan the Golden lay dead.

Oonagh wished for either silence or commotion; the in-between sounds of preparation that wafted up through her window were unsettling in many ways. For one, it was unclear just what was going on down below. Conversations were mumbles, without a word to which an eavesdropper could cling. Pings and bangs proceeded from every corner of the palace and plain, but no noise so sustained that its purpose could be determined. But what troubled her most was the fact that there were so few of them. Oonagh would have preferred it if Finn's enemies were in a frantic rush to prepare for his arrival. Instead the army stood in quiet confidence, needing only a tap or tweak here or there to get ready.

She rose from the tiny chair in the corner of her bower and went to the single, narrow window. The clouds were parting neatly across the sky, as though the Dagda were dividing the heavens in half with his hand. The air was cool and the wind whistled a story to whoever wished to listen. Oonagh had sung out whatever music was left in her, and the only tale she wanted was one that finished in Finn's arms. The parting clouds were tinged with pink, and she was amazed that there was any loveliness left on the Earth.

Suddenly she felt a presence. She was not simply being watched; this was more invasive, as if her thoughts were being read. She looked around the room, but Jack was not there.

Oonagh turned back toward the window. The sky had lost its grandeur of a moment before. It pained her to see it empty and bleak. In the courtyard below she spied the presence that unnerved her. He was not looking at her, exactly, but his huge face was turned up toward her window. It was Balar of the Evil Eye, loitering beneath the tower.

He was even more hideous in daylight with his bulging eye. She cast about for some horrible words to hurl down at him but she could find none, nor the ability to speak at all. Something in the Frost Giant's bearing whispered to her that he felt her hatred. The Fomorian radiated calm, as well as something like an apology. Oonagh was never easy to confuse, but this brute had baffled her twice in as many meetings – this time without a single word.

She let her eyes drift away from Balar, as if she had never noticed him at all. He was blind, she told herself, and he knew what he knew by trickery or lucky guesses. After several deep breaths and what she thought a suitable space of time, she glanced down once more to see if he had gone. The Frost Giant had not moved. His wolflike face was still turned up to her.

Oonagh could not look away. It was sickening to be so compelled, and she struggled vainly to free her mind and her gaze from this monster. Still Balar made no sound, and their silent embrace endured for more than a minute. Then at last the Fomorian was done with her. He nodded slowly and shuffled away.

The Giants had no more stomach for a fight. They carried Ronan up to a secluded place on the far side of the ridge. Each hewed his own stone from the rocks nearby. They buried him in as majestic a mound as they could manage. Finn found the black blade to be almost Breanain's equal in the task of cutting stone, and he laid a hexagonal offering on the growing tomb of the golden Giant.

"What should we do?" Clumberfoot said what the others were thinking.

"There is no question about it," Thumos answered. "We must return to the Canyon and prepare in earnest. This hastiness has cost us dearly, but there is still a chance to make amends."

"Return to the Canyon?" Finn protested. "Our task is that way!" He gestured at the ridge and toward the plain.

"Your task is your own, half-Great," the gray Giant replied. "You would trade us all to attain your ends. I can see you know nothing of omens, so please allow me to educate you. This omen is the worst we could receive. Ronan the Golden was a Great hero before you were thought of, and now a scampering rabbit has put an end to him. You would go on in the face of such a warning? Madness and carelessness, that is what I call it!"

"Insult me, so long as I live. But I know you will praise me when I am dead, as you now praise Ronan. I have not tried to disguise my own quest. If my love had not been taken from me, I would be safe and warm on my hill right now. But our enemy has a special place for me – you told me so yourself – so is the risk I take any less than yours?"

"Little fellow," the gray Giant scoffed, "do you not see? Every battle is won or lost before it is ever fought. Ronan was Great and but a small thing did him in. It is the poetry of the Gods, and we must read it right. Go back, it tells us, and prepare – not out of cowardice but out of wisdom."

There was a murmur among the Giants. "Well, speak up, the rest of you!" Finn looked at Onslow and Quint. "You two, for example – you have not spoken a word. What say you now?"

The two Giants stood the same height, side by side, wearing the same taciturn expression. They glanced briefly at one another, silently agreeing that Quint would be spokesman for the pair. "We say less than we think," he replied calmly, "while others think less than they say."

"What kind of answer is that?" Finn turned to the others. "I am the youngest and smallest here, so it may rankle some to take my counsel. But since none of you will speak yea or nay, let me do so. The enemy doesn't wait for us to be ready. My love and I weren't ready to be torn apart and have our home destroyed, but they did it anyway. And what about you? Did you find your way to the Canyon and the Vale out of choice or chance? Now we are here, and we are the right number, as the Banshee told me. I don't believe the Gods call for us to fail. But I don't wish us to plunge straight into darkness, either. Let us agree to succeed, and hang brave death! Wise and strong – a mighty army with hearts aflame! I would not share the glory of this victory with any greater number, so do not despair and look for reinforcements. What say you all?"

Absolutely nothing. The Giants had done no more than shift their feet and stroke their beards while he was talking. This dispirited Finn utterly, for he thought he had delivered his rallying call extremely well. He had posed his final question with a hand reaching to the heavens, and his palm remained pressed toward the skies as he looked at the dull faces of the company. Thumos sensed his chance to seal the debate.

"What you propose," the gray Giant told him, "can't be done, even with the best of luck. Shall we build a bridge to cross the river? How can we do so without being seen? It is all very well to talk of noble numbers and wise strength when we can't even reach the enemy!"

Finn and the Giants stood in silence before the tomb of Ronan the Golden, in such deadlock that the ground might have grown up over them before they moved. But then a squat little bird wandered into their midst. He cocked his head left and right, searching for some morsel of food. Then the tall shadows on the ground caught his eye and he lifted his gaze.

"Oh – hallo there," he said. Despite the size of those towering over him, the bird did not seem the least bit fearful. In fact, he seemed glad to have stumbled upon new friends. "I did not see you there. Hope I'm not interrupting!" None of the Giants spoke, so the little fellow continued. "Turducken is my name – what I am, I suppose – but since you're not likely to know any others, go ahead and call me so. My, what a big, handsome group you are!"

The Turducken was an odd sort of bird, evidently some mixed breed of fowl. With a flat bill and patchy feathers of black, white, and red, these squat birds had become quite rare, as they were widely known to be delicious. What is more, they were an easy target for predators. They were poor swimmers, and they could fly only brief distances, and never after meals. Their short legs and webbed feet prevented them from running fast, and their attempts to do so were ludicrous. A Turducken's only defense was the power of persuasion. When cornered, it might use any number of conversational gambits. If the attacker seemed corpulent, the Turducken appealed to his vanity – pointing out that dining on his fatty wings and breast would not be a step in the right direction. Or the bird might pose a number of skill-testing questions to tickle a hunter's intellect. Turduckens considered it a matter of survival to possess a wealth of intriguing facts. It should be added that they were not above using deception in the name of self-preservation, and had been known to offer magic wishes if they were spared – though they possessed no magical power whatever.

"Thank you," Clumberfoot replied, on behalf of the

Giants. "No, you are not interrupting at all." This earned him sharp looks from Finn and Thumos.

"Pleased to hear it," said the Turducken merrily, turning on his webbed feet and taking care to smile straight into the face of each Giant. "I've not seen you fellows round here before – you're chaps a body would remember, to be sure! What brings you by? Can I help you in any way?"

"That's a very kind offer to bigger creatures you've only just met," Thumos observed suspiciously.

"Well, when you're my size, pleasantness is the best policy. But no need to hear me babbling. Do you need help, or are you managing fine yourselves?"

"You are very good," Finn answered, "but I do not expect that those little wings of yours could carry this whole company across that river."

"Ha!" the bird laughed. "I should say not! Why, these puny things can barely hoist me to bed for a nap after a big meal! Besides, if you're looking to be on the river's other side – though I can't imagine why, with all the hullabaloo over yonder – this is nowhere near the spot to be crossing. Too deep, even for you fine folks. And fast, fast, like you don't know what!"

"Hang on," Iskander said, "do you mean there is a place where we can get across?"

"Why, sure there is. But I warn you – it's a bit of a waddle!"

"Will you show us?" Finn asked the bird. "That really would be a help!"

"Of course, of course! It's not all that far. You lads take larger steps than I do, so you may not notice at all. Follow me, if you like!" The Turducken began waddling away, but the thundering voice of Thumos stopped him cold.

"Just wait right there! Who said we were of a mind to cross the river?"

Finn threw up his arms. "Come on, Thumos! You'd just got finished talking about the poetry of the Gods when this wee bird hopped along. Can't you see he's a clever little rhyme? Let's go along and see where he leads, shall we?" Reluctantly the gray Giant nodded. Finn smiled down at the bird, bidding him, "Lead on, Turducken."

The feathered fellow headed off along the base of the hill. "No point going up and over," he advised, "before we're at the place we want to be. Lots of funny folks hereabouts, and not all of them as friendly as you big chaps." The Giants followed in a row, though they were obliged to take unnaturally small steps to accommodate the Turducken's pace. The sight of so many Great and ancient warriors trailing one fat little bird was ridiculous. It was not only for military reasons that the Giants hoped their enemies had no scouts nearby. "You were brave enough to contemplate crossing the river where I found you. It's the deepest and coldest in Albion, did you know that? Not everyone knows things, but I'm happy enough to tell them. Ah, here we are!" The bird stopped between two wide trees that grew at an angle from the base of the hill. A steep, narrow path ran upward through the gap and out of sight. "It gets a bit cramped here, sorry to say," the Turducken reported. "I should have thought of that, but you're tough and resourceful fellows – I'm sure you'll manage." He gave a huff that came right up from his feathered belly, and put his little legs to the task of climbing.

Finn was closest behind the bird as he led the way up the wooded hill. The half-Great could hear the plodding along of others. He smiled at Cuhullin's familiar cursing as the leaves flicked his face. True to the Turducken's words, it was a narrow path, not cut with Giants in mind, though the tall trees around it were welcome cover.

The top of the hill was like a razor's edge. No sooner had the climbers touched the summit than their toes were turned down again. They caught glimpses of the palace and the plain between the treetops. They were farther from the gate now, but facing it directly across an expanse of open field. The army and machines had broken into divisions, and different colors flew over them. The banner that caught Finn's eye featured a golden harp upon a green field. The design of the harp was familiar, and the heraldic use of it reminded him of something he could not place. Many of the companies flew the same banner that adorned the towers of the palace – a golden hen upon a blue field.

"Why do they have a chicken for their symbol?" Swynborn wondered.

"It's a proud bird," Thumos answered, as though it were obvious. "It wakes people up in the morning."

"Do not blame the rooster for the sunrise," Onslow added, to no one in particular. At the foot of the hill, the trees parted to reveal a flat clearing at the river's edge, hidden by drooping orange boughs.

"Here we are then!" announced the Turducken, waving his wing toward the shallows where the mighty river was no more than a trickle over yellow pebbles. To the left and right, the water was dark and deep as it had been at the place of Ronan's tragedy. Here it dwindled to something the Turducken himself could tiptoe across.

Finn whistled. "Astounding! Doesn't everyone know about this place?"

"I know only what I know," the Turducken replied, "and most of that I have forgotten. No, there's little use for this bit, except to approach the castle with convenience. It's not so happy a place that it draws much traffic. I must be off now. Good luck with your quest, whatever it is!" The Turducken popped into the underbrush and disappeared, lest anyone be thinking about teatime.

Finn and the Giants had some planning to do. The task was right before them now. Only a bit of riverbed stood between them and the enemy.

"Half-Great, let me speak to you a moment." Finn lifted his hands to Thumos, wondering what could possibly remain to be said. "Please," Thumos added, in desperation.

The other Giants grumbled among themselves as Finn and the gray Giant came together to one side. "You and I have disagreed all along," Thumos began, "but I hope we can agree now. We know where we can approach our enemy. Let's pocket that advantage and see to strategy. You would like to run at the enemy from here – you are a brave little fellow – but consider the lives of your companions. Spend some time seeing my side, and agree to come back here when we are better prepared to fight."

Finn pointed through the turning leaves toward the castle. "My love is in there. I will go myself, if you won't come along."

"Then you will be dead and she will not be saved," the gray Giant answered. "What good is that? Your friends have come this far with you, half-Great, and it wasn't to see you fail."

"Excuse me," Swynborn interrupted, stepping between them. "We're all wondering, what is the plan?"

"That," Thumos replied, "is what we are discussing."

"Well, hurry up about it!" Killorgin shouted.

"You have done a good deal of hollering," Timberfor told him quietly but firmly, "and I'm tired of the sound."

"I'm about to start hollering myself," Luboslaw warned.

"We stopped deciding things properly long ago. Who says you two should choose our path?"

"May I make a suggestion?" Clumberfoot offered hopefully. "It seems we are all the time talking about how we'll fight and when. But what about another way? If we could discover what our enemies want, and if it's not too dear, perhaps we could give it to them and avoid a fight. Wouldn't that be better?"

"This is silly," sighed Finn. "We can't stand here forever, too frightened to go forward and too proud to go back. We look a right bunch of dunders!"

"Who's frightened?" Cuhullin demanded.

"If I may," said Iskander, placing a calming hand on Cuhullin's shoulder, "we are not frightened so much as unsure." Finn began to interrupt but the Cyclops held up his hand. "I know, I know, my friend, you wish to rescue your Oonagh. And we'll help – that's why Ben and I came along. You are nowhere near handsome enough to find another like her." He chuckled at his own little jab. "But she will be all right a while longer, old friend. I see things sometimes, as you know, and I see you happy again. We have come this far – let us be wise the last little bit. Let us –" But before he could finish, there was a cry from the far side of the river.

"Ogres! Ogres!" A slender man was pointing a crooked finger at the Great Ones as he sounded the alarm. He was dressed all in green and his hair was snow white. His face was sharp and joyless, and something in his voice rang a bell for Finn.

"Well, that's torn it," Iskander muttered.

"Ogres! Ogres!" The man scrambled away, flailing his arms. When he reached the safety of his company, a tremendous roar went up. The men hoisted their weapons high as news of the Giants spread. Horns blasted atop Treryn's walls, and the war machine sprang to life.

None of the Giants seemed certain what to do. Thumos was wide-eyed, looking about for escape routes or high ground or some feature on which he could hang a hasty strategy. Cuhullin, though always ready for a fight, was confused. Iskander wisely took up a spot beside the Giant of Fyfe. Timberfor and Clumberfoot likewise paired up. The heroes were steady and stoic but none moved forward or back in any useful way. Even Killorgin was quiet, standing next to Korrigan and clutching his sword.

The war machines and formations of soldiers rumbled forward, closing in on the Giants with slow confidence.

"What ought we to do?" Clumberfoot asked Timberfor.

"We go down with pride!"

"Go down?" Finn protested. "You may go down if you wish. I am going *through!*" His face grew red and hot as he watched the formidable army approach. All fear left him, replaced by rage. "They took my love, and our hills, and our pride. Finn McCool owes them something fierce." Without a glance back, he strode across the shallow stretch of river toward the enemy.

Seeing Finn march off alone toward certain death, Iskander left the shelter of Cuhullin's shadow to follow. It was not more than a moment before the Giant of Fyfe came along too. The heroes took a little longer, but not out of cowardice. They only paused to admire the trio's valor before heading toward battle themselves.

"Lead on, Finn!" The call came from Clumberfoot, who had shuffled his enormous feet across the bank and was halfway over the river. Timberfor followed, though he had a fair time catching the tripping Giant. "We are with you! Let's pay them back! Pay them back!"

With not even a thought of a vote, the Treble Giant charged after their comrades, slowly at first, and then building

up speed and power. Trebiggen flung his arms wide and let out
a roar to rival the horns on the palace walls. He stomped across
the river, Caddock and Sprydon following in his wake. Taliesin
gave his bowstring a twang and a talking to, urging the weapon
to strike with truth, as he crossed the river with Swynborn.
Killorgin and Korrigan clasped one another's shoulders
and sloshed through the shallow water, followed by Quint and
Onslow, who made no show whatever of their firm resolve.

Thumos the Gray was no coward. He lingered alone on
the far side of the river, not out of fear, but still searching his
mind for any maneuver that could save his comrades in this
unfair fight. But as he saw his friends marching headlong
toward a massive foe, the only strategy that occurred to him
was to go himself, and lend a hand.

When Finn and all the Giants were across the river, they
spread out into something resembling a battle line. There was
a good expanse of plain, much of a mile, between them and
the main force of the enemy. At least a dozen machines
creaked toward them, along with a score of hooded Giants and
formations of soldiers, each made up of a hundred angry men.

Finn stood in the middle of the line, directly between
Iskander and Cuhullin, the black-bladed sword of the
Necromancer ready in his grip. As he braced himself to lead
on, like the point of an arrow for this small but mighty band,
the half-Great became aware of a burning in his free hand.
He looked down to see that his thumb of wisdom was
pressed against Durriken's horn, which was slung from his
belt. He had not thought of this bejeweled thing since
the Necromancer had passed it along. Finn remembered the
Necromancer's warning: he could sound it only once, in
direst need, and help would come. Unable to imagine a time
much direr than this, he took up the horn and set his lips to
a buzz before blowing.

A deep, full sound echoed across the plain. Finn held the note as long as he could, knowing he had but one crack at it. The ground shook with the blast. This horn had almost a voice in it – the call of something ancient and enormous. His face purpled as he ran out of air, and finally he lowered the horn.

Clouds and rumors of clouds began to form to the west and east. Then, from the north, a dark shape descended from the heavens. Both armies surveyed the strange sky. The clouds grew closer and their shapes were sharper than seemed natural. The shape to the north closed in fast with the sound of mighty wings and a burst of fire.

Huge, clawed feet slammed into the ground between the two armies, knocking many of the proud men backward. Even the mightiest of the Giants were frozen with alarm at the arrival of this massive creature. Blue wings whipped a mighty wind toward the army of men and machines before a familiar face turned and met Finn's eyes. The Wyvern had come to fight.

"I have been thinking about our conversation," the dragon called to the half-Great. The Wyvern's face was less cheerful now, his eyes filled with resolve. "There is a tussle that needs having! I am glad you called me. Let's get to it, Finn McCool. Fear no darkness!" The dragon turned his face toward the men and let forth a blast of fire that cut a line right up their middle. The soldiers who could escape hurled themselves to either side, and the fire caught one of the mighty machines full, sending it up in smoke.

"Brilliant!" Iskander whooped.

"Is he a friend of yours?" Clumberfoot called to Finn. Before the half-Great could answer, another blast of fire sprayed the enemy from left to right, breaking their proud squares and sending their hooded Giants running. Then the blue dragon let out a roar that was almost as fearsome as the flame. Several machines were now alight, and the army of men was heading for disarray.

"Call the red! Call the red!" From every quarter of the panicked army, the pleas went up to the captains in the castle. Then a new peal of horns sounded from atop the palace walls – a summons to battle.

Dark wings rose from a pit on the far side of Treryn. Straight up into the sky they went, trailing smoke. The Wyvern knew what the thing was, and he dug his claws deep into the soft earth of the plain to steady himself. When the dark wings reached their highest point between the sharp clouds gathering to east and west, they snapped back and dove straight toward the blue dragon.

The flaming, flying thing screamed and crashed full into the Wyvern, knocking him off his feet. When the smoke and fire ceased and the dust settled, a monstrous red dragon – much larger than the blue, and far more savage – stood between the armies. His armored body was covered with cruel spikes, and his massive, widespread wings blocked out the sky. He stretched and flexed his powerful neck before his yellow eyes settled upon the Wyvern, struggling to rise. The red dragon smiled wickedly.

"You were a fool to come here," he said, in a voice so deep it should have come from underground. "You cannot challenge me!"

"I can challenge you, sure enough," the Wyvern replied, wobbling to his feet. "Whether I can win is another matter."

"I will burn you to cinders and spread your ashes to the seas."

"When did you forget how to be civil? This is how you greet me after all these ages? Come along, Domovor, a fight to the death doesn't have to be impolite."

The red dragon did not laugh. He puffed his chest out and unleashed a spear of fire straight at the Wyvern, covering the blue dragon in flame. Finn and the Giants shielded their faces from the blast and were forced back by the heat. When the Domovor was done, he snorted a bolt of smoke and looked to see what was left of his opponent.

The Wyvern was still upon his feet but his head was bowed and his wings were tattered. Smoke rose from his shoulders and he did not move at all.

"Soon you will die," the Domovor promised. "I would have killed you earlier, but you and your brothers hid well. When you are gone, I will have only three left to hunt."

"No one can tell what the future holds," the Wyvern replied, his head still bowed. "You may hunt our brothers and you may kill them all. Or you may be inches from death yourself. I am not gone yet!" With that, his head snapped up and unleashed a fire blast of his own, catching the Domovor full in the chest. The flame was blue and strong and the unexpected attack knocked the red dragon back on his tree-trunk legs. His eyes went wide with shock.

Once the Domovor regained his wits, he answered with a solid yellow flame, beating back the blue fire of his brother. The dragons circled one another, trading comets of fury and beating their wings. They edged closer and closer, the force of their footsteps thundering through the earth. At last they were very close, and the Wyvern's bursts of fire began to fail.

Between blasts, the red dragon drew up his huge right leg and lunged with his spearlike claws. The blow caught the Wyvern across his face and neck, sending him badly wounded to the ground. There was no more fight in him. He lay wheezing and smoldering, his life seeping away.

The Domovor flew in a circle above the dying dragon, gloating, considering where to strike his final blow. He landed directly in front of the Wyvern and once again puffed out his chest to unleash a blast of fire. But suddenly a rumble shook the earth and every creature on the plain shuddered, including the red dragon himself. Each army looked across to the other, assuming this tremendous trembling was some trickery of theirs. But it was no doing of anyone above the ground.

The patch of earth between the Domovor and his prey began to pulse and rise. It spiked upward at a single point and a spire of stone burst through. The rock formation turned and grew until the shape of a hand and five fingers emerged. Another hand followed, as the crevice split wider. In a final explosion, the monumental digger was revealed. Standing between the Wyvern and the Domovor, his eyes fixed with cold determination upon the red dragon, was the Stone Giant.

"Who are you?" the Domovor demanded. He had never lost a fight. Even dwarfed by the Stone Giant, he did not begin to imagine that it could happen now. "You would be wise to step aside," he warned.

The Stone Giant did not respond. The Domovor's eyes flashed with anger. He lurched toward his new foe, drawing a deep breath right down to his belly. Slowly the Stone Giant spread his arms wide. With a roar of fury, the red dragon unleashed an earthly blast of hot yellow fire. The Stone Giant did not advance, nor did he retreat. He stood firm in his place, his arms open wide, taking the blast of fire in his chest.

Closer and closer the Domovor came, his hideous fire striking the Stone Giant hard. Still the Stone Giant could not be moved. Only when the red dragon stepped within range did his massive enemy strike back. In an instant the Stone Giant brought down his arms, catching the dragon in his embrace. The Domovor screamed. His flame flared so high that it hid both combatants from sight. Soldiers of both armies recoiled from the white-hot fire that blazed in all directions. Above the battle soared the horrible screeching of the dragon.

At last the screaming grew silent, and the deathly fire shrank to a smolder. When the smoke cleared, all that could be seen of the Stone Giant and the Domovor was a huge black stone shining like a diamond. The Stone Giant had been melted by the Domovor's hatred. They were both no more, crystallized in each other's dreadful clutch forever.

The Wyvern lay in the shadow of his enemy and his savior, unable to move. He stared at the shining monolith, astounded and grateful at this extraordinary rescue. Finn and the Giants peeled their fingers from their eyes. With both armies frozen in awe, there was a moment of opportunity for Finn and the Giants to pull the blue dragon to safety. Just as this occurred to them, they were amazed to see that Clumberfoot was already breaking from the line and making for the Wyvern with all the haste he could muster.

"Oi, wait up!" Cuhullin shouted, and he and Timberfor ran after Clumberfoot. Cuhullin was first to lay hands upon the Wyvern. As soon as he touched him, though, he snatched his hands back and stifled a curse. The dragon's scales were exceedingly hot.

"Gently, please," the Wyvern urged politely. With much wincing and blowing on fingers, the three Giants worked as one to pull the wounded dragon to their side of the plain.

Once the Wyvern was in relative safety, Cuhullin cast about for special plants. Finding the foliage he was after – a stout, weedlike stalk that a less trained eye could easily have missed in the grass – the Giant of Fyfe crushed several leaves into powder in his palm. Working quickly, he dressed the dragon's wounds with his hastily prepared treatment.

"That will have to do for now," he said. "We have some business here, and I can do a better job once it's finished."

"Thank you," answered the Wyvern weakly. "Thank you all." He looked round to all the Giants, halting his gaze upon Clumberfoot. "Do we know each other?"

"No sir."

"Yet you came so fearlessly to my rescue," the dragon observed. "There is rare character in you."

"Oh, I don't know about that," Clumberfoot demurred. "I only knew you were hurt."

"Even so," said the dragon, managing a smile.

A new sound rose from the army of men and machines. Slowly at first, beginning with the war drums, there came a single beat. The pulse was taken up by the soldiers, who banged their weapons upon their shields. The Wyvern had thinned their ranks and the loss of their own dragon had been a shock, but they were finding their courage once again.

Finn and the Giants heard the challenge. The blue dragon had begun their work for them and the Stone Giant had surprised all sides with his sacrifice, but now there was no more escape. The enemy was calling and the task lay before them. The Giants' time had come.

Eighteen heroes turned to face the foe. Huge machines rattled toward them, hauled by hostile men and hooded beasts. The odds were impossible and the omens were dire, but every heart in the company was willing. The earth trembled with the Giants' first step as, shoulder to shoulder, they strode across the plain to repay their debt to the ages. Finn led from the middle of the line, the black blade shining in his hand. Cuhullin and Iskander flanked him.

They crashed like a wave into the army of men. The mortal lines were smashed beyond recognition by the force of their attack, and more than a few of the men turned tail and made for the safety of the castle on seeing the sheer size of the Giants up close. Those who remained were dashed like leaves by the pounding fury of Finn and his fellows.

Each in his own way, the Giants showed the color of their courage. Cuhullin and Trebiggen gathered up groups of men in their mighty arms, tossing them high as they pressed on toward the palace. Caddock, with his whipping blades, put an end to scores of enemies at a time, crouching to destroy with the calm face of a cold soldier. Even Clumberfoot cut a path through the men, bringing up his immense feet one at a time, content to allow the berserking troops to career straight into them, and darkness. The Treble Giant were a wonder, their arms and legs moving in unison through the enemy's ranks. But it was Timberfor who led them all, working his mighty fists in a blur, pounding through one square of soldiers after another, straight toward the Giants Ring.

Finn and Iskander fought side by side, as was fitting for the two smallest. The sight of the first cutting machines gave Iskander a start, but he forged ahead. Then the swish of a blade came down from an awkward angle and the Cyclops fell on his back as he dodged it. At once a swarm of men was upon him, hacking and hewing, but Finn flew to the rescue. The half-Great dispatched the first wave of them with a single swipe of his blade. As he was rearing back to serve the stragglers the same way, another slash from the machine caught the black sword and sent him sprawling. Now Finn and Iskander were both down. This was always the aim of men fighting Giants – knock them off their feet.

But in this dire moment, fortune smiled on Finn and the Giants once again. The dark clouds that had been forming to the east and west since the half-Great sounded Durriken's horn now spread across the plain in a sparkling shower of light. As the men paused in their attack, puzzled by this strange phenomenon, one of the shining spots broke away from the others and flew in a broken path down toward the fallen Finn.

"Sorry we're late." The glowing speck hovered just over the half-Great's nose. "But there was no point in moving until we were all here."

Finn recognized the voice. "Quite all right, Dandee," he answered with a smile. "Better late than never!"

"Well said!" The Spriggan laughed. "Now then – let's see what we're about!" He darted into the air to join the cloud of his companions.

The Spriggans swirled like a tornado in the sunshine, radiant and fierce all at once. They crashed into the monstrous machines, hoisting them high, then dashing them to pieces upon the plain. Again and again they swarmed the dastardly devices, at times pulling the hooded Giants into the air with them. As they moved from machine to machine, it seemed only a matter of time before they did away with the entire fleet, clearing the field for Finn and the Giants to advance.

But just as quickly as before, the tide turned again. A blue bolt shot from the ground straight through the cloud of Spriggans. Another followed. Then the bolts came fast and furious, cutting the host of flying specks into clusters and wisps. All eyes turned to the source of the attack – an old man in a tall, pointed hat, standing just outside the gate of Treryn. His left eye was closed as he unleashed bolts from the wand in his bony hand.

"Marland!" Thumos announced the name without fear; indeed, the gray Giant shouted it with anger, as a call to unfinished business. He had been as fierce as the others in cutting through the army of men, but the sight of the wizard gave him new vigor. He let out a growl and pressed through the enemy toward Marland at the gate.

With the loss of the blue dragon and now the Spriggans, Finn and the Giants were back to fighting with courage and heart against a vastly more numerous foe. What machines had been spared the Spriggans' hoisting whirred back to life, as the hooded Giants who had not been dashed from the heavens resumed maneuvering them into position.

Timberfor led the fighting once again, charging fearlessly toward the inner circle of the Ring. The other Giants followed in his wake, impressed by his ferocity; indeed, Timberfor was within strides of the Ring's tallest obelisk before something stopped him cold. A group of men were assembled under a green banner bearing the image of a harp. One man stood apart from the others, glaring up at Timberfor – the cruel-faced fellow who had roused the army against the Giants. Timberfor found it impossible to move against him. As battle raged all about them, the two stood still, their eyes locked in some unhappy and silent conversation. The man's face twisted with hatred, while Timberfor's filled with sadness. After some moments, the other men beneath the green banner began to chant.

"Arvel! Arvel! Arvel!"

When Iskander heard the name, he turned toward Timberfor and the men. Finn too hastened toward the troubled Giant, as something about this sharp-faced man struck an ominous chord in his memory. But before they could get to Timberfor, one of the hooded Giants stepped out from behind a broken machine and took both the Cyclops and the half-Great by the throat.

The attacker's fingers felt like ice on Finn's neck as he lifted the two companions, squeezing hard. But just as the spots in Finn's eyes merged into darkness, the hooded Giant released his grip and went flying from view. Finn and Iskander landed sputtering on the ground, holding their throats and looking about to see what had happened. Clumberfoot stood before them, grinning, with one of his enormous feet still in the air.

"Well booted, brother!" Iskander gasped.

"Thank you," the tripping Giant humbly replied.

Finn and Iskander remembered Timberfor, but the melee was thick about them. They could not see him or what had come from the silent confrontation.

"Who was that man?" Iskander shouted to Finn.

"I don't know, but they certainly seemed to know each other."

Indeed, Timberfor and Dunbar were well acquainted. For all his ferocity, the troubled Giant could not bring himself to raise his hand against the father of the tragic boy, his departed little friend. Unhappily for Timberfor, Dunbar had no such reservations. To the howling approval of the other men, he plunged his sword into Timberfor's belly. Then he drew out his blade and slashed at the Giant's shins, bringing him to his knees. They were nose to nose now, Timberfor and his pursuer of so many years. Dunbar's face filled with cruel satisfaction. He measured his blade beside Timberfor's neck, ready to have the Giant's head for a trophy. Finn and Iskander burst from the crowd in time to take in this terrible sight but they were too far away to save their friend. Dunbar reared back for the death blow.

But just as Timberfor knelt within a blink of death, a great arrow caught Dunbar in his sword shoulder and sent him reeling. Had he been less consumed by hatred, the shot would have killed him at once. Instead, he shook off his shock and switched his sword to the other hand. Glaring at Timberfor, he staggered toward him and again prepared for the final cut. But another arrow shot through the throng, catching Dunbar in the other shoulder. He was astounded and angry, yet still he would not go down. More arrows followed, striking him in the torso. His eyes went from anger to disbelief and finally to darkness as he fell backward to the earth.

"Jolly good shots all!" Swynborn came bounding through the battle. He let out a low whistle as he surveyed the lifeless body of the man. Behind the filthy Giant came the archer, looking less surprised than his companion. Pressed by battle and blood and death, Taliesin had finally found his aim.

Slowly Timberfor rose to his feet, his hand holding his belly. The men behind Dunbar scattered but the troubled Giant did not give chase. Instead, he looked down at the body of his vanquished foe with a tear in his eye.

Despite Taliesin's deadeye aim and Clumberfoot's suddenly indispensable feet, the battle was not going well. Onslow and Quint, together with Killorgin and Korrigan, had formed a foursome, their backs to one another as they trounced all comers. Two of the four corners fought silently, while the other pair peppered their spectacular fighting with loud cussing at the enemy. Though the four Giants were fierece and brave, the men had them surrounded. Their defeat was only a matter of time.

The larger Giants, too – Cuhullin, Trebiggen, and the Treble Giant – had been slowed by weariness and wounds. The enemy crawled up about their shoulders, forcing them to their knees. They had made a brave showing, but the end was near for Finn and the Great Ones of Albion.

An explosion of water delayed their doom. Bursting from the deepest part of the river, not far from where Ronan the Golden had met his end, a dark struggling shape rose high over the plain. The figure whipped back and forth in the air, with

a terrible screeching like a song of hideous death. Then the
shape came crashing down amidst the armies.

Finn and Cuhullin recognized the Leviathan at once, but
even those who had never ventured to the Black Loch could
hazard a guess as to who this was. The Leviathan was even less
conversational than usual, for he held in his jaws a huge and
hideous snake. The Jorgumandr was long indeed, stretching
from the middle of the plain back to the river, with more of
him beneath the water still. His head was wide and gruesome,
with razor teeth that were taller than Finn. His scaly skin was
a patchwork of brown and green and yellow that spoke of
poison. He screeched as he tried to bring his jaws around to
bite, but the Leviathan had him firmly by the neck.

The battlefield cleared as these behemoths from the deep
rolled back and forth upon the plain. The Leviathan, it
seemed, had the advantage on land, as he planted his huge
girth and whipped the snake from side to side. Unable to
strike with his jaws, the Jorgumandr tried to coil around his
enemy and constrict, but every time he did so the Leviathan
would rear up with his neck, taking the snake's trapped head
along with him.

Impossibly, over it all, Finn could swear he heard a single
small voice. He could make out no words but he knew he
was being called. Only Oonagh could summon him away at
such a moment of crisis. He had come, after all, to save her.
This diversion was his chance.

Finn raced toward the palace. Iskander and Cuhullin, both
of whom had a keen touch of anticipation for the half-Great's
movements, saw him break and followed at once. No guards
stood upon the walls, all having poured out into the battle.
The wizard was gone from the threshold. Unchallenged, the
half-Great tore across the lowered drawbridge, his two companions close on his heels, and burst into Treryn.

Inside the courtyard, Finn did not trouble to admire the golden towers and splendid stonework all about him. Instead, he looked around for a door to where dungeons ought to be. There was a threshold at the base of a keep that seemed promising. He dashed to the door, kicked it down, and barreled in.

Cuhullin and the Cyclops were badly winded from the sprint into the castle. They had both paused, hands on knees, to catch their breath when Finn took off again. Before they could straighten up and make after him, a squadron of men led by a tall fellow under the blue banner charged into the courtyard and blocked their path. In the tossing and tussling that ensued, the half-Great was lost from their eyes.

The passage into which Finn had thrust himself led downward as he had hoped – he expected that Oonagh would be kept in some dark and secret place. Broad steps, lit by torches on the wall, descended into a black cellar. Gripping his sword with both hands, he leapt down.

It was a dank place filled with unwholesome smells. There was an eerie green glow and the sound of dripping water. The corridor was tall and arched, so that the top of the ceiling disappeared in the darkness, but it was narrow. It opened into a wider chamber from which several other tunnels led, each as dreadful as the others.

A low moan drifted up from the passage to his left. This made his choice a simple one, as not a peep came from any other direction. He followed the tunnel downward until it opened into another chamber strewn with bones and rotting food. This one felt and smelled even darker than the one before. Through the dim green Finn could see he was not alone. Lying on the floor, his back against the far wall, was the Bolster. The blinded captive was enormous – far larger than the largest Giant the half-Great had ever met. Immense chains bound his hands and feet. He was perfectly still.

"Hello?" Finn ventured.

"I know you're there, if that's what you mean."

"Oh!" Finn jumped. "I am Finn McCool. May I ask – are you . . . the Bolster?"

"I suppose I was," the Giant replied as he stretched.

"I see." Finn nodded. "Did you moan a moment ago?"

"I may have yawned," answered the Bolster. "Is that the same thing?"

"Maybe, to an ear in the dark. What brings you to this place? You know, you are no more than a legend to our brothers above the ground. How long have you been here?"

"I do not remember coming here, nor where I was before. I only know that I am here now and I have seen my last of the sun."

"But we are here now too," the half-Great announced, "your brothers and me. We are storming the castle and taking it back for our own!"

"Oh, is that what you are doing?" said the Bolster without interest. "I did hear some rumblings up above. Good for you, then."

"Do you not see? You're not a prisoner! Don't you want to be free? Will you come and join us? We saw you on the plain – you have no love for these mortals!"

"I do what little I must," the Bolster sighed. "They lead me out when it is time to kill, then they lead me down here again. It is a simple life."

"You can't be happy here! And you would rather be simple than good? How did you become a legend, if that's your attitude?"

The Bolster shrugged. "I am large. It seems that is enough."

"Enough for what? I may have misspoken. You are less a legend than a myth. That is one small step away from being forgotten. We need you! Whatever you were, please remember and join us!" Finn took hold of the black sword and cut away the chains from the Bolster's hands and feet. Only after he was finished freeing the Giant did he wonder if it had been a wise move. The Bolster was several times the half-Great's size and, blind or not, he would be more than a match for Finn if the conversation took a turn for the worse.

"Do you suppose I could not have done that myself?" the Bolster muttered.

"Well," Finn answered slowly, "there's a leap from *could* to *would*. You are free now, complicated as that may be. But, with respect, you are not why I came here. Have you seen or heard of a woman in these dark halls? Can you tell me where she might be?"

"I have seen nothing, clever fellow," the Bolster answered, rubbing his wrists. "I have been blind since before you were born. And I have heard nothing. I am not always alone down here, but what others they send never last long. They cower and whimper, or they boast and curse, until it is time to fight me – then they all fall silent. No women, though. I do not know where you should look, but there is only up from here."

"Thank you," said Finn with disappointment. "In that case, I must leave you. Come along if you will, or stay fading in the dark. Either way, farewell!" He raced back up the passage, but he found the route less straightforward than on the way down. There were choices to make as the tunnel forked out in all directions. Finn's margin for mistakes was narrow, so he wasted no time in bringing his thumb to his lips. At once one of the passages glowed gold, and he hurried along it.

Above ground, Cuhullin and Iskander were finishing

off the complement of guards that had been unlucky enough to come upon them. As soon as Cuhullin flung the final soldier away, they took off in the direction Finn had gone. They could hear more men giving chase behind them as they crossed the courtyard and rounded the corner toward the keep. Just then, a piercing sound filled their ears. It was a whistle coming from above.

"Boys! Up here, please!"

They raised their eyes to see Oonagh leaning out of the lonely tower's window, waving to them.

"Oh, hallo, lovely woman!" Iskander exclaimed. "What are you doing up there, then?"

"I'm a captive, aren't I?" Oonagh called back. "And heavens, lad, what's that on your face?"

"It's a jewel," the Cyclops replied, "and I can see all kinds of things. Now, sweetness, could you jump and let us catch you? We really should be going!"

Oonagh edged out of the window, making sure it was the Cyclops and not Cuhullin who would do the catching. Then she leapt with fearless grace, falling nicely into Iskander's arms. "Good show!" he said, setting her on her feet. "You don't happen to know the best way to run, I suppose?"

"Which way is my Finn?" she demanded.

"Well," the Cyclops mused, looking from side to side, "we seem to have lost him, just for the moment."

"Lost him? Meaning what, exactly?"

"Oh, he's in good health, don't worry," the Cyclops assured her. "Leastways, he was, last time we saw him."

"And when exactly was that?"

"Just a moment before we found you."

"I see," Oonagh said. "And hallo, Ben – thanks for coming along." Cuhullin nodded in reply. Before the pleasantries could continue, the sound of oncoming men

stopped them short. "This way!" Oonagh ordered. The
three ran toward the nearest door. Cuhullin hit it with his
shoulder, smashing right through, then Oonagh and her res-
cuers raced inside.

For his part, Finn was having no luck working his way
back to daylight. He wondered why he had been led to take
this particular passage, as it opened into an underground
chamber adorned with a glowing golden seal bearing the
image of a dragon. He sensed at once, as Oonagh had, that
this was a place of high history.

"Welcome, half-Great," a loud voice beckoned. Finn
whirled around but could see no one.

"Who is speaking, please?"

"An enemy," the voice calmly replied. Out from behind
a massive column on the far side of the chamber stepped a
hideous beast. Balar of the Evil Eye was even larger than his
father had been, but the resemblance was unmistakable.
Peaceful centuries had driven the memory of Ymir's appearance from Finn's mind, but one look at Balar brought it back.
Finn sensed that the Frost Giant was looking right through
him, seeing every deed he had ever done and every thought
he had ever had.

"Do we know each other?" he asked with alarm.

"I know you, certainly," the Fomorian answered. "I am
Balar, son of Ymir."

"That makes us enemies indeed," Finn said, readying his
sword and soul for a fight. Something like a smile crossed
Balar's face as the half-Great did so. He began to move slowly
toward him across the room. "No farther, I warn you!" Finn
called out. Balar's smile grew wide and grotesque. He stopped
and raised his claw.

"As you wish," he answered.

At that moment, Finn's feet became frozen in place

and his arms grew too heavy to move, as though he were immersed in thick mud. He struggled against this new weight while the Fomorian watched gleefully.

Balar crooked the forefinger of his outstretched hand, and the sword flew out of Finn's grip. The black blade soared through the tall chamber, flashing ebony against the glow of the seal. The sword settled, knowing its owner, into the grip of the Frost Giant. "Thank you for this," he said, with an evil grin.

Even with a proper weapon and a good amount of luck, Finn would have been hard put to defeat this much larger foe. Now, on top of being disarmed of a sword that he should never have trusted, he was practically paralyzed.

"I am sympathetic," the Frost Giant said sincerely, "to your position. My father killed yours, and you sought revenge. You were right to do so. And it is I who am in the right now. With that in mind, I hope you will consider what is about to happen as simply the way of things." Sword in hand, he resumed his slow approach across the chamber.

As Balar spoke, Finn became aware that his thumb was burning. Fat lot of good it would do, he thought, as he could not bring the blessed thing to his lips. Then he realized that his thumb was pointing down at the golden seal, and for the first time he studied its features. The dragon's ruby eyes were deep and imploring, and the "Immortal" pledge was familiar enough. But when the half-Great saw the words on the unfurled scroll in the dragon's claws, the burning in his thumb grew to a torturous sear. He lifted his eyes to see that Balar was shuffling his hideous feet toward the center of the seal, but his gaze was drawn down again by the pain in his hand. At last, instead of some incoherent cry of agony, Finn shouted the words that Fintan seemed to demand.

"NUMEN LUMEN!"

The dragon's eyes flashed red. The floor of the chamber shook and the glow of the seal grew as white as a small star. Whatever his ill-gotten foresight, Balar had not expected this. He spread his arms wide and braced his feet against the tremors beneath him, but there was little even he could attempt in the face of such powerful and ancient doings. The seal sent out a bright blast and Finn could swear he heard a roar. The half-Great was thrown across the chamber onto his back. His limbs were moving again, and he got to his knees just in time to see Balar consumed by the avenging light. Cursing in the tongue of his people, the Frost Giant shook his fists to the heavens, and in a flash he crumpled to nothing.

As quickly as it had come, the blinding glow faded back into the seal, leaving no trace of the Frost Giant, nor of his treacherous sword. Slowly Finn rose to his feet, wondering what to do next.

"FINN McCOOL!"

The half-Great's heart leapt into his mouth. He whirled around to see who had shouted. From behind the column opposite where Balar had emerged there came an even larger and uglier thing. Bergelmir had none of his brother's foresight, but he was the most vicious and savage of his kind. Unlike Balar, both of Bergelmir's green eyes were plainly visible, and they held all the awareness of a blood-hunting animal. Great gobs of acid slobber dripped from his jaws onto the floor, and his spearlike claws twitched eagerly as he descended on the half-Great.

This really was it, Finn thought. He could not hope for a single more spot of luck. Weaponless, alone, and lost in an eerie cellar, he clenched his fists for a fight he knew he would lose.

But fortune was not done with Finn yet. At the very instant Bergelmir launched himself toward the half-Great, a

monumental blur rushed past Finn and caught the Frost
Giant in midair. Two monstrous forms crashed to the floor in
a clinch – the Bolster had made his decision.

"Let me help you!" Finn called to the Bolster, who was
struggling to keep his arms from the Fomorian's snapping jaws.

"Not necessary, thanks," the Bolster replied through
gritted teeth. "But right about now, you may want to run."
With that, he lifted the Frost Giant from the floor and hurled
him headlong across the chamber. Bergelmir crashed through
a column, and dust and debris began to descend from the
ceiling. Finn took off up the nearest passage.

Meanwhile, Oonagh and the Giants had woven their
way through the queer construction of the castle, past a pair
of enormous doors and into a throne room. At the far end
stood a stone chair that would be too large even for Cuhullin,
and in front of it a small stool.

"Greetings, three."

Where the stool had stood empty a moment before, now
a little fellow in green sat upon it. Oonagh, of course, knew
him all too well, and with his garb and golden shears he
needed no introduction to the others.

"Jack in the Green," Cuhullin pronounced, "you have a
date with my fists!"

"Oh, I think not," Jack replied, smiling. Out from behind
the stone chair strode Gawain. As always, the little Giant
wore an indifferent expression, and he did not deign to look
anyone in the eye. "I believe you know this loyal friend of
mine. Cyclops, you do, anyway."

Iskander was perturbed to see Gawain approach, even as
he stood in Cuhullin's protective shadow. With his new,
jeweled eye, he saw the little Giant differently – there was an
alarming green glow about him now. Still, Iskander mastered
his fear and stood firmly beside the Giant of Fyfe, guarding

Oonagh. He turned his head back to her and sharply whispered a single word. "*Run!*"

Oonagh bolted down a tall passage to her right. Jack sighed and rolled his eyes, watching her go. He rose from the stool with theatrical exasperation and made a show of stretching his legs. Then he settled his eyes on Cuhullin and Iskander, who were braced for a fight. The indulgent smile he gave them was insulting. Twirling his golden shears on his forefinger, he turned to Gawain and issued one simple, casual order. "Kill them."

In a flash, Jack was gone. Gawain wasted no time, marching straight at the waiting Giants. Iskander's breath grew short, but before Gawain got more than a few paces across the room, Cuhullin pushed the Cyclops aside and stepped forward to take up the quarrel alone.

"Let me help you!" Iskander protested. Cuhullin only growled in reply, spreading his arms wide and barreling at his opponent.

The Giants crashed into each other in the middle of the floor. The first pass went nowhere near the way Cuhullin expected; Gawain lifted him clear off his feet and hurled him halfway across the room. When he skidded to a stop, the Giant of Fyfe scrambled to his feet with all possible speed and dignity and looked wide-eyed back at Gawain. The little Giant stood impassively in the center of the room, ready for the next round.

Cuhullin snarled and stamped like a bull. He charged headlong at his deceptively powerful opponent – a tactic typical of his fighting style and befitting his character: angry, swift, and poorly considered. This time, Gawain did not bother to meet him head-on; he simply stepped aside, leaving his toe in the path of his opponent. The Giant of Fyfe went hurtling to the other side of the room, landing on his head at the base of a mighty column.

Iskander had stood by long enough. He flew at Gawain, but the little Giant was more than ready for him. He slipped his hand straight through the Cyclops's flailing fists and took him by the throat. As their eyes met, the green glow Iskander had seen around Gawain turned to a burning red. For the first time, Iskander saw a look of anger in Gawain's face.

The little Giant lifted Iskander with one arm and brought their faces close together. His snarl grew to a seethe before he launched the Cyclops high into the air. Iskander came crashing down next to the little stool.

By now Cuhullin had regained his feet, and he leapt onto Gawain's back. Iskander too hopped up as quickly as he could, and launched himself at Gawain, plunging his shoulder into the little Giant's belly. With both Giants on him, Gawain twisted and grabbed for them until, with one grand heave, he sent them hurtling in opposite directions. When they looked up from where they had landed, they could see that Gawain was none the worse for wear. He wore a joyless smile – filled with rage – as he signalled them to try again.

Oonagh heard none of the rumbling in the room behind her as she ran, for the beating of her heart filled her ears. The passage opened to a chamber with towering blue windows, and glorious stars painted on the vaulted ceiling. This had plainly been a meeting place for the discussion of lofty subjects. She stopped at one end of the grand hall, and lost her breath. Staggering in from the opposite entrance was her own Finn.

The half-Great lifted his eyes. He shook to his soul at the sight of his love. He did not run to her, as he might have thought; rather, he leaned weakly in the doorway, taking her in and thanking all goodness she was there. "Hallo, my love," he finally said. That was enough to stir her. She raced across the hall, streaming tears of joy. Finn met her with arms wide in the middle of the beautiful place. She leapt up into his embrace and set about leaving no spot on his head uncovered with kisses.

"Where've you been?" she laughed, before planting her lips on his.

"The oddest places," he gasped, when she at last let him free for air. "Are you hurt?"

"If ever I was," she told him, "I could never feel it now."

"I love you, you know."

"I know it."

Roars and rumbles from the throne room and the battle-field shook them from their moment of happiness.

"There'll be a fair amount of rough work to get us out of here and home again." He gently lowered his Oonagh to her feet. As he did so, something rattled along the floor and came to rest next to their toes. It was a pair of dice.

"I am nothing if not reasonable."

Leaning upon the wall, in another of the studied, casual poses Oonagh had come to loathe, was Jack. "I gave you and your fellows a chance to avoid all this unpleasantness," the tailor said. "But here you've come along and blown your horn and given yourself the illusion of swift success. But even now, I would rather find a peaceable solution. You were no enemy of mine, half-Great. Coming for you and your hill was a con-dition of . . . allegiance. I do not think of you as a Giant – I want you to know that. But the Fomorians hold their grudges. All that said," he added, "yours is a lovely woman."

Finn fixed his eyes on the tailor. He did not address him right away; instead, he leaned his head to Oonagh and asked her one firm question.

"This is Jack?"

"Yes, my love, it is," she answered. "But you needn't quarrel with him. He took me from home, that's true, but he has not hurt me in any way. Don't mind him, my love. Let's be off!"

Finn heard none of her words past "yes." He dropped her hand and strode straight toward the tailor. Jack grinned and spun his golden shears. But just as Finn had the little fellow within pounding distance, Jack vanished. Just as quickly, he reappeared on the far side of the room, rattling the dice in his hand.

"I said we weren't enemies," Jack explained. "I didn't say I don't know you. I appeal to the part of you that is man, not ogre. You don't know what a favor I'm doing you. Not just by offering you my friendship – for I promise you, Finn, you do not want this contest – but by including you in a grand alliance. Are you a tremendous man or are you a puny Giant? These choices are important, Finn."

Finn had no interest in choices or friendship as he advanced on the tailor once again. As before, though, just as he came within range, Jack disappeared, only to reappear in the doorway, juggling the dice. "One toss," he offered, sauntering back toward Finn, "to settle all our troubles. If it lands even, Toothsome Oonagh stays with me and you go in peace. If it lands odd, I vanish, never to return, and you and she can see your way out of here and home. Either way, you and I need no quarrel. I can't be more sporting than that."

"And why would I roll bones with you?" Finn demanded. "You are a notorious cheater, I am told."

"He does cheat," Oonagh confirmed.

"So many ways a fellow gets a reputation," Jack laughed. "All I can do is make my offer. Perhaps I am a cheater – though I protest that I am not – does that make your other options more appealing? Does a fight you can't win outweigh even a small chance for freedom? That is what she wants, you know – freedom. She told me so herself. Did she ever tell you that?"

"Very well," Finn growled, "toss your dice one time." Oonagh's eyes widened with alarm, and she plucked Finn's shoulder with her finger. Gently the half-Great pushed her aside, as the smiling Jack came sidling toward him.

"You are wiser than your size suggests," the tailor said. "Shall we say, on three?" He pumped his hand thrice, and on the third motion he threw the dice high. Jack's eyes and Oonagh's were intent upon the bones, but the half-Great's were not. Just as the dice reached nearly to the star-speckled ceiling, he let his fist fly, catching the unsuspecting Jack full in the face.

"Who's the cheater now, hey?" Jack hollered, staggering on his heels, the back of his hand pressed under his nose.

"Let the angels be my judge," said Finn, "if you did not have that coming."

"Fair enough." Jack grinned and wiped a trickle of blood from his upper lip. He gave his shears one last spin and came straight at Finn. The tailor moved slowly at first, but he sped to a blur before coming into the half-Great's range, and he cut Finn deep across the chest. The half-Great stumbled backward and Oonagh rushed to help him. Finn did not lose his feet, though. He clenched his fists and cast his eyes all about the hall for the tailor.

"What do you want her for, if not to rule her?" Jack appeared directly in front of Finn, but tantalizingly too far for punching.

"She is my love," Finn answered. "What is it to you, anyway? Your time is almost up!" He lunged for the little fellow but Jack disappeared in a flash. Finn heard a swish from behind as the tailor laid another cut, this one on the half-Great's calf.

"You, you, you," Jack sighed. "It's always about you. Even now, you've abandoned your fellows on the battlefield to burst in here after your own ends. Isn't that right? Perhaps you are more Giant than man! You might be better off asleep, you know."

These last words coaxed a memory from Finn, of sleeping Giants and music and a grand hall long ago. He closed his eyes and brought his thumb to his lips. At once, he caught a glimpse of himself from above. He flung his free fist into the air and felt it hit home. There was a clang and a moan as Jack and his shears tumbled to the floor. The tailor was clutching his belly.

"A lucky shot!" Jack wheezed. "Well done." He threw his hand out to his golden weapon, but Finn was gratified to see it took him two grabs to find it.

"I'm a lucky fellow, Jack. But since you've seen my love, you know that."

"Charming thought," Jack coughed, staggering to his feet. "But there's not so much luck in the world." Again he disappeared, and once more Finn closed his eyes and put his thumb to his lips. This time he saw himself from the side, and he punched that way. As before, he caught Jack with the blow, but the tailor twisted as he did so and slashed him across the forearm. Both injured, they fell back to opposite sides of the hall.

At the same time, in the throne room, the two Giants were having a rough go against the unearthly strength of Gawain. They had lost count of their falls and leaned, bloodied and short of breath, against one of the huge columns. Gawain held claim on the center of the room, where he stood motionless save for his eyes, which moved steadily back and forth between them. He had not a trace of injury or exhaustion. Cuhullin and Iskander found his effortless appearance most discouraging.

"You know," the Giant of Fyfe gasped to Iskander, "I think you are a very good fellow."

"Why, thank you."

"You are a very good fellow," Cuhullin repeated, "but you are precious little use in this contest we're having. I would feel much better winning this fight on my own. You see what I mean? There's not much honor in beating a fellow two to one."

"Are we winning?"

"We will be, by and by. Besides, you ought to be looking for Finn and his lady. What are you doing lying about here? Help them, if you're their friend!"

"I am not as dopey as all that," Iskander laughed, coughing as he did so. "Brave Ben, you won't send me off so easily."

"Go after her, Cyclops, or" – Cuhullin pointed toward Gawain – "or I am switching to his side."

Iskander understood that he had as little chance of winning this argument as an arm-wrestle with Gawain. He smiled sadly and clapped Cuhullin on the shoulder. The Giant of Fyfe nodded toward the corridor down which Oonagh had run, and the Cyclops turned and raced for the passage.

But they discovered that Gawain was as quick as he was strong. He closed the distance between himself and the Cyclops in the blink of an eye. He was about to take hold of Iskander from behind when the full weight of Cuhullin hit him from the side. The little Giant went flying and Iskander dashed safely into the corridor, Cuhullin's roar of satisfaction in his ears.

Finn and Jack made several more passes, landing fists and

slashes. Oonagh was troubled to see her fellow in a battle that she did not imagine he could win. Again and again she begged him to let it alone, to flee with her down the nearest passage. He replied, adoringly yet firmly, that he would finish the fight, and that distracting him was not helpful. "Finn McCool is no quitter," he declared, and she threw up her hands. To make his point, Finn landed his cleanest blow yet on the tailor, who was shocked and angry to have one of his routine killings turned into a contest.

After circling the hall for several moments, his thumb to his lips, with no sign of his opponent, the half-Great got a clear glimpse of himself from directly in front. He shot out his hand, but not in a fist. This time he grabbed hard for whatever he could find, and he got something dear. He found that he held Jack firmly by the throat. The tailor wriggled and purpled, clawing at Finn's huge fingers, as life and light slowly ebbed from him.

Finn had the wickedest fighter in Albion at his mercy. Vengeance for his hill, his hounds, and his love were a simple squeeze away. He looked at Oonagh and was puzzled that she appeared more frightened than he had ever seen her. Then he turned his gaze again to Jack, looking him squarely in the eye, and took his thumb from his lips.

Before he could speak, Jack managed one last, hideous strike. Slashing with his shears-hand, he went straight for the half-Great's source of wisdom. A flash of pain shot through Finn as his thumb was cut from his hand. He released Jack from his stranglehold and fell to his knees. The tailor coughed, rubbing his neck before resuming his swagger and shears-spinning.

"My, that was close," Jack chuckled, a little hoarse. "Lucky for me there is no hatred in you, half-Great. There is plenty of anger, though, and that is perhaps worse." He slashed the crumpled Finn's shoulder, then disappeared again. Oonagh cried out but Finn held up his hand to keep her away. Again and again Finn suffered invisible cuts but, deprived of his thumb and reeling in pain, he could do nothing but bleed and wait to die.

It was a fine time for the Cyclops to appear. As he staggered in from the corridor, Iskander spent one precious instant in amazement at the beauty of the hall before the sound of Oonagh's distress snapped him into the moment. Jack was no mystery to Iskander's jeweled eye, and he saw the tailor creeping in for one final cut of his waiting victim. The Cyclops cried out three life-saving words. "BEHIND YOU, FINN!"

In one lightning movement, Finn rose to his feet, spun around, and unleashed his fist with a force that would turn a mountain to rubble. The sickening crunch of bone echoed through the hall, such that Oonagh and the Cyclops winced. Their eyes opened to see an empty suit of green clothes and a pair of golden shears twirling on the floor. Finn stood over the lifeless objects, his teeth bared and his fist still outstretched. Jack in the Green was gone.

Oonagh tore at her garments and at Finn's, swiftly applying makeshift bandages to his many wounds. Iskander hurried to assist, though he was not in good shape himself. Once Finn was patched past the point of peril, Oonagh took up the severed thumb of wisdom; though this repair might be beyond even her skills, she resolved to try. The dice, forgotten in the melee, lay on the floor. Jack had rolled a three.

"If you're all right, I need to get back to Ben," Iskander said.

"We're coming with you," Oonagh told him, leading her still-stunned Finn across the hall and up the corridor.

When they emerged into the throne room, there was no sign of Gawain. Cuhullin was seated with his back against a leg of the mighty throne, his hand on his aching forehead. "The darnedest thing," he reported as they approached. "Darned and darnedest."

"Where did he go?" Iskander asked.

"Oh, he's simply gone," Cuhullin replied, shaking his head with confusion. "Just as our battle was turning my way – I admit it might not have seemed like that to someone watching, but I fight with more strategy than people realize – he lost all interest. Just like that, he turned his back and walked away, down that corridor there. That was quite some minutes ago and he hasn't come back. I shouted some pretty strong things after him – not too harsh, though. He was a respectable fighter. But he's forfeited the match, hey? I hope he knows that!"

Before they could comment on Cuhullin's version of the rules of combat, the sound of cracking stone filled the throne room. Fractures ran along the columns, and mighty slabs began to slam down from the ceiling. Finn and Iskander hoisted Cuhullin to his feet, and the four ran with all the haste they could muster for the main door, the only passage that was not already filled with rubble. In all their limping and struggling, it was difficult to tell who was dragging whom. As they drew close to the door, they heard an explosion of rock. A massive beam hurtled down, bringing the rest of the roof with it. All four braced themselves for death.

After a moment they pried open their squinched eyes to find, to their surprise, that they were still alive. Blood fell in drops onto the floor around them, but it was none of theirs. Cautiously they looked up to see, standing above them with the weight of the tumbling room on his shoulder, the wounded but very welcome Bolster.

"Thank you," Finn croaked up to him, "yet again."

"Run!" the Bolster ordered, through grinding teeth.

"What about you?"

"I am quite safe," the Great fellow replied. "Now go – and do not forget!"

This last instruction seemed vague, but the growing shower of dust and debris left them no time to question him. No sooner had they raced across the threshold than the entire chamber came crashing down behind them. Finn felt a pang of pain for leaving the Bolster behind, no matter what safety the big fellow claimed, but he kept his wits and kept running. Taking the lead, Cuhullin smashed through every door in their path until at last they emerged into sunlight near the outer wall of Treryn. They did not slow their pace until they had scrambled over the open drawbridge and were clear of the crumbling castle.

The plain was an astounding sight. Wrecked machines littered the landscape, and several obelisks of the Giants Ring were knocked over. The men and hooded Giants had fled or lay slain. Most shocking was the carcass of an enormous snake stretching the length of the plain and on into the river. On the far side of the field, a gathering had formed around two towering, bluish shapes.

"He was not so fast as I was strong, it seems. Maybe a tad lucky, too!" The Leviathan's words were the first Finn and the others heard as they approached. The big fellow was wounded and weary, but he smiled down at the Wyvern as he spoke. Several Spriggans sat along the ridge of the Leviathan's back, nursing their hurts.

"I suppose I was just lucky," the blue dragon admitted. "And I shall never run out of thanks for that stone fellow." He gestured at the shining black rock in the middle of the plain. As he did so, he spotted Finn and the others. "Hey-ho – here they are!"

All the Giants were in terrible shape but high spirits as

they sat around the dragon and the sea monster, bandaging one another's wounds.

"What happened here?" Finn asked. Before he could take in a proper answer, Oonagh sat him on a boulder and set about improving his bandages. Dandee fluttered down to the level of Finn's face and pointed an approving finger up at the Leviathan.

"This fellow here," he insisted, "saved the day for the lot of us. In the nick of time he shows up – thanks, he says, to that horn of yours – and uses the enemy's own snake to scatter the field! Amazing!"

"It was the work of many," the Leviathan said modestly.

"But what of your people?" Finn asked the Spriggan, flinching as Oonagh went about her ministrations. "You were taking heavy bolts!"

"We are strong, though we be small," the Spriggan said with a wink. "There's not a wizard yet could do away with us!" Just then, Thumos came hobbling up, bearing many burned stripes across his cloak and body. "Where'd you chase him, anyway – that magician who fights from who knows where?"

"I chased him," the gray Giant said, leaning with his hands on his knees, "through halls of Treryn that I do not remember seeing before. But I did not catch him, my brothers. I am sorry." Without looking the others in the eye, he seated himself on a patch of earth near the edge of the group.

Clumberfoot and Timberfor were on the ground next to each other. The gash in the troubled Giant's belly had been well bandaged by his friend, who now knelt with his back to the gathering.

"What're you doing over there?" Killorgin asked him.

"Nothing," Clumberfoot called back. Timberfor waved Killorgin away. But he would not be put off. He looked over Clumberfoot's shoulder just in time to see him put the last, hasty touches on a splint for a terrified and battered mortal man. Seeing Killorgin approach, the man wriggled from Clumberfoot's kindly grasp and hobbled with all haste across the plain and out of sight. Killorgin let out a roar of protest.

"What did you do that for?" he demanded. "Did you not see he was a man?"

"Did you not see," Clumberfoot replied, "that he was wounded?"

Before the dispute could deepen, Caddock interrupted. "What remains of Treryn is ours," he said, "but who is best to rule us and restore it?" He glanced at Trebiggen. There were mumbles and murmurs as the Giants assessed each others' qualities and their own. The Treble Giant whispered among themselves, casting their eyes at this candidate or that.

"Finn McCool would have a claim," Clumberfoot suggested, over the din. This silenced the discussion for a moment. The half-Great was flattered to hear no immediate objections.

"I wish only to be home on my hill," he answered, "and even there I do not rule." He kissed Oonagh's forehead softly. In the course of her painful patching, she had sewn his severed thumb back onto his hand. It was not a pretty paw, and he could not move the thumb altogether well, but at least it was back where it should be. Finn brought the poor thumb to his lips. He saw nothing. Whether its wisdom was gone or the ancients were merely sleeping did not trouble him at this happy moment.

"I would hate to lose my friend Finn to a throne," Iskander chuckled. "But if I may say my mind, Cuhullin is King of the Giants." No one objected as they looked to the huge fellow of Fyfe.

"No thank you," Cuhullin said quietly, stunning them

all. "I am going home to Ben Cruachan." His face bore a thoughtful look.

Finn spoke up. "I can think of no better fellow than the one who has cared for our kind over the ages – our lives were dear to him all along. Who could lead us back to glory in better course than Thumos the Gray?" A ripple of agreement went through the group. Until he said it, Finn had not known he would speak so kindly of his quarreling partner. The only one who was uncertain about the honor was the gray Giant himself.

"Only if my brothers wish it," he answered, rising. "If so, I will put my poor wisdom to work straightaway." The Great Ones cheered, warming Thumos's heart to bursting. He bowed his head humbly, then turned his face to the shattered Treryn.

"Well done!" the Wyvern added. "Now, Benandonner – I know the site of your hill, if you would like a lift there."

"Ah, no," Cuhullin said right away, "I won't be going up into the air again soon. Thank you all the same."

"Let me stroll along with you," Iskander offered, "at least until your feet are steady. Besides, you might need someone to protect you!" Cuhullin smiled a little and clapped the Cyclops on the back.

"You took an awful walloping," Finn said to the blue dragon. "Are you really fit for flying?"

"We big fellows heal faster than you littler ones," the Wyvern replied, "and I'm as fit for flying as any day I've seen so far. If it's home you'd like to go, half-Great, I can take you as far as the near end of your Causeway. I stayed off this island for fear; now I'll call it home again. And you'll smile, I think, to see the place where I leave you."

"Thank you for that," Finn said, uncertain but grinning. He set about shaking hands and clasping shoulders with his assembled brothers, tarrying longest with Thumos. There were proper embraces for Iskander and Cuhullin, and the Giant of Fyfe did not protest at such affection in front of others, as he might have any other day. Oonagh then kissed the two Giants upon the cheek, unleashing furious blushes.

Finn helped his Oonagh onto the dragon's back and clambered up after her. Snorting a salute of fire, the Wyvern stretched his wings and lifted them from the plain of Treryn, soaring for the clouds and home.

The journey was swift and breezy. The blue dragon was not so talkative as he had been on their previous jaunt. He relished another day of life, and knew that the happy couple had earned a quiet snuggle.

When the Wyvern finally set down near the northern end of Alba, where Finn had last seen the ruined remnants of his Causeway, a very different sight greeted their eyes. Once more, the bridge to Eire stretched out into the open sea, and aged men clambered about it with hammers and sketched plans, shouting instructions at one another. As Finn and Oonagh dismounted, Wrisley came scurrying up to them, an unfurled scroll in his hand and a writing quill behind his ear.

"You're a wee bit early, but that's all right, that's all right."

"Early for what?" wondered Finn.

"We're almost done," Wrisley answered, "but we were counting on two more weeks, at least. It's perfectly safe now to cross, perfectly safe, but we Jobbers never leave a thing half finished, eh boys?" The aged men agreed in groaning chorus.

"Farewell, half-Great," the dragon said into Finn's ear, spreading his wings and rising swiftly out of sight.

"But look at that workmanship," Wrisley added, guiding Finn and Oonagh toward the launch of the Causeway. He made a swooping motion with his palm and let out a low whistle.

"It is very lovely," Oonagh agreed. "Thank you."

"I'll get some costs to you soon enough," Wrisley added, turning to Finn and lowering his voice to the tone of business, "but for now, you and your love scoot along home and we'll finish the job here."

"Thank you," said Finn, somewhat confused. Then he took his Oonagh by the hand and together they strode across the sea.

The most that could be said for the Jobbers' work was that they had indeed touched the islands to one another; their craftsmanship was not about to steal anyone's breath with its splendor. Finn and Oonagh felt whole clumps of rock drop away beneath their feet as they crossed, and many times they fell laughing into one another's arms. It was not until they spied the coast of Eire that Finn realized he had not prepared his love for the sight of their charred hill. Though their hearts sang to set foot upon their island again, the half-Great searched his mind for some way to spare her the shock. But she knew him well, and had already steeled herself for the worst they might find. She took his hand and led him up the muddy path.

A burst of joy greeted them as they reached the top of the path; Knockmany awaited, green and glorious as ever. Howls of greeting and the galloping of happy paws bore down upon them as Bran and Skolie leapt into their loving arms. Soon, all four in the family were rolling on the grass.

"They have been so anxious to see you, there's been no reasoning with them!" Finegas called as he came trundling from behind the hill, carrying on his hip an enormous satchel of seeds and seedlings. Behind the old man came the largest surprise of all – Goll mac Morna, tender of Tara, who had helped Finn build the Causeway. Goll the Great had always been gifted at tending woeful places, and he had used his mighty skills to ready Knockmany for its residents' return.

The Giant wore an enormous lavender scarf – a cherished garment that had not lost a single thread since Liath had given it to him centuries before. He waved warmly to the half-Great and his love.

"How did you fellows manage this?" Finn marveled, embracing his uncle and his old comrade.

"Teamwork and know-how, hey?" Finegas said, with a wink to Goll. "But that's not the most of it! Come on up and see what this big fellow and I have knocked together!"

With the hounds scampering circles around them, Finn and Oonagh followed Finegas and Goll up the side of Knockmany. A rough but happy house greeted them on the summit of the hill.

Finn whooped and clapped his hands to see it. "You fellows!" he exclaimed. "You fine, fine fellows!" Out of words, he hugged his friends again. Oonagh dabbed a tear that came too swiftly to stop, then threw her arms about the builders.

"By the by," Goll said, "I've had a look at what those Jobbers have done to our Causeway. You and I will fix it proper, hey? Once they're done making a mess and congratulating themselves on it." Finn laughed and shook the Giant's hand. Oonagh, the hounds on her heels, headed for the door and stepped inside.

The house was an astounding reproduction of what it had been before. Finegas and Goll hovered close to hear every word of her impressions.

"I love it," she sighed. True though this was, she made several quick notes in her mind of changes she would make once there was no one there to see.

"Thought you might, thought you might," crowed Finegas, and he pointed out the features of which he was particularly proud. Then, after more hugging and thanks and talk of the happiest days that awaited, Goll and Finegas took their leave.

Finn set a fire in the hearth and Oonagh cuddled up with him before it. Bran and Skolie stretched out on the floor and basked in the warmth of the reunion. Through flame and foes and war and woes they had come, to the place where happiness was measured out in barrows.

Finn and Oonagh were home.

glossary

Aillen	An Alfar minstrel who has seen his ups and downs
Alfar	Elven folk who have had a hard time
Alistair	Escape Goat
Arimaspians	Giants from the east, committed to the misbegotten project of stealing Griffins' gold to adorn their hair
Artek	Little King across the Sea
Balar of the Evil Eye	son of Ymir
Baldemar	Snow Giant, by his own insistence
Banshee	wise woman who sees more than she says
Benandonner	Cuhullin to friends, if he had them
Bergelmir	brother to Balar
Blunderboar	powerful Giant of Kernow
Blunderbuss	brother of Blunderboar
Bodhmall	stern aunt of Finn
Bolster	legendary Giant, huge but almost forgotten
Breanain	red sword of legend
Byrleigh	forest Giant
Caddock	warrior Giant with lightning blades
Caerleon	Treryn, to mortal men

Canyon of Heroes	home of the brave
Castimer	reasonable Giant
Clumberfoot	tripping Giant
Crystal Caves	home of the Ice Spider
Cuhail mac Art	Giant, father of Finn
Cuhullin	Giant of Fyfe
Dagda	King of the Gods
Dandee	Spriggan with a wonky wing
Demne	Finn, as a lad
Dolmen	burial monument made of standing stones
Domovor	red dragon, full of danger
Dunbar	bereaved father
Durriken	Necromancer, brother to the Banshee
Eire	daily miracle of a land, home to Finn
Escape Goat	A speedy fellow who is always being blamed but manages to be absent when repercussions come down
Fafnir	smallish, dragon-like creature
Fianna	Giants and Protectors of Eire
Finegas	kindly uncle to Finn
Finn mac Cuhail	half-Great
Fintan	ancient father of the Tuatha De Danann
Fomorians	Frost Giants, unpleasant and large
Garuda	known also as the Good Gracious Bird, as in "Good gracious, look at the size of it!"
Gawain	small Giant, loyal to Jack in the Green
Giant of Fyfe	Cuhullin, formally
Girvin	slender-faced Giant
Glindarin	enchanted harp
Gogmagog	King of the Giants
Goll mac Morna	tender of Tara, late of the Fianna
Grimshaw	hard-worn Giant

Harridan/Great Hag	tender of the spring-flowing hill of Clogher
Ice Spider	terrifying and invincible creature of the north
Iskander	Cyclops of the Arimaspians, friend to Finn
Jack in the Green	Giant-killer, formally a tailor
Jobbers	guild of slipshod workers
Jorgumandr	enormous snake
Killorgin	Giant
Knockmany	hill of Finn and Oonagh
Korrigan	spear-wielding Giant
League	about three miles
Leviathan	huge denizen of the Black Loch
Liath	slightly less stern aunt of Finn
Lir	god of the seas
Little King across the Sea	Artek, master of men
Lubomir	one side of the Treble Giant
Luboslaw	other side of the Treble Giant
Lutz	middle of the Treble Giant
Marland	wizard of Artek
Maudlin Vale	lair of regret
Mayhew	lumberjack Giant
Morrigan	scribe of the List of the Dead
Muirne	mother of Finn
Necromancer	Durriken, discourses with the dead
Nephilim	guardians of the Dawn of the World
Obour	bloodsucking ghoul
Onslow	deliberate Giant
Oonagh	beloved of Finn
Parthalan	farmer Giant

Peadair	pugilist Giant
Pengersick	sickly Giant
Piast	nasty snake, child of Jorgumandr
Quint	fifth Giant, friend to Onslow
River Horse	mount of Ronan
Ronan the Golden	heroic Giant
Samhain	Festival of Spirits
Shifting Stones	little-known sea passage of the Spriggans
Spriggans	mischievous faeries; beware the Spriggans!
Sprydon	speedy Giant
Swynborn	filthy Giant
Taliesin	archer Giant
Tara	hall of the Fianna
Tengu	keen-eyed bird, known for pranksterism
Thumos	gray Giant
Thunderbore	loquacious Giant
Timberfor	troubled Giant
Tir na Nog	Land of Eternal Youth
Trebiggen	huge Giant
Treble Giant	Lubomir, Luboslaw, and Lutz
Treryn	hall of Gogmagog
Tuatha De Danann	magical mortals; have seen Tir na Nog
Turducken	delicious and slow-moving bird; only natural defense is its affability
Wrisley	henpecked husband to the Banshee
Wyvern	blue dragon, full of smiles
Ymir	King of the Frost Giants; unpleasant in appearance and association